LIVING ON THE EDGE

RONDO BARNES

ISBN: 1439246408
ISBN-13: 9781439246405
Library of Congress Control Number: 2009906162

For Lou

PROLOGUE

I remember, as a little kid, I loved to compose tales of romantic adventure.

So I went on to study creative writing at an Ivy League college.

But my life story is the only serious work I ever put to paper,

And by then it was far too late.

THE PRELUDE

It can come in fragments or a single flash. This night it hits me complete and unabridged. As before, everything begins quite pleasantly.

"What're you waiting for, mister tall-dark-and-handsome? Let's go slippin' and slidin' with Little Richard."

Forget another beer from the useless bartender. It's time to dance with the love of my life, my favorite teeny-bopper.

Amidst the darting reflections from the crystal ball, we're doing the Lindy like I've never done it before. We move together in an alliance of motion that has me gasping with delight, our shoes just skimming the surface of the linoleum floor. Though the Wurlitzer jukebox is more comfortable with Glenn Miller and Billie Holiday, it plays the new rock 'n' roll with resigned gusto. Zina and I are swept up in the absolute joy of our moment.

I'm fascinated with the sensuous eurythmics of her body, perfect in every way. Entranced by her flouncing blonde tresses, I'm alive with the sensation of dancing on air. Guys and gals create a circle around us, clapping hands and shouting our praises. The pedestal of pride boosts us above the crowd. When we return to the bar through the enthusiastic audience, I've come to realize the full magnitude of my good fortune.

"Impressive footwork out there, you dancing fools. Deserving these fresh mugs of stout."

It's Lenny! My "pardner." My Ivy League brother, my medicine, my pilot. My good buddy till the end of time.

"So, here's to us. Fair maiden Zina . . . Sir Robbie Bender . . . and myself, your most humble and faithful servant. May our chalice last all the way to the final sunset."

We raise our glasses to honor our own esoteric ritual. And we drink from that sacred chalice. Lenny holds out his clenched hand and we tap our sapphire rings together. Brothers for life. I stand once more at the threshold, absorbing the blessing of everlasting love and friendship. I am humbled. How had I come to be chosen? What makes me deserving of such gifts and privilege?

Before I can dwell on such questions the crystal ball shatters into a million shards of flying shrapnel. I'm blinded by the bursts of strobe lights. My eyes squint at a psychedelic light show, fluid images and patterns of brilliant colors submerging the dark room in a spasmodic sea of amoebic distortions. Liquid, palpitating, foaming, Rorschach inkblot figures in diverging shapes and forms, drowning reality and reason in the undercurrents of delusion and madness. A surrealistic poster of stone-eyed Jimi Hendrix gazes through the haze. Janis Joplin's voice wails in tattered cries of agony above a reeling multitude of bohemians—hippies and folkies and flower children who've congregated at this Fillmore happening to enjoy the trip and pay homage to their culture queen.

Pegged pants and bobby socks metamorphose into bell-bottoms and tasseled moccasins. Ducktails and circle pins mutate into unisex braids and peace sign medallions. The banal odors of synthetic colognes, perfumed hair sprays and cigarette smoke are supplanted by mystical aromas of patchouli and incense, intermingled with a hint of forbidden marijuana. The drunken machismo air dissipates away to a perceptibly higher elevation of spirit.

Hold on. What the hell is happening now? Janis whacks the tambourine in tempo as Big Brother launches into a shrieking guitar interlude. I can *hear* the sparking strobes. They pulsate with the cadence, hard and fast and menacing like shots fired from a machine gun. Good lord, there's that ill-fated black sedan, a metal corpse shuddering in the grimy Saigon street as the bullets continue their relentless search for the human flesh inside. And I command my men with dilated red-rimmed eyes, acknowledging full well my own folly and dereliction of duty as I continue to pull the trigger.

The guitars engage each other in their own mortal duel. The singer's contorted face exudes the masochistic pleasure of being flagellated by her own hair as she whips it back and forth in time with the fierce rhythm. Now the explosion of the bicycle at the military bus stop reverberates in my ears. Mutilated bodies catapult across that rust-speckled boulevard in my brain. I run in panic back toward the frenzied commotion in the alley, fearing the worst and finding it there in the faceless remains of my most earnest compatriot. God Almighty, there must've been some way I could have prevented this.

Spotlights converge on the drummer as he pounds the skins. His sticks are like hummingbird wings, moving almost invisibly through the air. As the punished drums respond with thunder, the stoic faces of the orphans emerge from behind the stage. They remind me of those giant inflated plastic cartoon characters looming over the Macy's Thanksgiving Day Parade. And I'm stunned by the sting of discovery. I see the foreboding figure in the wheelchair, revisiting once again, a gloomy silhouette observing at the footlights. Olive drab helicopters traverse the blue backdrop sky, firing smoky tracer rounds. The orphan's Asian eyes are magnified and vacant. The skeletal girl-child in the center points her finger at me.

It is a hallucinatory show of sound, light and absurd impressions deliberately raging out of control. Creating its own lunatic universe while expanding its sphere of influence, it taunts me with my own sequestered demons. I jump at shadows, stumbling through the screaming gypsy crowd. I am angered when I encounter my President expounding about our noble cause and the integrity of our war effort in Vietnam; sickened as the hollow staring faces of the orphans melt into the napalm flames.

The strobe lights throb to the savage beat of the music as I peer into the rice paddy ditch. I recoil in horror when I behold my valiant cohorts lying there side by side, though their true faces are hidden behind the masks of Death. My head is lifted from that foul grave by the rim shot crack of the drumsticks. Once again I'm glued to the black-and-white picture on the TV screen, the topless limo rolling by the infamous grassy knoll, JFK bleeding from fresh gaping wounds and Jackie and the Secret Service agents scrambling in turbid shock. I stagger into the gale of outrage, my own confusion intensifying as they transfigure into my very own dear friends, the car swerving harum-scarum before veering off the road, crashing into oblivion.

Janis Joplin has returned to the microphone, her parched voice providing earthy anchorage for the lead guitar in its quest for infinite ecstasy. As the singer tears into the final verse, audience and performers are joined in a communal bond of reciprocal inspiration. Rhythm and instinct, melody and insight are melded in sweat and passion, everyone entangled in the search for utopian bliss.

My own bad karma prevails when my rebel hero James Dean returns. Driving that treasured Austin-Healey, he fails to bail out before flying off the brim of the sheer cliff. As the sports car plunges to the rocks below, I'm appalled to see once more the grim face of look-alike Lenny behind the wheel, prepared to meet his Maker. When the fire and smoke clear, my heart plummets into its own crevice of despair. Zina is lying there, prostrate and naked under a cruel light in a silent, sterile room.

Now the divine noise writhes and stretches for ultimate orgasm. Janis leans into the mike, the veins protruding in her neck as her voice reaches for the moon. The musicians merge in howling crescendo. Caught in the eye of the storm, I am helpless as the turbulence transports me to a field of stony pillars. Aghast, I observe my father laid out in an open casket descending into the cold hard earth. His ghostly face betrays a sadness that cuts me to the core. My mother stands over him, looking down in frigid contemplation. She grips a black leash in her bony fist.

The music stops in its tracks.

The blinking lights oblige. It's as though someone just pulled the plug on the jukebox. Amplified silence, emotion and anticipation hang in the idle air. My senses bristling, I become aware of the soothing warble of the river. The trill of the robin caresses my ears. Mother Nature comforts me.

I am back at the swaying footbridge. I cast my vision across the crystal rapids to the waterfall in the woods. Movement draws my eyes upward along the bluff, to the oak tree and the ledge near the crest. I see the little boy. Standing at the very edge. He appears to be confronting the danger. Now he raises his arms to the smeared red sky. And dances. Right there, at the brink of the precipice. My mind's eye, like a zoom lens filming a melodramatic movie, pulls the figure closer. His face displays the innocence of youth. He is smiling. Something about him is familiar. It must be Lenny, when he was just a lad on the farm. Or might it be my gung-ho Army bunkmate, the nature boy reared somewhere in America's rural heartland?

Wait. Is it possible? Could it be? I force myself to blink and concentrate, attempting to sharpen the focus. I find myself reaching back in memory to recapture a time long, long ago. I recognize him. Oh my god.

It is then that I hear the soft voice.

I'm here. I'm here for you. When you need me, I'll be here. You know that. I'll always be here for you.

I shudder. The hairs strain taut on the nape of my neck. My skin is clammy. When my eyelids rise to reveal the familiar ceiling, I feel the tickle of the tear on my cheek.

CHAPTER I

Bill Haley & His Comets rocked inconspicuously in the background . . .

"Hey guys, what're you up to? Hitting the high-octane to-night, eh? Mind if we join you?"

What a surprise. We swiveled around on our bar stools to find saucy Jane Lennox standing right there before us, squeezed into skintight toreador pants. A tough looking blonde girl I didn't know accompanied her. The glow from the jukebox's bubble tube lights accentuated their enticing bodies. I hadn't seen Jane in quite a while, since she'd been fooling around with some wise guy loser who had dropped out of school.

"Oh, yeah . . . this is my friend, Priscilla." As befitted her style, Jane tossed in the belated introduction as an obvious afterthought deserving no apology.

"Well, pardon me for tagging along," Priscilla responded, rolling her eyes upward.

Jane and I went back a long way. A fiery natural redhead, she resided on the border of the next town, about two miles from my house. She and her older sister Nadine lived with their divorced father, a freelance photographer. I remember one weekend when he was away, some five years earlier, in the spring of '52, when I had learned to play hooky in seventh grade. We added a hide-and-seek twist to the standard spin the bottle kissing game and found black-and-white glossies of nude female models in his bedroom.

I'd met Jane just a short time before that, when she happened upon the neighborhood post-dinner softball game we held on one of the few remaining vacant lots. She and another girlfriend had been out riding their bikes that evening.

As it turned out, Jane was a pretty spunky player, soon becoming a member of our informal sports group. She sure made an impression with her long flirtatious legs and perky breasts that jiggled inside her shirt, coaxing me to sneak peeks whenever I could. And her bold attitude and sinewy body made her an aggressive athlete who knew how to compete, even with the boys. She excelled at all the games we played back then. Too old now for "Oly, oly, in come free!" this included softball, kickball, stoopball, "Anthony over" and kick the can.

There had been an immediate magnetic connection between the two of us. In no time at all we progressed to the discreet hand-holding stage when apart from the other kids. Then Jane started coming by my house, which soon cued up my mother's curiosity. It didn't take long before Mom's effective detective work had me on the hot seat once again. It seems sister Nadine had an unsavory reputation for being a tart. And daddy Lennox traveled a lot—shooting those tempting models, no doubt—leaving the girls unsupervised for days. Mom didn't hesitate to turn Jane away from our door. She forbade me from seeing her, threatening severe disciplinary sanctions if I disobeyed. All of which, of course, fueled our defiance and desire to see each other even more.

Our covert liaison ended all too soon when one of Mom's bingo friends reported having seen Jane and me necking in a movie theater one Saturday afternoon. What this old spinster had in mind there in the back row during a kiddie matinee still baffles me. Jane and I had seated ourselves as far to the rear as we could, in the next to last row, where errant hands inside blouses and pants have a much better chance to elude prurient observation. The end result for me turned out to be a lengthy incarceration that had me considering running away from home.

"So, how's life treating you, Jane? You're sure looking good these days."

I often scared myself, being so glib in the social amenities. I was glad to see her again. Though we had long since run in different circles, I remained aware of her cheeky miniskirts and provocative charms. Observing her now I realized she'd gotten even sexier since those skinny junior high days.

"You're not looking bad yourself, big boy," she replied with that familiar gleam in her daring green eyes. "And how's mommy doing *these days*? I see she's let you back out on the streets. As a matter of fact, I hear you been up to a lot of your old tricks again. Better not get caught. She might just lock you up and throw away the key this time."

"Unfortunately for me, moms never change. My cross to bear. I just try to keep my distance."

Good old Jane. She still knew how to dish it out, and I loved her for it. Jane didn't take any crap from anybody. Her impetuous nature and flaming temper had often gotten her in trouble, especially with teachers, parents, and other authority figures. You had to respect her for own unique sense of personal pride. She gloried in the very act of rebellion. She was one of those broads who truly had a set of balls. I sensed the potential for another mad night.

The weekend crowd had crammed into every section of T&J Lanes, from the bowling alleys to the pinball machines, the pool tables to the bar. Phony IDs in pocket, we enjoyed the best seats in the house, the prime bar stools near the jukebox and facing all activities, our backs to the front door.

Street-smart Bobby Bennett proceeded to make his early moves on Jane's blonde friend. Slick Jerry Blakely sermonized boozer Eddie and cocky Speckles, so nicknamed for his coat of freckles. Jane's hand revived its favorite old habit, gently caressing my thigh. A gesture peculiar to her I will admit I've never objected to. Customers packed themselves together body to body, behind and around us. The noise level rose several decibels. Everyone reveled in rapt conversation and frisked about as space permitted. Bill Haley & His Comets rocked inconspicuously in the background, restrained by the jukebox volume control behind the bar.

"Hey, Bert, turn up the juke," I shouted to the bartender.

"Hold your horses there, Robbie," Bert growled with his back to me, waiting on some brave senior citizen clearly out of his element. "You're not the only customer in this joint."

The one essential not measuring up to my standards in this party atmosphere was the sound level of the music. Jerry and I had deposited most of the money in that machine. I wanted some value for our investment, especially since I'd been waiting to hear Ray Charles do his "Come Back Baby." Ray had been a favorite of Jane's when we were an item. I felt this more recent release by the great "High Priest" would be a real treat for her. I'd given my quarter and the jukebox number to one of my high school frat brothers who stood nearby, so I had faith it would be coming on. I've never found this soulful blues ballad on any other juke, not anywhere else in all my travels—ever.

Busy Bert, after I nagged him a few more times, eventually responded to my request. The tempo of the club picked up even more. Now this old bowling alley bar really started bouncing. Speckles and Jerry pontificated about who knows what. Bobby succeeded in facilitating the foreplay with his new friend, Priscilla, both of them perched precariously on their teetering bar stools. Eddie took his vodka collins and disappeared somewhere into the crowd. Jane and I drank it all in, snug in our exclusive cocoon.

When Ray Charles' anguished voice finally cried out from that music box the two of us already floated in total emotional intoxication, reciprocally buoyed like those kids back in that dark movie theater on a Saturday afternoon. Our bodies and bar stools seemed lashed together, and the song just lifted us up in a wave of nostalgic enchantment.

"Oh God, Robbie, it's so good to see you again. My scene's a real drag lately. It was pure luck I stopped in here tonight.

We were headed for the rides and shit over at the Palisades, and something in my head just told me to pull in here. Ain't that weird? It must be, like, fate or something, don't you think?"

Her eyes were moist. Where the hell had all the years gone since that fatal matinee? It felt as though I'd almost lost it to another lifetime.

"I sure ain't fightin' it. Now it seems like only yesterday we were slinking around and making out right behind my mother's back."

Bert announced last call. It startled me that the bar had nearly emptied, the bowlers were done, the pinballs quiet and most of the pool tables deserted. Debonair Jerry had found out-of-town ladies for Speckles and himself. Bobby still worked hard at figuring some way into Priscilla's pedal pushers right there at the bar. Bert had called a cab to cart drunken Eddie home.

"What do you say we all head down to the Rainbow for some vittles," barked Jerry.

We poured ourselves into our cars, bantering with each other and laughing about our inability to get an accurate head count. It seemed pretty obvious that the first to arrive would be equally inept at booking adequate table space at this popular all-night diner.

The Rainbow Diner had its usual brisk weekend business percolating when we arrived. At 2:07 Saturday morning this strategically situated eatery bustled. No doubt it prospered from its choice location, just off Interstate 80 by the George Washington Bridge in Fort Lee, the original movie town where silent films began, before Hollywood took over. Besides its own parking area, the diner sat adjacent to a huge municipal lot used by New York commuters. The covered bus stop to and from the city stood a mere block away. Odds were the owner of this grease palace had some drachma in the bank.

We joined the large late night crowd waiting for tables. It came as a bit of a jolt to see people in the harsh neon lights after the darker, softer atmosphere of a nightclub: sallow complexions, crow's-feet, moles, zits and other assorted wrinkles and blemishes. If I owned the place I think I'd have installed lighting that at least tried to be a little more merciful to the appearance of the customers, and the food. The characters we'd been thrown in with here looked downright frightening. But when I took a gander at ourselves I realized we were no movie stars either. Hell, maybe that's why they all moved out to LA. I bet folks don't even know what diners are out there, eating their fancy omelettes with some sort of guacamole sauce, in the refined milieu of a toney café with subtle indirect illumination.

Jammed together in the sardine can anteroom, I felt a moderate urge to take a leak. I also wanted to check out my ducktail. But I dreaded what I looked like in that men's room mirror. I'd been in that ugly room before. If it truly reflected my reality, Jane could soon be headed out the door. At any rate, I didn't want to deal with the potential dent in my self-esteem, so I opted to stay put with the rest of this flawed sample of humanity.

Finally the hostess led us to our tables, located all the way to the back, with the impressive panoramic view of the municipal parking lot below. I warmed to the touch of Jane sidling up next to me. I took hold of her hand under the table, recalling again that first time we held hands, when I'd walked her home after one of the neighborhood softball games. She'd been the one to take the initiative that time. Now it felt just as thrilling as it had then, maybe even more. I wondered how I'd stayed away from this girl for so long.

The Rainbow had again filled up with a rabble of eccentrics, for the most part sharing the common link of inebriation. So we fit right in. As usual, a sizable Jewish contingent occupied a center table. One lady in the group exhibited a towering bouffant stack of blinding orange hair and the biggest ruby to ever adorn a pinky finger. They all talked at once, each attempting to be heard over the others by sheer vocal intensity. The aggregate volume sounded incredibly loud. But if you'd mastered the art of selective hearing, you could easily have picked up anyone's words all the way over at the front entrance.

"Hoo boy, are you joshing me, Irving? You call this moxie? I'm telling you, the goy's a complete schmuck. He's going to run the business right into the ground, and then the market's wide open."

"Norma. You won't believe the diamond necklace Muriel finagled out of Barry. But you know, he deserves everything he gets after that little fling he had with Roberta."

"Oy vey. Would you believe they're out of lox? Talk to them, Sidney."

"What can I tell you, Myron, it looked like a decent deal. You know as well as me there's no guarantees with this type investment. And I don't appreciate that ganef, Bernie, kibitzing with you about it. Where does he get off thinking he can put the kibosh on what we do. Tell you what, I'll scope out the options on Monday and give you a jingle. All right?"

"So, what are you going to have, already. Saul, are you listening to me? We haven't got all night here!"

To the right of these folks, a cluster of kids much younger than us, probably in junior high, contributed to the hullabaloo. I couldn't believe they had permission to be out this late at their ages. They all seemed to be juiced pretty good, too. Either someone's parents had taken a little trip and a pajama party had invaded their house, good luck to all those naïve moms and dads, or these juveniles were simply prepared to pay the fiddler whenever they got home. Assuming they even had to worry about that.

"Those punks are going to put *us* to shame, if they're not careful," I commented, to the amusement of everybody at our table.

Jane gave my left nipple an appreciative hard tweak, like she used to do whenever I punctuated a savvy observation with some wise remark. I didn't even flinch this time. Rather, I savored a newly discovered titillation.

"Hey, don't look now . . . but it would appear we've got ourselves some goombah neighbors," Jerry said ever so softly behind his cupped hand. "Best we mind our P's 'n Q's if we know what's good for us."

"Yeah, I'm not that comfortable in cement shoes," Bobby snickered as Priscilla yanked on his shirt-sleeve.

Close to our tables, tucked into a protective alcove booth where half of them could face the action, sat the wiseguys, the real-life hoods. These goodfellas didn't dress up like us, in fifty dollar Elvis Presley style, saddle-stitched zoot suits and bright Mr. B roll-collared polyester shirts. They did, for the most part, outfit themselves toward the ostentatious. But in a more subdued, and definitely more expensive fashion. Their suits tended to be Italian imports, most often double-breasted Continental mode. Shirts boasted fine cotton or real silk, with long pointy collars that either hugged tight around the narrow knots of their chic silken ties or flared open enough to expose a hairy chest adorned with necklace, cross, crucifix, St. Christopher medal, or any combination thereof. They flashed a profusion of solid gold and silver jewelry on their fingers and wrists as well. I ogled the ornamental display at that table and imagined what hot wheels I'd be driving if I could hock just one piece from that collection.

Representation of this ethnic community has also been commonplace at the Rainbow. The Fort Lee area has a long-standing reputation as a Mafia stronghold, contributing solidly to New Jersey's image as a vibrant gangster state. Heck, Frank Sinatra's folks lived right down the road, just a few miles away, and Frank himself grew up in these parts. Of course, everybody knows him to be well-connected with the underworld.

It seemed these racketeers were all business this Friday night, with no adoring bimbos hanging on to them. I fantasized they'd assembled in the midst of some kind of sinister plot. Their behavior amounted to the very antithesis of the obstreperous Jewish conversations not that far away.

In between my participation in the tipsy antics going on at our table and cuddling with Jane, I kept glancing over at one brute in their booth who seemed to be the main man, judging from his arrogant mannerisms and the others' deferential responses to him. Yet even though he faced me, situated much closer than the kosher crowd, I could not, for the life of me, overhear any of his dialogue. They spoke English, as I could grasp snatches of phrases from others in the booth from time to time. But I could not even lip-read the words spilling from his petulant mouth. The guy looked like the heavy in a mob movie, speaking his lines into a dead mike. Then, when he caught me staring and locked his black eyes on mine, I realized it might be smart to get back, full time, to the dealings of my own nefarious group. A whole lot safer.

"Say, Jerry," Speckles nudged Blakely with his elbow. "Ain't that Bruce Tierney just walked in the door?"

Jerry sprung to his feet and yelled across the noisy room. "Yo, Bruce! How you doing!"

We all peered toward the cashier and spotted Bruce Tierney and three other older guys who'd graduated Denton a few years ago. Bruce waved to Jerry as the hostess seated them at a table near the counter service. Jerry made his way over to them to pay his regards. I think he and Bruce had been classmates.

Jerry's pick-up promptly started gushing to her girlfriend about how cool he was. "Oh, my God. Look at that cute butt. Says he's a bartender at the Clancy Street Tavern, back in Denton. You better believe we're going to be hanging out in that place."

Speckles nibbled on the girlfriend's earlobe in between popping oily French fries down his gullet. Bobby relished the progress he'd made in his persistent carnal exploitation of Priscilla, who now allowed his hands full exploratory privileges while she whispered scurrilous encouragements in his eager ear. All of this whet Jane's appetite for me as well. She began nuzzling my neck and shoulder.

I wondered how much more it would take before the owner or night manager came over and asked us all to leave.

Eyeballing the front to see if we might be the focus of any surveillance, I noticed a band of motorcycle riders had just entered. Their denim and black leather jackets flaunted numerous forbidding emblems. They started talking with Tierney and his pals at their table. Jerry stood alongside, looking on. Suddenly Tierney and his gang rose to their feet as well, and Jerry came hurrying back to us.

"Come on, boys, we got a little problem here. Those biker cats are saying Bruce cut 'em off somewhere on the highway. Want to settle things outside. I'll meet you out there."

Jerry stepped hastily toward the entrance. Bobby, Speckles and I all threw some bills down on the table for the girls to settle up with the waitress.

We ran past the preoccupied cashier, through the telephone vestibule, and out the front door. Speckles, who'd taken the lead, stopped and hopped on his toes, twisting to the right and left, trying to determine which way they'd gone. Their motorcycles remained parked at the curb. The sidewalks in either direction were empty.

After a brief perusal of the diner's parking lot, Speckles kicked into a trot in that direction, it being the most likely course they'd taken. "This way, you guys!"

The diner and this enclosure sat on a plateau above the municipal parking, separated by a chain link fence and the downward slope itself. The fence ended before the left rear corner, allowing for a short driveway, splotched with tar acne, to connect the two areas.

As we loped around the diner and moved toward this exit I looked up and waved to our girls, who pressed their faces against the rear windows and excitedly pointed their fingers out toward the right side of the far lot. Just as I began to digest this information, a series of shouts and curses erupted from that location. Bobby yanked my arm and pulled me along as he passed by. He dragged me forward toward the opening of the declining driveway.

"Let's go, Robbie! They're right down here," Bobby hollered at me. He'd now committed himself to this new objective.

Descending the driveway together I saw Speckles running to our right, directly below the diner parking.

And there they were—eight men already far beyond the parleying stage, scuffling with a ferociousness that nearly staggered me.

"Let 'em be, let 'em be!"

Jerry had already taken charge as the self-appointed referee. His arm extended toward Speckles, who might just have decided to tip the scales.

"Four against four. Let 'em duke it out, fair and square. Just keep your eyes peeled for a weapon!"

Soon Jane was there, at my side again, purring in my ear. "No wonder your mommy worries about you."

CHAPTER 2

Bruce Tierney knew how to take care of himself. The biker chief never had a chance.

"How do you like that . . . you goddam' son of a bitch! If I really wanted . . . to cut you off . . . you'd be lying in a ditch . . . right now. Instead, you're getting your . . . stupid brains bashed in."

"Fuckin' A, Bruce! Whip that bastard's ass. Make him ride home standing up," Speckles yelled, with his usual flair for humor.

The fracas rampaged fast and furious, the scuffle between the final two battlers stalemating on the ground, ultimately broken up by Jerry and the rest of us. The whole thing couldn't have lasted more than ten minutes.

Significant damage seemed evident on both sides, however: blood all over the place, ripped clothing, cut and swelling faces and fists. Probably some broken noses and loosened teeth. A couple of the bruisers received gashes that would need stitches, including one of Bruce's buddies who sustained a severely bitten ear. It wasn't easy to determine the full extent of injury under all the fresh plasma. And none of us had any inclination to play doctor anyway, with so much adrenaline and testosterone pumping.

It had been a real street brawl, though, far beyond mere fisticuffs. I observed many dirty tactics—kicking, clawing, biting, pulling hair, grabbing and squeezing gonads, smashing heads against the pavement. But Bruce and his boys emerged as clear winners, if such a term is even appropriate, by two unanimous decisions and two draws.

Bruce really impressed me. Though he looked strong, with a wiry build, he wasn't imposing in size. Yet he dominated a taller, heavier and very mean looking character. He beat him up so badly, and with such fierce intensity, that we pulled him off because we thought he might kill the guy. This just happened to be, of course, the asshole who started it all in the first place. The other winner really deserved a TKO, I guess, when he decked this leather-jacketed rowdy with one powerful shot to the head, leaving him defenseless to a flurry of hard punches to his gut and rib cage. We put a stop to that carnage as well.

In spite of their devastating defeat the bikers' mouths still worked well. Their battered leader issued an impromptu dare to Tierney.

"You dicks think you're so tough, let's find out. Next Friday night. You get all the muscle you can over to Teterboro Airport. We'll do the same. Nine o'clock, man. There's a big frigging empty lot on the east side. Red Neck Road, man. We'll be there. You will, too, if you're not a goddam' chicken shit motherfucker! Nine o'clock, man. Be there!"

"Well, listen to this ass-wipe. You know what? You're dumber than I thought," Bruce shot back. "After tonight's butt-kicking, you're looking for more? I'm not sure you losers are worth our time."

"Just be there, shit-heel!"

We stood tall, contemptuous smiles on our faces, as they collected their busted bodies and egos. They retreated up the diner driveway toward their bikes. As I watched them go, I noticed the rest of our ladies standing up above us by the fence. They must've been enjoying the show from that elevated position.

"Yeah, right, Teterboro Airport," Bruce said quietly, as an afterthought. "Come on, guys, let's get ourselves checked out. Before your ear falls all the way off, Pete."

"Teaneck Hospital's probably your best bet from here," Jerry offered as we all headed back in the direction of the diner.

There's something about a fight that doesn't lend itself to the festivities of wine, women and song. Even though none of our party had been directly involved in the tussle, we'd been affected by it. We all huffed and panted in a hyper state, but the glow of intoxication and sensual desire had burned out during the melee.

I should say with the exception of Jane, who seemed more turned on than ever. Yet she now had to deal with her friend, Priscilla, who'd had enough. While they argued about it I noticed horny Bobby had taken off. Speckles said he thought he'd gone to that intolerable men's room inside the Rainbow. Jerry had also left to make sure Bruce and his pals got properly mended.

"I can't hang around any longer," Priscilla whined. "I feel sick. My car's back at your place. We need to split. Ple-e-e-ease!"

"Okay, okay! We're outta here, you ridiculous candy-ass pantywaist. But next time, if I'm dumb enough to go out with you again, you better have taxi fare on you."

Jane bid me adieu with a wet French kiss and ran off, still bitching with her quirky girlfriend. So the night concluded and everyone went home, with the Teterboro challenge echoing in the back of our minds.

Isn't it funny how sometimes even the most illogical events come to pass because a groundswell of sentiment germinates from a little remark or story, then builds momentum to fruition? I would not have put a plug nickel on the Teterboro taunt actually taking place.

For one thing, Bruce Tierney was no fool kid, likely to respond to such a senseless provocation. I remember him as an elder statesman in Omega Gamma Delta when I first joined. He already functioned as a kind of mentor to the fraternal leadership at that time. The brotherhood respected him for his shrewd mind and pragmatic advice. You never saw him conducting himself in silly, attention-seeking buffoonery like I seemed prone to. He didn't need other people's approval or applause. In fact, it surprised me he'd been lured into the diner scrap in the first place. Then he astounded me even further with the brutal rage and combat skill he demonstrated in destroying his opponent. Bruce had not been an athletic hero in high school.

Somehow the fight and Teterboro became the talk of youthful Denton and Denton High in particular. Within a matter of days, all kinds of rumors, speculation and misinformation blew the events way out of proportion, contributing to an almost carnival atmosphere in the hallways and student hangouts in and around the school. The keyed up interest seemed a bit unusual, I thought, since Jerry and the combatants themselves had long since graduated. And Priscilla and the other two floozies who'd been with us weren't really known in town.

In spite of this the events received much publicity. The airport confrontation achieved spontaneous support from members of Omega Gamma Delta and the three recognized school gangs: the Court Jesters, the Denton Dukes and the Blades.

"Yo, Robbie! See you at Marty's Friday night," brother Bobby Bennett yelled to me across six rows of desks, right in front of our homeroom teacher. "Now *we* get the chance to lay some knuckles on those sorry biker bastards!"

I talked to him after the bell rang, on our way to the morning's first class.

"Don't think it's a good idea to broadcast this to the whole school, Bobby. We sure don't need the teachers in on this thing."

"Aw, excuse me, for crissakes. Forgot I was talking to the class VP. Hey, relax. Miss Tomascini's a cool lady. She's not about to rat us out."

A caravan had been planned to depart from the parking lot behind Marty's Soda Shoppe at 8:30 Friday night, to move en masse to the Teterboro rendezvous. It had all grown to spectacle proportions.

Before you could take a deep breath, like preparing yourself for the final period of a wrestling match or that crucial play at third-and-goal, Friday night arrived. We all waited there behind Marty's, watching the cars pull in. "Earth Angel" resounded from numerous dashboard radios.

Kids packed into every souped-up rod and straight family automobile beyond capacity. The large number of girls surprised me, I suppose coming for the thrill of seeing their boyfriends take part in a real-life rumble. I couldn't believe my eyes. Some of them actually waved school banners, as if they were headed out to the latest sports competition. Quite a few of the gang members wore their club jackets, promoting their own colors and identity in this massive collaboration. Our Omega president had put the terse word out to us frat cats that, if we chose to participate, no fraternal insignia could be displayed.

"Let's roll! Time to kick ass," someone bellowed from the mouth of the parking lot.

"Well, this is it, guys," I said. "Crank up the old rattletrap."

"Hey, don't be calling my jalopy no rattletrap," the driver bellyached.

"Biker balls, biker balls. We're off to bust some biker balls," one of my frat brothers in the back seat ad-libbed to his own melody.

As everybody pulled out into the street, remarkably only fifteen minutes behind schedule considering the inherent logistics, I was happy to note Bruce Tierney had not shown up. I knew he had too many smarts to be involved in these farcical proceedings. It pleased me also that the law had elected to ignore us this evening. I half expected the Denton cops would have been on to us, what with all the dialogue and hoopla of the past week. They must've been busy snacking over at Dunkin' Donuts or somewhere.

As for me, I decided to go only for the ride, out of curiosity more than anything else. I chose to attend with three more conservative pre-college brothers. Big brawny football players who'd opened holes for me to run through during Saturday's games, but bore no preconceived notions of valor.

Due to the extensive length of the caravan, other oblivious interfering drivers, the many turns, traffic lights, stop signs and other assorted travel impediments along the way, we all arrived sporadically at the huge open lot on Red Neck Road, next to Teterboro's little commuter airport. Despite the edginess we felt toward the possible consequences, we all found humor in the metaphoric irony of the street name. We chuckled about it.

"Who the hell are supposed to be the rednecks tonight?" someone queried with an accentuating snigger.

"Don't look at me. I ain't had no chicken-fried steak, hominy grits or corn pone since I visited my granny down in Chattanooga more'n two years ago," someone else quipped with a fake Southern accent.

When we arrived, many Denton cars and people already gathered along the road. Clumps of males roamed the lot itself, checking out the terrain. It appeared to be just dirt, weeds and some small bushes and scraggly saplings. I didn't observe any bikers or motorcycles anywhere.

"Looks like they had second thoughts about getting their heinies pounded again," I remarked.

We made a swift U-turn and parked on the opposite side of the road, like many others had been smart enough to do, putting some distance between our cars and the anticipated action. Aimed for a speedy departure back toward Denton.

Stepping out onto the road I noticed a larger, central group and strolled over in their direction. The others from our car joined me. As we got closer I saw the magnetic focal point of the muster. Standing in the middle, with two of his three buddies from last week, conversing calmly with everyone around him, none other than Bruce Tierney himself.

"Holy shit, guys. Look what we got here. Bruce Tierney has gone from chapter advisor to gang war honcho," I wisecracked.

"He always was Mr. Versatility," one brother observed.

It blew me away that he'd allowed himself to be goaded into this. But as we joined the rim of this circle I saw Bruce had been wise enough to summon stalwart support—Denton's most notorious thug, Hank Nolan, known by most of us simply as "Suburban," and some other monster hoodlum, whose name eludes me after all these years. These were real bad cats, well known in our area for their brawling prowess. I'm certain the tales of their violent exploits may have been somewhat exaggerated. Yet I had myself seen both of them lick hapless opponents, and could confirm they qualified as legitimate fearless bullies who fought with ruthless abandon. I shouldn't have jumped to conclusions. Bruce knew what he was doing after all.

Earsplitting thunder shook the night air as Red Neck Road suddenly filled with oncoming motorcycles. The time had arrived. The rumble was on.

"All right, my good brothers," I cried, "Let's stay in close formation on this one. Just like that super play when we won our last game together."

"Twins right, scram left, 585 crab, captain."

"All the way to the end zone."

The next few minutes exploded into total chaos, people running this way and that, depending on their reason for being there. It soon became apparent that many had come purely as onlookers, including a lot of self-professed toughies who'd dressed in grubby fighting clothes but now may have wished their girlfriends had worn their poodle skirts for them to hide behind. Confusion reigned since no spectator bleachers had been set up for them to wave their school banners.

In the midst of the madness the bikers drove off the road and onto the lot itself, gunning their engines as they roared through parked cars and frantic kids. The acrid smell of gasoline wafted through the air. They formed a large half-circle arc with their cycles so the headlights lit up the area for the impending clash. This deliberate, organized maneuver had an intimidating effect on the observers. Many vacillators began to back off, away from the tangle, some of them running for their cars.

"Jesus. Look at all those friggin' yellow-bellies," one of my blockers exclaimed.

I added some pepper to his observation. "That's it. Crap your pants and run. Run on home and suck up to momma."

The grumbled "Gutless fucking dipshits" sounded like a teammate regurgitating in my ear.

As the dust settled from this aggressive strategy and the re-treating response, it became clear the bikers were heavily out-manned. From my position at the periphery of the Tierney group I estimated they totaled between twenty to twenty-five cyclists. We had almost double that number on our side who seemed commit-ted to fight.

I also thought it significant that there appeared to be a great many more blue-collar Jesters, Dukes and Blades at the front line, supporting frat man Bruce and his two ruffians, than his own Omega brothers. I understood that Jerry Blakely had to tend bar and couldn't make it. But most of us who shared the secret grip hovered at the rear echelon of the Tierney brigade. Regarding my own posture and that of my entourage, perhaps the lofty prospect of college and future careers had not only begun to dilute our nerve, but degenerate our backbone.

Surveying the crowd, I felt a lump in my throat when my eyes collided with the brash verdancy of Jane Lennox's penetrating stare. It caught me by surprise since I hadn't seen her at Marty's parking lot. Then I noticed she'd brought her latest boyfriend with her, the one who quit school last semester. It made sense he wouldn't be subscribing to any student meeting plans, even for this underground activity.

Jane gave me a quizzical look I wasn't certain how to interpret or respond to. But it seemed obvious she found pleasure in every second of this personal encounter, within the dramatics of the pri-mary confrontation. She flipped a nod and smirk in my direction, coupled with a girlish wave of her hand, rolling her fingers. Then she turned and, pressing her body tight against her guy, whispered into his ear while maintaining eye contact with me. Capricious Jane Lennox. Truly one of a kind.

"Here we go, Robbie!" My right guard's thick voice jerked me back to the snarling scene before me. "Get ready to scrimmage. They're rolling and tumbling up front, by the bikes!"

"I see 'em! We're taking no prisoners tonight, boys."

"With you, cap."

Now the crowd surged forward in front of us. I could hear the curses, grunts and groans of physical combat taking place somewhere toward the spotlights of the motorcycle headlamps. The first reaction of just about everyone seemed to be an eagerness to get into the fray, especially with the advantage in our numbers. Yet this fervor dissipated in an instant. The ranks broke, with many halting, then turning to flee back in our direction and beyond, toward the parked cars.

Moving forward with my gridiron henchmen, sidestepping and sometimes colliding with stumbling bodies, the horror behind the panic came sharply into focus. The bikers had compensated for their lack of manpower by fortifying themselves with chains, tire irons and, perhaps, packing more concealed weapons. The front ranks of Jesters, Dukes, Blades and occasional Omega scrappers seemed to be taking heavy hits and going down fast, suggesting the likelihood of additional nasty armament such as brass knuckles, saps, maybe even knives. I couldn't see Tierney and his inner guard of roughnecks, but hearing the rattle of chains emanating from the front, I was afraid they'd gotten themselves caught in a serious losing battle this Godforsaken night.

"We're out of here!" I shouted, grabbing sleeves on either side. "We better get the cops here quick, before somebody gets killed!"

At that very moment screaming sirens and flashing cruiser lights enveloped us in a dragnet of shock and chagrin. The cherry tops of both local cops and state troopers came speeding down Red Neck Road, blockading the pavement and the ravaged lot that teemed with bloodied young warriors.

SUNRISE

The vibration and muffled ringing of the little alarm clock awakened the young boy. He'd been smart to place it underneath his pillow, where it would jar him from his slumber, but not disturb the rest of the household. He stifled the alarm and moved stealthily from his bed, putting on the clothes he'd placed on the chair after his mother tucked him in for the night. Even his toasty, lined jacket and cap awaited him, so he wouldn't have to visit the downstairs coat closet on his way out.

After zipping up his jacket, he picked up the flashlight he'd also placed there and moved with caution toward the bedroom door. This door always remained open so his mother could hear if he had problems during the night. But he had eased it closed after she retired to ensure his early wake-up went unheard. Reopening the door presented the problem of the squeak, two-thirds of the way through the doorknob rotation. He discovered this could be nullified by a quick turn after the halfway point. This went well, as he had practiced many times. He made his way six steps to the head of the staircase.

At this point he chanced using the flashlight, even though his eyes had grown accustomed to the dark. It would help him count steps to determine the creaky ones that would have to be traversed without the pressure of even his light weight. He allowed himself a tiny sigh of relief when he made it to the bottom. He listened for reactions from any of the sleepers in the house. It was quiet.

The last hurdle entailed passing by his grandfather's room, the only downstairs bedroom. The door had been closed as usual; the old man would not be up for another half-hour. He stepped across the living room, through the pantry hall to the kitchen, and out the back door.

The boy's exuberance at his successful escape coupled with the biting chill of the early morning air to raise goose bumps on his skin. He'd made it. Now the adventure could unfold. He calculated he had about twenty-five minutes before the sunrise would begin.

Still, he needed to be cautious getting from the house to the bridge. He couldn't risk cutting across the neighbors' properties, for any number of dogs would sound the alert at this hour. Selecting the safest route, he made his way along the side of his own gravel driveway to the street, careful not to crunch or kick pebbles as he would again pass his grandfather's bedroom, this time outside the house, by his open windows.

He fancied himself a comrade of Daniel Boone, the famous pathfinder of early American history, blazing trails through the dangerous wilderness of undiscovered territory. He was known himself as the imaginary Shelley Forrester. And so he made it to the bridge, undetected and without incident.

This trek of about a quarter mile warmed him to the morning briskness. He now felt compatible and comfortable with the environment. He did not tarry, as he would have on most occasions, to look over the side of the bridge at the dashing waters of Canadaway Creek. The headlights of some early worker passing by might catch him at this unusual hour. Rather, he moved with steadfast determination up to the fresh water spring just off the road beyond the bridge, where it appeared safe to again turn on his flashlight.

Here he paused to drink from the copper spout jutting out of the cobblestone fountainhead. Gulping down the cold water, it crossed his mind how inappropriate to call a river a creek, just because the name sounded better. This channel of water ran too wide and bountiful for a creek.

He'd become familiar with the trails that meandered through these woods bordering the river, for he spent much of his solitary time here. The flashlight functioned as a necessary tool once more, so he could see subtle landmarks to guide him. He wondered if the time could ever come when he'd be able to make his way blindfolded, determining direction by his knowledge of the fragments of earth he could see from beneath the kerchief. Certainly this journey to his secret place would be a good test, as he knew every nuance of the path almost as well as he knew himself.

As he moved along, an escalating clarity cast upon the rocks and foliage. He realized the dawn would not be far away. He hurried his pace and lengthened his stride, now embarking on a much steeper climb as he drew nearer to his destination. His feathered playfellows commenced their symphonies as though some fairy conductor had just flashed his magic baton.

It took another twelve minutes along this abrupt incline of forest, the rustling of birds and animals vacating the vicinity of the trail in front of him, before he finally reached the summit. He was close now.

This pinnacle heralded a hiker's challenge, the remaining steps requiring slow progress through dense underbrush. No semblance of a path existed here, only the natural identification points and trail blazes he'd established as beacons during previous jaunts. Nor did he see any of the normal evidence of other human presence: gum wrappers, matchbook covers or paper cups. He spotted the almost hidden outcropping of rock that served as his final signpost and veered toward it with intensified zeal. The overhead sky had gotten much lighter now, preparing for the ultimate morning ritual. The perpetual rush of the river grew louder.

The boy climbed over the outcropping and there it was. About eight feet below the rock nestled a secluded shelf of grass and stone, bordered by an immense spreading oak tree. He sat down on the rock where it formed a natural trough and slid down to the obliging ledge. Beyond this shelf a wide gap extended to the treetops that ascended from the other side of the river. From here the sound had increased to an emphatic roar. Yet from this posterior vantage point only mist from the cascading water below was visible. The musky odor of moist soil invaded his nostrils, inspiring his regard for the earthy aroma.

Straightaway, he had the sensation of being swallowed into an ethereal state of awareness. A sense of well-being about himself and his place within the cosmos. He felt at peace with who he was, how he fit into the universal scheme of things. This pristine place, his nirvana, remained unspoiled. True to him and him alone.

He hunched forward on his buttocks toward the edge, granting respect for the danger it imposed. He still suffered a twinge of vertigo despite his repeated visits here. As before, he would stop where his toes touched a jut of stone, some two feet from the brink. Then he'd gather himself into a kneeling position and carefully lean forward to take in the grandeur of the view beyond. The waterfall took his breath away with its powerful splendor. But he felt awed as well by the suspended footbridge downstream toward the bend. It was there that he'd first caught a glimpse of this sheltering mantel.

The curtain rose to a brand-new day. The gradual infusion of light that had been transpiring turned into an increasing incandescence. Before he anticipated it, a golden beam struck him square in the eye from between the trees beyond the footbridge. As the fiery globe emerged from behind these trees, it appeared to multiply in brilliant glinting rays. The timberland around him seemed to come alive, adding its vital signs to the pulse of the hectic water.

He was Shelley Forrester here in this wooded sanctuary. The majesty of the moment transcended his highest expectations. It had been worth the risk to sneak out of the house for this. To write credible stories, nothing can replace firsthand experience.

The boy felt certain that Indians lurked somewhere in that grove of glimmering sun-speckled trees, perhaps stalking the deer that came to drink from the river. Leaning forward, he marveled at the waterfall as it descended into a murky plunge pool. Here countless fish went about their own strange lives in a much different world. Down toward the suspension bridge, the banks along the river widened to accommodate numerous rocks of myriad shapes and sizes that harbored a potpourri of exciting creatures. Silverfish, centipedes, spiders. Toads, snakes and lizards. At the water's edge where the current restrained its frenzy, the keen eye could find scads of minnows, tadpoles and salamanders cavorting in their own treacherous little sphere of the planet.

The whistles and chatter of robins, chickadees, and many other species of birds now filled the bright air as they began their new day as well. They flitted about in search of their morning morsels of nourishment. And somewhere in the thickets, the calculating fox foraged for the many families of mice, rabbits, chipmunks and other squirrels that persisted to maintain their numbers in generous abundance.

Out of the corner of his eye the boy caught a flicker of movement by a protrusion of root from the nearby oak tree. He looked in that direction without turning his head, as he'd learned to do to avoid scaring away forest dwellers. An eruption of dandelions fidgeted in the breeze, but nothing of cerebral substance revealed itself. Whatever had caught his attention might very well have spotted him, too. He'd learned to be patient, like the Indians had taught his friend Daniel. He continued to stare at the spot, fixed in place.

Sure enough, after what seemed like a matter of minutes, a small, furry head with beady eyes poked up from behind the gnarled root. The boy did not flinch. He softened his breathing and slowed the pace of his blinking eyelids so he would not startle his newfound neighbor. Then, just when he felt the beginning of that unwelcome itch that always seems to make its rude appearance at moments like this, his diminutive guest jumped into full view. There he was, moving about in rapid twitches commensurate with his high-speed metabolism, a cunning young weasel with his long, slender body and a tail that had yet to mature to its normal bushiness. The boy was ecstatic with his latest acquaintance. This world certainly abounded in wonders. But quicker than he'd arrived, the weasel disappeared when a hawk swooped down out of nowhere before gliding away across the ravine.

Shaken back to the reality of his circumstance, the boy glanced anxiously at his watch. He'd been away now for well over an hour and needed to return to the security of his bedroom. He reached for his back pocket. His notepad and pen were there, as they should be. But he'd have to hold onto his idyllic observations until he got home. It would not be appropriate for Shelley Forrester to have to taste his mother's switch this miracle morning.

32 |

CHAPTER 3

"**M**an, this just might be the weekend of all weekends," Bobby Bennett exclaimed out in the kitchen, running his fingers through his sleek dark brown hair. "Hey, Tommy, did your old man ever show you how to make margaritas with this here tequila? Man, they say this Cuervo Gold can really screw you up. Ain't there supposed to be some goddam' worm at the bottom, to give it that hallucinating effect?"

We'd gotten together at Tommy Calderone's house on a Friday night. His folks had gone away for the weekend, and Tommy had been planning to host this 48-hour binge ever since they informed him of their intentions. Due to graduate from Denton High this June, this would be the first celebration to commemorate our official step toward independence, to bid a farewell to our high school days.

"My dad probably has some margarita mix somewhere in the bar cabinet, or out in the pantry. Just look around," Tommy called back from the living room, where he busied himself setting up the projector for a couple dirty movies from his dad's secret collection. "Don't really know what the deal is with the worm. But I did get some limes, so we could do shooters with salt. Seen my old man do it. We should try that before we watch these movies. Doing shots is faster, anyway."

The movies would kick off the bachelor portion of our special weekend party. We purposely, at least as I recall it now, did not have dates for this event so we could enjoy just "being with the boys." This way we had the freedom to chase down some skirts whenever we felt the urge. We planned to hit the T&J and probably a few other places we'd heard about over in Palisades Park later on in the night. If nothing panned out in terms of pickups, we figured we could always call up some old reliables if we got desperate along the way.

"So, Robbie, tell us about that big rumble you were in last week." Scrawny Tommy didn't fit the brawler mold and had not attended the Teterboro conflict. "I hear those bikers were armed to the teeth, and some of our Jesters and other cats are still in the hospital. I guess that Tierney guy got busted up real bad. So, our class Veep was right there in the middle of it? How come you got away clean?"

Of course I had to embellish my role somewhat as I told the story. Not anything too spectacular since I didn't even have swollen or cut knuckles, or any other supporting physical evidence to corroborate real participation, much less any act of masculine bravery. Besides, I also needed to be careful of firsthand contradiction since Tommy and some of the other guest partiers bore Court Jester credentials. There'd been more Jesters hospitalized than any other club present at the battlefield.

As good fortune would have it, no one got killed or brain damaged. The police confiscated not only the chains and tire irons I had myself seen, but a number of blackjacks and knuckle-dusters. Even some knives, just as I'd feared. A few kids remained in serious condition at Hackensack General, with cracked skulls, broken ribs and knife wounds. No one ended up worse than Bruce Tierney, on the critical list, and ironically, the biker chief who'd set all the insane wheels in motion back at the Rainbow Diner.

Reports indicated Bruce would be spending the rest of his life in a wheelchair. He continued to be paralyzed from the waist down, having sustained a fractured spine. His biker adversary ended up in rough shape, too—both arms broken, a dislocated jaw, cracked ribs and kidney damage. Word had it that both Hank Nolan and Bruce's other hired gun had been arrested for his injuries and those of a couple of other cyclists. I guess when these two maulers saw the weapons they faced, they both pulled bludgeons from their jackets. After Bruce went down from a blow to his back from the biker's tire jack, they'd joined in on working over Tierney's nemesis.

The motorcyclists that hadn't been hospitalized wound up in jail cells as well, for inflicting bodily harm with dangerous weapons. Local media reports praised the Denton Police Department for having alerted state police officials that a "large-scale youth altercation" might be imminent that night in the vicinity of Teterboro Airport.

"Well, enough of that horse shit, fellas. We're all lovers, not fighters, here," Tommy declared, taking a pull on his mentholated Kool. "We're going to have our own kind of rumble this weekend. Starting with this tasty little movie called 'Sally Loves Boys!' Now, let's be the first to toast the pending ending to our effervescent high school life. Here, take these shooters and grab a lime. I'll show you how we do it, Tia-ju-wana style!"

This had to be the first time any of us tried tequila. It endures in memory as my initiation to this perilous potion of warped sensibilities. The first slug of it really rocked me back. Feeling a bit nauseated, I thought I might have to run for the toilet bowl. But the salt and lime helped. I found the second shot much easier to handle. I remember doing three hits of tequila, then settling in with a much more palatable rum and coke that went a long way toward soothing the upset turn in my stomach.

After the lusty stimulation of watching sweet Sally do her thing, we all hankered for action. The time had come to hit the bars. I will admit I wasn't altogether cognizant of what went on during the trip to the T&J in Bobby's chopped and channeled '48 Ford V8. Other than we all seemed to be simultaneously yelling and laughing amongst ourselves in unreal amplification. Embraced by the crowd at our favorite haunt, we proceeded to elevate both the volume and zaniness going on there as well. Bobby and I had fun picking up two girls in the bowling alley. But to be truthful, I can't tell you who else we ran into. I know we had a marvelous time, as I had to endure Bert the bartender's involved yarns about our silly shenanigans for years afterward.

"Like that poor old Jersey wino, I been sleeping in a hollow stump!" Tommy dissonantly wailed, rousting us all from our comas Saturday morning with a droll rendering of Big Joe Turner's rock 'n' roll lyrics bellowing in the background.

While it didn't really help the hangovers, his voice was far more pleasant than the taste in our mouths. It served to motivate us for another day of frolics at that aged hulk of Tudor architecture on Clariton Road.

Tommy was a pretty amazing guy. He'd been crumpled up on the floor, in his own death trance, when I arose in the middle of the night from my tomb on the couch, wondering where the girls had gone before stumbling upstairs to an empty bed. Now he'd already made it to the kitchen on a sunny morning, fixing up bacon and scrambled eggs, toasted English muffins and coffee over a stack of hot R&B records. Too bad parents didn't take off every weekend like this. This was the way life ought to be.

Within the next couple of hours the rudiments of "Party Day Two" had been formulated. Bobby and I got in touch with Brenda and Grace, our new friends from the bowling alley. They accepted our invitation to return for more partying. Tommy also had success on the phone. He announced he'd gotten ahold of Ginger Jorgenson. She and Cynthia St. James would be swinging by, hopefully with some other girls, mid to late afternoon. I did a double take on that proclamation, for I'd had a secret crush on Cynthia ever since junior high. Everything had begun to hold the promise

of a historical weekend romp to memorialize our pending graduation right and proper.

"Looks like all the pieces are coming together," Tommy exclaimed with a snicker behind his spontaneous double-entendre.
He presented us his first batch of Bloody Mary's from his mother's
elegant silver serving tray.

Good old Bloody Mary to the rescue. I couldn't believe it.
By the time I hit the bottom of my second glass I'd gotten myself
together, ready to trip once more through the tulips. Just in time
too, as the doorbell signaled the arrival of our first guests. Tommy
went to the door and, in his own flamboyant fashion of manners,
ushered in Ginger Jorgenson, lovely Cynthia St. James—beware my
heart—a couple of other slick chicks and, oh, no, my favorite dance
partner, plucky Shirley McFarlin.

"Hey, Tommy! So, you guys are partying over here the whole
weekend. And you just decided to invite us now? How rude!
Shame-shame on all of you. You know the Tri Gams are the real
party girls at Denton. I can't beleeeve you thought you could do it
without us." Ginger's shrill voice pierced through the noisy room.
"Jeez, Bobby, how you doing? Robbie, what's happening with our
wrestling champ? There's my guy—"

She bolted past me and threw her arms around the neck of
one of her favorite Jesters. The force of her weight and momentum
propelled the two of them onto the couch, laughing hysterically.

Tall, blond Ginger served as president of Alpha Tri Gamma
sorority. Their party-hearty reputation and rallying cry motto of "Try Gams First!" had the other two sororities at school
tossing jealous moral epithets at them in futile attempts to compete. As far as this affected reactions from the boys, the tactic
worked in favor of the Tri Gams. It heightened their intrigue
and desirability. Their accusers assumed spiteful, petty, sanctimonious images, lending impetus to their social leprosy. Hence,
they only succeeded in further aggravating their physical and
psychological frustrations.

Ginger brought sorority reinforcements to accompany her and Cynthia. They epitomized the mature, core party girls of the membership. Each possessed a self-confident poise, humor and sensual charisma that belied their years. Any dirty old man would have gladly squandered his weekly pay in the solid conviction that, despite their circle pins and bobby socks, not one of these "women" was jailbait.

"Yo, Cynthia. Glad you could make it," I said, attempting to be suave but not counterfeit. Her curly cinnamon hair and flawless lily-white skin, like frail parchment paper, looked even better close up.

"How've you been, Robbie. Haven't spoke to you in awhile," she replied in her unforgettable delicate voice.

I acknowledged the subtle tremor somewhere far down inside me.

"Hey there, Robbie. How you doing? I hope you're ready for some serious dancing tonight." Shirley McFarlin stood on her tiptoes and gave me a kiss on the cheek.

Just then the doorbell rang. Tommy presented Brenda and Grace, to further compound my confusion.

Within two hours it became bona fide play time. Omega brothers Eddie Mazzoli and Speckles O'Reardon joined us, along with some additional Jesters. And Joe Turner, the Boss of the Blues, did another spin on the turntable, everyone showing off their practiced Lindy dance combinations to his catchy "Shake, Rattle and Roll."

I tried my best steering Brenda through my stockpile of steps. I'm sure she also did her best, trying to follow my lead. But I couldn't help peeping over at Cynthia, her saddle shoes interacting fluidly with her partner's penny loafers on the other side of the room. Then I saw Shirley, rocking so easy with Speckles. God, no one moved better on the dance floor than Shirley McFarlin. And where would I find my old pickup pal, blue streak Bobby? Over there, already making out with Grace in Mr. Calderone's huge TV chair, rooted from its traditional resting place in front of the big 19-inch picture screen to a remote corner of the room.

Now I found myself perplexed as to what course of action I should pursue. As Brenda smiled coquettishly and her eyes investigated mine, I realized she too had become an exciting opportunity, at least for the short-term. Cynthia seemed a precarious long shot gamble, but a seven-year fancy finally materialized. And Shirley embodied special booty herself, her flying auburn hair teasing the air above her dancing feet. I slugged down the last of my latest liquor research, a 7&7 this time, before heading to the kitchen for a refill.

The decision had to be no decision. Enjoy the party and everyone there, let the chips fall as they may. What the hell, keep the girls off balance. This system had worked in the past; let it work again. I found my way over to the record player and piled on a stack of fast rockers—Clyde McPhatter and the Drifters, the Crows, Chuck Berry, the Cleftones, Hank Ballard and the Midnighters.

"Come on, Shirley, let's dance."

I held out my hand, and we boogied just like our last date a year ago at the firehouse sock hop. Pert Shirley McFarlin had the feel and she knew how to shake it. Except for Bobby and Grace, everyone had gotten to their feet, moving and grooving to that nasty old rock 'n' roll.

In the midst of the bedlam, fulfilling my disc jockey role by searching for some fresh sounds from Tommy's record collection, I felt a soft touch on my arm. It was Cynthia.

"Robbie, could you put on Johnny Ace for me? You know, 'Pledging My Love'."

I took a second to compose myself and replied, as coolly as I could manage, "Sure, Cynthia, I think Tommy's got that in here somewhere."

"And Robbie, when you find it, do you think you could ask me to dance?"

I looked up. It seemed like she was staring right into my soul. Though I know I conveyed my pleasure to satisfy her request, I have no idea how I said it.

I found it impossible to stay calm as I plunged through the mounds of records. And with regret, the project made me aware of another problem I'd have to deal with. I'd begun to feel dangerously drunk.

"**F**at city!" Bobby shouted, competing with the bluster of his Hollywood mufflers. "That is one very hot young chick, any way you slice it. Now let's get back to the center ring of this rowdy circus."

He gestured wildly with both hands as he rolled down the road. I wondered if I should suggest I do the driving. It appeared that he and I had maybe traded places on the intoxication front. Then again, Bobby had never let anyone else handle his customized wheels, at least to my knowledge.

I'd gotten pretty upset with myself for letting him talk me into helping drive Brenda and Grace home early from the party. As far as I was concerned, the deciduous taste of the foreplay hadn't been worth the price of leaving a kick ass party right at the height of the lunacy. With immense possibilities pending.

The fact that I'd finally danced with Cynthia and everything turned out copacetic, despite my fuddled condition, convinced me that the chance of a lifetime with my dream girl had finally come to be. I could still hear her words whispering in my ear as we slow-danced to the sad, haunting voice of Johnny Ace. *Ginger and I are going to spend the night here, Robbie. We've already cleared it with our parents. We can party all night long.* I prayed that my imprudent absence during the evening hadn't altered the implications of that intention.

When Bobby pulled into the driveway at the Calderone house, I felt the prickle of my first hint that things might not pan out like I hoped. Although the hands on my Timex pointed to just 1:30 in the morning, I saw only two other parked cars. I jumped out the door while Bobby finished listening to some doo-wop on the radio. I leaped up the steps at the back entrance and into the kitchen. The stench of cigarette smoke welcomed me back. All right, the rock 'n' roll roared on, full volume.

"Hey, Bender, where you been, man? We missed you. Where's Bobby?"

A large group sat around the kitchen table, shooting the bull. Cynthia was conspicuously absent.

"Oh, he's coming in. He's out in the car," I replied to slurring Eddie, his eyes now as dusky and opaque as two chunks of char-coal. "So, what's happening? What'd I miss?"

"One helluva party," Speckles piped in, his copious freckles giving his face a two-tone effect in the stark kitchen light. "This one's right up there with the best of 'em. And we ain't done yet. Grab a chair and join us. Another toast to good old fucking Denton High. How the hell will she survive without us assholes."

Speckles poured a round of shots from the bottle of Cuervo on the table. I finally noticed its presence and the canister of Morton's Salt and plate of lime wedges. He held up a shaky, spilling shot glass of the wicked liquid, nodding for me to take it. A Tri Gam slid the salt and plate of limes over in front of an empty chair Tommy had fetched for me.

"Come on, Robbie, join us now in this sacrilegious ceremony. Our time together is running out, before our very eyes," Tommy pronounced. "We dare not minimalize the sacred nature of this hysterical event."

They all downed their shooters and went through the salt and lime bit. I hesitated, then followed suit.

"So where's everybody else?" I gasped, in between sucking on my lime wedge. "Who's in the living room?"

"We're it, old man. The rest decided to abandon ship," Tommy replied. "Now only us alkies are left to keep this boat afloat."

A moment later, with everybody preoccupied with their own hazy conversations, Shirley McFarlin leaned across the table and took my hand.

"Cynthia was upset you left, Robbie. She and Ginger took off with those east side Jesters. She got them to drive the two of 'em home, I guess."

This fine young gal with the mane that would put a lion to shame looked at me with the warmth of sincere and caring insight. The kind of look I wished I'd gotten just once from my doting mother.

"Pass me that bottle of tequila, Shirley," I said dourly. "Think it's time for another shot."

Her altruistic emerald eyes held me in an intimate embrace I could not fully appreciate at the time. Her satin voice squelched the raucous sounds that surrounded us.

"I'll do that, Robbie. Then maybe you'll play Johnny Ace. For you and me this time. I never did get that slow dance with you tonight."

I would've been glad to trade places with those damn birds singing in the trees, rejoicing the Sunday morning sunshine that streamed through the windows of my room in the old Calderone house. It had come to be their turn to celebrate the glory of life and they went about it in the manner God had intended, free of the masochistic crutch of alcohol abuse. Yet the fusion of their gay fragmented melodies and fragile whistling tones drilled the aching blood vessels in my brain with what seemed to be malevolent intent. It was as though they had decreed to rebuke me for the violations of their tranquility during the previous nights.

"Robbie, are you awake?"

I squinted in the direction of Tommy's whisper at the door. His appearance tugged me further toward painful consciousness. He wore a gaudy, oversize black and gold silk smoking jacket—I assume it belonged to his dad—which accentuated his narrow head and protruding Adam's apple poking out above the wide lapels. His skinny legs extended below the dangling waist sash.

"I got hot coffee ready, if you want. And some bagels and blueberry muffins."

"Oh, man, you look as weird as I feel," I replied, startling myself with a voice two octaves lower than usual. "Since when do waiters dress up like that." I attempted a laugh, but the pain in my head cut it short.

Fifteen minutes later I dragged myself into the kitchen to rejoin Tommy. I found him reading the Sunday paper with his muffin and cup of coffee.

"What's with the rest of the crew?" I asked, buttering my bagel and finger as if they were one. "Bobby and the others still sleeping?" It dawned on my ragged brain that I hadn't seen him since rejoining the party last night.

Tommy put aside his paper. He proceeded to give me a news update on an extravaganza now into its winding-down phase. Dashing Bobby had passed out sitting in his car. Tommy found him there this morning, asleep with the radio transmitting live gospel music from some Second Baptist church in Harlem. He reacted to the breakfast invitation by sliding down on the seat and curling up for a more comfortable recuperation. Speckles and Eddie and a couple of Jesters remained upstairs, in essence doing the same thing. One of the Tri Gams had woken Tommy over an hour ago, as she roused Shirley and the other girls. Since she had the car, they all left so she could attend early Mass.

"But she said you looked awful cute lying there next to Shirley. I guess Shirley had her arm around you, just like the two of you were going steady, or something."

I don't remember anything between that last shot of tequila in the kitchen and Tommy pulling me away from my morning contention with the birds. So, after all the fancy dancing, I ended up "sleeping" with Shirley McFarlin. I imagine Shirley felt pretty safe snuggling up next to a comatose ladies' man who demonstrated more adeptness in his courtship of alcohol than of the opposite sex.

"What do we got to eat?" Eddie inquired in an even raspier voice than usual, his squat Italian body wobbling into the kitchen. He looked as bad as I felt.

Within a half-hour Speckles and the remaining Jesters joined us, too. Tommy raced full tilt as the gracious host once again, pouring coffee, cutting and toasting bagels, making it all as pleasurable as possible, given the miserable shape we were in.

Finally, Bobby made his pathetic entrance from the back door. The side of his face displayed a distorted sample of the texture of his car's seat covers, a pattern of red lines and marks pressed into his skin. He ignored our humorous taunts and barbs. After settling in at the table with his coffee and bagel, he made his first verbal observation of the day.

"Hey, you know what, guys? We never did make it over to Palisades Park to check out some of them clubs we heard about."

"No," Tommy replied with a posed straight face. "I guess for some reason we just couldn't fit it into our schedule. I kind of think we did okay, anyway."

Speak for yourself, I responded, under my breath.

The Calderone binge proved to be the signal event for the final weeks of the high school lifestyle. In its wake came a time for planning more formal post-graduation family celebrations, scheduled school photography sessions, gathering platitudes and signatures from fellow students and teachers in autograph books. And, somewhere in between, studying for final exams.

The New Jersey weather cooperated on June 8, 1957, with an auspicious blue sky and a few cumulus clouds. The Denton High School graduation ceremony took place out on the football field. We did all our goodbye and good luck hugs and handshakes after the usual speeches about how we were now America's future.

The sunny afternoon then introduced us to a crystal clear evening, highlighted by a full moon, to honor our last night to howl. Tommy Calderone, Eddie Mazzoli and I crashed the various family affairs held in cramped backyards and verandas, their locations conveniently identified by strung-up party lights. We sampled punchbowls and hors d'oeuvres and imbibed the free drinks until we overstayed our welcome at each location.

Then we bopped over to the T&J, where we met up with a large crowd of celebrants, many not graduating from anything other than sobriety, to include Speckles O'Reardon, Bobby Bennett, Ginger Jorgenson, Shirley McFarlin, and the inimitable glad-handing hell-raiser himself, Jerry Blakely. We had our usual tumultuous time of it, raising our glasses in numerous preposterous toasts, everyone trying to outdo the absurdity of those previously proposed. The only damper on the revelry occurred when Bruce Tierney rolled up to the bar in his wheelchair. No one had a suitable toast for that.

CHAPTER 4

. . . and The Genius himself, Ray Charles . . .

In spite of my DA haircut, pegged pants and French toes with Cuban heels, I managed to get myself accepted at an Ivy League college. It seems the wrestling coach at Cornell University was impressed that I'd won the New Jersey State championship at 157 pounds. He pushed my marginally adequate scholastic record through to admission into the College of Arts and Sciences.

With no concrete career aspirations, I selected English as a tentative major, with an eye toward creative writing. I recalled the whimsical fun I'd had as a young boy, composing wild adventure stories. Wouldn't it be terrific to actually earn a living expressing your fantasies on paper?

Mom and Dad accompanied me on my trip up to Ithaca, New York, to attend frosh camp. It turned out to be a brilliant country day, temperate early autumn weather with a light breeze and a painter's blue sky. Enterprising pure white clouds accentuated the bright azure above us, tweaking the imagination with their innovative formations.

We took advantage of nature's blessing to stroll the main campus, visiting Willard Straight Hall, the student union, and the Arts Quad, the central square of the college I'd be attending. This quadrangle evoked in me feelings of homage to a vague power of enlightenment. In my mind's eye I stood alone on the threshold of a hallowed tradition, gazing on the statues of founding father Ezra Cornell and first president Andrew Dickson White as they acknowledged each other across the bisecting center pathway. The noble statues, the venerable stone buildings that framed the quadrangle, the stately trees offering shade to the poets and scholars of so many generations gone before, projected an atmosphere of intellectual eminence. It felt intoxicating, but intimidating as well. I hoped I would be up to the challenge.

"Pretty impressive, folks," Dad remarked. "So, this is going to be Robbie's home for the next four years. What say we check out the rest of the area."

Mom appeared to be in one of her distant moods again.

"Sounds good to me, Dad."

After retrieving the car, we toured the remainder of the campus and surrounding residential area. Driving across Triphammer Bridge we caught a glimpse of a panoramic view that caused us to park on the other side, at a little university café called Noyes Lodge. We walked back to the bridge and were captivated by a vista of waterfalls crashing down into a majestic gorge that cut far and wide beneath us.

Like many other visitors on the bridge, we approached the edge with caution, grasping the handrail firmly and peering over the side. I could look down for only a short while before a whirling lightheadedness seemed on the verge of paralyzing me. I found this dizziness would diminish if I looked straight out to flashing Beebe Lake, a mirror of water that fed the deluge from a sylvan background.

"That building over there by the falls looks like it could be a hydraulic power station," Dad observed, the sunlight glancing off his bald pate.

Another sightseer on the bridge confirmed that here indeed stood a university laboratory for just this purpose.

"Well, this is simply amazing," Dad concluded. "What a wonderful place for you to get your college degree, Robbie."

He wrapped his arm around my shoulders, as if he sensed my fear of both the immediate danger and the more comprehensive elevation this place represented.

"And you're going to be a good student here, too, making your mother and me proud."

Mom nodded absently, continuing to take in the view.

An hour later we said our farewells in front of the College Town boarding house where I'd be living, one of the money-saving perks made available to me by the wrestling coach. I walked my folks over to the car and went through the motions with Mom, exchanging stiff hugs and pecks on the cheek. I held the door for her until she'd settled her angular body inside. Dad and I shook hands. Then he threw his arms around me in a vigorous embrace.

"Goodbye, son. Best of luck in your new life. I'm just so happy for you. You're going to do just fine."

I stood at the curb and watched them labor up the street in the whimpering Nash. I was finally on my own.

"**L**et's go, Big Red! Let's go, Big Red!"

"Hit 'em hard! Knock 'em down! Push 'em back to Princeton town!"

Football cheers and college songs resonated through the pines. Frosh camp had begun at Sky Lake. And it seemed to me the sophomores and upperclassmen functioning as counselors had their work cut out for them. Besides the numerous off-key singers, I wondered about the conviviality of many more. But I did observe one charismatic character whose behavior piqued my curiosity and interest. I also fancied the detective-style fedora hat canted cockily on the back of his head.

Though he appeared different from the rest with his audacious attitude, and a bit rough around the edges, he didn't share my problem of being avoided by the group at large. To the contrary, he seemed to be in the thick of any laughter or frivolity wherever it chose to happen, sparse as it was. The outnumbered *coeds*—a term for college chicks to add to my vocabulary—wearing their bobbed haircuts and Bermuda shorts, generally did not measure up to the physical attractiveness or sensual sociability I'd been accustomed to. Yet their shortcomings didn't curb his mettle. He teased them and flirted in a jovial, affable manner. He liked the ladies and had a unique knack for eliciting responsive titters.

I made a few vain attempts to get near him, hoping some of his aura might rub off on me. But he was like quicksilver, an elusive will-o'-the-wisp. Just when I thought I'd succeeded in getting close, he'd vanished. Only to reappear, somewhere else in the crowd, spinning his charm.

"Hello, Robbie. Would you care to join me at the volleyball game?"

Before me stood my only significant college acquaintance, Dwight something-or-other, a fellow wrestler I met on the bus. "They're starting up in fifteen minutes, over by the dining hall."

I got the impression I'd attracted another lost soul, looking the Ivy League part in his natty clothes and eloquent demeanor, but with a yearning for acceptance running deep inside his polished appearance. He had to be feeling desolate himself to be seeking me out. We seemed odd birds of a feather in our divergent outer images, yet connected in our mutual isolation.

"Hey . . . Dwight." *I hope that's right.* "That sounds great. Thanks for asking. So, how's it been going for you?" I coerced my voice to convey a buoyant optimism as we walked together down the path toward the dining hall.

The volleyball game turned out to be our salvation. "Mickey Spillane," complete with his brown fedora, played on the opposing team to Dwight and me. He contributed a lighthearted gaiety to the event, as well as the winning score for his team. His presence was infectious, pumping exuberance and energy into participants and observers alike.

The boisterous atmosphere carried over to the closing night's "chicken in the basket" beer party. The college songs sounded a whole lot louder.

"We'll all have drinks at Theodore Zinck's! When I get back next fall!"

The counselors did their best. But the singing was deadly. I doubt Cornell's cherished hymns ever took a worse beating.

Before we knew it, even Dwight and I became recipients of the wizard detective's catalytic blessings. We chatted amicably with everyone at our table, festive in its exception to the university's one-third coed population.

"What's our Cornell motto?" the counselors shouted, urging us on.

"Freedom with responsibility!" we obediently answered, with elevated inspiration.

Later, as a local country rock band pretended to be Buddy Holly and his boys, we did our best trying to adapt to the varied dance styles imposed by expanded geographic and cultural backgrounds. I conjectured that the lackluster individual techniques most likely indicated inhibited lifestyles that involved grueling honor society study habits.

"Mickey" lost his hat a few times as he steered a number of partners through some intricate extemporary routines that had the nearby crowd buzzing with amused reaction. I don't think many of these people had ever experienced, much less appreciated, anyone like him before. As seasoned as I felt in the party boy arts, I had to admit that neither I, nor all the noteworthy personalities I'd ever known, could rival this human phenomenon.

He came near me once to retrieve the suitably rambunctious hat. I noticed he looked rather small in stature. Maybe 5 foot 8 at the most. Yet he was well built and handsome, with strong, chiseled features, crystal blue eyes and a broad, tanned forehead contrasting the flaxen hues of his sandy blond hair. I understood why the ladies didn't shy away.

"Roll me over! In the clover! Roll me over, lay me down, and do it again!"

Wow. Where did that come from? The strident voices rang out from one of the tables somewhere to my right. *But I'll take corny over tight-ass any day.* At least some male inhibitions appeared to be crumbling. Even our mentors seemed caught by surprise.

"Don't forget our motto," a masculine voice exclaimed. Probably a counselor.

"Freedom with responsibility!" a mixed chorus responded, tainted with a splash of inebriation.

Dwight and I finally got into the swing of things. On a muted scale compared to our extroverted motivator, of course. But finding some measure of renewed confidence in our own social graces. We secured the interest of two moderately attractive coeds who agreed to dance. While my partner couldn't match up with the likes of Shirley McFarlin, we did manage to hold our own, compared to the limited expertise of this collection of reserved personalities. Dwight surprised and impressed me when he proved to be a very good dancer himself. He showcased a few Lindy moves I thought I might want to add to my own repertoire. He taught his new acquaintance some interesting steps to expand her restrained technique.

I was having fun, at last. And I wanted more than ever to get to know the rascal I felt could be my patron saint in this rigid new world. With renewed vigor I felt ready to meet the man. I excused myself from my group and meandered through the festivity in search of the wicked fedora. Upset when neither could be found, I realized the spirited level of the party had subsided as well, in all likelihood a result of his absence.

Despite my thorough search I could not locate him, even after extensive backtracking. This time he'd totally evaporated. It mystified me as to where he might've gone. Conceding my inability to make him materialize, I returned to my table. Still distracted by his disappearance, I reacquainted myself with my new companions.

When the party closed down, Dwight accompanied me partway back to my cabin. I asked him if he'd met the mystery man in the brown fedora.

"Oh, sure. His name is Lenny Morrissey. Quite a character, isn't he?"

"Yeah, he really is. What do you know about him?"

"Oh, nothing, really. I just introduced myself. I believe he's a townie. Well, this is my turn. Goodnight." He stepped away to the left path and I continued on my own.

I mulled it over a few minutes later as I lay on my bunk. So, his name is Lenny Morrissey. And he's a *townie*. What does that mean, I wondered, as I slipped off into a restless sleep.

On my initial expedition to downtown Ithaca, I stood at the apex of Buffalo Street, somewhat startled by its precipitous decline. Besides scouting out "the city" for the first time, I figured I should be able to find a barber and some clothing stores. I'd decided I needed to cut off my ducktail. I also wanted to initiate a conforming college wardrobe. Nursing the bite of a hangover from the previous night's investment in Johnny's Big Red, an ostentatious College Town bar and restaurant I investigated after a disappointing Frosh Open House, I felt grateful for the luxury provided by the downward slope.

As soon as I crossed Eddy Street on my gravity-enhanced journey, my path took on an intriguing artistic allure. All of a sudden I became aware of unconventional little houses and duplex apartments, porches with hanging plants and wicker furniture, windows decorated with stained glass ornaments and potted flowers. The faint tinkling of wind chimes pirouetted on the fragrant breeze. An Indian motorcycle rested in an alleyway leading to a rear cottage.

"Good morning!" The sprightly greeting of a young girl surprised me as she passed by on the sidewalk.

I froze in place, turning as she climbed the hill behind me, catching the smile she tossed to me as she went.

"Yes, nice day, isn't it." She acknowledged my belated response with a wave of her hand before continuing on her way.

I watched her go. She had lush sable hair and long ballerina legs extending from her cutoff jeans. Books peeked out from the top of her chockablock knapsack. Another off-campus student, just like me. The ache in my head got lost in my excitement as I resumed my walk with a renewed spring in my step, tilted once again toward town.

And then I saw the car. It was parked on the hill below me, its front wheels canted in toward the curb to prevent it from rolling. A spiffy '54 Olds convertible, painted a lavish turquoise with a white top, folded down. Shiny dual exhausts poked out from under the rear bumper.

As I got closer, I noticed the car also vaunted tailor-made features. It had been nosed and decked, lowered in the back, with sleepy chrome eyelids mounted on top of the headlights. A unique custom-forged grill had been set in front. A capable craftsman had deftly painted flagrant orange and gold flames on either side of the louvered hood. The seats were re-upholstered in supple matching turquoise vinyl; the owner had even acquired a fluffy turquoise steering wheel cover. Orange and gold fuzzy dice hung from the rearview mirror, coordinating with the flaming hood. The mock license plate on the front bumper read "GO 4 IT."

I observed that the driver also had nerve, parking in front of a fire hydrant on a steep hill. The only practicality employed was the safety turn of the front wheels. I looked over at the house facing the car, further amused by its long, level, available driveway. Then I made another big discovery. A sign on the house identified it as an Ithaca College dormitory annex. A light bulb flashed in my fettered brain. No wonder this neighborhood has charisma. It's a student housing area for the down-to-earth college kids who live in the shadow of the blue blood Cornell elite. I hastened down the hill with my spirits soaring. I just might fit in here after all.

By the time I tripped upon Rudy's Barber Shop I'd already begun to procrastinate about going through with the college boy conversion. Change is never easy. Especially when you've grown into a certain role in society's game of life and become typecast in that part for a good portion of your existence.

"I'd like a flattop, please," I said to my barber, almost choking as I said it.

The back of my throat had become the Sahara, just like when I exercised my muscles on the warm-up mat for the state wrestling championship. Funny how a simple haircut can invoke such a profound effect.

"So, we're saying bye-bye to the beautiful ducktail, are we?" It surprised me the old coot with the scissors even knew what to call it.

He shook out the cutting cape from his previous client. "Time to be the college man, I guess," I mumbled as he secured it behind my neck.

Sitting back in the chair, I attempted to sort out my mixed feelings and the convoluted reasoning that had conspired to bring me to this consequential crossing in the road. It seemed that my visit to Johnny's Big Red had been the final factor in the decision. As soon as I walked through that door, I realized I'd stepped into a world of pretentious gentility I'd never experienced before. But I stayed right there till closing, flaunting my DA and sideburns to the bitter end. I left those pompous drunks wallowing in their own self-indulgence, walking out as straight as I could. manage, never ever to return.

"You're all done, son," the barber whispered in my ear, alerting me back to reality.

I refused his offer of the hand mirror. Better to postpone seeing the damage than instigate the return of the headache on top of my upset stomach. I beat it out of Rudy's Barber Shop like some fugitive on the lam, looking about for a clothing store to complete the disguise. If anyone had observed me coming and going from that shop, they would have concluded it had to be two different people, albeit wearing the same hood-style clothes. I now looked like some goofy pinhead and my body language reflected my newly acquired lack of confidence.

It didn't take long for me to spend a fair amount of Dad's hard-earned money in three clothing stores on State Street that competed for the contents of collegiate wallets. And I got a little frightened looking at my new image in the dressing room mirrors. My slender shaved head thrust out from button-down collars and V-neck sweaters; the feet beneath my khaki-clad legs were wedged into tasseled loafers.

Contemplating how I'd explain these expenditures to my parents, I now faced the task of getting back up the formidable hills that lay between downtown and College Town, gripping shopping bags loaded with my purchases. Standing at the base of State Street hill, I pessimistically stuck out my thumb. I got lucky after just six passing vehicles.

"Where you headed?" The male driver's razor blade voice sliced through the dusk of early evening.

"Just up the hill. College Town."

"Hop in."

I'd never known a ride like this before. The sports car was a gunmetal gray two-seat roadster. The top folded down inside a nifty black leather boot, displaying matching leather bucket seats. I discovered that the tiny area behind these seats provided just enough storage space for my bundles.

After checking out my sharp-toed shoes and tapered slacks he shifted into gear and stepped on the gas. "Hold on there, Rocky Guitar."

We bellowed up State Street hill lickety-split. The car seemed so low to the ground I could conceive how close my fanny came to being toasted by the friction with the street's hot red bricks. The snarl of the engine impressed me. Not the pulsating throb I'd grown accustomed to hearing from eight-cylinder American hot rods, but the rich sonorous monotone of a powerful six-cylinder beast.

"What kind of car is this?" I asked the obvious upperclassman. He'd outfitted himself in a tweed jacket and madras shorts. Bare knuckles lewdly protruded through the circular air vents in his leather driving gloves.

His manner and everything about him oozed the elitist credentials of the snobby fraternity man, right down to the bronze crest and Greek letters signifying Alpha Delta Phi mounted on the dashboard. For all I knew, he may very well have been in Johnny's Big Red last night.

"Austin-Healey," he said, loftily. "3000. British."

I couldn't be sure what he meant by "3,000." The car had to have cost more than that. It probably referred to the model number. I filed it away for future reference.

As we climbed with ease up into College Town, a whole new perspective relative to automobiles began to crystallize in my mind. The customized Olds parked on Buffalo Street shined as a work of hip Americana to be admired. But this tiny foreign sports car represented another class altogether. I vowed right then and there that someday I would own one, too.

CHAPTER 5

"*Uno momento*, amigo. People are going to think you're loco if you keep talking to yourself like that."

Wrenched from my brooding train of thought, I stared at the smirking tawny-haired fellow with the expansive smile and air of cocky self-assurance. We stood there, face to face in the middle of the Arts Quad.

"Want to join me at the Ivy Room for a cup of coffee? Name's Jack Darling. Looks like we're going to be Spanish compadres this semester."

I did have an hour before my next class. And I needed someone to share my concerns about the advanced Spanish instruction that had just overwhelmed me. At least this total stranger would have firsthand knowledge of the dilemma I faced.

Jack Darling became my first experience with a full-fledged *preppie*. When he boasted that fact to me I pretended I knew what it meant, although it had been another of the new terms I heard bandied about at frosh camp I intended to investigate. I was fast learning how little I knew about a lot of things, how provincial my upbringing and background, despite my adventurous nature and proximity to big city life.

Jack had a number of steps on me, in just about everything—clothes, vocabulary, self-confidence, polish. And his seductive way with women. Even as we sat across the table from each other in the Ivy Room, as he embellished his plan to help both of us through Spanish 103, he acquainted himself with available coeds. One would have thought him to be an upperclassman, for he handled even the mature sorority women as deftly as the eager freshmen girls. He pocketed a couple of telephone numbers during the hour's break I spent with him.

Watching him in action, I realized he presented an impressive persona, a combination of masculine charisma and shrewd social talent. He had a distinctive look about him, handsome despite bearing a number of atypical facial attributes. A long, slender ridge of a nose jutted low on his head, sloping to the tip as if it had been designed using an architect's compass. Even in my agitated state of mind I could envision my tiny landlady and a bevy of Lilliputian friends ski-jumping with glee off the end of that incomparable proboscis. Above a pronounced cleft chin his wide canyon mouth bore the suggestion of an endless horizon.

Viewed independently, each feature seemed peculiar in its glaring uniqueness, not to be found on the plastic surgeon's recommended contour charts. But the composite face, set upon broad shoulders and lending expression to the imposing personality, merged its deviant characteristics to manifest sensuality and power.

"So, combining my verbal expertise with your reading and writing capabilities, we can be one hell of a Señor Beaner in this course," he concluded, collecting his books and rising to go to his next class. "Here, give me a call tonight. We'll get together on the first assignment."

He tossed a small card on the table and strode over to an attractive coed who'd apparently been waiting for him at the exit door. I watched them leave with his hand steering her at the small of her back. I picked up his offering, astonished to find myself looking at his personal business card. It had been professionally arranged and printed in raised letters that announced "Jack O. Darling, Student of Life, Cornell University." The card indicated his address and telephone number at the freshman dormitories.

All of a sudden I woke up to the fact that my English Comp course had started in Goldwin Smith Hall. I rushed out of the Ivy Room in a dither. It isn't prudent to be late for your first class, especially in your chosen major.

I'd just survived my first wrestling practice at Teagle Hall. As I pulled off my wet sweats in the locker room, my frosh camp pal Dwight slapped me on the shoulder.

"Hello, Robbie. Good to see you again. Congratulations, I noticed they had you working with the select few at the back. I guess they have high expectations of you."

Before I could respond, a vaguely recognizable voice spoke out from my other side.

"Yeah, saw you over there, running with the big dogs. Looked like you were holding your own with that tough Canadian."

I turned in the direction of this second visitor. He looked familiar, standing there with only a towel wrapped around his waist, his hair still wet from the shower. But I needed some time to place the face.

He extended his hand. "Hey there, I'm Lenny. So what happened to your duck's ass hairdo? Trying to get close to some sorority honey already? It ain't worth it, I'm telling you."

Recognition pierced my brain. Behold that sculpted face again, those crisp blue eyes, the square jaw and prominent forehead. Only the blond locks vacationed from his classic countenance, thanks to the shower spray. It was none other than the mystic man I'd sought in vain at Sky Lake. Now Lenny Morrissey stood before me. And he'd taken it upon himself to shake my hand.

I had no idea the motivation maestro of frosh camp shared my penchant for wrestling. The two of us hit it off right from the start, both of us talking incessantly about everything imaginable, oblivious of everyone else in the locker room. Poor Dwight gave up trying to put in his two cents' worth. He took off on his own, after we ignored his invitation to drinks from the vending machine.

Lenny possessed a super wit, with an uncanny ability to dredge humor out of the most mundane subject. I found myself chortling away like someone losing control at a cocktail party. Lenny seemed to sense the impropriety of our exuberance so early on within the sober athletic climate. The moment we were dressed, he offered to give me a ride to the dorms. He appeared pleased when I told him I lived in a boarding house in College Town.

"That's even better. Right on my way home. Let's go crack the books," he exclaimed with a wink, his tongue pushing out his cheek.

Lenny led me out of Teagle Hall and into the parking lot. We chuckled about his dance improvisations at frosh camp, the stupefied reactions he'd gotten from the crowd. He recalled the response of one conservative coed partner who couldn't follow his Lindy lead at all, so he'd resorted to a bastardized version of the Charleston.

"She was bewildered at first. Then she smiled this sheepish little grin, handed her horn-rimmed glasses to another chickie to hold for her, and showed all of us how it should be done. The only thing missing was the flapper dress. I spent the rest of the night trying to keep her from time-warping me all the way back to the twenties. But turns out she definitely knew the back seat boogie, too."

I decided I'd toss in one of the highfalutin Cornell-isms I'd heard around campus. "So that's where you disappeared to. You *cad*. I was looking all over for you that night, since you were having more fun than me . . . and you just left me there, high and dry."

"Hell, I couldn't afford being seen with some city slicker hooligan with a duck's ass hairdo. I got to start building my Ivy League image if I want to succeed, you know. Well, here we are."

I stood gaping at the car in disbelief. There it was, again. The turquoise paint job glimmered in the flush of the evening.

The chrome headlight shields reflected a seductive wink as we approached. The decorative flames along the hood flickered in the waning twilight. That customized '54 Olds convertible I discovered illegally parked on Buffalo Street belonged to my inscrutable new acquaintance, Lenny Morrissey.

When we pulled out of the lot I tried to blindside him with the surprise of this knowledge. I asked if he'd been at the Ithaca College dorm annex Saturday afternoon.

"The police are looking for some guy who was there with a customized green convertible," I lied. "Apparently some . . . coed . . . was found spread-eagle naked on her bed, handcuffed to the bedposts."

He played along with my contrived tale, his lip curling impishly as he countered my banter. "A faulty fabrication if I ever heard one, Bender. First of all, I always use rope. It's kinkier. Secondly, it was me they found tied up. Let me tell you, those IC honeys are something else."

We laughed. I settled back in my seat, relishing the comradery I'd been missing.

Rolling right by my boarding house, Lenny downshifted gears, generating a staccato back blast through his Smitty steel-packed mufflers. I imagined my landlord, seated there in his inner recluse, opening his oversize eyelids in annoyance.

"Okay. So now I know where you sack out. Do you like greasy burgers and fries? Let's grab a bite to eat at the best goddam' diner in Tompkins County."

Now he sped down the hill, taking corners with squealing tires. The cool night air caressed our faces as we both slipped into the euphoria of the ride itself. I anticipated the wail of some cop's siren penetrating and bursting the tenuous rapture. But Lenny kept to the back streets, making many turns as he weaved his way across town, knowing just when and where to either accelerate, gear down, or swerve to avoid potholes. Then we bounced over railroad tracks and screeched to a halt before an old railroad car with a wavering fluorescent sign on the roof identifying it as "Obie's Diner."

It came as no surprise to me that Lenny seemed to know everybody in the place. Starting with the beefy owner and chef, Obie. The old guy in the apron performed like a one-man sideshow at the carny, up to his armpits in Crisco filling orders for hamburgers, omelets, grilled Taylor's ham and cheese sandwiches, tuna salads, deep-fried onion rings, hash browns and French fries. I took his gruff manner for a façade, as he appeared to enjoy the spotlight. The one available mini-table in the back turned out to be five minutes away, Lenny glad-handing and conversing with all kinds of locals as we went.

I noticed most of the customers fell into the category of blue-collar workers: plumbers, electricians, mechanics, a smattering of farmers—at least they wore denim coveralls. A few businessmen in cheap neckties and young rowdies flaunting their angry duds and tattoos stood out in the crowd. The women ranged from older ladies wearing too much lipstick and perfume to coarse country girls trying their best to appear refined beyond their earthy cultivation. At long last I'd gotten educated on the meaning of the term *townie*.

Of course, some college kids had come to hang out there as well. But the ones Lenny hobnobbed with all attended Ithaca College. I assumed the others, seated together in their neat button-downs and London Fogs, had to be student representatives from the genteel culture that reigned from the lofty hill across town.

"Look like goddam' Psi U's," Lenny muttered, half under his breath. "Frigging snotty preppy snoots."

His sudden invective startled me. My first glimpse of his concealed temper exposed a side as volatile and surly as his outward manner gleamed carefree and clever.

I squeezed between tightly spaced tables to the far side of the two-foot Formica square that would serve our bonding banquet, allowing Lenny the privacy of turning his back on his targets of malice. We jockeyed into synthetic chairs.

"They booted me out of one of their parties I crashed last year. 'Cause I was having too good a time with their Dee Gee honeys. A couple of those sneering faces look familiar."

We had a lot to talk about, getting to know one another. I was glad Obie had only a single waitress working this night, one of those who always seem to be busy somewhere else. It gave us plenty of time to lay the foundation of our friendship.

Of course I'd already learned from Dwight that Lenny resided in Ithaca, certifying him as a local, or townie, as they say. His parents had escaped a hard rural life when they left the family farm some years before, his dad gaining a sales position with the local Pontiac dealership. The eldest of three children, all boys, Lenny had flourished as the apple of his daddy's eye. He'd been a leading athlete at Ithaca High School, starring on the soccer team—too small for football—as well as wrestling and track. I'd come within an inch of having guessed his height at frosh camp. He actually stood at 5 foot 7, and weighed about 135 pounds. Like myself, he only lost one match during the course of his senior year, and won the 130-pound sectional championship. He fully expected to be the starting wrestler at that weight on Cornell's freshman team.

Lenny had talked me into the "Obieburger." It turned out to be a skyscraper of ingredients perched on top of a half-pound hand-formed beef patty, inside an inadequate-size bun. He looked at me with a mischievous grin.

"You know, coach wouldn't be too happy seeing us eating all this grease. Especially you, working out with the big dogs in the back."

My response came out muffled by the mouthful I'd just begun to chew. "Yeah, wehh, I don' expec' I be dancing with those guys for very wong, anyway."

I managed to swallow. "That air back there is a little too thin for me. If you know what I mean."

"A rarefied atmosphere, to be sure," Lenny replied. "Those boys don't even have sex the week of a match. Afraid it'll sap their strength. To be honest, beyond the books and wrestling, they don't have a life. One nice thing about it, we won't have to worry about running into any of 'em at the places we'll be getting our extra training. Kicking it off this Thursday night down at the Chanticleer."

"You mean you'll be wearing your Mickey Spillane hat again, investigating some underground activity . . . with your slick new sidekick?"

"You got that right, pardner. And you better believe 'my gun is quick'," he ad-libbed at blazing speed, referencing the author's trashy bestseller.

On the drive back to College Town I listened to the rumble of the Oldsmobile's mufflers as I again enjoyed riding shotgun up State Street hill. I recalled the lighter growl of the fleet British sports car during my previous ascent. Despite the lure of that incredible automobile, I knew this was where I really belonged—with Lenny. I had no idea an inconceivable odyssey had just begun.

CHAPTER 6

I'd always considered the pace of my high school days to be the fast lane. Yet those times pale in comparison to the frenetic tempo that characterized my college world. Now my unbridled temperament became the governing force, renouncing my controlled early upbringing. I became my own worst enemy in perpetuating the pedal-to-the-metal velocity of my life, my disposition spurring my physiological functions to the extreme. There were not enough hours in any day. And no one to tell me, "Time for bed."

My choice of new associations, just like the friends I developed in high school, further fueled this helter-skelter lifestyle with their own high-powered personalities. Jack Darling not only convinced me to commit to his joint venture approach in conquering advanced Spanish, but join him Wednesday night for pitchers of whiskey sours at the notorious Jim's Place.

"Time to get your dicky wet at a real college hangout, laddie-buck. Might want to have a rubber on you, too. I've already struck it rich there. Got your pick of lovelies . . . Cornell and Ithaca College."

At wrestling practice the next day Lenny and I also made arrangements to hit the downtown bars Thursday night, starting at the Chanticleer.

"I'll pick you up at your house around nine. That'll give us a couple minutes or so, after practice, to crack them books, heh, heh, before we head out. Ain't nothing happening before then, anyhow."

Coach had secured me a cloakroom job at the student union and the schedule had me on duty that night. But I'd met a wimpish bookworm who also worked there. I figured he might help me out.

Jack Darling ditched me at Jim's Place Wednesday night, staring at a half-pitcher of sours. He favored a petite brunette who wore her sweater inside out to hide her Kappa Kappa Gamma pin after downing her fifth glass.

Lenny Morrissey arrived right on schedule Thursday, his turquoise Olds slam-banging to a stop in front of my boarding house at exactly nine o'clock. My head felt cobwebby from the previous evening, but I was too excited about doing the town with him to let that interfere.

"It was like duck soup!" I bragged to Lenny as we sped down the hill. "This nerd I got to sub for me at the Straight actually thanked me for asking him. And he's handling some big professors' conference that'll keep him busy most of the night. I'm taking his Sunday afternoon spot. That should be nice and quiet, so I can catch up on all the reading I should've been doing this week."

"Way to go, pardner," Lenny yelled back at me, as we careened around a corner to the harsh whining of his Dunlop tires. "I knew you could do it. Where there's a will, there's a way, or some such shit. Now I'm going to introduce you to the underbelly of the good old city of Ithaca. And the Chanticleer's just about the best place to get baptized."

The tacky old bar on the corner, with its neon rooster perched at the top of its vertical sign like some antiquated arts cinema, hummed briskly. Just as Lenny said it would. Of course everyone knew him, like they had at Obie's Diner.

I felt a little surprised it didn't turn out to be a college hangout at all. The crowd seemed predominantly older locals. The male patronage wore badges of the working class, their weathered necks and callused hands sticking out of plaid flannel shirts. There also happened to be a couple of groomed fellows sporting ties, who might've been neighborhood retailers having just closed up their shops.

The women were older too, like the music they played on the haggard jukebox, Glenn Miller's "In the Mood" and "Little Brown Jug," along with other catchy dance tunes from the big band swing era. Most of them had dressed in simple print dresses. They appeared to be having a rollicking good time, four of them dancing with each other and flirting with the men. It seemed obvious everyone was enjoying themselves as long accustomed to doing here, with no pretenses.

"Things are just getting going," Lenny advised, after introducing me to some of the geezers at the bar. We'd moved down to the far end of the counter. "Let's settle in at my old bar stool at the edge of the earth here. If you sit long enough, you'll eventually see it all. What're you drinking? This one's on me."

After we'd been served he caught me off guard with a momentous personal toast.

"Welcome to infamous Ithaca, Robbie. May your time here be an education beyond the musty halls and ivy walls of that holy institution up on the hill. And here's to good times and true friendship, 'cause that's what it's all about. Most folks never get to even sample that sweet nectar. And if they are that lucky, the cup usually empties pretty quick. So, here's to you and me, taking that first sip together. May our chalice last all the way to the final sunset."

Beyond the symbolic poignancy, I'd never before heard anyone make a deep soulful pledge like this with such improvised eloquence. Prone to being emotional, I could feel my eyes begin to fill. I looked away to hide my embarrassment. But unable to fabricate some charade to warrant the action, and feeling the intensity of his presence beside me, I returned to the disconcerting ambiance he'd created.

He looked straight at me, right through me, a brazen glint in his eyes. Then his mouth curved into a half-smile, half-smirk, and he flashed an almost imperceptible wink. Finally grasping his roguish drift, I surprised myself reacting with a hearty spontaneous laugh. Lenny followed in turn, until we both began convulsing with howls of delight that spread to our neighbors at the bar, who adopted the mirth without question. Tears of joy now fell unrestrained from our eyes. It was a strange occasion I shall never forget, much less explain.

As the place continued to fill up I noticed many younger townies began to arrive, joining their elders without regard for the generation gap. Rather, there appeared to be an affection that transcended their mutual respect. The only item of significance I could discern between the age differences was the more contemporary clothes on these new arrivals: form fitting jeans or sheath skirts on the girls, stylish shirts or sweaters on the guys.

And they all mingled at once. Two youthful men who'd just entered politely broke in on one set of middle-aged lady dancers, who amiably accepted their new partners. The couplings hoofed the floor for more than double the pleasure. Their friends gathered at the edge of the dance area and encouraged the romping pairs with good-natured hollers, clapping hands and stomping feet to the tempo of the music.

"Come on, big Dave, show 'em how you won the 'Tall Man's Two-Step' at the state fair!"

"Yeah, give 'em your Paul Bunyon 'loop her through your legs' trick! The folks always like that."

"Just don't let her bump her head this time!"

"That's right. You remember how that hurts. E-E-E-E-HAH!"

I turned to Lenny, to express my enjoyment of the spectacle taking place before us. He was gone again. This time my eyes caught up with him, over at a far table. He whispered in the ear of a heavyset gal whose rippling giggles added to the merriment. The next second they too began high-stepping with the other dancers, somehow avoiding collision until they got their act together. I felt reluctant to plunge into Lenny's world, not having the security of my own inner circle of conspirators. So despite some rather conspicuous encouraging glances from a number of decorated eyes in various corners of the club, and a few alcohol-inspired urges to respond, I held my ground on my corner stool.

After a series of lively numbers, a mawkish ballad put an end to the daredeviltry, summoning dewy bodies to more intimate dalliances. A moment later Lenny came back. He pointed out the dancing rotund lady he'd just left to a gangly spindly-legged man in worn corduroy trousers. The guy appeared to be starving for the nourishment he might leech from her plump flesh. They were quite the contrast out on the floor, beyond their divergent body types. She overtly affected demure rejections, sniggering her mock distress at his pursuit of a closer, more romantic posture.

Soon people became aware of this bizarre pair. A swelling of raucous hoots and halloos commenced. As the woman played up to the room, I thought it ridiculous that the man became so intent on his obsession he seemed oblivious of both her demeaning actions and the taunting clamor from the audience. I felt sorry for the jerk. The insipid music eventually concluded. Then the entire establishment gave the couple a standing ovation. They took extravagant bows and curtsies and blew kisses to the enthusiastic crowd. Lenny stuck two fingers in his mouth and vented shrill whistles of appreciation.

"What a couple. Yeah! All right! Give 'em a hand, ladies and gentlemen. What a show! What a show."

I finally realized the only dupe in the place was me.

"Hi, Lenny. Fancy meeting you here, of all places."

In the midst of the confusion, two stunning young blondes stood before us. Their porcelain smiles confirmed their warm regard for my new "lifelong" buddy. It seemed like the four of us floated on a cloud somewhere in the atmosphere. I hoped that when I blinked we would all still be there. I did, and we were.

"Hey, it's Margie. Imagine that. Hi, Zina. Well, I'm equally shattered to see you two lovely ladies exposing yourselves to the likes of the old 'Rooster.' On a Thursday night, no less. Say, I want to introduce you to my newfound friend here, Robbie Bender. He and I are both going to be wrestling for good old Cornell. You're going to come out and cheer us on . . . at least when we meet IC, ain't you? I know how you both love wrestling."

"You've got such a nasty way of saying things, Lenny Morrissey," Marjorie replied as she nestled into his arm. "Don't you start misleading your new chum. Hi, Robbie, I'm Marjorie."

She gave me a smile that made me feel we could become true pals.

"Lenny's showing you the ropes, eh? Hope you're having a nice time rubbing elbows with all us local yokels in our little Peyton Place. You'd do better to get to know Zina here . . . she's come all the way from Holland, just to learn our wonderful American ways."

I looked at Zina and she returned my gaze with matching interest. She held out her soft hand to me. "I'm very pleased to meet you, Robbie. So you're another one of those smart Ivy League college boys. I'm sure Marjorie and I would love to see you and Lenny in your wrestling tights."

Zina had this ostensive girlish innocence about her that sparked my most secret fantasies. But she obviously possessed a keen inner resourcefulness, confirmed the moment she spoke, her Dutch accent adding a smidgen of Continental polish. Her straight blonde hair fell halfway down her back, framing an oval face accented by pouty red lips and lustrous blue eyes. She'd been blessed with a slender, athletic body, well promoted by the snug blue jeans and tight sweater she wore. In a word, she was a fox. I felt captivated by her enticements.

Given the opposite paths traveled by my bruised conceit and aggravated self-consciousness, I would probably have resisted temptation. At least for the time being, obeying my fears of not measuring up in some regard, not articulating with humor, intelligence or worldliness, or just not looking cool. But fortified by the alcohol, the glow of the night's diversions, and my accomplice's confidence, I stepped up to the occasion with a fervor that had deserted me since those daring days back in Denton.

Now we all talked and laughed together, Lenny assuming the role of the moderating host. Except his obvious intent was to discard all moderation, as he made certain everyone had drinks and instigated outrageous conversation and behavior. Swept up by the pace of the action within our circle and beyond, it seemed like I'd been transposed to the good old T&J. I caught myself shifting back, more than once, from the memory of that favorite haunt to the reality of the present. Now I'd become an authentic college man, cutting up in a wild country tavern with my new companions. I rejoiced in the realization that the transition had at last been accomplished.

"Let's do it, Robbie. I'm ready to dance with my first American boy."

Back in full stride once again, I flew to the dance floor with Zina. I found myself further beguiled by her impassioned, graceful moves, her natural feel for the music. Beyond our complimentary styles, there seemed to be a reciprocal rhythm and flow somatic comprehension, as though we'd shared a childhood as next-door playmates. I exulted in the ether of the moment, realizing the frail, temporal nature of opportunities like this, savoring it like the drink that has boosted you to the intoxicating pinnacle.

It seemed obvious to me and, I felt certain, every other male in the place, that here indeed was the beautiful queen of the hop, the luscious girl/woman vision of seductive innocence and uninhibited youth. And, brother, did she know how to groove. While I believed I'd evolved into one of the better dancers of the original rock 'n' roll generation, I celebrated the sweet taste of elation when Zina stayed right with me. She seemed to absorb the very essence of the music into the marrow of her bones.

We danced as though possessed, our feet gliding over the floor. I was barely cognizant of the audience around us until everyone got up on their feet, saluting us with cadenced hand claps as we whirled and pranced to Little Richard's "Slippin' and Slidin'." Only then did I realize Lenny and Marjorie had slipped out there too. Zina and I were just part of the backup choral dancers, performing with the headliners.

"Where are we going?" Zina cried with a look of astonishment.

"I'm ready for a booze break," I sulked, yanking her by the hand.

"But we were just getting into it out there," she said. "Come on. We're really good together."

"You're a great dancer, Zina. But right now I need a drink."

We slid through the crowd back to the bar.

I felt somewhat slighted so much attention had been directed at Lenny and his partner, rationalizing it had happened because he was the local hero and I the newcomer in town. But as I watched from the bar I realized he deserved the adoration. His ability to incorporate an endless variety of steps and moves with little repetition could only be considered phenomenal. And he did it with perfect timing, allowing Marjorie adequate notice of his intentions so she could respond to the innovations fluidly while infusing her own embellishments.

As each new musical selection replaced the old I became aware of an even more astounding aspect of his talent and the approach to his craft. Despite the free expression, every performance was unique unto itself. Close observation revealed a fresh choreography exclusive to the individual piece. Lenny's creativity provided each dance its own distinct identity.

Clamorous applause. Observers leaned toward the vortex. The other dancers encircled Lenny and Marjorie, everyone clapping and chanting "Hey, hey, hey" as the pair conjured up exaggerated struts and flounces to "Flat Foot Floogie"—"with a floy, floy."

The four of us felt the wacky urge to chortle those lyrics when we stumbled out of the Chanticleer almost two hours later. The chimes of "See you later, Lenny!" echoed in our ears.

"Time for a nightcap," Lenny announced. He led us around the corner to a battered door a half block away.

The crackled gold lettering arched across the front window identified the Sunset Bar & Grill as a place that had earned its presence over many years. As soon as Lenny swung open the withering gate I knew I'd like this joint. The heavy bass progression of some old blues standard invited us into an entirely different environment. Inside, a veil of smoke and darkness enfolded us, the scanty illumination provided solely by the dim lights from the bar, a jukebox, and one hooded bulb hanging over a pool table. My pupils activated emergency dilation measures, like when entering a theater with the movie already in progress, even though we'd come in from the shadowy city streets in the middle of night.

As we moved toward the bar, my eyes continuing to adjust, I observed we just happened to be the only white people in the room. The Sunset was a colored club. We stimulated some curious looks from the patrons. It seemed obvious they were not accustomed to seeing Caucasians, much less three blonds, in this refuge from the daily agony. Lenny nonchalantly escorted us to one empty barstool located at the very center of the bar.

A male on the left started to get up, offering his seat. Lenny placed his hand on the man's shoulder, saying, "Hey there, friend, thank you very much, but you stay right where you are. We just need the counter space to get ourselves some serious drinks from good old Chester over there."

Hearing his name, the bartender glanced over from the far end of the bar, where he waited on another customer. A big smile creased his face.

"Well, well, well. Look who's granting us the honor of his presence tonight. Good to see you, Lenny. Give me a minute here. I'll be right with you."

The husky voice on the juke yowled, "Listen to me, brother. Get yourself together. The time has come for a change."

With the closing hour fast approaching, Lenny made use of the few moments we had left. He introduced us to Chester and a couple of other characters he knew. Then he secured drinks for the road and played some records on the reposing jukebox. I heard Albert King's sorrowful "Bad Luck Blues" for the first time, thinking it a peculiar choice coming from the blond boy with the catching smile.

I got real bold and took hold of Zina's hand as we stood at the bar. I felt relieved when she answered with a tender squeeze, looking straight into my eyes with anticipation. As Lenny and Marjorie got into a lengthy conversation with Chester, I finally had the opportunity to talk to her. The first shock hit me when she told me she still attended high school. A 17-year-old foreign exchange student into her senior year, she had her own room in an American home somewhere on the edge of town.

"Until now I've lived my whole life in Holland," she confided. "With Mamma and Pappa. And my older brother and sister, before they left the house. They're both married now. And I just became an aunt!" she beamed.

"They really didn't want me to do this. Coming to America on my own, I mean. Mamma's taking it the worst. Pappa's office is in Amsterdam, and he has a long commute. Now she's home alone a lot. She misses me bad already."

"So, now you're finishing high school here in the States . . . living with Marjorie and her family."

She laughed, flipping her long hair back over her shoulder with a casual flick of her head. "Not exactly. Yes, I'm finishing . . . high school, as you call it. But I plan to go back to Holland for the university. And no, I'm not living with Marjorie. She's a student at Ithaca College. I met her when I was shopping in town one Saturday afternoon. Can you believe it, we were both interested in the same dress at the store. We became accidental friends, just like that."

I was so fascinated with Zina and her story I didn't think to ask who ended up with the dress.

Chester started to close up and turn on lights. It surprised me that quite a few existed. So we said our goodnights and nice-to-meet-you's as everybody took turns departing. I reached for my drink to drain the bottom of the glass.

Lenny grabbed my arm, looking at me with a crooked grin. "So here we are at the Sunset, Robbie. And we've drunk the nectar together. Let's leave something in that chalice for next time."

A moment of silence as big as the future weighed heavy while I swallowed on the intention of his words. The only sound was Chester stacking chairs to clear the floor for the morning mop. Even Marjorie and Zina seemed suspended in mute curiosity. Then Lenny and I fell into a fit of laughter that contagiously had the two girls, and even Chester, caught up in the absurdity.

"You son of a bitch, Lenny! You are something else, you know that? Goddam'! You set that up right out of the shoot, over at the Chanticleer. What a frigging con man you are," I blurted in hysterical gasps.

"No," he replied, struggling at grasping his own composure. "I'm serious. I really mean it. I believe it . . . don't you?" The flames of deception raged in his crystal eyes.

"All right, you idiots. This here joint is officially closed," Chester cried. "I need all your white asses out of here, so I can lock her up. Just make sure you bring your friends back for a longer visit next time, Lenny, you crazy goddam' honky."

We tumbled out the door telling Chester how much we loved him and promising we'd all come back.

"Let's tour," Lenny exclaimed, as we Lindy-hopped together out on the sidewalk. We decided to leave Marjorie's car there and retrieve it later. We hustled ourselves down the street to Lenny's turquoise masterpiece.

Within minutes we'd driven up into the hills, taking winding two-lane roads at breathtaking speed. Lenny had the top down, so Zina and I in the back found ourselves holding onto each other for both warmth and stability. And, just like that, we were out in the country, with the earthy clarity of rural air enhanced by the faint, aromatic fragrance of horse manure. For a moment I got lost in a vague earlier time, when life had been simple and beautiful and wondrous, when both terrestrial and celestial worlds had beckoned, eager to reveal their ancient mysteries to anyone brave enough to enter with an open mind and thirst for enlightenment. It was as though the magic and power of the universe had summoned me once again, even inside this reckless speeding automobile, reminding me that the challenges are forever and the answers eternal.

"Look out, Lenny!" Marjorie shrieked at the top of her lungs, as he swerved all the way across the opposite lane, sending stones flying at the far shoulder of the road.

The car fishtailed as he fought to regain the pavement. The rear tire bit onto the hard edge and we lurched back to the right side.

"What was that?" she yawped, looking both shaken and excited as she turned around, kneeling on the front seat to look back at the fleeting tarmac.

"A goddam' Guernsey," Lenny shouted. "Yeeoow! That mother was right there, looking to re-customize old Betsy. How you doing back there? Did I get your hairs up? Thank God for automatic reflexes . . . we could've been at our final Sunset tonight, after all. You see, good thing I didn't let Robbie take that last sip."

Lenny slowed the big Oldsmobile down enough to allow the fuzzy dice a comfortable waltz beneath the rearview mirror. Shortly thereafter we pulled off the road onto a gravel embankment that commanded an impressive view of Lake Cayuga, glistening in the distance. It became obvious this would be the highlight of the tour. As soon as our guide cut the engine he and Marjorie had their heads joined at the mouth.

I felt a bit awkward about the abruptness of all this. But when I turned toward Zina her delicate face shone right there in front of me, her eyelids at half-mast, those inviting moist lips already parting. We kissed the kiss of dreams, as though each of us was searching for the secrets of the other's soul, timid and gentle at first, then increasing our courage for deeper revelations, as the lake slowly slipped from our view.

I'm not certain how long the shameless hot rod shimmied on that lofty perch, rocking easy in the midnight breeze. But after a time of indulging in the heavenly inspiration its mufflers throbbed once again. Then it leaped back onto the road, in a churning cloud of dust. We raced back down the hillside, as furiously as before, the wind lashing our faces and the dashboard dice, now strung out taut in a quivering Saint Vitus' dance.

"Watch out for that cow," Marjorie reminded us. We all laughed together, Lenny accelerating even faster until we reached the outskirts of town.

We bid goodnight to the girls at Marjorie's crusty old DeSoto. Zina's departing kiss lingered on my lips as we followed them to Marjorie's dorm, making sure they got home safe. Marjorie had elected to live at the Ithaca College dormitories, seeking independence from her parents. She and Zina had made arrangements to spend the night there together.

Ascending Buffalo Street I realized it could've been Marjorie Lenny had been visiting when I first discovered his car. Sure enough, as we approached the dormitory annex the DeSoto slowed down and pulled alongside the last open parking space. We exchanged honks and waves as Lenny gunned the Olds around them. I added the vision of Zina blowing me a kiss through the dirty windshield to my list of divine recollections.

Minutes later, Lenny skidded to the curb in front of my boarding house.

"See you at practice, lover boy," Lenny hollered, as I slid out the door. He peeled out into the street.

I ambled up to the house, climbed the steps to the porch. I stood there, reflecting on my fabulous first night out with this astonishing human being. Behind my thoughts I heard the intermittent, ever more distant scream of those abused Dunlops as he made his way home.

CHAPTER 7

"Hello, laddie-bucker. Ready to fight for women's rights? At least their right to be with us."

Jack Darling's evil smile seemed wider than ever as he approached me at the front steps of Willard Straight Hall. This fresh spring Friday evening he kept me and my hangover waiting twenty minutes beyond our agreed meeting time. Everyone else had already departed for the protest rally over at Sage Hall. I'm sure he could sense my irritation and edginess about having had to wait, wondering if he'd show up. But I'd already learned not to expect any apologies from my Spanish class "compadre," and he didn't disappoint me in this regard.

He also had someone with him, and they'd both dressed up like they intended to go to Johnny's Big Red for a fancy dinner. Jack looked like a fashion model from *Esquire* in a swank tweed jacket and his shorter companion appeared quite dapper himself in a camel's hair version that could've been styled by the same designer. They both sported suede elbow patches. Once again I felt odd man out, though I'd long since made the effort to look the Ivy part. This night I wore crisp khakis and a brown boat neck sweater.

"So, Robbie, say hello to Preston here. He's a bud of mine at the dorms. Not someone you'd want to introduce to your sister, I might add."

Preston gave Jack a playful shoulder bump in response to that remark before greeting me.

"Nice sweater."

His eyes and facial expression conveyed the insolence his voice perjured with the pretense of banter. He did not offer his hand.

"Well, let's be off, then," Jack announced. "Time to do all we can for our repressed feminine minority."

I fell in behind the two of them as we strode off in the direction of the amplified voice now resounding from the other side of Barnes Hall. The protest rally had just started, and I had the inkling I was about to broaden my college education.

The crowd outside Sage Hall had already gotten larger than I expected. And the organizers had gone to surprising lengths preparing for the rally. They'd set up a makeshift platform to enable the speakers to stand above the aggregation. They'd also equipped themselves with microphones and a sound system. A huge banner hanging at the rear of the platform stated simply, "FREEDOM WITH RESPONSIBILITY," the Cornell motto explained to Dad and me during our registration appointment, later drilled to memory during frosh camp orientation.

Standing in conspicuous locations, protesters waved placards, denouncing the university administration and its controversial new legislation. Representative examples included "WHO REALLY CARES ABOUT STUDENT AFFAIRS?" "FREEDOM FROM IRRESPONSIBILITY," "DEAN(E)S CONFINE WITH DIRTY MINDS," "EQUAL RIGHTS FOR COED NIGHTS" and "FREEDOM TOSSED BY BOSS DEAN CROSS."

A mobile generator provided lighting and a number of kerosene torches flamed in the background. Most of the clustering undergraduates, like myself, seemed to be there out of curiosity and for the fun of it. But a good number of participants made their die-hard presence known, apparently serious about the issue and committed to supporting the malcontent leadership. The campus security force had also invited a number of "Ithaca's finest" to join them in monitoring the event.

"Looks like we're going to have ourselves a real jim-doozy here," Jack observed, with a touch of cynicism.

He and Preston scanned the area for social prospects. While I wanted to learn what the protest was all about, and the spokespersons on the platform were eloquent, the two of them showed more interest in scouting out the honeys. As a result, I'd get absorbed in a piece of substantive oration, glean some information, then find myself playing catch-up with my wayfaring friends as they assessed the coed action from another perspective.

The offending new regulation, as I understood it, prohibited female freshmen the liberty of attending off-campus private parties, or even visiting men's apartments. Unlike the boys, coeds had to sign in and out of their dormitories every evening. They also had to indicate in the register exactly where they would be. They had curfews as well. The discovery of a spurious entry in the log could subject a girl to a loss of privileges for a period of time, or even more grievous penalties, if considered appropriate. The new offense of getting caught at off-campus housing, which would also indicate falsification of the sign-out ledger, would be cause for severe disciplinary measures, to include possible expulsion from the university.

The final whip at the microphone, a young master at motivational public speaking, riled up the audience with inflammatory remarks that might've cost him dearly in a court of law. He concluded his plea by leading his listeners in a chant of "We will fight for coed rights!" The response spread through the agitated gathering.

Cheers accompanied the chant as activists hoisted a male mannequin into the air, dressed in a dark suit and strapped to the end of a long pole. A sign pinned to the dummy identified it as "Dean Baldwin." A second incantation of "The dean of men is not a friend!" intertwined with the first, eventually extinguishing its predecessor.

Soon it too came to be alternated with yet another catch phrase, "The dean of men can never bend!"

At this point I noticed I'd been left on my own. Jack and Preston had disappeared somewhere in the multitude. But it didn't matter anymore. I was swept up by the excitement of the occasion. This event went beyond any other student issue incident I'd ever engaged in, like the fatuous "grimy day" protest against the banning of dungarees in junior high. When I blinked in response to the flash of a camera I also realized I'd become involved in a volatile situation with potential media implications.

Even in my observer role, participation in something of this magnitude was rousing. I speculated about the influence such an experience might exert on malevolent inclinations within the psyches of susceptible individuals. I saw changes already occurring in the moods of many around me. They weren't acting like the complacent *crème de la crème* I previously observed strolling the campus.

Another mannequin rose up, this one outfitted in a long, flowing dress and identified as "Dean Cross." Someone at the microphone bellowed, "What do we have to say to the dean of women?"

This prompted the loudest crowd reaction yet. A new mass intonation, "Get lost, Dean Cross!" erupted with seeming spontaneity. The collective sound climbed to a higher fever. Then it mutated into assorted angry shouts. Cheers and whistles ensued as a party of collegians brought forth a torch and fed the flames to the scorned images on the swaying poles. That peculiar sour taste made its way back into my mouth again. I'd never witnessed anyone burned in effigy before.

You could feel it coming as surely as a hurricane. The amused assemblage that first arrived had deviated into a blustering throng, rising up in blind emotion and indignation, a rage beyond the control of the protest chiefs.

Someone in the midst of the whirlwind, without the aid of a microphone, yelled, "Let's take a shot at Deane Malott!"

The latest rhyme, like a bolt of lightning, received ratification as the new rallying cry, repeated by a horde galvanized into action.

"To the presidential palace!"

I felt myself pushed forward with the rest. Then we began running madly across campus, a mob on the move, racing like rabid lemmings toward the gorge at Triphammer Bridge. Policemen hurried alongside us, horseless cowboys in blue trying desperately to head off the stampede. Or at least deflect it to some possible containment area.

The bridge appeared right in front of the rampage. The police had established additional ranks at this funnel, a single file across the mouth of the structure, brandishing billy sticks as deterrents to any further progress or conflict. But it was too little, and much too late. The swarm of scholars never hesitated, charging straight through the line. Photographers' flashbulbs lit up the area like electrical discharges in a storm. I observed one policeman knocked to the ground as I ran by.

The show of force seemed to be the extent of campus security's pre-event strategy. The officers exercised great restraint toward a number of abusive young people. I didn't see any billies cracking heads. Allowing myself to be swept along in the deluge of run amok lunatics, I made certain I stayed dead center in the middle of the bridge, nervously keeping my eyes focused forward to the other side.

Halfway across, I was horrified at the sight of two imbeciles just ahead who had climbed up onto the side railing. Right about where Mom and Dad and I had tentatively glimpsed the waterfalls and hydraulic power station during our campus visit. They laughed like circus clowns imitating high wire acrobats as I passed them. I felt a tinge of nausea just thinking about the grim reality of a terrifying, flailing plunge. A consequence it seems they deemed inconceivable.

The rabble slowed its pace when it advanced from the far side of the bridge, down to an easy trot. Then to a brisk walk by the girls' dorms and sorority houses. Startled coeds on lawns and sidewalks belatedly realized the purpose of the parade. They waved their encouragement while others cheered and applauded from windows and doorways. It appeared obvious the leaders of the pack intended to boast the success of the rally, basking in the publicity of the moment in front of the very gender that was its cause.

A short while later our ragged voices jogged past the landscaped private homes of university staff and faculty. We turned right and left, up and down gently rolling hills and dales, before descending upon the ultimate destination. The impressive house of President Deane Malott, Cornell University's esteemed headmaster, stood in solemn splendor before the madding legion of youth. The area in front of the house was lit up like a Hollywood film set. Campus security and the city police were already in place. Clubs in hand, they waited on their marks.

To this day the details of that confrontation remain a blur of recollection. So much happened so fast, while my mind spun out of control. I do recall my observation that I was undoubtedly the only student there concerned about the well-kept lawn and sculptured shrubs being trampled by so many barbaric feet.

While ralliers and inquisitive bystanders continued to straggle to the scene, the mob hollered its latest metered creation, "We want Deane Malott! We want Deane Malott!"

Policemen formed human barricades before the entrance to the house. Other cops attempted to maintain some semblance of perimeter control. They were overwhelmingly outnumbered. And they knew it.

Many minutes passed with no response from within the house. I wondered if the president was even at home. Interior lights beamed from downstairs windows, though. And I presumed that the police would've informed the organizers at the front if our trip had been in vain. The volume and measure of the activist chants and the accompanying malicious epithets and curses continued strong and unabated. After a few more minutes the front door opened. The tumult stopped. The silence seemed louder than the din preceding it.

All eyes focused on the open door for what seemed another full minute. Finally, a single figure emerged, stepping into the light at the front stoop. The anxious congregation greeted university president Deane Malott with a haughty roar.

As the noise subsided, the president responded to questions and charges posed by the protest honchos. From my position toward the rear of the large assembly, I had trouble hearing all the dialogue at the front steps. No microphones had been set up. During this question and answer phase, another man and two women came into view at the front door. They looked to be about the same age as the president. With grave faces, they stood behind him.

Deane Malott initiated an extemporaneous speech about the issue. He raised his voice in response to insolent cries of "We can't hear you!" repeated from various locations within the audience. It soon became obvious to the crowd, from his evasive answers to the direct questioning and the equivocal rhetoric of his address, that no satisfaction of demands would be forthcoming during this encounter with the university's chief executive.

"Say something significant!" a male voice shouted from somewhere in the middle of the crush. When this met with further nebulous verbiage from Mr. Malott, yet another protest slogan had been born.

Many dissenters joined in, elevating the volume of the plea while expanding the scope of its articulation. A chorus of "Say something! Say something!" drowned out the president's ambiguous eloquence. He fell silent against the assault of sound.

The backlash of insurgency finally vented its pent-up hostility. Without warning a flying object splattered against the house, not far from the entrance door. More of these missiles followed in rapid succession, striking various portions of the façade. The mob bustled and simmered, convulsing again in a ferocious outrage.

I saw a jock-type, not far from me, pull an egg from his pocket. He hurled it at the house. Following its trajectory, I saw the primary target, Deane Malott, hurry back inside with his colleagues.

The projectile disintegrated on impact with the doorjamb. Chaos ran rampant as others joined in the mutinous spectacle, ignoring admonishments rasping from a police bullhorn. Many more saw fit to flee the howling tempest. Somewhere down the road I snapped out of my personal panic to discover myself racing with the exodus, hellbent for the safety of my little room inside my College Town boarding house.

It took me quite a while to get to sleep. The last thing I remember was thinking about how easily the staid, moderate Ivy Leaguers had shed their restrained personas to relish the thrill and emancipation of raw rebelliousness. They didn't seem to be that different from me after all.

I made a special effort to pick up the early edition of the *Ithaca Journal* first thing Saturday morning. The terrible event at President Malott's home had already made front-page news. In the article I learned that the associates with President Malott had been his wife and a wealthy alumnus who just made a mammoth donation to the university's athletic department, to enhance the facilities for the renowned crew program. The newspaper quoted the well-heeled benefactor as having asked the president, "Are these the kids I'm giving the new boathouse to?"

The publication also exhibited a number of photographs of the rally itself, the incident with the police at the bridge, and the confrontation at the president's home. I was shocked to discover that my face had been caught by a camera amongst a clump of open-mouthed maniacs racing across Triphammer Bridge. I didn't know whether I should be proud or ashamed.

Sunday night my parents made their traditional weekly telephone call. Mom seemed especially concerned about what she'd seen in the papers pertinent to the protest. True to her nature, she fired the bullet right at me.

"The headline in one of the New York City papers reads 'Cornell Classmates Riot for Sex!' I certainly hope you weren't a part of that disgusting affair."

"Oh no, Mom. I was working at the student union that night. I heard about it, though."

CHAPTER 8

Welcome home for summer vacation, hotshot collegian. The big news around town was that Bruce Tierney committed suicide. I couldn't believe it.

As Eddie Mazzoli put it to me, "They found him in his apartment, sitting in his wheelchair, by the kitchen stove. The poor bastard must've turned on the gas and just sat there till he was gone."

Eddie's words detonated like hand grenades in the suffocating air. I felt a shiver shinny up my spine. Then the taste of bile gathered in my mouth, from somewhere way down in the pit of my stomach. It's one thing to read in the newspaper that someone chose death over life, or to hear about it on TV. But to have known that person, to have looked up to him as a flesh and blood leader, a true pillar among pretenders, is something else again. It's difficult to fathom how this kind of individual could be done in by such a senseless, irrelevant happenstance. Of course I was not the person relegated to a wheelchair for the rest of my life. That had to be rough. Real rough.

Despite the jolt of Bruce Tierney's death, I stood proud to be home representing myself as a sophomore Ivy Leaguer. Somehow I'd made it through my freshman year. Which is more than I can say for my roomie and fellow wrestler, who "busted out"

of the Ag school midway through the second term. I felt grateful just to have survived.

"Robbie! What's happening with the old college man?"

The voice on the phone sounded remotely familiar.

"It's Maury. Maury Weisenstein. So how's everything going at Cornell? Are you wrestling up there?" Etcetera, etcetera, etcetera.

Maury was a sharp little guy I got to know as a fellow high school teammate. Our relationship had slowly grown to an unassuming, yet abiding, real friendship. He'd just completed his senior year at Denton High and invited me to his graduation party. I gave him a capsule update on my first year in college, sparing him many dubious details. Such as the unsavory campus reputation I acquired as a hard drinker at weekend fraternity parties.

Infatuated with Zina, I'd gone out of my way to see her at every shining opportunity. But when Lenny and I both pledged Delta Upsilon, underage Zina had been refused admittance to the fraternity's alcoholic elixir mixers. An absurd ruling by the strait-laced house officers, I griped, based on the thinnest technicality. Zina would be eighteen at the end of the semester. It was then, I suppose, that the booze became more attractive to me than the desperation dates I regretfully resorted to invite in her place.

Zina returned to her native homeland right in the middle of my final exams. I sacrificed valuable study time to ride with Lenny and Marjorie to see her off from the house of her host family. The memory of our parting remains ensconced in my brain.

I'll be writing you, Zina. You can count on that. Until the day we're together again.

My sweet Robbie. I'll write you, too. You know I will. Oh, this is so hard.

We wept, we hugged and kissed on the front porch for many toots of the car horn. I remember she stayed snug in my arms until Marjorie pulled her away.

C'mon now. We need to go. You're going to miss your plane.

I got the last word in, calling to her just before she eased into the car. *Look for my letters. I'll never forget you.*

Then I watched with anger when she and Marjorie drove away with the family, not understanding why they couldn't have made room for one more.

Though I managed to squeak through my freshman year, I barely eluded scholastic probation. Collaboration with playboy Jack Darling helped me get past my Spanish nemesis. I set new personal records cramming for final exams just to pass my other courses as well. And my wrestling team performance complied. I registered a lackluster record of six wins and three losses.

When I pulled Dad's embarrassing Nash into Amanda Hardwick's driveway that first Saturday night home, I found myself brimming with apprehension about my choice of date. But I was stuck. After talking with Maury I thought about who I might bring to his graduation party. A thorough review of my sacred black book and the high school yearbook combined to offer only a handful of possibilities. It seemed scary so many girls waved red flags of inaccessibility. I'd already burned my bridges with quite a few, while others were either going with someone, engaged, already married, not presently in the area, or I'd lost track of them.

I tried to get in touch with Shirley McFarlin, but her mom informed me she'd already left to work the summer up in Cape Cod, bar-waitressing with one of her Tri Gam sisters. Word had it that Jane Lennox had gotten pregnant and planned to raise her illegitimate kid on her own. Of course, she would still have the chutzpah to accompany me. I imagined what the expressions on everyone's faces would've been if we arrived together out on Maury's patio. Mom suggested Mandy, who attended our family church. I remembered she not only had a pretty face, but that special look in her eye—the look that had nothing to do with saying her bedside prayers at night.

"So nice to see you again, Robbie Bender. We've missed you at Sunday school."

The moment I saw her I felt mesmerized. Her beauty went beyond anything I remembered, from her long chestnut hair to her Lana Turner legs. I caught my breath as those provocative hazel eyes held me in her spell.

"Gee, Mandy . . . you sure have grown up. You look terrific."

Maury's party turned out to be terrific too, though I'd already become so entranced it wouldn't have made any difference. Maury and his friends seemed equally impressed with my date, a few of them salivating and fawning over her. So I came to experience the heady joy of escorting a gorgeous new female to a social event of established, and in some cases stale, acquaintances. And Mandy knew how to play them all, making coy small talk, laughing politely at even the bad jokes, nibbling on kosher hors d'oeuvres with her pinky finger extended like sipping at high tea.

What a pleasant surprise to find Mandy also had dancing skills up to the talents of Shirley and Zina. Our styles immediately meshed. We became the focal point of a crowded dancing frenzy as the celebration slipped into high gear down in Maury's finished basement.

Then, somehow, we found ourselves in a paneled alcove of framed Weisenstein family photographs, leaning into each other against the wall and exchanging hot kisses. Until we knocked one picture off its hook and it crashed to the floor. We hastened away through the swell of tipsy revelers, to a darker corner of the room, where we resumed our personal adventure in more privacy. As we embraced, my hand scraped against a door latch to what proved to be an even more secluded haven. Within seconds we found our way into the unlit utility room. Here we further elevated our amorous pursuits to a breathless culmination, with the support and assistance of the washer and dryer and ignored by the hibernating furnace.

After the party I drove Mandy home one-handed. We lingered together at her front door, keeping each other warm.

"I had a super neat time, Mr. Robbie Bender." Seduction seeped from her whisper. "I sure hope I'm going to see a whole lot more of you."

We held each other and kissed while the moon in the sky leisurely crossed behind several branches of the nearby dogwood tree.

Later, I made my way back to my house with caution, both hands firmly committed to the steering wheel. I wondered if it was possible to fall in love with more than one girl at a time. I also wondered what it'd be like when I graduated from the dry hump, coming to know the bliss of going all the way.

Maury's party and Mandy Hardwick turned out to be the only positive highlights of that first summer home from college, however. Besides the trauma of Bruce Tierney's suicide, I also experienced one catastrophic night at the negative end of the spectrum.

It seems I'd antagonized Denton's ruffian bad boy, Hank Nolan. I'd made the mistake of inviting his allegedly former girlfriend, Glenda, to join me in Ithaca for a college weekend. In truth they continued to be a couple. I'd been the recipient of erroneous information that their relationship had turned past tense. Word had it that "Suburban" was "looking for me." So I took extra precautions to try to avoid the confrontation. I succeeded for a few weeks. Until one sorry night in mid-July.

Tommy Calderone, Eddie Mazzoli and I dawdled over our drinks at the old T&J. I looked over toward the jukebox as Fats Domino rolled into his "Ain't It a Shame." Three strangers in black leather jackets stood across the bar from us, doing straight shots with beer chasers. They didn't look like friendly types. Just as I focused on the particulars of our neighbors, the entrance door swung open. A single figure entered, joining the objects of my scrutiny. I stared as if thrown into a catatonic state. Their new compatriot just happened to be Hank Nolan. The encounter I'd been avoiding was now at hand.

"Hey, look who just walked in," Eddie whispered at me with gravel in his throat. "Think we ought to buy him a drink?"

"Not funny," I replied softly, coming out of my stupor. "Let's just keep talking together, like we don't notice 'em. Maybe they're just in for a quick one."

Tommy tuned in that something was brewing. "What's going on here? What's the problem?" He obviously had no knowledge of the potential fight rumor circulating Denton. Fisticuffs had never been his forte.

"Never mind for now," Eddie said. "Let's just take it slow and easy here. No commotions. Maybe it'll all blow over."

Nolan didn't seem to be paying any attention to us, conversing with his buddies across the way. We played our hand at the same game, trying hard to come up with anything innocuous to talk about. Working diligently at a lame recollection Eddie manufactured just to keep the conversation moving, I jumped when a heavy hand fell on my shoulder.

"What do you say you and me go outside for a little chat." The odor of Hank Nolan's liquored breath escorted his threatening words.

I don't have any idea what I said at that point. I do recall following this *man* across the barroom and out the front door, turning left on the sidewalk leading to the rear parking lot. As I moved along behind him I observed his thick neck and broad shoulders. The muscled arms and legs strained inside his clothing. I had to find a self-respecting way to talk myself out of a fight with this redoubtable bully. Knowing his reputation, it wouldn't be easy.

Nolan stopped and turned around just before the sidewalk deferred to the parking lot. He folded his arms over his prominent chest. The thunder of bowling balls and racket of crashing pins on end lanes 15 and 16 emanated from the nearby wall.

He didn't mince words. "So, I read the cute little letter you sent my woman. You sure got a set of balls moving in on another guy's bitch. Especially my bitch! Guess you think you're pretty hot shit . . . college boy and wrestling chump, and all that crap."

As Nolan raved I couldn't help but notice the crowd we'd drawn, bloodthirsty vultures anticipating the thrill of an imminent kill. Apart from Eddie and Tommy standing nervously behind me, I didn't know anyone in the drooling crowd. And their numbers exceeded the patronage that had been at the bar. They all seemed to have incarnated out of the evening vapor. The three goons in leather jackets stood alongside Nolan, gruesome sneers on their predatory faces.

Aware of the pounding in my chest, I tried to control the quiver in my voice.

"Hey, Hank . . . listen to me. I heard you'd broken up with Glenda. I'm not the kind of guy to go after someone else's girl. You got to know that. And if I was trying to be sneaky, I sure wouldn't have put it in writing, man."

He had no intention of listening. "And then, we're out for a drive. And who cuts me off, right in the middle of town? With that same piece of shit Rambler you got parked right over there in the lot? You, again, bozo!"

What a crock that was. It seemed obvious he wanted to make something out of nothing. The night I'd passed them in his truck I purposely stayed in my own lane, making a left turn away from them at the first available intersection. Doing my best to maintain a low profile until I could put some distance between us.

"And I also hear around town you're looking for me. Well, here I am, asshole!" He got so smug and confident that he unfolded his arms, extending his right hand to lean against the brick wall.

My mind raced. It seemed he was spoiling for a fight, no matter what I said. My best option might be to strike without warning, while he remained exposed and comfortable in his cocky attitude. He'd already verbally abused me; the physical beating would follow, given the one-way street we were on. This might be my only chance to catch him by surprise.

I made one last-ditch effort at reconciliation, hoping for sympathy from the kicks-seeking onlookers while appealing to his ego. All the while hoping to maintain some measure of dignity.

"Hey, man, you got to believe I wasn't out looking for you. A punk teenage kid hunting down a badass grown man, with a rep for being the toughest guy around? I mean, I can handle myself all right. But I'm not crazy, either."

His response snarled as cold as his blood. "Yo! Look at the little creep squirming in his goddam' boots! You know, this is going to be more fun than I've had in a long fucking time."

I focused dead center on the middle of Nolan's flaunted belly. I hit him square with my right fist, throwing everything I had behind the punch.

When I looked up, that familiar stucco ceiling reappeared through the gloom. The same little nooks and nodules, crests and crannies I grew up with. As a boy, they'd represented a detailed topography of an imaginary place grown from small town simplicity to a complex urban sprawl. The fairy tale woods and farmland, rivers and streams, swamps and trails, had transformed into a metropolitan environment. The plaster now mapped a maze of never-ending commercial districts, dissected by concrete streets and asphalt alleys, saturated with neon-embellished buildings and crowded neighborhoods. As I got older, the intrinsic features of the ceiling had been relegated to helping me focus out of my early morning lethargy, be it the result of too little sleep, the overindulgence in alcohol, or, most likely, a combination of both.

In this instance I couldn't be certain if it was morning, afternoon or night. And the anguish went far beyond weariness, headache or hangover. Every move I made, or thought I made, evoked a searing pain.

The ceiling was there, and though it appeared shaded, the contours remained recognizable. Yet somehow different. As I lay in my bed, afraid to move for fear of inciting more stabs of agony, I realized that the difference related to dimension. The ceiling had become two-dimensional. I could make out the expected details, but they'd lost their depth. They existed in their usual individuality, but had been somehow shaved smooth, planed to a flat appearance.

"Well, now, look who's finally decided to rejoin the living."

I knew the voice and, on this occasion, felt comforted by it. I was home, with Mom tending to me. But when I tried to turn my head in her direction spasms of angry shooting stars flared across my brain. My neck rebelled with an aching twinge, as if it had gotten snared in a steel vise.

"Just lie still now, Robbie. You've got to take it easy for awhile."

My summer job had come to a quick conclusion. Six weeks ahead of schedule. No way could I handle a lawn mower, or hold electric power clippers to trim bushes while mending two broken ribs and a dislocated shoulder. After a time, with Mother Nature working her miracles, I began to see normal again. I stopped bumping into things with my sprained knee. My left eye came to be only partially closed as the swelling subsided. As a result, the bedroom ceiling had also been restored to its proper relief.

Looking at my reflection had been a horrifying undertaking in the beginning. I'll never forget my shock when Mom acquiesced and brought me a hand mirror. She stood over me with her knees pressed against the mattress, as though she intended to be the protective side frame should I lurch from my crib in hysterics after the grisly discovery.

It appeared even worse than I anticipated. Though I'd gotten accustomed to the lacerations and bruises all over my body, and I knew my eye had been swollen shut, I still found myself unprepared for the view of even the reduced swelling, the discoloration and facial distortion. I was aghast to see the 5 inches of stitches from my temple to my forehead. My God, my head must've been sliced wide open.

While I had a hard time recalling the fight at the beginning of my recuperation, fragments of details continued to emerge from the recesses of my mind during the long hours and days I remained bedridden. Tommy and Eddie filled in the remaining gaps, after I gave in and agreed to let them stop by the house.

To this day I prefer not to belabor the specifics of the encounter. The old aches have a way of celebrating the event anyway, without the added stimulus of addressing the reminiscence. Suffice to say, after I connected to Hank Nolan's rock-hard stomach he fell back a few steps, genuinely stunned. According to Eddie, he growled, "Why, you sorry ass sack of shit!"

He then charged me like a lanced bull, throwing a flurry of punches as we fell together into the gutter. Though I somehow got in a couple more good licks, he proceeded to whip me unmercifully. Restrained after a few kicks to my rib cage, Bert the bartender joined Eddie and Tommy to pull him away. Bert had also called the cops, who arrived right on schedule, minutes after it was all over. I spent the rest of the night receiving treatment, tests and observation at Holy Name Hospital.

Mandy Hardwick called me every day during my early recovery. I looked forward to her gentle voice and soothing words visiting me across the wires. When the mirror and my anxious anticipation joined forces to convince me it would be all right to let her see my altered appearance, she made the trip from Ridgefield whenever she could get the family car. The tender hours she spent at my side went by all too quickly.

We got to really know each other during this period. The agenda had to be confined to talking, or playing cards or board games. One evening I told her a funny story about a pledge prank Lenny and I had been a part of, both of us having become "official brothers" at Delta Upsilon fraternity. Mandy reacted with that bubbling laugh that was uniquely hers. I giggled with her, aggravating the soreness in my fractured jaw, broken ribs and so many other injured places.

I cried out with cracked, hacking chortles. "Ooh, ow! That hurts! How bad is that? Torture for the crime of laughter." All of which just added to the tickle, and the pain, of the moment.

She put her arms around me and hugged me delicately.

"Oh, my poor hero. Let Nurse Mandy make it all better."

She then proceeded to kiss each and every wound, while I kept my ears alert for Mom's footfall on the staircase.

After two weeks I got myself out of the house. Mandy borrowed a girlfriend's car and picked me up right after lunch so we might share "some fresh air and a change of scenery." Mom and I were both pleased, I think, just to get away from each other for awhile. She played her role to the hilt, however, cautioning Mandy to drive extra careful with me.

We headed toward Ridgefield. "I gotta stop by my place first," she said. "It'll just take a minute. I forgot something."

When we parked in front of her house, she invited me in. Catching my reluctance and analyzing it correctly, she added, "No one's home to see your pretty scars, Robbie Bender. They're visiting with friends across town. Come on, I'm not going to bite you. Besides, you need the exercise."

The family cat greeted us at the door. Inside, Mandy made me comfortable in the living room. "Why don't you just relax here on the couch. How about a beer?"

On her way to the kitchen she turned on the record player. The 45 at the bottom of the stack dropped onto the turntable. The Dell-Vikings got things rolling with the toe-tapping "Come Go With Me."

A minute later she glided back with two Budweisers. As the Moonglows harmonized "Sincerely," we picked up from where we left off after her last bedside visit.

"I sure wish all my nurses treated me this good," I sighed, after a deep soul kiss. "I'd probably be out fighting all the time, just for the therapy."

"Yeah, but today's prescription's for a breath of fresh air, remember?"

She pushed herself away and stood up. "Enjoy your beer, troublemaker. I'll be right back." She sashayed across the room to the music before whisking nimbly up the stairs. In between records I could hear Maxine purring as she brushed back and forth against my legs.

The Chantels had gotten into a few bars of "Maybe" when Mandy frolicked back into the room. She stood before me, smiling demurely, one hand on her hip. She wore delectable diaphanous, black chiffon lace-trimmed lingerie, complemented by matching pumps, stockings and garter belt. The fragrance of perfume woke up my nose. I was astonished and swept up in the sheer fascination of this remarkable spectacle. It seemed as though a living, breathing professional model had just stepped out from the glossy photograph of an enticing magazine. And she looked as luscious as any picture I'd ever seen.

"Come on, tough guy, I see that look in your eye," she coaxed, in her best Mae West. "Leave that beer and get over here. It's time for some real fresh air. This affair's headed upstairs."

I didn't know what movie we were in. Nor had I rehearsed my lines, much less found the rhyme. But I felt more than ready to play my part.

"Yes, ma'am," I ad-libbed meekly, lifting my aching body off the couch.

She led me into her parents' bedroom, with its blatant king-size bed.

"Take your pick."

She held up two pairs of silk, or satin, men's pajamas.

"Whose are they?" I asked, still reeling from the pace of this unexpected turn of events.

"They're yours, lover," she replied. "Here, let's both go black, for starters. That adds to the mystery, don't you think? You can change in the bathroom, behind you."

I learned more about love and sex that day than I had in all my previous years. It seemed fitting that rays of sunshine bestowed their warmth upon our naked yearnings, commemorating the surrender of my overage virginity in a wondrous afternoon delight. Maxine roamed the bed, her fur occasionally caressing my skin, as The Five Satins praised us and blessed the historic occasion, singing their glorious doo-wop anthem, ironically titled "In the Still of the Night."

When Mandy dropped me off at my house that evening, we languished in our precious final kiss. I walked to the front door healed of all pain, knowing I would never ever be the same again.

CHAPTER 9

"**O**-o-o-h, Da-ha-na, O-o-o-h, Da-ha-na!"
The soiree was in full swing and I in full bloom, as the designated "piano man" of the brotherhood. By default, since no one else could play. Just another drunken Saturday night party at the old Delta Upsilon house. Though the group vocalizations continued to be horrendous, the spirit and intensity prevailed. And that's what really mattered.

The piano became my wedge toward a more comprehensive fraternal acceptance, beyond my camaraderie with Lenny and the other hellions in the membership. Though I didn't stack up to the likes of Jerry Lee Lewis, everybody got their money's worth in the collaborative efforts. I compensated for my lack of technical artistry with pounding rhythms and pretentious staccato key work, leading the extempore ensembles with my own Ray Charles-influenced melodic vocals. I had to conclude one lengthy and vigorous intoxicated performance when my ravaged fingers started to bleed.

This happened to be one of the few areas of my individuality not altered by the influences of Cornell's Ivy League mien. While I'd made reluctant changes in my physical appearance, acquiescing to social conformity during that fateful visit to Rudy's Barber Shop, my peers continued to view me as a campus scamp. I was a weed in the garden of couth. My Jersey accent, working class language and demeanor, lack of solid educational or career interests and manifest immaturity certified my lower socioeconomic status, relegating me to the fringe of the pure Ivy culture.

I remember one coed reacting to my alcohol-enhanced antics at a particularly jovial frat party, saying, "How gauche."

Suspecting this might not be a compliment, I had to refer to the dictionary in the house library while I remained sober enough to remember the word. Finding it in my condition without knowing the correct spelling turned out to be no mean feat, either. We both kept our distance for the rest of that evening. I continued to plunge headfirst into the spirits of the night anyway, getting totally inebriated. The next morning I couldn't recall the word.

But long term, a subtle, cumulative subconscious process took place. Little by little I learned to tame the excesses of my words and actions to better fit the occasion, or at least the particular setting, taking into account the characteristics of the immediate audience. In my own way, I managed to adapt and flourish in the cultivated nourishment of that loamy intellectual soil, entangled in the stems of Ivy, yet rooted in my own unique identity.

Lenny and I disposed of two pitchers of beer at Jim's Place, each surprising the other that we'd both decided, independently, to quit the wrestling team. He'd become frustrated by the prospects of warming the varsity bench. Beyond the concern about my physical fitness after the beating I sustained, I also suffered from a lack of motivation. Hell, there's no professional future unless you're some hulk with a zest for primitive stunt acting. Oh, and what with all the time on my hands over the summer, I'd started smoking. We clicked our mugs together in the joy of our correlated decisions.

After a group of our frat brothers joined us, Lenny mentioned he'd heard about a party somewhere in College Town.

"I don't know how good it'll be, especially since it's not the weekend. But this cute little artsy chick I met at the library told me about it. She hangs out with all those freaky fried eggheads who live in the Music Room at the Straight. Ever go in there? A whole nother world, man. They're cracking the books to Brahms and Beethoven and all those highbrow classical records."

The address had us crooking our necks to the upstairs apartment of an old house, just a half-block from the district's off-campus doors of student commerce. Entry could be gained by means of a flight of stairs on the outside of the building. Lenny wasted no time making his way inside, the rest of us lingering on the small balcony.

Sure enough, the Willard Straight Music Room crowd had assembled there, in force. A quaint collection tuned in to its own esoteric Pied Piper. The gossamer strains of Mendelssohn, or some such classical composer, lilted within the dark atmosphere. Scores of candles provided a teetering light. My nose detected the hint of a unique, musky fragrance that was new to me. Devoid of dancers, this bundle of peculiar folks occupied either the floor or the furniture, sitting in small circles or lying about at random. Several had their eyes closed and appeared to be sleeping, though not necessarily in the traditional prone position.

My eyes searched the haze for Lenny. I finally found him, on the other side of the main room, chatting with a frail young girl with dark braided hair, wearing a long print dress and sandals. This was so like Lenny, already adapting and fitting in with this eccentric gathering. Clearly the most versatile individual I'd ever known, or would ever come to know.

I decided the time had arrived to let the doorjamb support itself. Since Lenny looked occupied, I crushed my cigarette stub under my shoe and rallied our reluctant soldiers behind me, intent on a more thorough reconnoiter of this campy bivouac. We also needed to fortify ourselves with whatever alcoholic refreshment we might discover.

Stepping over bodies strewn through various rooms, followed by a fairly uniform defile of my skeptical frat friends, I marched our troop through and into the kitchen at the far end of the apartment. To our dismay, no beer or hard liquor anywhere. All we did find amounted to a few bottles and jugs of wine, most of them empty or approaching their demise. A lot of dubious foodstuffs lay about: breads and cheeses, raw vegetables, crackers and dips.

"Looks like this is it, guys," I groused in disgust. "Don't know about you, but I think it's past my bedtime. Ain't nothing happening here."

My entourage grumbled mutual accord. So we all strode back through the languid entanglement of dreamy souls. I tapped Lenny on the shoulder as I passed by, indicating we'd decided to leave. He gave us a casual salute of farewell before returning to his new acquaintance. I hesitated when I got to the door and looked over in his direction. He was deep in conversation with the little cherub of the Music Room.

The wrestling coach sat there in his office chair, a vacant stare on his face. I became aware of the throbbing ache in my temples, most likely a deserved reprisal for last night's consumption of beer. But I think my state of fatigue may have helped me through this dreadful meeting. At least I was able to say what I had to say without breaking down, as I have a proclivity to do in sensitive situations. And the coach fulfilled Lenny's prophecy with his response, condemning fraternities with an almost dogmatic religious fervor, pretty much word for word as my new brother had facetiously predicted.

"Well, I guess that's it, then," Jimmy said, getting up from his chair.

He held out his hand and flashed his celebrated smile at me. This time it came across forced, unable to mask the intersecting shadows of disappointment and insincerity.

"Good luck with the rest of your life."

"Thank you, Jimmy." My eyes were glued to the floor as I walked out of his office. I eased the door closed behind me.

Zina and I mailed each other a few letters across the wide Atlantic, attempting to keep our flame burning. But as the weeks turned into months its intensity became tempered by time and distance, the new demands and interests in our respective lives.

Her third letter was noticeably shorter, more descriptive of her own excitement of attending some Dutch university than reiterating the attachment between us. My own passion now leaned more toward recollections of the summer's hedonistic adventures with Mandy, reinforced by earthy phone conversations. I realized, with resignation, that the wavering affection Zina and I shared had been shunted to the obscurity of a pilot light.

I started to write a return letter in the library one evening, struggling to come up with something interesting to say. After managing a single tedious paragraph, I tucked it away in my knapsack to continue at a more creative moment. I later found it there, crumpled and torn after weeks of injury inflicted by hyperactive notepads and textbooks. Taking a look at its boring verbiage and subject matter, I tossed it into the nearest trash basket. That turned out to be the unceremonious conclusion of my correspondence with Zina, my irresistible nymph from across the sea.

"Hey there, pardner. I want to know how a gaper like you ends up with such a hot babe."

Lenny might've been the tenth brother to come up to me at the party, complimenting me on my choice of Fall Weekend date.

"Jeez, that randy Mandy's something else. You mind if your old friend Leonard asks her for a spin around the dance floor? Damn, that chick can flat shake it."

I strutted proud as the proverbial peacock, swaggering around the frat house with my hometown lady love.

"What's mine is yours, dear brother," I declared. "Outside of lewd violations of the flesh. By the way, whatever happened with that Music Room honey you hooked up with over at that dopey party in C-town? You have to admit that was one strange scene."

"Hey, you got to learn to be a little more open-minded, my man. Variety is the spice of life, or so they say."

Lenny glanced in the direction of the restroom, to be sure our girls were not within earshot. "I'm still working on that little number . . . and getting an education on classical music at the same time. Forever expanding those horizons, Robbie."

"Yeah, well, I want to see how you boogie to that beat, O man of the world. Say, while we're on the subject, did you happen to notice the funny smell in the place that night? Expand my horizons on what that's all about."

Lenny looked at me like I was born yesterday. "You got to be kidding me. You never smelled incense before? All them bohemian types are into burning that stuff . . . all the time. Hell, Jocelyn has a stick of that shit fired up in her room even when she studies. I don't know, I kind of like it myself."

"Hi, boys! Did you think we got lost?"

Mandy'd come back from the girls' room with Marjorie. She cuddled up to me, giving me a taste of her naughty hazel eyes. "I think I could use another drink, Robbie Bender."

"Not until you show me all your fancy steps firsthand," Lenny exclaimed, offering his arm with extravagance. "You don't mind if I get a dancing lesson from your fine-looking sweetie, do you, Rob?"

Before I could respond the two of them skipped off to the dance floor. I thoughtlessly left Marjorie standing there while I headed to the milk pails for two more "whiskey flings."

The weekend was a blast, from start to finish. Mandy turned out to be the ultimate party girl, affecting everyone around her with her irrepressible free spirit. She even smiled away the incessant rain that, after a month, had transfigured the peaceful campus gorges into conduits of audacious waterfalls and rambunctious run and tumble rapids. We both romped and pranced on clouds of impulsive pleasure—laughing, dancing, shouting, singing—high on the pace of the music, the drinks and the action. Fortunately never relegated to the ugly edge of inebriation.

I banged out my repertoire of rocking songs on the piano while Mandy performed a comical spur-of-the-moment role as choral director, to the delight of even the stodgy faction in attendance. And Lenny and Marjorie amazed everybody once again as whirling dervishes of the dance floor, creating and incorporating new moves to their infinite inventory.

A crack of downtime enabled me to tour Mandy around the main campus and College Town. We hit Jim's Place for a pitcher of sours. Jack Darling and Preston just happened to be at the bar with some other Dekes. I took advantage of the opportunity to flaunt my pretty lady.

I knew I'd scored a hit when Jack summoned all his preppy wit, offering Mandy his bar stool. Preston ogled her, confirming his reaction through the daze in his jaded eyes. I obliged the invitation, allowing Jack the privilege of paying for the pitcher, to further enhance his prosperous image. So Mandy got her first chance to savor the aroma of Ivy League bar life. We had a fine time, Jack motivated to show off his lecherous humor. Until Preston had to be removed from the premises after barfing on one of the barmaids. We thanked Jack for the sours as he and the other Dekes helped his friend stagger out the door.

Emptying what was left of the pitcher into our glasses, I put my arm around Mandy. "Now that you've met the high priest of preppies, allow me to fill you in on Cornell's self-proclaimed 'student of life'."

Mandy had been impressed with the cool savoir-vivre Jack honed in his privileged upbringing. It seemed obvious she'd been beguiled by his con artistry. I filled her in on his background, from the elegant house in affluent Scarsdale and his two sets of wheels, including the Thunderbird sports car he always kept under a dust cover, to his education at the exclusive Hotchkiss School. A world she and I could only imagine.

"The guy's been spoiled all his life," I remarked, lighting a fresh Marlboro. "Given everything on a silver platter. Yet his life is kind of sad . . . mom's an alcoholic, dad's never around."

I told her about my experiences with Jack and the many facets of this complex character. How he'd bailed me out of a thorny cutting class academic imbroglio I'd gotten myself into, providing me answers to a prelim I'd missed and phony infirmary documentation to deceive a professor and salvage credits necessary for graduation.

"Whether it's women, grades, whatever, Jack knows how to score. And he's the master of the shady deal."

I regaled her with the story of one dark night when I assisted Jack and Preston in stealing a cow and sneaking it into their frat house as a pledge prank.

"Yeah, Jack calls me on the phone one night, back when I was living in this boarding house. Says he needs my help with some pledge class project he's working on. Seems he's got his hands on a truck somehow, and he and Preston are planning to steal a cow and dump it off at the Deke house. You remember, I told you about that time Lenny and I screwed with our DU brotherhood, spiking the coffee urn with Ex-Lax and taping cellophane paper underneath all the toilet seats. The pledges are always trying to pull something off against the brothers.

"Anyway, they pick me up in this rusty old Ford pickup. It's like after midnight, and the three of us head over to these buildings at the Ag school. There's this barn at the end of a little road. Jack pulls out a key, and it actually unlocks the barn door. Sure enough, the place is full of cows . . . just standing there in their stalls.

"Next thing I know, we've got this big fat Holstein out at the truck. Preston slides down a metal ramp, and we somehow manage to get this stupid animal standing up in the back, hitched to the side posts. Then we're rolling down the road, just like that."

Sensing I may have increased the volume of my voice in the excitement of the recollection, I looked around the bar. Mandy smiled her appreciation of the tale, encouraging me to go on.

I lowered my voice. "So I'm worried we're going to blow a tire or bust the shocks on this old truck. We're riding real low to the road, and listing to the right, where the cow's standing. Somehow we make it to the Deke house without breaking down.

"Now it's, like, two in the morning. There's only a couple lights left on in the place. And we've got this major problem, 'cause the damn cow's got its ass facing out! We can't get it to back up. Well, I guess we get lucky pushing and pulling, with Jack whispering sweet nothings in its ear. All of a sudden it gets offended by his obscene suggestions, or something. And it just bolts . . . backwards right on down the ramp, almost crushing Preston and me, catching us by surprise."

Four students standing next to us at the bar had picked up on the story. They attempted to stifle their chuckles, I think fearing they might intimidate the telling with their uninvited participation. I continued undaunted, enjoying my moment.

"So, it takes us forever. But using the ramp, we finally get this frigging cow up onto the porch of the house. I'm grungy, worn out and happy we got this far, figuring this is a perfect spot to leave it, tied to one of the big support columns. But now Jack tells Preston to check the place out. And he goes on in to make sure no one's around. We end up getting this cow through the front door, into the house, and rope it to this big old chair by the fireplace in the living room. I couldn't believe it.

"Then we're running out of there . . . trying to muffle our insane laughter, all the way back to the truck. And it seemed like a lifetime getting that damn thing started. Finally it cranks up, and we're chugging on down the road!"

Mandy was really into it now. I baited her and our eavesdroppers, pretending to close the book on my narration.

"Well? So what happened afterwards? The brothers go nuts when they found that cow? Did they ever figure out who did it?"

"Hey, all Jack told me was the entire pledge class had to clean up a bunch of nasty cow pies off the living room rug. I guess that mother did a real job in there. Anyway, they never did find out it was Jack and Preston. With little old me giving 'em a hand!"

Sunday night we held hands on our way to the airport with Lenny and Marjorie. The rain had returned. We shared misty eyes and held each other, saying our goodbyes. Fall Weekend 1958 had become an asterisk in my life. I speculated the same was true for Mandy as I honored my reflections riding back through the drizzle headed toward campus.

CHAPTER 10

After Zina departed Ithaca, I'd gone out with a number of other girls at college. Only Mandy, my Jersey squeeze, shared compatibilities to sustain a relationship beyond a couple of dates. I guess she evinced a mirror image of myself, really, standing on the other side of the sexual boundary, yet committed to the very same raptures I held dear. Or most other males I associated with, for that matter. She lived for the good times: dancing, drinking, laughing, raising hell, probing eros. Any manner of cavort representing an escape from the travail of the everyday existence. She liked fast cars and fast men. The impetuous, the irreverent, the immature were hers to champion. She was a girl, but she was also one of the boys. I simply could not get enough of her.

I'd considered trying to touch base with Shirley McFarlin, to invite her up for one of the big weekends my sophomore year. I berated myself for not taking the initiative to make contact, having located her through her mother the previous summer. My old Denton buddies, Bobby and Speckles, individually surprised me with the news Shirley had had a "secret" crush on me when we were classmates. I myself had neglected an interest in her, too, all through high school.

"According to my old lady, she's still got the hots for you, pal," Bobby told me. "You better get on it. Get her up there for one of those drunken college orgies. We're talking about Shirley McFarlin, man. This is not just another broad."

"Nobody in their right fucking mind would pass up an opportunity to get something going with a super-babe like Shirley," Speckles advised.

But the magnetism of my relationship with Mandy could not be ignored. I'd asked her instead. Each of her visits turned out better than the previous one and we reveled in our limited time together. It came as no surprise to me that she heightened her stature with everyone, joining Marjorie as one of the special weekend honeys at DU, the bad boy faction of the fraternity putting her on a pedestal that elevated both our egos. In fact, she was so well received by the brotherhood at large she improved my own rapport with the bluenose contingent of the membership. "When's Mandy arriving?" became a stock question put to me by many brothers as we approached any significant party occasion. I treated her acceptance and popularity as my own, for she expanded my platform of endorsement as well.

At the start of my junior year I volunteered to be a member of my class's social committee. I hoped to expand my meager college credentials in some notion it might enhance my career-seeking opportunities after graduation.

The primary function of this diverse assortment of students was to conduct the class party. One area of expertise where I could contribute, given my track record in the field. But despite elaborate preparations commencing well in advance of the events' spring target date, I soon found myself relegated to the periphery of committee participation. My trivial assignment: a ticket taker at the door. How could I say no. It was, without question, the very least anyone could do.

The committee voted a Roman toga party as the concept theme. Which had me conjuring up all kinds of prurient anticipations. Site selection went to the domed sculpture lab on the top floor of Sibley Hall, at the College of Architecture. With its high ceiling and unconventional creations in chiseled stone, welded metal, and other three-dimensional forms of expression, this location articulated the theme.

I enjoyed myself in my simple, mindless role, greeting people and taking tickets in my wrinkled—but laundered!—white bed sheet, which insisted on falling off my shoulder. I'd also gone that extra mile, standing under the shower to allow the spray of the water to leave my hair matted forward, Julius Caesar style. Of course, not owning a pair of sandals, my sneakers barked their rebellion against any serious attempt at costume authenticity.

"Greetings, Marcus Brutus. What good fortune it is to find a friendly conspirator at the entrance door."

There he was, in all his splendor, standing tall before me in an exquisite maroon robe with gold trim and accessories. A statuesque, equally well-draped blonde goddess clutched his arm. He wore a wreath of gilded fig leaves on his head, complementing the ringlets of flowers interwoven with braids accenting his lady's apricot hair.

"Hey! How's it going, Jack? Long time no see."

In fact, I now racked my idle brain trying to remember just when Jack Darling and I had last seen each other. It had been a while. By the looks of his date, no Cornell coed. I would've remembered this one on campus. He hadn't lost a step in the world of petticoat connoisseurs.

Jack got right to the point. "Need your help, laddie-bucker. I left my goddamn tickets back at the house. You're not going to ask an old compadre to go all the way back for them, are you?" The big Cheshire cat grin stretched wider than ever.

I could feel the skepticism emitting from the "Dee Gee" coed handling the table with me. I also heeded the high-ranking committee staff members and faculty advisors standing a few feet away, including the subcommittee chairperson who'd entrusted me with this token participation.

"Well . . . this is a class fund-raiser, you know. We can't just let everybody—"

He cut me off in mid-sentence. "Robbie, my boy. It's me. Your old friend, Jack. Remember? You're starting to sound like you don't believe me."

Leaning forward, he dropped his voice to almost a whisper. "Let's just say this is for that poor sick kid who had to spend all that time in the infirmary. Thank God he's all better now."

There it was, out on the table. Jack chose this tactical moment to play that old card.

It didn't matter what position he might be putting me in. I owed him, and that was that. I now realized full well he didn't have any tickets. It all came down to playing the game. Beating the system. Money was not the issue here. He'd driven up in his new Thunderbird and he and his *Cosmo* queen wore expensive costumes he'd undoubtedly rented. Yet he had to impress her he could con his way in without paying the measly cost of admission. I saw another facet of my perfidious friend and felt soiled by the reality of our relationship. He had no qualms about forcing me into a conniving public act to satisfy his thirst for cheap thrills.

"Yeah, okay, go ahead on in. I . . . I remember you bought those tickets. No problem." I stamped their hands.

"Thanks, gumba. I'll see you inside?"

Jack patted me on the shoulder as he and his lady friend sidled on by. I gave him a self-conscious nod in return. My Delta Gamma co-worker gave me a look of disgust and proceeded to take tickets from the next in line.

I spent another hour peeping at skimpy costumes. Then another committee couple spelled my partner and me. She looked pleased to get away from the stench of my indulgent behavior. I grabbed a beer from one of the portable bars and joined the party. The crowd started noisily reacting to some activity near the dance floor. So I worked my way in that direction, around a knot of jabbering celebrants.

An imported blues band had gotten into a competent version of Bo Diddley's "I'm a Man." The clamor escalated as I wormed my way through the swaying congestion of merrymakers, losing half my drink in the process. I managed to circumvent a gangling basketball type, rocking to and fro. Only then did my eyes behold the source of the commotion.

To one side of the dance floor I saw Jack Darling in his princely gown, dancing on top of a lab table. A gaggle of students, I believe all males, swarmed around him. They waved their arms and raised their splashing cups in concert with their discordant Diddley-mimicking voices, chanting bawdy encouragements. Jack's beautiful model woman stood nearby, her arms folded in front of her, a bewildered expression on her face.

Then I realized the reason for the uproar. It had nothing to do with Jack's dancing ability. The attraction was born in the observation that he wore nothing underneath his toga. It seems Jack had decided to pay literal tribute to the Bo Diddley anthem, recurrently exposed and fully aroused in the stimulation of the circumstance.

In the days and weeks that followed, I may have been subjected to a few more disparaging stares and comments from certain committee members and other classmates possessing inside knowledge of that incident, and the unfortunate free admission leading up to it. But I felt content to endure that judgment compared to the fate of my "amigo" from Spanish 103. Subsequent to the investigation by campus police and a hearing before the Men's Judiciary Board, Jack Osgood Darling, after almost three years of Ivy League schooling, was expeditiously expelled from Cornell University.

CHAPTER 11

I looked forward to Mandy joining me for yet another Spring Weekend, just a month after that ignominious junior class party involving Jack Darling. Relishing the expanded base of fellowship I'd developed since my inductions into two social "honoraries," Mummy Majura and upstart Fessor's Majura, and feeding off the inspiration of a spring fling in Fort Lauderdale, I felt more than ready to party hard with my female alter ego. Beyond the fraternal cocktail hours and dance parties, Fessor's Majura scheduled a Sunday morning milk punch bash out at the lake. This bourbon-spiked beverage, with its ceremonial significance, would serve as the catalyst at the infamous "Last Chance," the retreat where "Fessor" himself, the club's founding father, resided.

This time Mandy got ticketed on an earlier Friday flight into Syracuse, rather than the later options into nearby Tompkins County Airport. Now we wouldn't miss the limelight at the opening happy hour at the house. I cut three classes in order to make the trip to pick her up, in Lenny's borrowed "Turquoise Terror," naturally. But I rationalized I wouldn't be able to focus on studies at that point, even if I attended. I always felt Friday and Saturday classes during a major party weekend should be canceled, anyway.

As it turned out, I enjoyed the longer drive in Lenny's hotrod. It also gave me the chance to bring Mandy up-to-date on the latest happenings. Of course I gave her the raunchy details of Jack

Darling's expose at the class party, and resultant dismissal from the university.

"Why, I can't believe that lovely man could ever do anything so outrageous," Mandy remarked with eyes wide. "He seemed like such an innocent and decent human being."

I looked at this extraordinary female. It felt good I had the travel time to absorb her refreshing presence, without the interference of others. It seemed she never looked more entrancing. I felt fortunate to be the object of her interest and desire.

The Friday and Saturday sessions once again lived up to the hype and expectation of a super extravaganza. Mandy and I willingly returned to the center ring of the social circus, pleasing the crowd with our expected impulsive carnival acts. Sticking to standard format, we cavorted with Lenny, who unleashed his latest untamed townie tigress. Rupert "Mad" Madigan and all the other swinging DU daredevils joined in the pomp, performing absurd stunts with their high-flying honeys.

Sunday morning Mandy and I piled into the top-down Turquoise Terror with Lenny and new "spunky lady" Charlene. We drove by the Psi U house to pick up drinking buddy Mike Gorman and his date, on our way out to the Fessor's Majura party on the lake. I looked forward to this special social, closed to members only and their girls. It would be my first time at the renowned Last Chance party chalet. Mandy was excited as well. I'd told her all about the exploits of this uninhibited coterie.

As we came to a screeching stop alongside the Psi U house, muscled Mike emerged from a small gathering standing near the entryway. He was all by himself and obviously upset, evidenced by his idiosyncratic raised elbows as he approached the car. Lenny confirmed the observation.

"I can tell by your strut, you're all pissed off about something, Mikey boy. Did you lose your girl *again*?"

We all laughed at that. Charlene offered him a Bloody Mary from our breakfast thermos.

"Son of a bitch! She got so polluted last night she passed out in the pisser! Now she's so wasted she's still sacked out and I'm on my own. Some Spring Weekend party girl. Shit."

"Well, today's another day. And you're with us now. So everything's going to be just fine. Hi, I'm Mandy."

While Mike climbed into the car Mandy took it upon herself not only to make the introduction, but bestow words of encouragement on the perturbable Mr. Gorman. What a class chick.

Before Mike got himself seated Lenny hit the accelerator pedal. The Terror left rubber in the Psi U parking lot, tumbling him down on top of Mandy and myself in the back seat.

"All aboard! Next stop, Last Chance," Lenny shouted. "Hello, Fessors. Goodbye, you Psi U snoots."

Even Mike joined in the laughter, as the car dashed away. "Yeah! You Psi U snoots," he screamed back at his own fraternity house. He'd confided to Lenny and me that he sorely wished he'd been offered a bid from our brotherhood.

We enjoyed another insane ride down the hill and through the residential back streets of Ithaca. Lenny pumped the clutch and shifted gears, putting the transmission through yet another rigid stress test. The Olds jerked and jumped to the commands, Bloody Mary's sloshing everywhere.

"Damn good thing I'm not wearing my Sunday best," Mike hollered, attempting to take a swig of the medicinal brew, only to spill a good portion of it down the front of his Hawaiian shirt.

Once again Lenny made it all the way across town without so much as a hint of a cherry top. Then we rattled over the tracks of the Allegheny Railroad, saluting the garbage pails behind Obie's Diner, squealing around the corner and accelerating out onto Route 89 North.

"Is that the new boathouse over there? The one us sex fiends tricked that alumni fool into buying for us?" I yelled into the wind as we passed the training area for the crew, at the south end of the lake.

"That's it, all right," Lenny replied. "And speaking of tricks, I hear all our poor freshmen honeys are now doing it in there with the crew, since they ain't allowed into apartments anymore."

We all toasted the driver for that smartass remark. Leave it to Lenny to make that connection to Cornell's scandalous protest rally.

I'd been out this way only a couple of times before, for "weeds parties" at Taughannock Falls. I never fully realized the natural beauty of the drive until this golden Sunday morning. Rising in elevation along the western ridge of Lake Cayuga, we passed an abundance of little bungalows facing out on the water, their tiny separate garages just off the shoulder of the highway. Beyond the lake Cornell University stood on the eastern hill, its landmark Old Library tower exuding the dignity of honored tradition and noble endeavor. Further north the houses were fewer and farther apart. The forest stood tall in its lush timber, beaming in the glory and radiance of the morning dew. Like a dog with its head stuck out the window, I held my face up to the torrent of air, imbibing the fresh pine scent.

"Here we are." Lenny's voice yanked me back inside our fleeting convertible. "This is Glenwood Pines. The Last Chance should be just down this side road."

Everyone settled down, alert with anticipation. Sure enough, as the restaurant and state highway crested behind us we came upon numerous cars parked along the edge of the road, many adorned with Cornell bumper and window stickers. Lenny slid us into the first available space.

Then, as we climbed out of the Terror, Mike and Mandy suddenly crashed down the embankment. They disappeared into the vegetation.

"Last to the Chance gets ants in his pants," Mike called back through the bushes, with mocking juvenile inflection.

"And forgets how to dance!"

Mandy improvised the rhyming tease from somewhere in the rustling thicket. Their laughter drifted through the trees.

"Well . . . let's old farts take the trail on down to the ranch, I guess," Lenny sputtered, doing his version of Gabby Hayes. "Don't want to be late for this here hoedown."

The house could not be seen at first, through all the greenery. But as we descended the meandering path it finally became visible. To my surprise it wasn't a chalet at all, but rather a small cottage with a screened-in porch almost the size of the interior floor space. The side lawn provided ample recreational room, already hosting a number of Fessors and their weekend girlfriends. I negotiated the final series of flagstone steps to the grassy plateau and joined the action. It appeared Mike and Mandy were going to suffer ants in their pants. I didn't see either of them anywhere.

Lenny and Charlene and I ladled ourselves some milk punch from the large dairy pails sitting by the porch. Taking my first sip, I noticed the neatly engraved wooden sign hanging over the door, announcing "Last Chance." Other than that it looked like just another little summer house on the lake.

"Hey, pal. Can I have a taste of your milkshake there?"

Mandy wrapped her arms around me, nuzzling up from behind. "How the hell did you guys beat us down here? Guess you really were afraid of forgetting all those fancy moves I taught you, huh?"

I must admit I'd gotten a little peeved about her running off into the underbrush with someone like Mike Gorman. But she was such a cute, perky minx. And she was my playmate. I released my suspicions to the sweet spring air and kissed her on the forehead.

"Why don't you just take mine here, hon. I'll pull out another one for myself." Her bright hazel eyes seemed more compelling than ever.

Just then music blasted from the nearby porch screens. Hi-fi speakers had been set up out on the deck.

"Let me teach you all over again," Mandy kidded. We displayed no modesty as first dancers on the grass, rocking to Duane Eddy's twangy guitar.

It became a Fessor function for the ages. The milk punch was strong, the music rousing. One of the Phi Gams living at the Chance served as deejay. He shared my taste in sounds, playing many of my favorites, from Elvis's "Good Rockin' Tonight" and Buddy Holly's "That'll Be the Day" to Little Richard's "Good Golly, Miss Molly" and The Genius himself, Ray Charles, doing his spellbinding "What'd I Say." Everybody danced and played silly games with each other. And the dairy pails provided milk punch aplenty, more than enough to slake our party thirsts and soak our clothes as well.

The day turned out picture perfect weather-wise, too. The afternoon clouds had yet to materialize. The clear sky cloaked itself in a rare deep indigo, surrounding a brilliant, toasting sun.

Taking a break from the tomfoolery, Mandy and I strolled over to the front yard. The view dazzled us. We stood high above Lake Cayuga, a blue diamond reflecting the bashful sunshine. The far side of the lake daydreamed in the verdancy of its woods and meadows, yet unspoiled by the interference of man's progress.

"Oh!" Mandy cried out in surprise, looking down beyond our toes for the first time.

The cottage nestled on a bluff overlooking the lake. A narrow railed walkway of wooden stairs led down the cliff to the sheltered beach and boat dock. A small viewing platform provided a less elevated perspective halfway down.

"My God, Robbie Bender, this place is Heaven."

Mandy was enchanted. I felt myself swept into the spell with her. We stood there for a long while, basking in our simple joy, at the same time rejoicing in the noise of unrestrained merriment buffeting us from behind.

The woodland festival of Fessor party animals continued to celebrate the rites of spring as the morning sun rose toward its zenith in the sky. The milk punch and music continued to flow in an endless supply. It seemed apparent no one had any concern about commitments to his respective fraternal activities scheduled for later in the day.

Mad Madigan persuaded another DU brother and me to join a ludicrous game of badminton. After skidding on my rump through a patch of mud in a vain attempt to avert the final losing point, I ran over to the house in search of a towel to clean myself up. And there he was, the man himself, Fessor, coming out the kitchen door.

"Hey there. How you-all doing? You and your precious lady-love having yourselves a real good time, are you?"

His accent reminded me he came from somewhere in the South; his words reminded me I hadn't seen Mandy in a while.

He appeared to be a real Southern gentleman too, going back inside to find me a towel to wipe the dirt off the seat of my pants. I thanked him, cleaned up out in back of the house and rejoined the party, intent on locating my Jersey girl.

She didn't turn up among the groups capering on the side lawn. I didn't see a jolly soul in the front yard. No one had taken our cue to admire the view. Maybe she'd gotten sick or something. I returned to the cottage to see if she might be in the bathroom. Three couples goofed around in the kitchen. But the bathroom was unoccupied and the rest of the place quiet. I felt a little uneasy about nosing around, but decided to check the other rooms anyway. Perhaps she didn't feel well after mixing drinks and decided to lie down. Beyond the vacant living room there appeared to be just two other adjacent rooms. I tiptoed over to the first, on my left, and stuck my head inside. A bedroom. No one there. I leaned into the other room. Another bedroom. Empty. *Where the hell could she be?*

I went back outside and mingled with various clusters of people, all the while scanning other gatherings for her long, ruddy-brown tresses. I must've seemed already stewed to those who tried to converse with me; unable to focus on the gist of conversations, or even direct questions, I realized my words sounded incoherent even as I uttered them. Maybe I was crocked. But unlike my other drunken escapades, this feeling hit me more like my mind fracturing into pieces. Still Mandy could not be found.

After a time I walked over to the front lawn, stopping at the head of the steep wooden stairs. I looked down to the dock below. *Could it be she'd gone all the way down there to check out the beach? It would've been nice if she'd thought to take me with her on that exploration.* I saw no one on the dock, either.

Then a flicker of movement caught the corner of my eye. It pulled my vision to the left and back up the cliff to the halfway point, where the staircase turned in its final descent. Where the scaffold provided a private lookout.

There they were. The couple stood on the little platform, her back against the railing, her hands clasped behind his neck. Their bodies pressed together in the embrace, his right hand disappearing up inside her blouse. No need to see their faces to identify them. I recognized the Hawaiian shirt. I found Mandy, all right. Found her in the arms of Mike Gorman. Then I couldn't see anything. My mind splintered apart and my eyes were swimming in the dark undercurrents of despair.

CHAPTER 12

Lenny Morrissey once again stepped up as the man of the hour. From the moment I informed him of my plight, he took over in my behalf. He isolated me from the party in one of the bedrooms at the back of the cottage, where he did his best to calm me down from my hyperventilating mind. Agreeing it would be best to get Mandy out of there, he gave me his car keys. He was adamant I keep the Terror for the rest of the day.

"Don't worry about me. I'll get a ride with someone. Do what you need to do. Just don't do something stupid. Remember, you've almost completed your suspension on your license."

He then retrieved Mandy from her tryst, catching her at the top of the stairs, stealthily returning by herself.

The weekend agenda had come to a premature conclusion. Although Mandy's return flight departed later that night, in an hour I had her packing her suitcase back at the frat house. Then we went through all the motions of goodbyes to my brothers and their girlfriends, expressing our regrets that we couldn't stay for the final party, enduring various articulations of "See you again next year, Mandy!"

The return trip to the Syracuse airport seemed twice the distance compared to Friday's breezy pleasure drive. As in the case traveling from the Last Chance to the DU house, no words broke the silence during the first half of the journey; we both kept our eyes on the road ahead.

After a while, Mandy turned toward me. Her tears began to flow. Her voice trembled. "I'm sorry. I know that sounds pretty ridiculous. There's no excuse for what happened. I can't explain why it happened . . . it just did. Maybe I had too much to drink. I don't know. I guess that sounds even more ridiculous. What can I say . . . I'm just sorry."

That was that. We managed to book an earlier flight back to Newark. Mandy reached her mom on the phone to arrange the pickup. We said our final farewell at the gate. This time only one set of eyes misted as we parted. Before I could turn away she grabbed me and hugged me. I froze, rigid and awkward. We stared at each other for a moment. Then I left her standing there. I dared not look back.

I'd barely gotten beyond city limits when I tasted salt from the tears trickling down my own face.

When I returned the Terror to Lenny later that evening he greeted me with his right hand in a cast. He'd broken it, and Mike Gorman's nose, after I left. Lying in bed that night I realized I still had one everlasting friend in my life.

A couple nights later, sometime during the wee hours before dawn, I experienced this haunting dream. *I'm back in high school, on a date with Shirley McFarlin at the Kiwanis sponsored "Teen Fellowship Sock Hop," in the old Denton firehouse. Everybody's there, having a monster time at this big long table. Eddie, Bobby and Speckles. Oh yeah, Tommy Calderone, too. We've got dates with all the hot honeys. Besides Shirley there's Ginger Jorgenson and her inner clique of Tri Gams. The real party girls of Denton High. We're all laughing and laughing there at the table. Then I'm out on the dance floor with Shirley, cutting a rug like I'm Lenny, realizing for the first time that she's the greatest of any girl I ever danced with. In an instant our whole table forms a circle around us. They shout words of encouragement and appreciation, clapping their hands. All of a sudden we're dancing together in Tommy's living room. It's that weird pre-graduation weekend fling at his house, when his folks are away. "Bowling alley Brenda" scowls at me. My secret centerfold, Cynthia St. James, trips the light fantastic with Speckles. Forget about them, now Chuck Berry's singing "Maybellene," and Shirley's getting me into it. I hear it. I feel it. Then, somehow, Shirley's face becomes Mandy's. Oh, Mandy, why couldn't you be true? Now I've got to get past all those times I had with you.*

Waking up that morning the dream's right there, in my mind. One of those dreams you remember the next day, clear as water from the fountainhead. Like it actually happened. Like it all happened all over again.

As I strolled by the bright windows of the Clancy Street Tavern, I noticed some sort of celebration going on inside. Balloons floated above an assemblage of active tables alongside the dance floor. Shrill rejoices of feminine voices could be heard transmitting through the glass.

My last summer break from college before I'd have to join the real world. I'd just completed the third day of my substitute position at the post office, working the noon shift driving the local mail pickup and special delivery truck. The time frame kept me on the job into the early evening, affording me the benefit of being excused from the tension of Mom's supper table. I felt content on my own, grazing in leisure through the leftovers, free of that family torment. It seemed my absence agreed with my digestion. This night I decided to incorporate a pre-dinner tipple into my new schedule.

I speculated the women had gathered to mark some female occasion. Maybe one of them having a baby, or some such thing. What an awful rowdy place to be holding this type event, I thought. I entered the tavern from the side door bar entrance.

"Hey, Robbie! Welcome home, my man. Good to see you back."

Jerry Blakely stood at his customary post behind the bar. I grabbed a seat and he remembered my usual without having to ask. We scratched the surface on each other's lives, in between the typical interruptions as Jerry catered to others' impatient cravings. He informed me about a couple of recent local doings.

The ladies' party got more hysterical out in the front lounge area. Pitch seemed to elevate in proportion to the increased voice volume.

"Say, come to think of it, Robbie, that party over there is for one of your former girlfriends." Jerry nodded in that direction. "In fact, if I remember right, I think you dated quite a few out of that ol' gang."

I swung my swivel stool around and took a better look, through the crowd, trying to catch the faces under the cruising balloons. Sure enough, I saw Ginger Jorgenson standing by one of the tables, laughing about something just said. She looked like she'd aged, more mature I guess, perhaps a tad more sophisticated, her blonde hair cut in a shorter pageboy.

"Jesus! Ginger Jorgenson's over there." I toed up on the bar rail, attempting to gain a better view. "Come on, Jerry, don't jerk me around here. Whose party is it?"

Jerry summoned that special twinkle in his eye. In keeping with his style, he took his time wiping a glass, for dramatic effect.

"You remember Shirley McFarlin? I think you were running with her, for a little while there."

"Is Shirley over there, too?" I could feel my blood rising.

"Hell, yeah, she's over there. The party's in her honor, for Christ's sake."

Sitting back down, I reached across the bar and grabbed his wrist. "Don't make me grovel for bones here, Jerry. What's the goddam' story? What's the party for?"

It's apparent to me now he had no idea what an impact his next words would have on me.

"Okay, okay! Relax! It's a bridal shower, man. Shirley's getting married to some cat from Edgewater. I think the wedding's sometime next month."

I sat there stunned, stuck to my stool. After a while I picked up my glass and threw down the rest of the contents. I waited until Jerry got back to my side of the bar.

"Jerry, do me a big favor. Don't tell any of those girls I was in here. I'll see you later."

The time had come to slip back out of there, to return to Dad's Nash, parked up the street. I noticed a curbside space available right alongside the establishment's lounge room windows. Moving fast, I backed the car into the spot before anyone else took it.

I turned off the lights and sat in the dim recess of the automobile for maybe ten minutes, observing that party of high school girl friends inside the Clancy Street Tavern. Most of the female side of the old gang was there, all right. And they didn't look like they'd changed that much. Except for Shirley. She still had her long, luxurious auburn hair. But she'd become even more attractive than I remembered her. Pulling away from the curb I wondered if the discomfort in my chest could be my sagging heart. Or maybe indigestion, anticipating Mom's reheated well-done pot roast, with all the fixings.

CHAPTER 13

What the hell. I'll do it.
When I got back to the DU house for my final year of college I found a note taped to the door of my new frat room, telling me to get in touch with Rupert Madigan as soon as possible. Tall, slender Mad, now a grad student, had moved out of the house and into a cottage on the lake, similar to the Last Chance. He left me his telephone number. It seems one brother fell out of the deal, deciding the place too far from campus. Mad invited me to fill the vacancy and join him and two other DUs living out there.

So I came to boast the "Nitecap" as my senior year residence. The house was some twenty plus miles from Cornell, out on the western side of the lake, on Route 89, but closer than the Last Chance. Besides Mad my roomies would be Wayne Shockey, nicknamed "Lectric," another Mummy Majura party boy, and Grant Blankenship, a member of both Mummy and Fessor's, like Mad and myself. The Nitecap looked to be a dangerous piece of real estate for the 1961 school year.

"Do you like the name we came up with?" Mad asked me, the usual hyper-excitement in his voice. "Check out Webster's!"

He ran for the dictionary and came back brimming with enthusiasm, like a parent getting ready to read to his first born.

"Listen to this! 'Nightcap. One, a cap worn in bed, especially formally, to protect the head from cold. Two, colloquialism, an alcoholic drink taken just before going to bed or at the end of an evening of partying, a night on the town, etcetera. Three, colloqui-alism, baseball, the second game of a double header.'

"That's it," he raved. "This place is 'The Nitecap.' It meets all the criteria. I can just see the first party out here . . . ."

I could sense Mad's inimitable imagination cranking up again.

"We'll have all kinds of farcical festoons embellishing the cas-tle. And hordes of guzzling gapers will be snarfing up truffles, with smidgens of squid and crispy crustaceans. Feasting on sea-soned sides of Burgundy beef, savory shanks of mulberry mutton, luscious loins of pickled pork. Even licking their delectable drip-pings. And swinging huge drumsticks of pheasant and fowl . . . all the while swarfing down tankards of stout and goblets of ale!"

He led me on a grand tour of the grounds.

"Now out here on the lawn, where the heavenly honeys are rol-licking at a game of croquet, Lectric Shockey's again lost the puck in his jockeys . . . beating himself at old nooky box hockey. And in this great garden of glory, that prankster General Grant and his silver spoon are dropping trou, flashing gotcha's at the moon . . . scaring off all the quivering loons."

At this point Mad flailed his arms about, finally directing a forefinger at a thicket of fern intervening the grass and woods.

"Whilst you, Sir Robert Rapscallion, why, you're planting your seeds over there in the weeds, making a flick on a safari for chicks. Finding those cups of sweet honey pups . . . and searching their clothes-es for little pink noses!"

The man was amazing. "And what will you be doing there, O great Lord Mad?" I interjected, attempting to keep the well pumping.

"Hmmmm. What will I be doing in the midst of all this loony festoonery?"

He stroked his chin, in mock meditation, enjoying the invita-tion for a rapid-fire retort.

"Why, of course. Don't ask. I'll be copping some rays in the Ithaca haze. Fighting off trolls trying to crash our bed rolls. All the while quaffing the liquor, 'cause we all know it's quicker . . . to chase down young trollops in their frilly white knickers!"

"Yeeeooww! I love it! I knew I had nothing to fear . . . coming out here . . . for my big senior year. Let's all give a cheer." Like everyone else, even Lenny, I was no match for Mad. But he definitely furnished incentive.

Rupert Madigan had to be one of a kind, a fascinating original social being unlike anyone I'd ever met before. It never ceased to astound me how he could go on like that, brandishing his toothy smile in a non-stop chant of nonsense and illusion. Sprinkling in tongue-in-cheek dashes of Cornell-isms to the bubbling brew, in hilarious concoctions of alliteration and rhyme.

It seemed someone up above at long last decided to look out for the unfortunate Robbie Bender. Mad Madigan, Lectric Shockey, Grant Blankenship and the Nitecap. I'd survived the shadowy tunnel. I was back in the light. Somehow I'd made it to my senior year. Now I'd be living on the lake with Mad and his boys, and the golden promise of a brand new sunrise.

I should've known it couldn't work out like I expected. Despite the good times during weekends at the lake, the luster of living at the Nitecap wore off fast. Ithaca's winter season dragged on long and cold, the snow and ice never seeming to melt.

Without my own car, I slept at the frat house on many occasions, forced to wear the same clothes to class on consecutive days. And I couldn't find anyone to replace Mandy Hardwick, thus inflating my reputation as an incorrigible drinker.

Ivory Tower, the female "Honor Society in Joyful Living," the coed counterpart to Mummy and Fessor's Majura, voted me as one of six nominees for the disreputable distinction of Spring Weekend King. The *Cornell Widow*, the university's lampooning humor magazine, characterized the King as an "excessive party animal with negligible redeeming features." The only good news: thankfully, I failed to prevail over the scoundrel candidates touted alongside me.

As if this wasn't bad enough, I also found myself placed on disciplinary probation by the Men's Judiciary Board, for a drunken escapade at Keuka College, a nearby girls' school where I'd hoped to find a last minute Spring Weekend date. I had to write a letter of apology to the president of that school to avert police charges. That black cloud followed me even beyond my anticipated graduation day.

So, as the snow, sleet and circumstances continued to perpetuate my descent into depression, I found myself spending more time alone. I waded in self-deceit, foundering in the silhouetted ecstasy of my own pity and praise. Casting myself in the empathetic lead role as the hero of the drama, I created a noble character plunging into purgatory without a parachute.

I found solace in music, drowning despair listening to trumpet, saxophone or flute, piano, bass and drums at Leonardo's, a be-bop jazz club Lenny had introduced me to. As this true American creation took hold of my aesthetic sensibilities, I wondered how I ever missed the emotion, the profoundness, the poignancy of it. And with Lenny absorbed in his relationship with Charlene, I often bummed a ride across town and threw down a few Jack and sodas at the Chanticleer, occupying his "bar stool at the edge of the earth."

On one of those solitary occasions I found my favorite selection on the old jukebox. Somehow, from that night on, hitching home to either the frat house or the Nitecap, everything seemed just a little bit better after listening to Joe Williams singing, "Every Day I Have the Blues."

Just like that, it seemed, finals week was upon us and then behind us. To my relief I saw all my passing grades posted on the various bulletin boards, later receiving my official invitation to participate in graduation exercises. No communication from the Men's Judiciary Board updated the status of my probation. I felt content to let that sleeping dog lie.

Since Mad, Grant and Lectric weren't participants in this year's ceremonies, I ended up the last man at the Nitecap. This entailed the responsibility of turning in four sets of keys to the landlord, who happened to be an administration official at the university.

We'd already done a complete cleanup of the cottage. This included removing an extensive entertainment console a brother built for us, with lumber he'd swiped from a campus construction site. We all loved that piece of innovative furniture. It broke our hearts to have to tear it apart. No easy task, I might add. But we couldn't figure any other way to get it through the doors. We piled it up behind the cottage and I'd been entrusted to somehow get rid of it. Afterward, my three roomies split.

Mom and Dad drove up to attend my graduation, with my younger siblings Barbara, Patti and Donny in tow. We'd been sequenced two years apart, and Donny, the baby of the clan, grumped as Mom's latest victim. She refused to let him take the wheel with his New Jersey Learner's Permit and "put five-sixth of the family in jeopardy." When I made introductions at the DU house, even those frat brothers I considered my biggest detractors treated them graciously.

On the morning of June 12, 1961, proud Dad took my picture in my cap and gown, Bachelor of Arts degree in hand. That afternoon he photographed ROTC commissioned 2nd Lieutenant Robert S. Bender, Military Police Corps, United States Army, and 2nd Lieutenant Leonard B. Morrissey, United States Marine Corps, holding our heads high in our uniforms, hats tucked under our left arms, spit polished bills pointed forward. I look at that photo a lot more now than I did back then. Lenny and I look so cocky. And so young.

After that last picture, hugs and handshakes exchanged all around, Lenny took me aside.

"Well, pardner, we made it. Now it's time to celebrate! And, you know, I been more than a little concerned about you for some time now. It just ain't right seeing my good friend looking so down in the mouth. So, as your bona fide soul brother, I've got you hooked up with one of the finest young ladies to grace this earth with her voluptuous presence. In fact, the two of you will be accompanying me and Charlene to a little farewell party . . . to be held out at the prestigious Nitecap itself."

"What do you mean, party at the Nitecap?" I replied, incredulously. "Mad and everybody already left. We cleaned the place up. I just need to get our deposits back from the landlord. We can't be using the Nitecap."

"I thought you wanted to lose all that stolen timber out there," Lenny shot back. "What better way than partying around a cozy bonfire."

Having no easy way to get out to the Nitecap until Dad's Nash arrived, I'd forgotten all about the lumber in the excitement of graduation. I now lived back at the frat house, with its many available bunks. It also slipped my mind that I'd mentioned the console to Lenny, asking if perhaps he knew someone locally who could put the wood to good use.

"Damn! Why, of course. Why the hell didn't I think of that," I said. Then, rejoicing in my best friend's ingenuity, "Well, that's why you're the wizard, Lenny. Brilliant. You're the man!"

It was perfect. I'd just turn in the keys tomorrow, instead, before we left for home. A crafty way to flout Mom's emphatic "bright and early" declaration.

When I arrived at the lake house with Lenny, tantalizing Charlene, and my "voluptuous" blind date, Debbie, I twitched at my first surprise. I saw a number of unfamiliar hot rods, pickup trucks and junkheaps parked along the road.

"What's going on, Lenny? Whose cars are these?"

"Hey, Robbie. This is my surprise party for you. Your last chance to get together with a bunch of *genuine* dyed-in-the-wool true-blue townies."

He pulled the Terror into the single driveway spot they'd had the consideration to leave open for us. "Come on, folks, let's go have ourselves a good old *gradiation* celebration."

We followed Lenny down the path toward the house, skipping like little kids. I could hear the rock 'n' roll clanging through the trees.

The drama unfolding as we approached the place challenged even my imagination. The yard was a beehive as guys and gals went about their assorted tasks. I recognized many of Lenny's friends from the Chanticleer. And Chester, the bartender at the Sunset Bar & Grill, had made the scene, too. Everybody looked committed to a major production, setting up a hi-fi system, kegs of beer, decorating the picnic table, lawn chairs, and nearby bushes and trees with streamers and flying colored balloons proclaiming "HURRAH!" The balloons reminded me of Shirley McFarlin's bridal shower at the Clancy Street Tavern. Someone had carted in a cookout grill and two men fixed to fire it up to barbecue the chicken and ribs stacked on nearby platters.

But the towering creation in the center of it all really astounded me. Three fellows placed the last pieces of the ill-begotten console cabinet to a well constructed woodpile that stood at least ten feet tall.

"You said you needed to get rid of some timber. Well, we gonna' have ourselves a weenie roast tonight!" Lenny cackled.

The lumber must've been well seasoned as the flame caught quickly. The searing heat soon took the nip out of the evening air. And everybody got to know each other real well too, if they hadn't already. Before I knew it, many doffed their clothes and went skinny-dipping in the lake.

"Let's join 'em, Robbie! Let's go swimming, too!"

Debbie pulled on my sleeve, coaxing me to accompany her in the arctic aquatics. My objection had more to do with the cold water than taking off my duds, and I said so.

Now Charlene got in my face. "Oh, Robbie. Don't be such a stick-in-the-mud." She jumped up from the grass, pulling her sweatshirt up over her head. By the time she had it off Lenny was up too, with Debbie, all of them shedding their things right there in the quivering glow.

"Let's go, Robbie." Lenny joined the two of them in chiding me. "I've already seen you in the shower, so you don't need to be shy with me."

He and Charlene ran to the water, leaving poor Debbie standing there with her arms wrapped around her, impatiently hopping in place as she waited for me to show some courage.

"Come on, fella. You can do it! Just get into your bare skin and join the crowd," a male voice cried out from the group seated hearthside, emphasizing his pun.

He found reward in the many laughs and a chorus of slogan sanctioning supporters, who refrained, "Bare skin. Bare skin. It's no sin to wear your . . . bare skin!" A multitude of dissonant voices now, from the fire worshipers.

Five minutes later Debbie and I joined the exposed dock dwellers, laughing and splashing our feet in the water, as much of my body as I felt willing to immerse in that frigid lake. Caught up in the spirit of the moment while tending to my own lusty curiosities, I didn't notice the briskness of the air. It was all good clean fun.

Subsequent to a frolic in the water with other naked townies, Lenny and Charlene joined us on the pier, dripping wet mementos of the historic occasion all over us.

"Hey, big guy," Lenny shuddered. "Let's go up by the fire and roast our weenies."

"I want to see that!" Debbie giggled, as I helped her up from the deck.

Some time later all the water lovers ended up back at the fiery centerpiece, most of us remaining in our birthday suits. It became a strange sight to behold, worthy of special notice, when everyone got to their feet to twist to the beat with Chubby Checker.

"You better be careful there, Robbie," Charlene teased. "You don't want to hurt yourself."

I figured buxom Debbie should be more concerned about that than me, considering the effect of the temperature. But I held my tongue, accepting the compliment.

After the consumption of much food, drink and merriment, the shiver in the night air advanced upon the gathering once again, taking advantage of the opportunity provided by the capitulating flames. Soon clothed and unclothed scavengers searched the premises for anything they could find to feed the dying embers.

Before I knew what was happening, pieces of furniture from the cottage had been added to the resurrected bonfire, carried to the smoking fetish by a file of jubilant townies. I must've been a few sheets to the wind myself, caught up in a trance as more furniture marched to the burning stage, sacrificial offerings to nourish the combustion. I snapped out of my daze when I saw the kitchen table on fire. Racing to the crackling blaze I snatched it away, screaming as I dropped it to the ground, the flames French-kissing the base of one leg.

"No more! That's enough! You can't just—"

My words were quenched by a resonant voice from the darkness beyond.

"Hello there. Mr. Madigan? Are you there, Mr. Madigan?"

People ran for cover. Like wild jackals interrupted by the lion at the site of the kill, most everyone, naked or not, dove into the bushes or hid behind the house. Peering out from the concealment provided by a lawn chair, I had no idea where Lenny, Charlene or Debbie went, or where I'd left my clothes.

The furniture continued to burn, projecting an eerie luminescence across the lawn. I looked up toward the highway and saw two wavering lights shining out from the vicinity of the path. *Why hadn't I turned in those damn keys this afternoon?* Realizing I represented the person responsible for the property, I summoned the gumption to call out to the intruder.

"Mr. Madigan is not here. Can I help you?"

The reply was prompt. "This is Mr. Thackeray. Who are you?"

I tried hard to control the tremble in my voice. "I'm a roommate, sir. We're having a graduation party here tonight."

Without hesitation, "I think you had better come up here and talk with us, young man."

"Yes sir."

I glanced around the yard for something, anything, to wrap around me. I spotted a plaid blanket on the ground, toward the restless fire, some twenty feet or so to my left. Taking a deep breath, I stood up from behind the chair. I hurried over to the blanket and draped it around me. Then I hastened across the lawn to the hillside path to meet the owner of the ransacked Nitecap.

CHAPTER 14

The next morning I'd just begun to get my act together when my family arrived to pick me up at the frat house. I'd squeezed into the lobby pay phone booth, rubbing my aching temples and trying to reach Lenny when the five of them walked through the front door. Lenny came on the other end of the line just as they saw me sitting there.

"Lenny? Yeah, I know what time it is!" I tempered my voice as Dad approached me. "Look, do me a big favor. Call me back at the house pay phone number. I'm low on coins, and we need to talk awhile. Give me ten minutes to get my tribe some coffee or whatever. Stay awake, man. Please don't make me call you back."

Lenny mumbled something about feeling rotten and I hung up.

"Hi, Dad. How you doing? Would you like some coffee?" I walked him back over toward the rest, acting as casual as I could.

Mom cracked her whip. "Didn't you bring your suitcases down, like I asked? It's nine o'clock, and we have a long trip ahead of us."

"Everything's ready to go upstairs," I lied. "But there's a couple loose ends I need to tie up before we can leave. So let me take everybody to the dining room, and you can have some coffee and breakfast."

"We've already had our breakfast."

The venom trickled from her words. She pointed a spindly finger at me. "You didn't mention any 'loose ends' to us yesterday."

"Well, a little situation has come up with the lake house, where I was living. I'm expecting a phone call any minute, so I can get that straightened out."

Mom started her inquisition as I got them settled at a table with coffee, juice and jelly rolls. I avoided direct responses, using the rest of the family as conversational buffers, making sure they had everything they needed. Then Lenny's return call saved me from further interrogation. I ran back to the ringing phone.

Lenny began ranting about his hangover.

"I know you're hung over, Lenny. So am I, man. But we've got a real problem here. You know the Thackerays are giving me today to clean up from the party. Then they're coming back to inspect it at six o'clock. Let me tell you, they weren't happy discovering a bunch of nudes dancing around a bonfire on their lawn. And they had friends with 'em, too."

I heard a groan from Lenny on the other end.

"So what the hell are we going to do about all that burnt furniture and stuff?" I snarled. "You know, this guy works for the university, man. Like, if this gets back to the school, with him checking up on me and finding out about the probation and all . . . they might just take action and rescind my goddam' degree! And you could be in the same boat too, you know."

"Hey! Hey! Calm down, brother. That's total bullshit."

Lenny's brain cranked up into operation. "We've got our fucking degrees, man. They can't do anything about that now. The horses are already out of the barn."

"Yeah, all right, maybe so. But how about this?" I jumped to my next worry. "What good will our degrees be, and our officer commissions, if we're charged with arson! You don't have to burn down the whole house, you know, to do jail time for setting fire to other peoples' property."

This time Lenny didn't have an answer. I thought I heard an exhale.

Just as I started to ask if he was still there he said, "Okay. I'll pick you up at noon. I'll get us some friends to give us a hand out there. We'll fix it up . . . somehow."

I went through hell with Mom and Dad the rest of the morning, after telling them the lake house had not passed inspection. I tried to sidestep Mom's relentless search for specifics and questions about any relationship between the inspection and last night's party. It wasn't easy. I got Dad to secure new reservations at the motel for an additional night while Mom went into orbit.

"Well, I'll tell you one thing, Buster. You sure have put a damper on your graduation, that's for sure."

We reviewed the maps of the campus and Ithaca area and I pointed out some places they might like to visit, beyond the sightseeing we'd already done. I managed to get them out of the house fifteen minutes before Lenny arrived. The plan was to meet my folks back at the frat house, targeting seven thirty. Then have dinner downtown.

Lenny and I grabbed a light lunch and got out to the Nitecap sometime after two o'clock. We proceeded to work on the inside of the house first. It didn't look that bad, considering all the party people that had trudged in and out, insanely searching for additional "firewood," and using the kitchen and restroom facilities. Someone had gotten sick and didn't quite make it to the commode. Yet, other than the kitchen table, only small pieces of furniture had suffered the banishment to Hades. Most of the casualties turned out to be incidental items from the porch—folding chairs, a coffee table, a magazine rack. Thankfully, the tables, chairs, sofa and davenport in the living room remained intact.

Nonetheless, the project turned out to be a more arduous task for two people than we'd imagined. What with necessary beer-chugged hangover breaks, we still had much left to do at five o'clock, when Lenny's pals thought they could get there from their respective jobs. We'd yet to clean up the ashen remains of the huge bonfire, and figure out what to do about the charred furniture.

"I need to take another breather for a couple minutes," Lenny said, lying down on the grass next to a partially scorched chair.

We both stretched out for a short rest. I stared up at the lifeless sky. *Man, what a disaster this turned into. I always seem to find a way to get myself in trouble, even for the special events in my life.* The sky looked like mercury creeping across a steely ceiling above me.

"Hey, you guys. What do we got to do?"

I heard the voice as though in a dream. Then the words and the reality of the situation hit me like a sledgehammer.

"Holy shit! What time is it?" I jerked up into a sitting position.

"It's a quarter to six," one of Lenny's townie chums replied.

"Let's go, Robbie," Lenny shouted. "I guess we must've nodded off. We got a lot to do, and no time to do it."

Fortunately, two of Lenny's buds had been trusty enough to show up. They busied themselves cleaning up the remains of the fire while Lenny and I disposed of the damaged furniture we'd collected and separated into two piles. We returned the salvageable to the most inconspicuous places we could find inside the cottage, sticking the shortened leg of the kitchen table toward the far rear, against the wall, hoping it would not be noticed until the Thackeray's summer vacation.

As we completed our final project, heaving the irreparable pieces down into the gully beside the house, we heard voices coming from the entrance path up behind us. I tossed down the last ruined chair and we raced to the front yard, just in time to see Mr. and Mrs. Thackeray heading in our direction down the wooded hill. Treading cautiously behind them were Mom and Dad, with Donny, Patti and Barbara.

The old Nash rode low to the pavement as we rolled home to New Jersey. Driver Dad and five passengers had squeezed into their traditional seating positions. The straps securing the luggage and boxes to the roof carrier flapped in the wind. The trunk had been tied down to keep from coughing out the incremental baggage. It impressed me that this working class product of American industry displayed such durability. Despite its laughingstock appearance it had proved to be dependable transportation over the years.

"Thanks, Dad, for helping me out with the landlord last night. The place really was pretty neat and clean, considering four college guys had been living out there all year. And, like you said, a little grass seed and that burnt lawn is right back to where it was. But that was a great argument you brought up when he got nasty about some things. Cripes, I never really thought about the legal aspects of renting out a summer place in the winter, with no furnace or heating unit. He was a whole lot quieter after you made that point."

Dad smiled, continuing to focus on the winding country road before him.

"From the sound of things you and your fraternity brothers will be mighty lucky to get any of your deposits back," Mom remarked, her words striking me like icicles. "If they have any common sense they'll insist you pay them back yourself. And don't think we're giving you the money for that."

The blizzard intensified. "It's hard for me to understand how you continue to be so damned irresponsible. After the good upbringing your father and I worked so hard to give you. Thank God your brother and sisters know better than running around with no clothes on, burning up other people's property. My lord, what were you thinking?"

"Everyone just decided to go skinny-dipping, that's all," I protested. "It wasn't my idea. And we didn't invent it. Kids have been doing this forever, you know. And I didn't throw any furniture on the fire, either. I was the one who stopped people from doing it."

"Sounds like a whole lotta' fun, if you ask me," Donny blurted. "Sure wish I coulda' been there."

"Get off his case, Mom," Barbara added. "We are talking about college frat boys, after all."

The time had come to broach a question burning in my mind. I looked over at Dad.

"So, I'm curious. How did you happen to meet up with the Thackerays, anyway?"

"Oh, they came by your fraternity house while we were waiting for you. They mentioned your name to one of your brothers there. We just introduced ourselves, and ended up following 'em out to the lake."

When we got onto the I-81 toward Binghamton, Dad broke the enduring silence.

"You should be proud of yourself, Robbie. You've gotten yourself a first-class college education. Now you can decide what you want to do with it."

I thought about this for a minute before I answered.

"Yeah, I got an education, all right."

CHAPTER 15

. . . I sang along with John, Paul, George and Ringo . . .

"Care to buy an old friend a drink, big boy?"

I sat by myself on a Sunday night in T&J Lanes, facing the juke and the front door. The ancient voice and fragrance surprised me from behind.

" 'Course, if you'd rather drink all alone . . . ."

Stubbing out my cigarette butt, I turned my head to find Jane Lennox standing there, one hand resting on her hip with the practiced intent of provocation. Those perilous green eyes and the mischievous ruby smirk challenged me to not only take notice and appreciate, but to whet my social skills for the fast lane repartee certain to follow.

"Stud, you and me got to find a more discreet place to meet," she whispered, leaning in to me and resting her arm on my shoulder. "Seems to me this is the same dump we started at the last time I was with you, umpteen years ago."

Jane had been bowling with three girlfriends. She dropped them on the spot, not even finishing the game they'd gotten halfway into. This time she was the one to play Ray Charles on the music box for us, surprising me during the refrain with a deep soul kiss, right there at the bar. I spent the night at her apartment, feeling a bit awkward about her 2-year-old son sleeping in the next room. She told me she still saw his dropout father from time to time, that on rare occasions he took the kid off her hands. But she essentially raised the boy on her own, and of her own volition.

" 'Daddy' does his part, when I ask," she said, straight-faced. "But we're both better off going our separate ways. Doing our own thing."

That was as far as she wanted to discuss that issue. She mentioned a number of baby-sitting crutches, from neighbors to girlfriends, who helped her maintain her uninhibited lifestyle.

From that point forward I pretty much hung out with Jane when not working my night shift at the local post office. Uncle Sam had been kind enough to allow me a summer respite between college and my military obligation, and I felt pleased to have some kind of gainful employment during this interim period. I'd go home after work, at the break of day, shower, change clothes, have breakfast with the family, and drive over to her apartment, a few towns away. Grab some shut-eye there. Later, we might enjoy an afternoon delight, maybe take in a flick, or picnic at one of the nearby parks. Just goof off together, one way or another. I don't know where Jane got her money, she never had a job that I know of, and I never asked.

The PO assigned Sundays and Mondays as my weekend. So they became our nights on the town. Though not many others subscribed to this schedule, outside of the diehard drunks and for-saken loners, we had ourselves a ball. We didn't need anybody else. We had each other.

Then came that fateful occasion when I returned home late, after another long Monday night cruising the bars with Jane. It must've been around 4:00 a.m. when I fumbled to retrieve the house key from under the milk box. Feeling a bit unsteady, I removed my shoes and tiptoed through the dark house to the staircase.

As I ascended the steps to my bedroom the living room lights flashed on. Mom and Dad sat there on the couch, solemn and gaunt in their long robes. The ensuing confrontation went beyond any logical expectation or explanation; the sordid details aren't even worth mentioning. Suffice to say Mom had never been one to let even a moth-eaten issue die gracefully. Disreputable Jane would not be the exception to this cold reality.

"So you're back in the gutter with those wayward sluts again. Since you're now supposed to be a man, and paying us room and board, I guess this time you expect us to just swallow it and look the other way."

"What are you talking about?"

"You know what I'm talking about. Those Lennox girls. The one who wanted to play doctor with you in junior high. Nadine . . . no . . . the younger one. That's it . . . Jane."

How does Mom know these things?

"And what if I am?"

My speedy trial convened and concluded in just a matter of minutes. Of course Mom was masterful in assuming the roles of plaintiff, judge and jury in the farcical proceedings. She summarily dismissed all arguments from my stunned defense, rendering an instantaneous unanimous verdict of guilty. Some regrettable choice words of invective got hurled from both sides of the searing altercation.

"You're headed straight for Hell, Mister Robert Bender," she yelled.

"Good for me. Could I borrow your map, please? Christ Almighty, this is so much bullshit."

"We may have to put up with you and your filthy, sacrilegious mouth. But that Lennox tramp's not welcome in this house."

"She never was. I get the picture."

I had some basic necessities packed within the hour, ignoring backpedaling pleas for reconciliation from Dad.

After loading my cankered suitcase into the trunk of the '57 Impala he'd advanced me the money to purchase, I drove back to Jane's apartment seething with anger. I lived with her for the remainder of the summer. I stopped by the house only to gather additional personal items and raid the fridge, when I felt certain Mom and Dad wouldn't be there.

"Well, look who's decided to come back home. And loot the pantry in the process."

"Oh, hi, Mom. How you doing?"

This time I got caught, red-handed with a fistful of chocolate chip cookies and a glass of milk.

One week later I strolled back into that kitchen, to have breakfast with the family before hitting the road for Georgia. A half-hour earlier I'd said goodbye to Jane and kissed her as she fell back to sleep in her queen size bed. It seemed illusional, like I now lived inside someone else, as I bid farewell to my own flesh and blood. I drove away to begin another chapter of my life, not knowing what to expect in the world of life-size soldiers.

With the enlisted ranks of the armed forces bloated from the heaviest conscription since World War II, due to the Korean War and escalating Vietnam conflict, the Army welcomed me with open arms. Along with all the other green lieutenants being commissioned in record numbers off the college campuses.

For those of us destined to become military cops, they cranked us through the MP Officer's Orientation Course at Fort Gordon and shipped us out to operational assignments around the world in just eight weeks' time. I'd barely book-learned the rudiments of military police procedures when I got assigned as a platoon leader right there on post, at one of the enlisted training companies within the 4th Training Regiment-Military Police. On occasion you couldn't be certain who was teaching who. But I soon became enlightened about fundamental military protocol. I also learned the hard way to be punctual for all formations, with special attention to those chilly dawn-breaking reveilles. The "old man's" tongue-lashing still dwells in my brain.

"Don't you ever be late for duty again, shavetail. If you can't cut the mustard, you'll be just another soldier saluting your own platoon leader before you know what hit you."

My escape from Army discipline took the form of driving around off-post in my "new" Impala. I found the nearby city of Augusta to be an interesting sociological study, all by itself. I'd never before seen the ugly face of segregation up close and personal. I remembered the separate restrooms at gas stations and restaurants along the interstate, on the drive to and from my one spring break in Fort Lauderdale. But I hadn't focused on the fact I never saw colored faces being served anywhere. The cruel racial separation in this town was distressingly obvious. Yet no one seemed upset about it, on either side of the fence. It existed as a fact of life, accepted without question.

The town did have a commercial section for *coloreds*. Seldom would you find a Negro customer outside its boundaries. Or vice versa. Even entertainment centers, like movie theaters and playgrounds, bowed to segregation. In the white areas, both downtown and in the neighborhoods, Rebel flags could be found on display. It appeared the Confederacy remained alive and well, merely resigned to some temporary state of suspended limbo. The flags served as a constant reminder that the Southern white attitude endured beyond the war in spite of the military defeat.

One of the most popular white bars in town, located in a lovely hotel on a shaded boulevard of tall willows and maples and dignified houses, bore the proud name of "The Rebel Room." Word had it even the mayor enjoyed happy hours there. The local radio stations played Patsy Cline and George Jones for the shiny new Corvettes and Cadillacs when they pulled away from the curb, brim full of mirth. Over on the other side of town, along Twiggs Street, rusty Dodge pickups and primer-spotted Fords squatted in rutted red clay driveways. The aching soul of Solomon Burke and Ivory Joe Hunter floated from ramshackle windows, catching the breeze beyond the faded cotton curtains and escaping into the ragweed air.

I refused to acknowledge the segregation, though I represented no champion of minority rights. My protest amounted to stopping in at a colored joint when the notion hit me, as I'd grown accustomed to do at the Sunset Bar & Grill in Ithaca.

Once, on my way back to the base and needing to replenish my mini-fridge at the BOQ—Bachelor Officers' Quarters—I popped into a small Negro food mart. Looking into the meat case it amazed me how many presentations of pork they had on display, and the imaginative names of dishes reflecting specific pig anatomy. I saw ham hocks, of course, and ribs. But they also advertised "chitterlings," pig intestines, pronounced "chitlins." And "fat back" and "hog jowl." Also something called "barebooty," spelled exactly like that, handwritten on the sign. A multitude of pig parts could be purchased in either bottles or plastic wrap, labeled "trotters" and "rooters," even "switch-a-bouts." Hog hooves and knuckles, snouts and tails. Of course, they had jars of pickled pig feet, too. I reckoned there wasn't any part of that animal they didn't consider edible.

Standing in line at the cashier, with my mundane loaf of white sandwich bread, sliced baloney and mayonnaise, I became fascinated by the little boy in front of me.

He held out his dime to the clerk. Pointing to a jar of candies on the counter, he petulantly asked, "Gimme a dime's worf o' Mary Jane's. How much dat be?"

I chuckled to myself, *Why, ten cents, of course.*

Not until I'd gotten a block away, riding in my Impala, did I wake up to his point. He wanted to know how many Mary Jane candies he could get for his dime. Man, sometimes you wonder about the value of that Ivy League education.

Jane and I continued to communicate, on the telephone and with an occasional postcard, since both of us hated to sit down and write. She caught me at the BOQ one Wednesday night.

"Hey there, lieutenant. How they hanging? This is your Yankee bitch calling you from that polluted swamp better known as New Joisey. You keeping your boots spit-shined down there with all those frigging rednecks?"

I realized how much I missed Jane, just hearing her irreverent words and Jersey accent. A far cry from the sweet Southern belles and their frilly subterfuges. Not that she was any less dangerous; I guess I just felt more comfortable with her hard-edged, upfront approach.

"What's up, Janey, babe? Good to hear your dainty little voice. You can bet I'm missing your ass down here, hanging out with all these whiny Georgia peaches. And mealy-mouthed Rebels who still think the Civil War's up for grabs."

"Well, big boy, Momma's got good news for you-all. She's a-gonna' take care of all your cotton-pickin' frustrations, if'n you-all can just hang in there an itty-bit longer."

Impressive. She knew how to do a pretty damn good Southern drawl, given she'd never been beyond Philly.

"Got myself one fat ticket to good ol' Augustee, Geo-gia," she continued, pouring it on. "You-all better be saving your strength for your juicy Joisey gal, 'cause she been saving up a whole bunch o' big wet kisses . . . just for you, lieutenant."

"So, when're you-all flying in those purty punkins?" I responded, getting into it myself. "Your lover boy is droolin' just a-thinkin' 'bout all them there tasty freckles."

"I'll be on the six o'clock train, this Friday, honey dripper. Then Momma's got a whole week to cuddle with her soldier boy."

"You're taking the train?"

"That's right, sweetie. Old lady Lennox's 4-inch spikes are as high as she's ever going to get off the ground. After twenty-two years of rooting around this here earth, I ain't about to be flying in no stratosphere."

This surprised me. I never pictured Jane having any fears in her hellbent life. I guess we all have our inner trepidations, no matter how self-assured the facade we exhibit to the world at large.

On-post visitors' billets were located not far from my BOQ. I reserved a room for her there. I was afraid to take her to the nearby officers' club, however, for fear she'd say or do something outrageous, just to stir the pot. Staid formalities and starched tradition easily provoked her volatile nature. So we did the town of Augusta every night, establishing "our table" right in the middle of the raucous Rebel Room. We had a frisky time of it, making superficial friendships with many of the local folk that frequented the place, wobbling our way back to post in the wee hours of the morning. And Jane and I made energetic love as a yellow moon cast its Southern hospitality upon our squeaky double bed inside the military guest house.

The big crash came just one day before Jane's scheduled return to New Jersey.

"Jerry? You mean Jerry Blakely? What's he got to do with you and your kid?"

I'd just stopped over at the visitor billets to take Jane to lunch at one of the snack bars on post. We were both hung over from the consecutive nights of drinking and partying. Her careless mind made an intriguing slip triggering a red flag in my own sluggish brain.

"Well . . . I just needed some help taking care of Adam while I was gone."

Fidgeting, she attempted to choose her words with more caution. I knew her too well.

"Jerry was nice enough to give me a hand with him. Dropping him off at baby sitters, and stuff."

"I don't get it. You mean Jerry's got your kid at his place, while he works the Tavern? And he also carts him all the way over to your sitters in Little Ferry? Sounds logistically infeasible to me." My callow military knowledge had already started creeping into my everyday jargon.

Jane's short fuse ignited. Fragments of razor-sharp insults flew through the air of the small room. "Cocksucker mother fuck, you goddam' shithead! All right, asshole. You have to know every fucking detail of my life? Jerry's staying at my place while I'm gone. To give me a break. So I could come down to this craptown Army base to be with you. Not too many people I know in this screwed up world who'd go that far to help out."

"So, what does this mean?" My selfish male conceit smelled more than generosity in the wind. "Jerry's just doing all this out of the goodness of his big heart?"

Now the skirmish erupted into a full-scale battle.

"You son of a bitch, Robbie. You frigging guys are all alike. You can fuck around all over the place yourselves. But all your sweet girlies are supposed to just sit home and wait for their big man to come on back so they can wait on him all over again. You want to know the truth? Think you can handle it, big man? All right. Jerry's been staying with me. And I been sleeping with him. What did you think? You've been gone for months."

Jane's face had gotten closer to the color of her hair.

"You think I'm going to close down my whole life for you? Did you ever make any promises to me? That you were going to be true to us? Did you ever say anything . . . ever . . . to make me think we had any kind of a future together? Fuck you, Robbie Bender! I'll tell your whole frigging Army world here, so everybody can know the truth."

She whirled around and crashed through the door into the hall, yelling as she went. "Hey! Listen up, all you Army bastards.

I been cheating on Lieutenant Bender here. What do you think of that?"

Halfway down the hall I tackled her from behind. I dragged her, kicking, screaming and cursing, back to the room. I needed to resort to some of my old wrestling tactics just to fend her off, sustaining some deep, bloodletting fingernail scratches during the scuffle.

Two hours later I left her at the train station. Then I went to a car wash to see if the scuff marks she'd left on my Chevy would come off. As my luck would have it, they were into the paint. Worse yet, she'd also dented the outside of her door and the dashboard with her vicious kicks.

That night I went into town and hit all the bars, getting royally juiced. Of course I ended up back at the Rebel Room, where my new waitress friend sat with me and commiserated, in between servicing tables. The next thing I know, I'm staring at a cop knocking on my car window. I'd passed out sitting at a traffic light.

The Augusta Police deferred to Army jurisdiction. Within a week I stood before the commanding officer of the MP training regiment, charged with "Conduct Unbecoming an Officer and a Gentlemen," subject to nonjudicial punishment in accordance with Article 15, Uniform Code of Military Justice. The reprimand would become a permanent part of my personal military file. He also restricted me to work, mess hall and billets for a period of thirty days. And I was reassigned, "away from direct trainee contact," as the colonel put it. He gave me the dead-end job of Motor Officer, in charge of the regimental motor pool.

I noted, with a touch of contrition, that it hadn't taken me long to get back into trouble once again. This would be a large blot on my military record. Disturbing, had I any career aspirations. Which, of course, I didn't.

Looking on the bright side of things, I felt very fortunate the civilian police did not cite me for drunken driving. At least I'd be able to get behind the wheel again with a clean license, after the month of confinement.

NOONTIME

He hoped he would find "Wee Willy" waiting for him. The name had come to him on his way home, after their sunrise encounter. The boy felt certain his new friend would relate to it. But subsequent visits to the ledge proved fruitless. The weasel did not reappear. Nonetheless, he remained patient and optimistic, as all frontiersmen had to be. For Shelley Forrester it had become second nature.

Yet something seemed different about this return to his refuge. He felt a nagging discomfort somewhere deep inside him that he could not explain. All the distinguishing features of his private retreat remained in their abiding relativity—the grand oak tree, with its intricate web of surface roots offering shelter to so many elfin creatures; the projection of craggy rock two feet before the cliff, ever serving as a reminder of the impending danger; the thunder of the crashing water just beyond, its vapor billowing into the air.

With brand-new boldness, he stepped over the warning protuberance of stone and squatted, having grown more comfortable with the risk this involved. He scanned his attention downstream, across the ravine. The suspended footbridge was there, as always. An integral component of the whole, though, of all the elements of this magnificent place, it alone bore the burden of human creation. Canadaway Creek sparkled in the noontime sun as it continued its steadfast northbound dash. It was all there, as it always had been. Yet something seemed wrong. He just felt it. Somehow it had been compromised, no longer virgin purity, no longer the exclusive domain he'd come to cherish as his own.

He attempted to recapture the pleasures of previous experiences here, to absorb the serenity inherent even in the chaos of nature. With legs folded, Buddha style, he looked out from the edge of the precipice. But the sense of violation continued to prey on his mind.

Moving back to a patch of grass, he faced the aged oak. Time to attend to catching Wee Willy absorbed in his perpetual forage. Sitting immobile, the boy moved his eyes to pan the area, focusing on the most probable action places while maintaining a peripheral vision to note movement within the panorama. Shortly into this process he saw the first hard clue to his gnawing apprehension. He stared at an unnatural crease in the soil to the right of the tree. From where he sat it appeared to be a footprint. A footprint of a shoe.

The boy abandoned his plan to wait for his delinquent acquaintance. The moment had come for active investigation. He got up and moved to the spot to confirm his conclusion. Yes. A large shoe had pressed into the earth, pointed south, toward a hummock of shrub behind the tree. A second partial print, just before the ground firmed with moss and stone, corroborated the direction of movement toward this knoll.

He threaded his way through the thicket, as swift and light-footed as an Indian stalking prey in his moccasins. He stopped within the cover of foliage at the fringe of a small clearing of grass and rocks. The shock of discovery froze him in place. Much of the lanky grass had been matted, thrashed or broken. The refuse of an intense human habitation glared everywhere. Not the rubbish one might expect from some sorry vagabond living off the land. This unfortunate glade, this sacred earth God bequeathed all of us in His infinite benevolence, had been ravaged and defiled by the drunken dregs of humanity. He saw beer bottles everywhere, and the ruptured cardboard cases from which they'd been eagerly extracted. A circle of charred grass and wood, much of it reduced to shivering gray and white ashes, served testimony to the scorching blaze that had raged here.

Lingering in the camouflage of his hiding place, to be certain the perpetrators had fled the scene of their debauchery, he swallowed back the bile rising in his throat. Convinced he was alone, he stepped out from the bushes and further surveyed the area. Crushed pretzel boxes and restless empty snack bags had been strewn about. A stomped tin can of potato chips now attracted a file of disciplined ants into its greasy makeshift mess hall. Cigarette butts littered the ground, many of them bearing red lipstick marks. Bordering trees and bushes displayed the pruning of limbs, branches and twigs, amputated to feed the flames of a frivolous campfire.

The boy imagined the terrified eyes of his innocent wildlife friends, watching and listening to this fiendish event from the shield of darkness beyond. How frightened they must've been, unable to comprehend what it might portend in terms of the principles of order they understood and shared and lived by, in the sanctity of their natural world.

The wanton abuse of this meadow in the heart of a splendid greenwood suddenly overwhelmed the youngster. He bent over, resigned to the impulse to have to contribute to the pollution with a nauseated retch. But only an agonizing dry heave resulted. He straightened back up and stood, unseeing, for what seemed a very long time. Then, resigned to the realization he would not be meeting with Wee Willy this day, he trudged away from the burned earth and the broken bottles. Troubling yet powerful grist for a story. But, once again, his notepad would have to wait till he got home. He slipped back into the embrace of the forest.

CHAPTER 16

Like a bit part actor bent on hyperbole, he exaggerated his vocal disguise, playing the role of some high-ranking officer involved in an investigation of my activities. I recognized who it was at once, feeling renewed inner spirit welling up inside me, and played along with the game. Either my old friend possessed psychic powers, or coincidence ran rampant. I had not discussed my situation with anybody. I took no pride in my current state of affairs.

"I'm sorry, sir, what investigation are you talking about? I haven't been off post, much less drinking in a bar, for a month now. You must have the wrong man."

I felt a tingle of reprobate excitement as I injected a piece of my secret sordid truth into the role-playing. It also felt like providence inspired this call, right at the conclusion of my period of incarceration.

"Well, then, I do apologize. I thought I'd located *the* Lieutenant Bender who's dedicated his life to wine, women and song. I happen to have some very loose lady friends of his looking to celebrate Mardi Gras in New Orleans. Thought he'd be interested to join the parade. Sorry to have bothered you."

"Lenny, you old mother humper! How you doing there? Where are you?"

"Learning to hover a chopper over those Florida beach babes," he replied.

I couldn't continue the charade any longer, I felt so happy to hear his voice again. The very next week I tested the long distance mettle of the Impala convertible for the second time, rolling through the heart of Georgia in the direction of the naval base at Pensacola, where he attended flight school. It seemed my tires were airborne, knowing Zina and Marjorie would be there too. Slicing across the southeast corner of Alabama toward Panama City, I still couldn't believe it was all happening.

Zina had taken a semester's leave from her university studies in Holland. She'd arranged a reunion in the States with Marjorie and the folks she'd lived with during her foreign exchange schooling in Ithaca. Waxing nostalgic with Marjorie one evening, they decided to call Lenny. The conversation turned into extending the scope of the reunion to include a Mardi Gras adventure. Lenny agreed to try to contact me to join them. I thought about how fortunate I was that my disciplinary confinement ended just in time; I don't know what I'd have done if I'd still been restricted. I would've found a way somehow, I knew. Even if it meant fabricating a death in the family and swearing to it on my mother's life. I had to see Zina again.

After driving straight through, I arrived at Lenny's BOQ just as the sun's first rays peeked out from behind the horizon. It took a few knocks on his door to get a response. Five minutes later my old buddy and I settled in at his kitchen table. We shared red eyes from the previous night.

"How about a Bloody Mary, pardner?" Lenny asked, getting back up and opening the refrigerator door.

She was an exquisite gem. Zina went beyond even my fond, distorted recollections of her, in both appearance and personality.

Of course, she'd matured a lot with the cultivation of her university years. She still exhibited the capacity to appreciate good times, and lit up her surroundings with her energy. But now she approached it all in an even more sophisticated manner, like a true connoisseur tasting the nuances of fine wine, possessing a wisdom and intellect beyond her years, yet also maintaining a wild, visceral imagination.

On the physical side, she'd become more alluring than before. Riding with her in the back seat of Lenny's Merc convertible, he'd sold the tired Turquoise Terror, I found myself staring at the curve to the bridge of her nose, the protrusion of her full red lips. With all due gratitude to the balmy Gulf breeze, she wore short shorts, and I realized why she'd looked so good in jeans and skirts in Ithaca. She had unbelievable well-shaped legs, toned to perfection, with just a hint of freckles. The sun highlighted translucent blond hairs above her knee.

Instant mutual attraction captivated us all over again. Lenny and Marjorie appeared equally bewitched, acting like there'd never been a Charlene in between. And New Orleans proved to be the perfect setting to rekindle the romance of our shared pasts.

"Oh, Rob. Just look at this lovely city," Zina remarked, with a gentle squeeze of my hand. The eclectic skyline of architecture slid across our view in slow-motion as we traversed the bridge from the scruffy outskirts motel we'd checked into. We realized, after occupying the last available room, why it claimed the distinction of the only vacancy sign still lit up within thirty miles of the city. "We're going to have so much fun here. And this time I've got my camera with me, so we'll have more than just memories of each other."

New Orleans was already jam-packed. You could hardly move, by foot or wheels. We dumped the car in one of the few remaining spaces at a remote parking lot, and hoofed it all the way to the French Quarter. Needing to quench our thirsts and rest our aching feet, we popped into the nearest nightspot. Guzzling cold bottles of beer and watching the stage show, none of us realized the stripper didn't represent the traditional gender until we saw the male G-string. Marjorie's exclamation of "Oh, my God!" elicited a big laugh from the crowd and granted us immediate acceptance by the diversified group of deviates in attendance. I echoed Marjorie's outcry under my breath a half-hour later when the very same person high-heeled it into the men's room. Dressed in a halter top and imitation leopard skin miniskirt, the transvestite entertainer stood right next to me and took a pee in the trough-style urinal.

Another interesting encounter took place at a female strip club on Bourbon Street. One of the bleached-blonde dancers on stage seemed to have an eye for Lenny while she performed. After shaking her fanny to the audience, she bent over, and looking between her splayed-apart legs, beckoned in his direction with an inviting finger, smiling and flicking her tongue. The big surprise came later when the girl approached our table and asked Marjorie for a rendezvous, after she got off work. Furious Lenny hailed our waitress, picked up the tab and hustled us out of there. Of course I didn't pass up the opportunity to bust his chops about it afterward. I also stuffed it into my sack of digs for future reference.

When the clock struck midnight it became Shrove Tuesday, signifying the official advent of Mardi Gras, the last day before Lent. The city went berserk. Even conservatively dressed women and girls agreed to conform to the custom of baring their breasts in return for some kind of ceremonial bead necklaces.

After Zina and Marjorie refused a number of obstinate necklace peddlers, protected by Lenny and me in cantankerous verbal sparrings, we ducked into a rowdy corner joint by the name of Old Absinthe. The loud blues band rolled the sweaty crowd with a heavy minor chord progression. A Muddy Waters replica rasped his jubilant pain. We pushed into the flesh-packed saloon. I'll never forget the wall behind the bar, every square inch covered with ragged paper currency, a few Confederate bills interspersed amongst the greenbacks, from ceiling to liquor cabinet.

As we polished off our mixed drinks Lenny took the initiative. "What do you say we take the next round to the bandstand. Show these *gapers* how to boogie."

It pleased me to hear our Cornell education ringing its distant bell in his verbiage.

"Yes! Let's pretend we're back at the Chanticleer," Zina chirped at me. "Let's see if we can still dance like we did that first night we met."

I felt happy to know she still remembered the name of that townie bar. It seemed she treasured our inaugural evening together as much as I did. Loving instinct moved my hand from the nape of her neck to stroke her cheek. Her responding lips were as soft as down. Inside the clamor the call of the nightingale beckoned.

Although too many people were packed into the noisy room to really kick up our heels, we had a great time there nonetheless, moving our bodies together and making momentary friends with all the absolute strangers enveloping us. Two hours after having wedged our way inside, we tipped the waitress for her courageous service. We fought the battle back out onto Bourbon Street, resolved to return to our grubby motel.

A few steps down the street the water balloons hit us.

"Jesus Christ! What the f—" Lenny yelled, as all four of us got soaked. A clutch of partiers stood on a balcony above us, laughing at their successful bombing venture.

"Thanks a lot, you goddam' idiots!"

"Aw, come on now, it's all in good fun," one of the male bombardiers hollered back. "Your girls don't have beads around their necks, so a wet T-shirt contest is definitely in order."

After some bantering between us, they invited us to join the revelry up in their hotel suite. This group no doubt had some money. We left a trail of drips through a classy marble lobby and rode an elegant brass embellished elevator up to their floor. The same fellow from the balcony met us at the suite entrance, now decorated himself with layers of the beaded necklaces.

"As beautiful as you-all are, I can't let you in without doing the Mardi Gras thing. I mean, it's not like there's a bunch of leering lechers standing here with me, you know. By the looks of you girls, you ought to be proud to do it."

I couldn't be sure whether I should like this guy or punch him out. I responded with a disconcerted smirk. Lenny appeared perplexed himself, babbling some incoherent gibberish.

"Oh, for God's sake. Give me some of those beads," Zina exclaimed. She opened her blouse and unfastened her brassiere. "Here. These should qualify me for a handful of those things."

We all stared at her luscious breasts. Although I had had the privilege of touching them before, I joined Lenny and our host at viewing them for the very first time. They stood out as distinctive as Zina herself.

"Well, all right then. If that's what it takes." Marjorie followed suit, exposing a larger pair, not as perkily aesthetic, but attractive in their own right.

"Okay! Welcome to the party. Come on in. Let's get you some drinks, and I'll show you around. Oh, let's not forget your beads, girls."

Our guide removed his necklaces, divided them in half, and draped them over Zina and Marjorie's heads with obvious care.

This turned out to be an affair unlike any I'd ever attended before. Besides the disparate personality types, I observed the stark contrast between the ornate French Provincial furniture, Persian rugs and luxurious décor, and the weathered sleeping bags and wilted mattresses taking up wall and floor space throughout the four rooms. An expensive system of hi-fi components had been set up on a coffee table. Piles of records and reels of tapes were strewn around the equipment, along with waxed cups of used drinks and opened cans of beer.

I recalled my high school days as the Cadillacs serenaded our brief expedition with their toe-tapping old doo-wop hit, "Speedo." In each room people were dancing, drinking, shouting, or making out. Some dozed or appeared to have passed out. We stepped with polite feet over mattresses and sleeping bags, some empty, some occupied. Every piece of furniture supported at least one human being in various stages of alertness, from the hyperactive to the obliterated. The balcony wrapped around the corner of the building. It too was jammed with animated socializers—talking, singing, smoking, drinking—many of them interfacing in boisterous glee with the mobs of disorderly pedestrians in the streets below.

"I guess you could say dat we've gone to da mattresses," our escort quipped, doing a painful imitation of a Mafioso I bet he'd been trying to perfect with any number of new guests. Then, back to his regular hospitality voice, "We're going to be here for a few days, so you're welcome to stay as long as you like." Tour complete, he disappeared into the lunacy.

After fetching our belongings from the trashy motel, we spent two days and nights there in Suite 316 at the Hotel L'Impériale. One could rely on a mattress, sleeping bag, couch or floor space to cop a few z's, if you felt tired enough to negate the racket. We pretty much did that as our own private party within a party. We came and went, for food, new faces and places, as we felt the urge. Now, when someone asks me what I thought of the famous Mardi Gras parade, I have to sheepishly admit, *Oh, I never really got around to see that particular event.*

Before we knew it, and much too soon, it was time to go. Lenny and I took the girls to the New Orleans airport for their return flight to Syracuse. Zina and I hung onto each other through the final boarding call. My heart ached like never before.

"I'll write to you. I'll never stop writing. Promise me you'll write me, too."

"I will." She snuggled closer into me and hugged me tighter. "I'm going to miss you so."

My arms drifted up her back and I clasped my hands in her hair. "There'll be something down the road. You'll see. This can't be the end of us."

She looked up at me, her eyes searching mine. It felt like our hearts beat in sync against each other's body. The kiss began soft and easy. I saw her blue gaze glistening as my eyelids closed. It was that first kiss all over again, back in the Turquoise Terror with Lenny and Marjorie, high above Lake Cayuga. That kiss of dreams. Tender, yet eager, at the start. Then the torch of desire igniting passion, seeking fulfillment . . . .

I heard her voice like a whisper on the wind.

"Goodbye, my dear Robbie."

Lenny and I shared a rare time together on our return trip to Pensacola. We ascended into spiritual brothers with an innate understanding that defied explanation, and the need for conversation. Lenny understood my mind remained with Zina. We bonded together in our mutual silence for most of the journey. Sunbeams skipped and pranced across the Gulf of Mexico. The bracing smell of salt sea air filled our lungs.

Back at the Navy base, we slapped each other on our shoulders as we parted.

"Look out for yourself, Jasper," Lenny said. "Stay in touch."

I climbed into the Impala and cranked up the engine, annoyed it chose this moment to take three turns of the ignition switch before it fired up.

He gave me that intriguing expression of his, relating to the drama of the occasion. "Great car you got there. Hey, super times as always. Drive safe, lieutenant. We'll do it again."

Then, as an afterthought perhaps intended from the very start, he leaned forward. "I know you still got the hots for Zina, mister. Take it from someone who ought to know. If you want her that bad, just go for it. Don't let her get away."

A few miles beyond Pretoria, Georgia, my headlights began to dim. Then the Impala stalled out. I couldn't get it started again. After several cars ignored my frantic wave for assistance on the narrow, unlit road, a colored gentleman in an old flatbed drove me into the town of Albany. I arranged for a tow truck. With just about everything else closed up, I had no choice but to check into a motel.

It seemed I lay awake that entire night on the sagging bed, worrying about my car, my impending AWOL status, and my nebulous future with Zina. A gray depression fell upon me like a shroud. I longed to be back with Lenny and Marjorie and my adorable sweetheart. Why couldn't loving friends just stay together? Why did life have to be so hard, so fraught with sacrifices to happiness?

I recalled Zina's hushed words as we lay together on that soiled mattress in the midst of rowdy celebrants. They tortured me now, even more than when she'd said them.

You've brought me to the turning point I so wanted to avoid. I didn't want this to happen. But I had to know. Now I'm torn between what path I should choose. I have a boyfriend back at school. We've been going together almost two years now. He's been wonderful to me. More than I deserve, really. We've been very happy.

I remember how she leaned in to me in the midst of her confession. She reached up with her hand and caressed my face. Her fingers were feathers on my skin. I opened my mouth, but nothing came out.

She went on, my ears offering rapt audience to her voice inside the din. *All the while I've had this tiny, lingering doubt inside. I went on sabbatical just to get away. I never forgot you. You were always there, even after we stopped writing. God, why does it have to be so complicated?*

I guess now that I've seen you again, I really need to be by myself. To sort things out. To see where I'm really going with my life. I'm doing some traveling through Europe after I leave Ithaca. Hopefully I'll find some answers. I won't go back to Amsterdam until school resumes in the fall.

Caught in a spindrift of intoxicated emotion, I had no adequate response to her reflections. I couldn't even remember what the hell I'd said to her at that crucial juncture in our lives. I just knew it was totally inadequate to the opportunity.

The next morning, while a mechanic replaced the distributor on the Impala, I called in to report why I was late returning to duty.

I felt lucky when I received only a verbal reprimand from my new boss, the regimental S-4, for my technical AWOL. Not long after that, however, I received my second Article 15 from command headquarters. This time they singled me out as the scapegoat simply for attending a drunken bachelor picnic that somehow went awry, involving not only student nurses, but alas, once more, the Augusta Police. As before, my punishment restricted me to work, mess hall and quarters for thirty days. Worse yet, Colonel Slater announced he would be taking steps to recommend revocation of my officer's commission.

CHAPTER 17

It appeared this time I'd slipped over the edge, tumbling straight for the bottom of the abyss. I recalled my earlier fears of flunking out of college. My dramatic solution then entailed running away to some nondescript oblivion where I could linger to my dying day in the ego massage of martyrdom.

This situation presented the added dimension of more eternal consequences than the forfeit of reputation and career aspirations. If I were to lose my officer status I would undoubtedly be drafted back into service as a private, to fulfill my military obligation. I would not only be forced to endure the embarrassment and hardship of enlisted boot camp, but could very well end up as an infantryman, susceptible to a terminating Viet Cong bullet in the tangle of Vietnam. Ultimate martyrdom, to be certain. But lacking the delicate pleasure of the melancholy psychological rub.

The second 30-day confinement did allow me the time to write in earnest to Zina while I sniveled in self-pity, contemplating the unfairness of my circumstances. My spirits came to be further dampened, however, when I received only three postcards from her, each from a different exotic location in Europe, in return for my soul baring letters.

They epitomized the typical superficial patter, consistent with the cramped writing space and lack of confidentiality inherent in this form of tourist communication. "Having a wonderful time!" "Wish you were here!" "This place is fabulous!"

Even the photographs depressed me, comparing the engaging scenes to my own austere environment. They underscored the vast difference in the scope of our worlds, from my restricted repetition of routine steps to the refreshing freedom of her adventurous miles. Of course, I rationalized, she had not yet received my letters, gathering at her mailbox while she traveled the Continent. I could only hope that, behind the shallow postcards, she was "finding herself," and her self-discovery included me.

One morning robin redbreast appeared at my windowsill. A perfect blue sky provided harmonious contrast, like the backdrop to the *Oklahoma!* musical we'd performed years before at Denton High. The weather had been beautiful ever since Colonel Slater moved on to his next assignment. His replacement saw fit to give me a chance to redeem myself and prove my worth. First I'd been granted the opportunity of regimental training officer, under the tutelage of the inspirational S-3 operations officer. Now I marched direct to center stage on my own, as the newly appointed commanding officer of Foxtrot Company. The suspended polished sun shone brighter than ever.

Just like that, I emerged from the darkness into the light. At the same time, I felt saddened by the infrequent correspondence from Zina. She'd returned home from her travels, now completing her education, but made no direct reply to any of the observations, feelings and idealistic notions I attempted to share. While I composed pages of romantic ramblings, her belated responses remained brief and more informational than anything else. I suppose I didn't want to admit it to myself, but the handwriting was on the wall, as they say. Yet I continued to send long letters, hoping for any kind of heartfelt response.

One Saturday afternoon I drove into Augusta, the car radio tuned to the local race music station. A premonition of impending reality jolted me.

The epiphany appeared through the medium of song, from soul balladeer Chuck Jackson. I'll never forget the title, "Any Day Now (My Wild Beautiful Bird)." The piece expresses the contemplation spurring a lover's regretful resignation. The prophetic lyrics emanate from a man crying out from the very depths of his heart because he senses his beloved is about to leave him. My own truth became clear in the image of my own gorgeous wild bird already flown, leaving me to cope all alone.

The message exposed my denial of the obvious. Zina's personal search no longer involved me. I needed to move on, for my own sake.

Ten days later I received her Dear John letter, telling me she'd gotten engaged to her Dutch boyfriend, asking that we remain friends, that she will never forget me. She included a photograph Lenny had taken of the two of us, holding hands out in front of the Old Absinthe gin mill on Bourbon Street.

The constant responsibility and challenge of the company commander's position not only helped me get over the loss of Zina, but allowed me to more or less "keep my nose clean," as Mom would've put it. I did maintain my social life, primarily off post, dating a couple of Southern lassies. One, the randy young daughter of a fire and brimstone Baptist preacher. The other, Heather Lake, the pretty, peroxide blonde, ever-popular waitress at the Rebel Room. They helped to assuage the pain.

Toward the end of my active duty obligation, the summer of '63, Uncle Sam rewarded my "rehabilitation," promoting me to first lieutenant. Shortly thereafter, he played his old hand at the standard *re-up* game, offering me the opportunity to stay on for a choice European reassignment. I considered the proposal for awhile, thinking how great it would be to experience the enchantment of that part of the world. But I also harbored concerns about extending my military commitment while the Vietnam conflict escalated and demanded additional troops. I had no interest in this kind of adventure, risking a fateful date with that Viet Cong bullet.

I called Lenny to see how he was doing, brag about my new grade status, and tease him regards my impending escape from military life. I knew he'd committed to a longer active duty obligation with his enrollment in flight school. After a few minutes of verbal jousting with each other he mentioned a situation he'd just learned from Marjorie, pertaining to Zina. It wiped the jester grin off my face real quick.

As soon as we hung up I found myself dialing Marjorie to verify the news. She sounded her usual vivacious self when I reached her at her apartment in Ithaca. We exchanged fond recollections of Mardi Gras. Then I charged straight to the impetuous point of my call. Her response sent tingles up my spine.

"Lenny had it right, Robbie. Zina and I keep in touch, as you might imagine. Like sisters, we talk about everything. She's been engaged to Lars for a while now. He's just gone on to medical school. So she's pretty much supporting him, with her marketing job in Amsterdam. But he wants to put off getting married till he's finished all his schooling. Which means years. I know she's been upset about that.

"But the last time I talked to her, she was acting kind of like it could be, you know, a blessing in disguise, or whatever. She talked a lot about you. Asked me to find out what you're doing . . . if you're still in the Army. All that kind of stuff. Anyways, she's definitely having second thoughts about everything. I kind of figured you might be interested."

After setting the phone down, I lay on my narrow Army bed, contemplating this crucial pivot in my life. My mind raced out of control. *I'm now a first lieutenant. I survived the threat of Colonel Slater's intolerant actions. I still have no idea what I'll do for a living in the civilian world. Lenny will be in the service another couple years himself. Of all the exciting places on this planet to visit, I've always dreamed about experiencing the romance of Europe.*

Zina lives there. She's asking about me. She's at a crossroads in her life, too.

Zina. There's no one else like Zina. She's the woman I always wanted. She's the one who makes me whole.

I clicked on the little radio on my night stand. Otis Redding had just started singing "I've Been Loving You Too Long (To Stop Now)." I'd heard the tune before, but never really listened to the words. When the song was over I got up and went over to the bookshelves across the room. I'd made my decision. I picked up the informational material I'd been given relative to military police operations in Europe, and stretched back out on the iron bed.

On Friday afternoon, 22 November 1963, I stood once again in front of my troops on the parade field. The weather had turned a bit cooler since previous exercises under the Georgia sun. This time the barracks across the street didn't look warped by undulating waves off the hot asphalt. And while the march entailed the standard ceremony I'd performed countless times before, this one held personal significance for me. It represented my last parade at Fort Gordon.

But something seemed amiss up at the parade stand. The major who'd been designated as this ceremony's parade commander had us all standing at attention for an inappropriate long period. He appeared to be absorbed in a lengthy discussion with soldiers in a jeep that had driven up in front of the stand, right in the middle of the proceedings. It was unusual we hadn't been granted the *parade rest* command for such an extensive length of time. I couldn't check my wristwatch, obviously, but I estimated we'd been left in this position for at least five minutes. During the summer months you'd be hearing the soft thud of trainees' bodies as the less stalwart slumped to the ground.

I muttered a few curses under my breath, relative to the merit of the acting commander. I heard a few disgruntled comments from within the ranks behind me. Eventually there came a tapping on the microphone. The major spoke, slow, deliberate. It seemed he remained unaware we still stood at attention.

"Gentlemen. It is my grave duty to inform you that our commander in chief, the President of the United States, has apparently been shot. There is no word at this time as to his condition other than he has been taken to a hospital for treatment. There is no information at present as to any details of the shooting. Under the circumstances the remainder of this ceremony will be canceled. Commanding officers . . . take charge of your units and proceed to your respective areas for further instructions. Dismissed."

Not until my battalion commander issued his command did I realize where I was and respond accordingly to his direction.

Few of us left the BOQ television that weekend. We all watched with a disquieting apprehension, over and over again, as every channel repeated its news coverage of the appalling event. At times there would be some new detail to add to the ghastly story. It seemed impossible President John Fitzgerald Kennedy had been shot to death in a motorcade in Dallas, Texas. We reacted like stupefied zombies sitting in front of the blue picture tube in a strange, never ending twilight. Most of us stayed up all night, watching and conjecturing.

I escaped my Transylvanian quarters late Saturday night, meeting Heather at the Rebel Room and following her home. The two of us cried together in front of her set, while her sleeping kids curled up with their innocent dreams. We held each other for a long time at her front door before I drove back to the BOQ. The stars had just started to fade as I pulled into the parking lot. The TV screen could still be seen flickering inside the day room.

A few hours later I again sat in front of that television with my BOQ mates. We watched Jack Ruby gun down alleged assassin Lee Harvey Oswald—live, and in black and white.

Another Yankee lieutenant rode home with me for Christmas. He looked forward to joining his family in Connecticut and resuming his civilian life. I intended to try to patch things up with Mom and Dad before I caught my Navy transport ship to Germany. We stopped by Heather's apartment to drop off the key she'd given me. It was about 0600 hours.

I tiptoed into the bedroom. Heather remained sound asleep. Checking her kids in the other room, I found them slumbering peacefully, too. I went back to Heather and leaned over the bed, kissing her on the cheek. She gave a little moan and turned in the opposite direction. Fare-thee-well my Georgia belle.

I left the key on the night stand and slipped back out the door, the sense of *déjà vu* lurking in the back of my mind.

"You-all set?" my friend quipped, displaying his mastery of the drawl after two years of Southern exposure.

"Yassuh," I replied, as we slowly pulled away from the curb.

CHAPTER 18

When I traipsed into the Clancy Street Tavern I found myself nursing a sizable urge for a Jack and soda the way Jerry Blakely made them. Strong on the Jack with just an accenting fragrance of the mixer to soften the bite. It felt good to be back, where the accents hit hard and the language is direct. There's no euphemistic country masquerade abiding New Jersey. After my first little tête-à-tête with Mother Bender, regards my "asinine" decision to postpone a civilian career in favor of serving my country in Europe, I needed a strong one.

The place was crowded with all kinds of people already enjoying the holiday spirit. But Jerry didn't appear to be working this evening, I didn't see any of the old gang hanging out, and a new face confronted me from behind the bar.

"Jack and soda, please." I settled in at the one available stool, at the far end of the counter, near the entrance to the restrooms. The odor of pine scented disinfectant reeked especially strong this evening.

After surveying the scene I realized the only face I recognized was the owner, busy serving customers on the other side. When the new tender delivered my drink, I could tell by the color it didn't measure up to a "Blakely," I fired my question before he could get away.

"So, where's Jerry tonight? Got time off for Christmas shopping, or something?"

He looked at me like I'd just got off the boat. His tone spurned common courtesy. "Where you from? If you're talking about Blakely, he's long gone, pal."

The bar jerk walked away from me to refill a tap beer a half-dozen customers away. I finished the pathetic drink and, still not finding anyone I knew, made my way over to the owner at the other end of the bar. He was busy as hell, so I just butted in.

"Oh, man. Look who's gracing our doors tonight," he responded, surprised and seeming genuinely pleased to see me, though we'd never been close. "How you doing there, Robbie."

I got right to the point, his time being precious. "Friendly new bartender you got over there, Ted. I hope your manners rub off on him pretty soon. So, where's Jerry?"

He set down the liquor bottle he was holding, wiped his hands on his apron. "I take it you just got in town?" I nodded and he leaned toward me.

"Jerry was killed in a car accident Thanksgiving night. They just had the funeral two weeks ago."

It felt like somebody hit me across the chest with a two-by-four. I was stunned. The second blow staggered me.

"And Jane Lennox is in Hackensack General. She's still in a coma. They say it doesn't look good, even if she pulls out of it."

In between serving customers, Ted filled me in on the distressing details, polite enough to answer whatever questions my fractured brain conjured up after the initial shock. Then I needed to get away, to drive; it didn't matter where.

For about a half-hour I rode around aimlessly, steering to old familiar places by rote memory, as though the Impala had been set on some kind of automatic pilot. Then I pulled over into a park at the edge of the Palisades cliffs, with a view of the distant George Washington Bridge. I sat there, staring at the fog that hung at the upper reaches of the bridge's tall stanchions, swathing the contouring lights in a gauze of vaporous haze. The hulking influence of New York City loomed in the background.

Jerry Blakely is dead. Just a matter of days after Kennedy's assassination. I had trouble grasping the enormity of either catastrophe. It seemed inconceivable, yet I understood it was reality. Jerry hit a light pole head on, at high speed. Police reports stated he'd been driving under the influence of alcohol.

And Jane lay near death's gate herself. I recalled how we'd parted under the worst of circumstances. Now I felt pangs of guilt about how our relationship ended. Who was I to expect her to adhere to chaste standards of virtue and commitment that didn't apply to me? That final ugly scene between us came about as the product of my own selfish disposition. If only I could find a way to at least mend the wound, to ease the hurt I'd inflicted.

My fingers had already anticipated the move to the ignition key. I started the engine and drove to Hackensack General Hospital in the grim night air.

"I'm sorry, sir, but visiting hours are over. And the patient has not been cleared for visitors beyond the immediate family."

"Look. I'm her boyfriend. Wouldn't it be possible for me to . . . just sneak a peek at her for a moment?"

"I'm sorry, sir."

"If I come back at regular visiting hours?"

"I'm sorry, sir. Not until there's authorization beyond her legitimate family."

I suppose, then, that excludes Adam, her own son, I thought, as I tromped away, my hackles resounding in the hall behind me.

Christmastime turned out to be worthwhile from the standpoint of seeing the family again. I couldn't believe the changes in my brother and sisters.

Strait-laced Barbara had graduated from college, putting her degree in sociology to good use as a secretary with a local insurance company. It wasn't Dad's firm, but he'd helped her land the job. She'd also become engaged to her old high school boyfriend. Former prom queen Patti continued to be an honor student, now attending NYU, majoring in drama and theater arts. I envied her, living in Greenwich Village. We all submitted our early requests for box seats at her first Broadway performance. Little Donny wasn't so little anymore. Although he stood at least 2 inches shorter than my 6 feet, he weighed a lot more than I did. He admitted to 210 pounds, though I'm certain he went beyond that. As I might've guessed, he struggled as a freshman at Fairleigh Dickinson, with no concept of what he might be interested in. He still lived at home and commuted to classes.

Dad, in contrast, looked like he'd lost some weight. He'd started chain-smoking. I figured it was symptomatic of the various stresses he had to bear, from his job, putting four kids through college, and sharing life with Mom. She remained the shrew she'd always been, if not more opinionated and peevish than ever.

I didn't find many of my old pals around. Of course, one could always rely on boozer Eddie Mazzoli, now a self-professed "mechanic" at the town Sinclair station, but merely handling the gas pumps whenever I pulled in. I settled for joining him and two random chicks he knew for a disastrous New Year's Eve at some gaudy banquet hall in Moonachie. I considered it just desserts when his date threw up on his only suit.

The day before my scheduled ship out to Europe, I made one last attempt to see Jane at Hackensack General. A different head nurse granted me visiting privileges without a hassle.

She lay in the bed, all alone, still in a coma. I hardly recognized her. It was Jane, but she looked trapped inside the ivory veneer of a stranger. I stood there for about ten minutes. Then the nurse confirmed it would be all right to touch her hand. As I did so, an elucidating flare flashed inside my head. Jane and I sat together at the bar in the old T&J, and Ray Charles sang "Come Back Baby" on the juke. I held her hand until I couldn't take it anymore. I walked away, embarrassed by the tears in my eyes.

The next day I boarded the USNS *Rose*, a Navy transport ship sailing for Bremerhaven, Germany.

The voyage across the Atlantic Ocean in January did not fulfill my expectations as a between-duties vacation adventure. I thought I might just sit back in a deck chair on the officers' level, bolstered by Dramamine to avert seasickness, enjoying my first cruise on the high seas. For one thing, the weather didn't resemble warm Georgia; and I'd underestimated the persistent task assignment orientation of the military. So, being the sole MP officer aboard, they perfunctorily assigned me the role of provost marshal of the ship, with police responsibility for all Army personnel.

The Navy assumed the support role of navigating the barnacled leviathan of steel. They also provided routine services such as mess, bar, vending and purser. An ad hoc organization and chain of command had been set up by the Army for its troops in transit to various European assignments. In essence, the passengers represented one enormous organization of various branches and missions and destinations floating together from one continent to another. We all fell under the command of the highest ranking officer, who, as far as I know, existed only on the official manifest. Functioning as the officer in charge of security and police matters, I never had the opportunity to even salute the man, wherever he was.

My provost marshal duties included apprehending and locking up seven drunken soldiers who'd started a fight amongst themselves. I had to separate them in manacles inside the brig during a roiling squall, after they sneaked into an off-limits officer/NCO bar.

But, for the most part, I did have time on my hands to contemplate the most recent devastating events surrounding my life, and consider my future plans. The deaths of President Kennedy and Jerry Blakely, and Jane Lennox's tragic condition, propelled my mind further in the direction of living life to the fullest. No guarantees existed that tomorrow would be there for you, regardless of who you were. Certainly John F. Kennedy's violent departure from his position as leader of the free world and the demise of the "American Camelot" he'd created, furnished credence to the viewpoint.

The ghost of Bruce Tierney, still slouched in his wheelchair by the kitchen oven, hovered over my thoughts, a dark vulture I felt determined to avoid. I would not waste any time getting on with my own life. The moment had arrived to absorb the culture of Europe, to sink my teeth into the rapture and pathos of new worlds, to take that deep, soulful swig from the chalice.

The first step in the venture would be to find Zina. To capture her heart, once and for all. I requested Germany for my tour of duty because it neighbors the Netherlands. Unfortunately, I'd been assigned to a battalion headquartered in Munich, closer to the southeast border, near Austria. Nonetheless, I felt optimistic that the journey to Zina would be accomplished with ease in the speedy new sports car I planned to purchase.

CHAPTER 19

I waited for what seemed forever for the phone to make the long-distance connection. At last I heard the curious Continental ring as the call went through.

"*Goedemorgen.* Gunther-Verhoeven. *Waarmee kan u van dienst zijn?*"

"Hello there. Is this Helge?"

"Er . . . yes, this is Helge. Do I know you?"

"Well, no, not really. I'm an old friend of Zina Baerg. And I was hoping you might help me surprise her. I'd like to stop by on Monday and take her to lunch."

"Oh. I don't know."

"Please? I just need to make sure she will be in the office Monday. I'll take care of the rest."

"Well, she should be in the office, but . . . what is your name?"

"Very good, then. I'll come by at noon and say hello. Thank you, Helge. Oh, and please don't say anything to Zina. So it can be a real surprise. See you Monday."

I hung up before she could react further.

Marjorie had provided me all the details I needed to put a plan into action. I figured Zina would not be away when Lars attended medical school classes. I could contact Zina at work, take her to lunch, and hopefully convince her we're meant for each other.

Her admission to Marjorie that she was "having second thoughts" about "him," at the same time asking questions about me, gave me confidence there could be a reasonable chance of success. I remained fortified by her words back in New Orleans as well, when she confided, *I've always had this tiny, lingering doubt inside. I never forgot you. You were always there. Even after we stopped writing.*

I'd locked those words inside my head. When I needed them I'd turn the tumbler, open the vault and hold them out to scrutinize and cherish. And it turned out perfect that Marjorie not only had Zina's work phone, but had somehow gotten the receptionist's name as well. This gave me just enough information for the personal approach, to verify Zina would be there after I made the long trip, and to do so without tipping her off that I was coming.

My first leave from my new assignment with the 508th MP Battalion headquarters in Munich had been scheduled for the following week. The Friday telephone call allowed me the weekend to drive to Amsterdam, get settled into a hotel, and locate an intimate and discreet restaurant not too far from her workplace. I felt certain this would be my one chance in a lifetime. It was imperative we meet face to face for such a consequential occasion. After all, this just happened to be *our destiny* at stake. If it all worked out as planned, I had the remainder of the week to be there with her.

When I climbed into my freshly washed *forst*-green Austin-Healey 3000 early Saturday morning, with my luggage and my maps and a full tank of gas, I had to be as excited as I've ever been in my life. My past, present and future shone brighter than ever before.

Although the sky remained overcast during the trip I sustained my state of euphoria, testing the fast lane of the unbridled autobahn in my consummated State Street vision quest. My dream car performed more nimbly and with greater muscle than I'd even imagined.

The first neighbor I'd met at my McGraw Casern BOQ apartment had introduced me to the fresh British pop sensation, the Beatles, incessantly playing their music in his perpetual beer can party pad. After crossing the border checkpoint into Holland, I realized I knew all the lyrics to their hit, "I Want to Hold Your Hand." With liberated gusto, I sang along with John, Paul, George and Ringo on the car radio.

A light rain fell as I arrived in Amsterdam, looking for the American Hotel, where I surmised they spoke English. After working up a sweat, I found the place. I felt a bit apprehensive leaving my new car keys with the doorman before checking into my first European hotel room. Though the lights of nearby nightclubs beckoned, I fell asleep in my stuffed chair, later climbing under the puffy, quilted comforter on the bed for a good night's rest. Sunday I paid too much money for an umbrella in the hotel gift shop, and checked out "Wiedengaart" in the continuous drizzle, a restaurant the hotel concierge recommended not too far from the offices of Gunther-Verhoeven. I made reservations there, concurring that it satisfied my notion of the perfect place for a rendezvous.

I will never forget the astonished look on her face when she walked tentatively into the reception area at her office and saw me sitting there. Nor the raised eyebrows from Helge behind the desk when Zina threw her arms around my neck, and we did one complete twirl in the middle of that small room.

"Oh, my god! Robbie! What are you doing here? How did you find me?"

"Hey, I'm a cop, Zina. We're supposed to be able to track people down. Besides, I promised you in New Orleans I'd see you again."

"I can't believe this is really happening!"

I whisked her out the door before anyone else could get involved.

Now we were back together again, in an artistic Dutch restaurant, as though we'd never been apart. Gazing at her across the table, she looked striking, as beautiful as ever. She had an unadorned, natural loveliness about her that transcended lipstick and eye shadow and jewelry and hair styling. In fact, on this rainy Monday she'd dressed quite simply for her workday, in a rather plain blue skirt and beige blouse, her hair pulled straight back and bobby-pinned in a loose French twist. She wore just a hint of a pale lipstick. Taking it all in from the other side of the lonely white orchid standing in its ceramic bud vase, I knew this was the girl for me.

We acted like teenagers bringing each other up-to-date on our lives, careful to edit out the relationship most contrary to us, of course. Focusing rather on the good things you want to share with someone who occupies an exclusive place in your most personal world.

Chatting away, we took little time for a breath or bite of food. I still see the glint in her sunshine eyes as we imbibed in the joy of each other's presence. All of a sudden I became aware that the white orchid no longer stood between us. I'd somehow moved my chair next to hers. Our hands touched lightly, then snuggled together on the table. I knew the moment had come.

"Zina—" A parching drought invaded my throat. This wouldn't be as easy as I thought.

"I have to tell you. The reason I'm still in the Army. So I could get to Europe. So I could be with you."

There. I got it out.

"I know now that you're the girl for me. We're absolutely right for each other. We're on the same wavelength. We laugh and we cry at the same things. We're into each other, like, in a whole different realm. Beyond boyfriend or girlfriend. And we dance together better than anyone else. Well, at least as good as Lenny and Marjorie!"

We both laughed together at that silly point. She put her other hand on top of mine.

"Robbie—"

Her face was right in front of me, and I wanted to lean forward and kiss the tears about to cascade from her eyes. I restrained the impulse as they trickled onto her cheeks.

She hesitated, then continued. "You don't know how much I wanted to hear this. And see the words coming from your lips."

I plunged on with my little speech. "I was such an idiot in that hotel in New Orleans. I've thought back so many times to when we were together on that mattress on the floor. With all the noise, and people stepping over us. You shared all your feelings with me . . . opened the door for me to answer. And I blew it. I just flat ass blew it. I don't know where my head was. I know what was in my heart all along. But I just couldn't say it."

Folding my other hand on top of hers, I looked deep into her eyes. "But I'm saying it now—"

There goes that throat closing up on me again. And why is it so warm in here? My skin is all prickly heat. My stomach's sour.

"I love you, Zina. From the very first time I saw you . . . in the Chanticleer. And this will never change."

We kissed and clutched each other right there in the restaurant. I'm certain people must've been staring at us, thinking we needed some lessons in etiquette. I didn't care. At last I'd said all the things I should've said way back when. I had said them, and she cried and she held me, and it wasn't too late after all. Something like a drip of perspiration scooted down my spine.

"Will there be anything else, sir?" The waiter stood at our table now, perhaps sent over to break up this uncouth public display.

"Just a check, please. Thank you."

We managed to get our emotions under control and straighten ourselves up a bit.

Zina glanced at her watch. I didn't like the looks of her furrowed brow. "Oh, my God, Robbie, we've been here an hour and a half! I have a big meeting at 2:30!"

"That's okay. I'll see you tomorrow. Same time, same station."

She looked straight at me with the most despairing eyes I've ever seen. It seemed as though her radiance evaporated into the posh restaurant atmosphere. Even before she spoke I knew it wasn't okay. It wasn't okay at all. I began to feel sick deep down in my gut.

"Robbie. I'm so sorry. But I can't. It's not fair to either one of us. Damn, I wish I had the time to explain it all to you. The way you deserve. If I'd only known you were coming—"

My face sizzled like a frying pan the chef had left on the hot stove top.

Zina's tears were back again, and my eyes responded in kind. "Well, you see, Lars invited my family over to his family's house for a dinner last month. You got my letter, right? The letter I sent you saying I was engaged?"

I nodded, already having a good idea where all this would lead.

"Well, he surprised me. And everyone in my family, at least. Announcing he was ready to set a wedding date right away, for as soon as possible. Even though he'll still be attending medical school. And, just like that, everybody was toasting us, and then the calendars were out. By the time we left, the date was set."

She paused, as if gathering courage. "Just two months from now."

The waiter acted even more edgy this time, overtly laying the check on the table. "Whenever you're ready, sir!" he said, so loud I first thought his words were intended for another table.

Zina sobbed now, uncontrollably. I felt frozen to my chair. "I'm sorry, Robbie. I'm so sorry. But it's too late now. It's just too late."

It seemed like I'd been transported all the way back to that mattress in New Orleans. I stared at her. My lips parted. This time my dumbness was deafening.

She went to the ladies room to try to get ready for her office meeting, chagrined when she tripped on an area rug along the way. I noticed she'd left her purse by her chair. I took the opportunity to remove the cardboard coaster from under my wineglass, grabbed the pen from the waiter's checkbook, and hastily scribbled a note on the bottom of the coaster. Then I slipped it into an outside pocket of the purse. A moment later she returned to retrieve it, seeming even more upset that she'd forgotten to take it with her. She made the long walk back to the restroom, this time being extra careful to negotiate the rumpled rug in her path.

A few minutes later she stood before me, an anemic smile on her face. The pallid lipstick now accentuated her wan appearance. I'd gathered my senses and attempted to coordinate my brain and motor functions to at least say something, realizing it was all slipping away again, this time for good. She looked at me, purse in hand, obviously anxious to leave. I got up and reached out to grasp her shoulders.

"No, Zina, it's not too late. You're not married yet. And we were meant for each other. We both know that. We owe it to ourselves to be together."

This time she bowed her head. She didn't say anything right away. Then she looked back up at me. Her voice sounded worn and weary.

"I can't do that to Lars. Or our families. It wouldn't be fair to any of them. And . . . right now I don't know what I feel anymore."

My titanic dream submerged into despair. I could hear the wailing in my heart like two thousand lost souls crying out for salvation.

I don't remember too much after that. I guess I handled the check without a problem, hoping I paid the waiter the correct amount, still learning to calculate foreign coin. Somehow we made it back to her office. We embraced each other briefly at the door. She kissed me on the lips with particular tenderness.

Then she pulled away. Her words resounded inside my head, though her voice released little more than a whisper.

"I'll never ever forget you, Robbie."

She ran inside, before we lost our composure again.

I decided I didn't want a cab this time. Instead, I took a long walk back to the hotel. My expensive umbrella kept me dry, but it rained torrents in my heart.

On the way, I contemplated the note I'd left her. *My darling Zina, I will love you—forever. Robbie*

It's too bad I waited so long to express those words. It was just too late.

CHAPTER 20

Hanging around Amsterdam for another night, I fell into a blue funk compatible with the constant precipitation. A cabby dropped me off at the notorious red light district. I walked the sopping streets of that sad neighborhood, with all the leering perverts and lonely outcasts. How pathetic they were, obsessed by their desperate searches for erotic gratification and fantasy substitutes for their own failed relationships and empty lives, staring at the spotlight windows of tempting painted ladies in their stiletto heels and tawdry lingerie. A small tour boat slid by me on the rain-drizzled waters of the contiguous canal. A loving couple giggled and cuddled under the canopy, caught up in the bliss of their own warm ecstasy and amused by the garish peep show exhibits before them. I envied their shared good fortune, imagining them to be Zina and myself, having just found each other at lunch this very afternoon, now nestled together in the rapture of a swirling paradise.

The raindrops continued to fall as I drove out of the city the next day. I had a strong suspicion they would've just kept coming as long as I stayed. I also had the urge to put as much distance between that place and myself as I possibly could. The time had come to pick myself up and start all over again.

So I played tourist for the rest of a cloudy, but dry, week in Germany, developing a confidence and companionship with my new car and visiting age-old cities along my return path. I spent the first night in Stuttgart. There I mourned my lost love in a small, downtown *Gasthaus* with a belly full of bratwurst and the bitter taste of many steins of nut brown *dunkel Bier* coating the inside of my mouth. The next morning I decided to seriously test the handling of the Austin-Healey, threading my way along the twisting mountain roads down in the Bayerische Alps, along the border of Austria. I rested overnight at the U.S. Armed Forces Recreation Center in Garmisch Partenkirchen, dreaming of Zina after curling up under the covers in the fetal position.

Following a late breakfast, I continued my attempt to escape the reality of my most recent debacle. I resumed my sports car rampage through the southern Bavarian mountains and countryside. The roads became even more dangerous as I made my way northeast from Garmisch, by Walchensee and Kochel and Bad Tolz. I experienced the goose flesh thrill of a few close calls with oncoming traffic at some blind hairpin curves. It was my therapy. The joy of the responsive automobile and challenging fresh terrain provided both the diversion and release I so badly needed at this juncture in my life. I spent another night in a cottage overlooking the placid waters of Tegernsee.

On Friday I headed back to Munich, my BOQ and the Beatles, fully pledged to find a way to gather up the shattered pieces of my life.

In the weeks following my *coup de grâce* farewell with Zina, I tried to reach Lenny on the phone to talk about it. He was the one person who could always give me another slant on things when I most needed it, and I craved that with real hunger now.

But our active schedules and the huge time differential separating us made it impossible to coordinate a successful phone call. I finally wrote him a letter, of all things. Beating the odds, he responded with a few pages of his own, scrawled almost illegibly on U.S. Marine Corps letterhead.

It's time for us to do it again partner! I can't believe how much our lives stay right in tune. Margie and I have just had the big bust up too. I still see her face when I'm all alone. And I don't ever want that to stop to tell you the truth. That's something so many people never get in their humdrum lives.

It just makes me happy to know she had some of the best days of her life with me—and me with her—maybe the best she'll ever know. And that gives me all I need to go on through new gates into other soul pastures—feeling blessed and strong about where I already been.

So you speed things up when you need to get past the pain. You get involved in new things and new scenes and fresh faces. And you fill up every day with them. Pretty soon your back in focus somewhere else with different people and you just know its going to be good again—maybe even better than before.

You got to feel great about what you had with Zina man! Not too many cats I know can say they ever had a long term scene with anybody that beautiful. In her looks and in her mind. And you know she wont ever forget you neither. So take the power you earned from that and take it with you wherever you go. Take it now to a new soul pasture.

By the way, the pix inside is my latest game! And you should just see the honeys hanging out at the track!

Remember good brother—you and me still have many more green fields to graze together.

Later, Lenny

Enclosed inside the letter I found a photograph of Lenny, wearing full racing gear and standing next to a stock car. His face beamed for the camera. He had his helmet tucked under one arm, the other raised as he held a trophy over his head.

Taking Lenny's advice I attempted to locate my old high school buddy, Bobby Bennett, reportedly now a sergeant stationed somewhere in Europe. I contacted Eddie Mazzoli, who did some checking with Bobby's hometown best friend, Speckles O'Reardon. The word was that Bobby had transferred back to CONUS, continental U.S., for specialized advisory training prior to combat duty in Vietnam. I had one final question to this news, and it took almost six weeks for me to get a reply from Eddie. The answer, which I had hoped I would not hear—*infantry*.

Munich's June flowers had flourished to full bloom when a major corps reorganization inactivated the 508th Military Police Battalion. The battalion colors were lowered for the last time at McGraw Casern and folded away in a box for shipment to the Pentagon. I have no idea what they do with it there. The following week I drove my Austin-Healey due north on the autobahn, prepared to assume yet another assignment in my deciduous olive drab military world, and anticipating new friends in a different pasture.

CHAPTER 21

One of the people to befriend me in Nürnberg was the banquet manager at the local officer's club, another redhead, a classy German woman named Heidi Mayerhoff. She provided some measure of medication from the loss of the irreplaceable Zina.

But I discovered, early on, that bearing the label of Heidi's boyfriend put me in an equivocal position of controversy I hadn't foreseen. I knew many of the officers who frequented the club admired her, for both her good looks and her proficient manner. I also observed any number of married men, even the higher field grade ranks, attempting to flirt with her. Whatever the source of the provocation, I was astonished when my battalion commander, Lieutenant Colonel Bradbury, blindsided me in his office.

"I must say I am very uncomfortable having to ask you this, lieutenant. But it concerns the Sunday brunch my wife is giving this weekend. As you are aware, all the wives will be attending with their men. Well . . . er, ah . . . some of the ladies were inquiring if you would be bringing Miss . . . Mayerhoff, I believe her name is. You know, the woman at the Kalb Club."

Just what the hell is this all about, I asked myself, shaken by the unexpected question and wondering about its implications.

"Why, yes. Of course. I've been dating Heidi for some time now, sir. She's a very nice person."

The colonel continued, unusually hesitant. "I'm certain she is. It's just . . . you see, the point is, perhaps it's not really fair to the wives, if . . . well, if your intentions with this woman are not, shall I say . . . honorable?"

What a crock of shit. I'd always held Colonel Bradbury in high regard, a man of polish and stature. Now he'd begun to shrivel up right there in front of me. It seemed obvious to me his wife had put him up to this, after "the girls" discussed it at their coffee klatch. What a bunch of sanctimonious connivers. They couldn't hold a candle to Heidi Mayerhoff in terms of appearance, poise, or manners. Maybe that was it. She represented a threat to them. They'd seen the lusty looks in their husbands' eyes. They didn't need some peon lieutenant flaunting this slinky *Fraulein* at their prissy little party.

I tried to keep a lid on my indignation. "Miss Mayerhoff is a perfect lady, sir. She comes from one of the best families in Nürnberg. Her father owns one of the most successful restaurants in the city. As I'm sure you know, she's part of the management staff at the club. And she's always conducted herself in a very professional manner. I'm certain the club manager would verify this."

I paused for the colonel's response. His silence threw me off balance. He just stared at me from the other side of his desk.

"I'm not exactly sure I understand your question, sir. But I guess I would respond by saying Heidi and I are dating. Just like the married officers dated their wives when they were still single. I can't say if I'm going to marry Heidi or not. I don't know. But I can tell you my intentions with her are, honorable, whatever that means."

Resentment churned inside me. I hoped it didn't show.

"Well, then. That's fine. Very good, lieutenant. There's nothing more to be said. We'll see you at the house at 1000 hours on Sunday."

I think he felt upset himself, by what he had had to do, glad it was over, though the answer would not be well received.

Stick that in your collective craws, I thought to myself. Later, I debated whether I should tell Heidi about this, for fear of hurting her feelings. But my outrage howled so loud I could not contain myself. Knowing the situation, she wouldn't have missed that stilted affair if it meant getting up out of her sick bed.

So it was that we attended, arm in arm, inspired by the contention of our very presence. We had a "fine" time, as the colonel would say, enjoying the food and the other young people in attendance. Everybody smiled courteously and said all the proper small talk things, though I'm certain I missed a few raised eyebrows and catty side remarks. Heidi and I exulted in the satisfaction of rising above it all, and after the initial anger, felt kind of amused by the whole episode. Looking back on it now, I realize how swift and dangerous the pious currents of hypocrisy run. Especially when fear, ignorance and jealousy feed it enough power to plow leaks even in the staunch levees of leadership.

If the wives of the 793rd MP Battalion were upset with my choice of girlfriend, and my "intentions" with her, their husbands might've been even more concerned, had they insight into my growing record and tape collection.

Now enjoying a few surplus bucks in my pocket, I invested in the innovation of a *stereo* sound system, the latest technology to antiquate Grampy's treasured Victrola. I spent much time, as well, expanding my music library. Beyond the Beatles and traditional rock 'n' roll, I'd started delving into the emerging folk music sector. Much of this genre contained pacifist left-wing protest lyrics, led by a prolific new singer/songwriter named Bob Dylan. I found myself seduced by his profound words and intimate, dusty voice. Never before had I heard such wisdom expressed in a haunting backwoods singing style.

Jazz also recaptured my interest, after I'd lost track of it during my R&B time in Georgia—where the choices beyond that had been country, gospel or trite white pop. Reminiscent of those nights at Leonardo's in Ithaca, I came to dig the sounds of Miles Davis, Thelonius Monk and John Coltrane. The music brought forth feelings and emotions I couldn't share with anyone around me, especially my military cohorts. In my world at that time, only Lenny and I would've been able to discuss the subject with intelligence. My roommates at my off-post apartment couldn't stand the music, convinced I qualified as certified eccentric.

Imagine what impressions and comments I might've evoked from the lads and ladies of the battalion if they'd been subjected to my budding musical tastes. I would've loved the opportunity to cohost some kind of tea party at my place, exploiting Heidi's substantial hospitality skills. We would sit them down to tea and crumpets and treat them all to a musical enlightenment of Richard Rodgers' and Oscar Hammerstein's "My Favorite Things," followed by Irving Berlin's "Russian Lullaby." Melodies and songwriters they would be comfortable with. Only this time these conventional classics would be performed by master jazz saxophonist John Coltrane, closing with his own composition of "Giant Steps."

I can just see everyone trying to take their cues from the colonel and Mrs. Bradbury as the musician sweeps them all into uncharted musical waters. The visceral voyage sets sail in routine tradition, a slow majestic glide through a placid harbor. Wave by wave, we transcend the familiar coast line into complex improvisations on high seas. With no trace of land in sight, we gain speed, rising and falling in unpredictable dexterous navigations of sound and passion, ultimately cresting in an enigmatic Bermuda Triangle of creation from which there is no return.

Before my guests regain their landlubber legs, I'd have them make the quantum leap to a ration of Bob Dylan. Protest songs "Blowin' in the Wind," "Masters of War," and "A Hard Rain's A-Gonna Fall" would conclude the program. I'm sure the expressions on their faces would be priceless as Heidi and I thanked them all for coming.

Lenny said he'd meet me in Nice. Marine Corps Lieutenant Morrissey would be finagling an Air Force ride all the way from somewhere in Florida to the French Riviera. He had only a week's leave time before reporting to his new assignment at almost the other side of the world, in southern California. "No sweat," he said, when I asked him how he thought he would accomplish that.

I didn't have anywhere near the distance he had to cover. But it did entail a rigorous exercise, driving my trusty Austin-Healey from my post in Nürnberg back to Munich, cutting west and southwest down through Austria, Liechtenstein and the Swiss Alps into Italy, then on to France.

The high altitude driving stimulated me. I enjoyed even more strenuous riveting thrills after I passed through the Tunnel de Tende, a dark, narrow, burrowing passage through the stony side of the mountain separating Italy from France. On the French side recurring road signs greeted me, forewarning the number of *lacets* to follow. I soon understood these to be 180-degree turns lying in wait as the slender, unguarded roadway made a crisscross traverse down the treacherous mountain side. I recall one sign signaling the arrival of as many as nine consecutive *lacets* in one series. Determined to keep my foot off the brake, I used only the engine to control the car as I shifted gears through the hazardous turns.

Ah, what a superb car I was driving. My little limey treasure electrified me once again with pinpoint responsiveness and remarkable agility. I yelled out my thanks to the Cornell frat snob who'd arrogantly granted me that ride up State Street hill my freshman year, introducing me to this impressive automobile. The wind carried my exuberance across the wide-open spaces that flirted with the road as it snaked its way toward the crystal waters below.

Halfway down I came upon another sports car, a top-down Alpha Romeo driven by a pretty brunette. We toyed with each other the rest of the way, passing one another, back and forth, in between *lacets*, entangled in a game of cat and mouse. Arriving at the bottom, we stopped fast for a red traffic signal and the Mediterranean Sea, both shining right there before us. My Healey's chrome grill gleamed in the paint finish between the Alpha Romeo's bright taillights. The girl put on her left turn signal, indicating she'd be heading east toward Monte-Carlo. I realized, wistfully, that we had mere seconds before we parted. When the light changed to green, we exchanged a flurry of farewell waves and a toot of our horns. Though we never shared a word we'd been joined forever by the occasion, and I knew she knew that, too. I made my opposite turn in the direction of Nice, and my appointment with Lenny.

That's him! Even from a block away and across the street I knew that self-assured posture. Lenny said he'd meet me at the American Express office. As usual, he was a man of his word. It seems pretty amazing we could hook up that easy, considering the miles we both had traveled.

"How you doing, pardner!" Lenny and I embraced on the sidewalk. His skin was tanned, his close-clipped Marine cut hair bleached to a golden hue from the Florida sun. He looked fantastic. "How was your trip?"

"Incredible. You should've been coming down that mountain with me, wheeling one of your stock cars. I want to tell you, that is some friggin' drive up there. And what about you? I can't believe you made it over here, man! And you're right on time, waiting for me . . . all the way from 'Gatersville', USA."

"Damn tootin', brother." I could tell Lenny had geared up for the occasion. "I figure it's about time you and me got back into the swing of it. What're we waiting for? Let's go somewhere and *parlez-vous francais* at some chic cabaret. We got a lot of catching up to do. Makes sense we do it where we can ogle it with some sweet little Froglets!"

L ooking back now on the week Lenny and I shared in Europe, it seems like it all happened in the flit of an eyelash. We fell in love with France's Mediterranean seashore. Vibrant St-Tropez, with its exotic restaurants and laughing cafes. And the uninhibited *au naturel* Île du Levant, an island escape where nudity prevailed in all aspects of its liberal society.

Beach lovers let it all hang out, naked jaybirds, as expected. But we were surprised to find everyone in town, to include waiters and waitresses in the bars and restaurants, clerks working at stores and gift shops, wearing only the teeniest of loincloths, barely covering their privates. Posted regulations required that these so-called "articles of clothing" be worn outside the beaches. A matter of modesty and common decency, of course. The pygmy pieces of material were even considered the propriety of fashion and conduct for church services.

"Lordy, lordy. What do you make of that?" Lenny commented. "Far as I'm concerned, these village folk ain't wearing no clothes, neither."

I wondered if there might be a courthouse somewhere on the island, fantasizing what a public trial would be like, conducted in the buff.

As a result, Lenny and I found it necessary to purchase our own G-strings from one of the town's tourist shops. We decided it would be more interesting to get involved in the novelty of these semi-nude community activities, so we spent only an hour or so at the beach. In fact, we enjoyed ourselves so much we stayed overnight at a small inn. The bartender there recommended a restaurant a few streets away, where we appreciated the good food and the service of a well-endowed waiter.

When the young man scuffled off to the kitchen with our orders, Lenny leaned toward me. "Did you see that? I do believe that guy's hung better than you!"

"Astounding," I shot back. "Well, Leonard, it does look like he's wearing Extra Large, just like me. I guess if he can prove he's packing at least another *minimeter*, someone better inform Guinness and Ripley."

We continued west from Le Lavandou, destined for Barcelona, Spain, where Lenny had nearby Air Force connections for his return flight to the States. He persuaded me to let him take a leg of the trip, proceeding to scare the shit out of me with his fearless driving tactics. I guess it bothered me more on this occasion because these were my sacred wheels being subjected to his aggressive, often risky, maneuvers. But it seemed he'd gotten more daring than ever since his involvement in stock car racing, passing even long lines of vehicles on curves and hills.

"Dammit, what're you doing?" I yelled.

"C'mon, my sweet Brit buggy, I know you got it in ya'! Yes! Yes!"

The blaring of panicky horns from oncoming traffic rose in crescendo before scattering in the wind as the cars and trucks whizzed by.

He uttered mad, ranting exclamations during and after each unnerving stunt, referring to my car as his "baby," comparing it to various "badass" stock cars he'd driven in competition. He also mentioned having totaled one, then walking away, unscathed. We didn't have an accident, but I was a nervous wreck when we checked into a roadside hotel somewhere west of Montpellier.

Barcelona seemed the perfect city to complete our adventure. More cosmopolitan than I'd anticipated, it reminded me of New York in terms of its diverse neighborhoods and peoples. Despite the ritual of the afternoon siesta, when everything closes down for a few hours right in the middle of the day, it's a vivacious metropolis with a bold temperament, an energy you feel you can reach out and touch. We spent our time mixing sightseeing with saloons, sangria and *señoritas*.

Lenny had heard about a resort town just south of the city known for catering to the Continents' younger generation. So we took a short train ride down to Sitges, where we rented a seaside beach house. It's an incomparable little town, where you can literally bar hop Western Europe to your choices of native liquor, language and social custom. We ordered *"zwei Bier, bitte"* in a German *Bierstube*; *"vin rouge"* at a French *bistrot*; *"Proseco"* from an Italian *'inoteca*; *"Ceres"* inside a Danish *vaertshus*; and countless pints of bitter while we foraged a British pub. We did jiggers of *"Fundador,"* a potent Latin version of Germany's *"Steinhager"* schnapps, in more than one Spanish cantina. Lenny and I had a roaring good time during our brief stay here. Of all my European travels, I think this tiny oasis of youthful exuberance remains my very favorite.

Sadly, the week ended far too soon. Before we knew it, it was time to go. Lenny and I hopped a cab to the Sitges train station. I needed to return to Barcelona to retrieve the Austin-Healey; he would take the next train in the opposite direction, to catch his flight back to the States.

We stood together on the platform, quiet in our own thoughts. I reflected on the unique experiences we'd just shared, realizing that, in an ironic twist, I seemed to have traded places with Zina. Now it was me visiting Europe's vacation meccas in a search for answers. Now she faced the restraints, shackled by her situation. Yet while Lenny and I had enjoyed the company of a number of European girls during our Mediterranean escapade, I understood more than before that, for me, no one could ever take the place of Zina.

I took the initiative and cracked the silence. "Once again, it doesn't get much better, brother. Take care of yourself out there in the land of fruits and nuts. Let me know where to reach you, so we can do it again when I get back."

The train whistle blew, not far away.

"Yeah, safe trip to Krautsville, lieutenant. Go easy on my little sports car there. I expect to see both of you in one piece next time we go riding together."

He picked up his duffel bag as the train grinded into the station. At that moment he surprised me, employing an overhook with his free arm and sliding his hip in front of me in a mock takedown move from our long gone wrestling days. I reacted with the traditional leg counter. We both released our holds as the train screeched, hissed and shuddered to a stop. He hoisted his bag and climbed the steep boarding steps to the platform at the rear of the nearest car. When he reached the sliding entrance door, he turned back toward me. Our bloodshot eyes masked any embarrassing emotional vulnerabilities, but it was one of the rare times Lenny looked self-conscious.

"Later, pardner." He disappeared inside.

In spite of the hellacious summer traffic, I made it back to Nürnberg with just a single stop along the way, driving almost twenty consecutive hours before catching a brief snooze in the parking lot of a roadside restaurant. After returning to my military duties in slow-motion, I played the role of Rip van Winkle my first weekend back. I dreamed about Lenny, which conjured up abstract visions of Zina. At long last, I awakened from my infinite sleep knowing I missed both of them more than anything else in this big old world of ours.

"Hey there, *Captain* Bender!"

The battalion executive officer hollered to me through his partition window, emphasizing my recent promotion as he motioned for me to join him in his office.

"Got something in today's mail I thought might interest you."

As much as he attempted to ease the shock, stressing how my "outstanding performance" had earned me this "professional opportunity," the bad news was that the Pentagon had decided to deny my request for release from active duty. My next destination would not be back home to New Jersey to pursue some vague civilian vocation, but rather to take command of a company destined for Vietnam. I sat in my chair and stared at him, my mind and body refusing to react further.

Shifting in his seat, he interrupted the pregnant pause. "Like I explained, Robbie, it's a great opportunity. A lot of captains would—"

He caught himself just before he said it, modifying his choice of words as best he could, ". . . *give anything* for this assignment. It really puts you on the fast track for career development."

I think he knew his pep talk approach wasn't helping much.

The XO took me to happy hour at the Kalb Club that evening, and the boys of the battalion toasted me for my impressive reassignment. Of course, the Reserve lieutenants camouflaged their personal satisfaction that they would most likely be returning to the safety of civilian life after their European tours. Long after the major and his lackeys departed, a couple of barfly friends drove my car and me to my apartment to sleep it off.

Just shy of a week later, as though some kind of cosmic connection had occurred, I found a message on the kitchen table, left for me by one of my roommates. It stated, *Robbie, Call Zina at 287-2900, extension 431.* It was a *local* number.

CHAPTER 22

As I walked down the hall of the dignified rococo hotel in downtown Nürnberg, my heart thumped inside my chest like it wanted out. The place oozed an imposing aura in its classical grace, also revealing the withering decadence of many years of courtly service to the sovereign and affluent minority. I acknowledged my shoes sinking into the deep pile carpet as I passed a small table displaying a vase of coral-red gladiola.

Brass plate 425, 427, 429—and there it was. Room 431. The door, like all the others, was embellished with a contouring ornamental molding. A small brass-framed glass peephole glistened in the center. Situated on the right-hand side of the main fourth floor corridor, it stood in the very center of the row of mimicking portals.

Yet this door was not like the others. Behind it breathed the love of my life. The ravishing creature who had fascinated me for more than eight years, who I never expected to see again, after the rain and tears of Amsterdam. My palms were sweaty. I couldn't remember the opening line I'd crafted and tried to memorize during my drive to the hotel. I prayed that somehow I would say and do everything right this time, if there was any chance at all . . . .

As if they had impatient minds of their own, my knuckles rapped gingerly on the heavy door. After a moment it swung open, and there stood Zina.

Like a mythic goddess before me, with her flowing blonde hair, her indigo eyes and entrancing smile, she looked compatible with the extravagance of my memories, the idealism of my dreams. I felt transfixed in place, my legs and feet stuck as though they'd been glued together, a toy soldier standing woodenly at attention.

"Well, don't just stand there, Robert Stephen Bender. Come on in. Don't you know I've missed you?"

Robert Stephen Bender. She'd used my full given name. I didn't remember having told her that. Sweet Jesus, somewhere along the line she'd made the effort to find out. And she remembered. Maybe, just maybe . . .

She garnished her voice with peppery cheerfulness, but I sensed she felt as edgy and apprehensive about our tryst as I did. With a wisp of hesitation, she moved back into the room, toward a small sitting area with two stuffed chairs and a coffee table. I noticed the grand four-poster bed a short distance away.

"Please. Let's sit down over here together," she continued, motioning toward the chairs. As she did so, her diamond ring caught the setting sun from the window. Like a prism, it cast a refractive beam in my direction. "We have so much to talk about."

I felt disappointed we hadn't kissed, or even hugged each other.

Then I noticed the bottle of champagne in a standing ice bucket, a white cloth napkin draped around it. An assortment of cheeses, cold cuts and crackers graced the table. Two elegant long-stemmed glasses waited side by side next to the food platter, their bases touching with seductive insinuation.

We sat down opposite one another. Zina gave me a timid smile that mirrored my own anxiety.

"Would you please do the honors for us, Robbie?" she said, nodding toward the silver bucket. "And make sure it foams all over the place, just like those handsome leading men do it in the movies!"

That seemed to break the ice a bit, and we both laughed together, the tension in the air beginning to dissipate. I managed to fulfill her wish by losing a good portion of the bottle on the plush rug. We giggled some more. She didn't seem to bat an eye when we clinked our glasses together and I made my suave, eloquent, diplomatic toast.

"To us!"

We talked as though we'd never been apart. She told me she'd come to town for some kind of marketing convention. She was convinced its scheduled location represented a sign she should make contact with me.

"Marjorie and I still write, and she got a San Diego postcard from Lenny. He told her you were now here in Nürnberg. She said she had to laugh because she never saw so much news on one little card. He wrote notes on both sides of it, right across the pretty photo. And he told her to give me your new telephone number. He even put it right in the middle of a California cloud, where it was clear to read. So, here I am!"

I privately thanked my lifelong brother for again going out of his way on my behalf. Before I knew it, Zina had moved to my side of the coffee table. She fell into my arms and we kissed and entwined as though we'd traveled back to that hill overlooking Lake Cayuga. Only this time our faces got salty and wet with our mingling tears. We murmured rejoices in each other's ears, exchanging praises of the wonder and joy each held for the other. I refrained from reiterating my love for her, the scars of Amsterdam still fresh, not wanting to upset the balance we held on the slivery thin emotional high wire we now traversed.

"Robbie, Robbie," she exhaled. I could feel the vibrations of her delicate voice flowing from her temple into mine, as we held each other close. "I've missed you so much. You're always there, in the back of my mind. The times we've spent together just keep playing, over and over again, in my head. I hope you don't think I'm a terrible person. I don't know why I'm doing this. I just had to see you again."

I couldn't tell her how simultaneously euphoric and agonizing this was for me, how much she also consumed my thoughts and dreams. Besides the worry that I would just crumble and cry like a child, it required an eloquence beyond my capability. I tried to keep it simple.

"My lovely, lovely Zina. You're always with me, too. It's been more than eight years we've known each other, and I feel stronger about you now than I did when I first met you. When you dazzled me at the Chanticleer. You've lived in my thoughts ever since."

We kissed and hugged some more, then finished the bottle of bubbly.

"Robbie, this champagne is going right to my head! Let's go somewhere nice for a cozy celebration dinner."

A short time later we walked together in downtown Nürnberg. It was one of those refreshing evenings when everything seems to have a magical clarity to it, like the romantic scene in some exquisitely photographed cinematic masterpiece. We held hands like brand-new lovers who'd just found each other, blinded by the rapture of virgin discovery, walking right by the restaurant the hotel desk recommended, laughing together when we realized our mistake and ran back the extra block we'd traveled.

The meal must have been magnificent. I recall my taste buds relishing the rich flavors. Yet I have no idea what we ate, other than we both ordered the same thing. We did have a bottle of some expensive French wine, and floated away to the hotel on a cloud of enchantment.

Returning to her room, she took my hand and led me to the bed. We lay down on top of the brocade duvet, side by side, gazing up at the Baroque ceiling. I welcomed the sultry moisture of her palm merging with mine.

She turned to me and held my face in her hands. She looked straight into me. Somehow I knew a sublime moment was poised to become an everlasting blessing.

"I love you, Robbie. I love you. I've always loved you. I just never had the courage to tell you before."

The power of those words caressed my raggedy soul. It seemed the two of us had begun to levitate somewhere between the mattress of that stately bed and the ornate ceiling.

The chains that had bound me when we first met were cast aside. I glowed in the freedom to say those marvelous words to her again. "I love you, Zina. You know that. It's as certain as the sun and moon. You've captured my heart forever."

"My darling Robert Stephen. Let's do it. Let's make love." She pressed her body tight against me. When she spoke again, her voice had diminished to a sigh. "Let's make a beautiful baby."

Make a baby? Yes, of course! How could we not be together if we share our own child? Her marriage to Lars would become nothing but a sham.

On this epic night of my life, after all the virtuous years of our relationship, Zina and I made unbitted love together. The ancient bed creaked and moaned; the bedposts swayed in harmonious jubilation. Of course, inspired by the fever of my own soaring ecstasy, I reached the pinnacle of our passionate journey all too soon. We withdrew to rest in each others' arms on an intimate plateau. Some time later we attained the summit together. After rejoicing in the grace of our achievement, we entered a sanctuary of tranquility and peace that enveloped us in its reverence and affection. Resting inside her golden nest, I experienced a comforting inner warmth unlike anything I'd ever known before.

The next morning I took care of some military matters in half my usual time, finishing up just before noon. Zina slipped away from her business associates and the convention to meet me at the hotel for lunch. After sharing plates of veal schnitzel and sauerbraten, we took the Austin-Healey for a drive out in the countryside. An hour later we parked at Hitler's infamous Zeppelin Stadium and strolled along the shoreline of the nearby lake. We snuggled together on a shady park bench where the water lapped gently at the roots of a bowing willow tree. For a few sweet moments we talked about the miracle of just being alive at the same point in history, finding each other among the millions of people. Then Zina confronted the heavy presence that had shadowed us ever since we'd gotten together.

"I have to go home tomorrow. And I need to tell you where I'm at in my life. My marriage is good. Lars loves me, and he takes special care of me. We're happy together."

She faltered for an instant and I felt her hand shiver ever so faintly in mine.

"We are also facing a complication. I need to have an operation. Within a year, or two at the most. Female business. When it's over, there's a good chance I won't be able to have children. We are both very sad about that."

Words of concern spewed from my mouth as the trauma set in. "Oh Zina, I am so sorry—"

Her whisper from the previous night bellowed inside my head.

"But . . . last night. You said you wanted us to . . . make a baby?"

She looked startled, as though she didn't remember saying that. Then she appeared to get hold of herself. She looked me in the eye. Her voice seemed far away, yet her words hit my ear crystal clear, like wind chimes from a neighbor's porch.

"Robbie. I know this sounds crazy. But don't you see, this is our one chance. For our own special kind of *ever-after*."

I remained silent for a moment, letting that sink in. The concept behind the statement boggled my mind. "Wow. But . . . but, with your medical condition . . . couldn't having a baby be hazardous to your own . . . safety?"

"Yes. But we only get one shot at this life. I'm willing to take that risk."

Our eyes locked in a reciprocal focus that seemed to connect our aching hearts. Mutual compassion flowed freely along an invisible shaft of love. I heard her voice continue, seeming to echo somewhere inside the intensity of the moment.

"I am scared. Lars has been my rock through all of this. You see, I love him, too. For his kindness, his inner strength. He's so committed to us, to making it all work. He has this devotion to everyone and everything in his life. His studies, our marriage, our families, our friends.

"He's so considerate, and it touches everyone around him. Especially me. But, I don't know if this makes any sense, maybe it's some flaw in me, but I love you as well, Robbie. In a completely different way. Is this possible? Can someone be in love with two people at the same time? There must be something horribly wrong with me."

"Are you kidding? There's absolutely nothing wrong with you. You love . . . your parents, don't you?" *I wish I could say the same for myself.* "Your brother and sister? Other relatives and close friends?

"It's perfectly natural to love more than one person in your life." *Oh, c'mon, just get right to it.* "I love my father, and my sisters and brother. And if you really analyze it, without the stupid sexual inferences, I love Lenny. Because he is my best friend. But I love you, Zina, on a whole nother level."

She looked at me with skepticism in her eyes. "I understand that. But you don't love . . . you don't have, another . . . sweetheart, do you?"

The question caught me by surprise. I'd chased so many skirts I hadn't given it any serious thought. But the answer was right there.

"No. No one like you. I have told some girls I loved them. Because maybe I thought so at the time. Or knew they needed to hear it. And I have dated some girls in my life who I'll always remember for the good things between us. Even though it didn't work out. But never the overwhelming feeling I've always had about you."

Her burgeoned blue eyes seemed the size of the two decorative plates hanging on Granny's kitchen wall. I sensed she wanted to respond, struggling hard with her emotions.

"Well, it sounds like you've made your choice," I said, filling the void. "I'm happy you've found someone who'll take good care of you. I know you'll come through everything A-OK."

Having regurgitated religion forced down my throat as a kid, the unexpected blaze of insight crossed my mind with all the wonder and power of a fiery meteor. Perhaps Zina's comment about "our own *ever-after*" inspired it. The words slid off my tongue. "But if you believe in—"

I stopped. I couldn't even think about spending the rest of my time on *Earth* without her.

"Robbie. I love you more than I can tell you!" She began to cry, and she threw her arms around me. "But I can't leave Lars. My life is in Amsterdam. It's who I am, and where I belong. If our worlds weren't so different. I don't know . . . ."

I felt a dank hollowness swelling inside my bones. Swallowing back a surge of nausea, I conceded reality, resigned to the deepest hurt. That sense of *déjà vu* struck me once again as my eyes joined hers in streams of tears. We held each other without another word, for a very long time. Then I gathered myself together to the point where I felt I could talk without breaking down.

"I understand. I wish I could change your mind. I wish I could change a whole lot of things. But that's not the way it is. And I accept that now. At any rate, I'm not going back to New Jersey just yet. The Army has other plans for me. I'm headed to Vietnam from here."

The news twisted her face in a fear I hadn't anticipated. Right away I felt angry with myself for having mentioned this superfluous information. It served only to upset her even more. She looked at me, unable to speak. When she tried, her lips trembled. Then she threw her arms around me, resting her head against my chest.

"Oh my god. My dear Robbie."

After a while we drove back into town. I noticed a jewelry store as we walked from my parked car toward the hotel.

"Come inside with me. I want to buy you something you can keep forever. So every time you look at it, you'll think of me—"

I conquered my own quivering lip to get the rest out, ". . . and remember how much I love you."

"No," she said, soft as her velvet touch. "I don't need anything like that. You've already given me something priceless I will treasure forever."

"But I want you to have something you can hold onto."

"I already have that," she replied, reaching into her purse. She pulled out the cardboard coaster from the Wiedengaart restaurant. "And it's personally inscribed in your handwriting. Look."

I remembered those words as if I'd just written them.

My darling Zina, I will love you—forever. Robbie

That evening we never left the hotel. We ordered the most expensive items off the room service menu, to include a $125 bottle of wine. Naked, we fed each other off our plates. As before, we made love flesh to flesh in that wonderful four-poster bed, again and again and once more in the early morning, before I had to leave. We must've kissed each other for half an hour at the door, both of us hanging on to the very end before I made my way through, and it gently closed between us. Turning away, I knew we shared flood-water eyes one last time. The steps I took to the elevator turned out to be the longest walk of my life.

When I got back to my apartment to get ready for duty, I found a surprise in the satchel I'd taken with me. In the midst of my change of clothing nestled the empty bottle of wine we'd consumed on our final night together. Across the label Zina had written, *Dearest Robbie, You have made my life complete. Love eternal, Zina*

Not long after Zina had gone, I wrote a quick letter to Lenny. I advised him of my final hours with her, thanking him for making it all possible. I neglected to mention her intentions for me to get her pregnant, or her anticipated surgery. I didn't want to even think about the possible consequences this might entail. I did inform him of my promotion and Vietnam assignment.

Just before I left Germany I received a slipshod scribbling back from him, inside a tacky Christmas card. He expressed his sorrow about my ill-fated relationship with Zina. He congratulated me on my promotion. I later learned he'd been promoted too, but he never flaunted his own successes. With flamboyant scrawls, he told me he'd be seeing me in Vietnam, where he was destined as well. He even gave me the name of the Marine helicopter squadron he would be assigned to.

Though I found it difficult to decipher large portions of his handwriting, he also mentioned his continuing excitement with stock car racing. Plus new thrills in hang gliding. He didn't stop there. *Next week my friend—I'll be free falling miles above the sunny California coast! Something I been wanting to do for many years. See you in Vietnam good buddy! Later, Lenny*

I admired Lenny for his pluck and his boundless spirit. He wasn't afraid of anything. But I was afraid for him, worried I might lose yet another special, essential person in my life.

CHAPTER 23

P A-PA-PA-PA-PA-PA-PA-PA! POW! POW! PA-PA-PA-PA-PA-PA-PA! POW!

The earsplitting racket of the automatic MI6 rifles and .45 caliber pistols shattered my marijuana haze. As if my mind wasn't screwed up enough already, I had to respond to my first combat confrontation with the enemy after having smoked my first joint.

I was no better than the mess hall cooks and orderly room clerks when it came to an itchy trigger finger. POW! I fired another round into what remained of the bullet-riddled black Peugeot sitting in the street below.

Wouldn't you know they'd choose my company billets for an attack, less than a month after our arrival? Select the very night I tried smoking the weed.

Peeking apprehensively over the edge and looking down at the smoking car from our rooftop advantage, it appeared the driver had been killed. I could see him lying on the floorboards by the front seat. He wasn't moving. *Jesus Christ. What now? If that car is rigged with explosives, it could blow sky high any second.* The bastard hadn't made it past the manned security kiosk and perimeter barrier of sandbags and sand-filled oil drums guarding our building. But that bomb on wheels was still close enough to do serious damage. Besides taking out everybody on the street.

WHAT THE HELL ARE WE SUPPOSED TO DO NOW?

After the hullabaloo, I came down with a case of the shakes. My mind resembled a dull machete trying to slash through a jungle of disconnected thoughts, swarming with fears past and present.

God. That was louder than that day on the practice range at Fort Bragg. When I'd fired my first weapon during ROTC summer camp. And a whole lot scarier. I wonder if the grass has anything to do with it. It's supposed to magnify the senses. Damn. If I hadn't gone out drinking that "33" brand pisswater Vietnamese beer the other night with a battalion staffer, I might've handled it better. That brew tastes like they put gasoline in it, anyway. And who would expect an officer handing out drugs as a welcoming gift. I wasn't ready for this crisis straight, much less stoned out of my head.

That first episode in Saigon set the tone as to what we had in store for us in the strange, protracted conflict called the Vietnam War. It was an endemic struggle of will between opposing political and sociological ideologies in a steamy, unpredictable third world country, unlike any other military enterprise in American history. We would find our previous experience and tactical training, to include the combat readiness exercise at Fort Lewis, Washington, hadn't begun to prepare us for the unconventional nature of the engagement. My men and I survived this early orientation without any physical injury. Yet we suffered the psychological embarrassment of overreacting in our first operational test. We looked pretty foolish, not to mention the South Vietnamese lieutenant we crippled forever.

Circumstances leading up to the event had stoked the fire for our blunder. Intelligence reports received from the provost marshal's office warned of a planned Viet Cong attack on one of our battalion's facilities. The tactic employed by Communist Hanoi's guerrilla force, nicknamed "Charlie" as a spin off the NATO phonetic alphabet for "Victor Charlie," would be to crash an explosive-laden vehicle into a military police building. Though our billets were located in Cholon, the safer Chinese district of the city where this wealthier ethnic presence paid Charlie off to protect their homes and businesses, we represented the vulnerable new kids on the block.

My MPs were working the provost marshal's duty roster that evening, leaving me with a sleeping shift of soldier policemen and a bunch of overanxious support services personnel to defend the castle. Fortunately, I received more than enough support and an array of authorities and decision makers at the scene within minutes, from my own on-duty MPs, the provost marshal himself, his duty officer, my battalion commander, to a host of other key battalion personnel.

The bad news was that we'd mistakenly shot up a friendly "Arvin"—Army of the Republic of Vietnam—officer. He had the misfortune of stalling his car on the wrong night at our front door. Compounding my personal quandary was the fact that my company XO, Lieutenant Chudzinski, had caught me toking on that joint when he rushed into my private quarters to warn me about the impending incident.

Even in my abstract state I remember his panic-stricken words as he crashed through the door.

"Captain Bender! There's a vehicle refusing to obey our security warning at the kiosk! It's stopped out in front of our building right now!"

I dropped the remainder of my hand-rolled "cigarette" in the ashtray by my chair, grabbed my pistol belt off the bed. We ran out of my fragrant room into the hall.

"Let's hit the roof!" I cried. We bolted toward the staircase.

"He's already ignored the first and second phase warning whistles," the burly lieutenant shouted as we scrambled up the stairs.

Just as we reached the top we heard the whistle blow the third phase triple blast. If there's no reaction after three triple signals, the kiosk cops would offer a warning shot before opening fire.

Running toward the front, I saw my supply sergeant and some of the mess hall personnel with their rifles aimed down in the direction of the street. The whistle in the kiosk blew another three shrill signals. Then one of the weapons prematurely discharged. Hair-trigger responses yapped from the remaining rifles on the roof. As the lieutenant and I arrived at the parapet, I heard many more rapid bursts from the windows below us.

Looking down, I observed my kiosk MP and his South Vietnamese *canh sat* partner emptying their magazines as well. The black car rocked in place as the bullets shattered the windows, blew out tires, and penetrated the metal exterior. I noted with satisfaction that this Vietnamese policeman did not choose to run when the terror began. We'd been advised they had a proclivity to do this. The remedy, sanctioned by the Vietnamese National Police—shoot them in the back.

Caught up in the delirium and adrenalin rush, I added several rounds into the target with my Colt .45. I have no idea how many shots were triggered, but I imagine a number of weapons unloaded their entire cartridge clips into the vehicle during the horrifying seconds of the assault. I shall never forget the deathly stillness that descended upon us all after the last, belated shot had been fired.

En route to Vietnam, I'd savored the joy of anticipation during my flight from Frankfurt to Newark. I looked forward to my holiday respite with the family in New Jersey before going to war. As usual, Mom brought me back down to earth.

"I hate to say it, young man, but this time you've got yourself in a real fine fix. You wanted to be the playboy in Europe so bad you forgot about your responsibilities to your own family. And even yourself. The obligation, the consideration you might have shown us for the sacrifices, the cost of raising you and giving you the special educational opportunity so few can afford. So now you can throw it all away and go get yourself killed in Vietnam. And leave us all standing at your casket . . . crying about what you could've been. It just makes me sick."

Welcome home, Robbie. Christmas is coming and Mom's on a roll. Some things never change.

Escaping behind the privacy of my bedroom door, I'd lain down on my old bed. I stared once more at the stucco ceiling. My make-believe suburbia remained intact. The labyrinth of busy streets and neighborhoods just as I'd conceived during my youth. I thought about the landslide of distressing events I had to confront since my departure from Germany. The transitory revisit to Denton didn't help to salve any of the wounds I brought home with me. If anything, my misery became exacerbated by the changed environment and traumatizing personal updates. The town had died, as far as I was concerned.

Speckles O'Reardon had become a full-time husband and dad, having to marry some girl from Teaneck. Tommy Calderone, classified "4F" by the military for his innumerable health problems, had appropriately taken to pursuing a pharmaceutical career down in the D.C. area. I could only speculate as to what he was into now. Eddie Mazzoli got fired at the gas station, caught with his hand in the till. I guess he needed to augment his meager "mechanics" pay to support his chronic alcoholism. He'd left town for somewhere on Long Island, where he now sponged off his sister and brother-in-law.

I stopped in at the T&J twice, once before Christmas, once after. Couldn't find anyone I knew. Even Bert the bartender had departed. The Clancy Street Tavern was not only missing Jerry Blakely, God Rest his Dashing Soul, but had been liberated from the obnoxious bartender who replaced him. Ted had split as well, the establishment now operating under new ownership. A vaguely familiar old drunk at the bar told me Ted sold the place and moved away. He didn't know where. Both clubs were glutted with pimply-faced kids pumping beers and acting like assholes. The girls still looked good, disregarding their tasteless clothes and mouths full of gum.

With nothing to do between Christmas and New Year's, fighting my frayed emotions as they chafed in the Santa Claus opulence of seasonal joy and the barren realities of my personal world, I decided to track down Jane Lennox. I needed to find out how she'd progressed since the car accident with the late Jerry Blakely. I remembered holding her wilted hand while she lay in a coma at Hackensack General. How I had to leave when I started crying, abashed to display my weakness to the attending nurse.

After some frustrating detective work, following a number of dead end leads, I found out she now lived with her older sister and family up in Nyack, New York, by the Tappan Zee Bridge. My Austin-Healey had just arrived at the pier in Port Elizabeth. I picked it up and gave it a test drive direct to Nadine's house.

I felt gratified that the car still performed as it should. But my satisfaction came to be short-lived when the sister led me inside her home to visit my original girlfriend. Jane sat like a mannequin in a chair, hardly moving the entire time. She knew who I was, but had trouble conversing, putting together only the most simple sentences and speaking in a monotone. Her green eyes had lost their luster. Saddest of all, her impulsive inner flame had been relegated to ashes.

Nadine brought Jane's son, Adam, into the room. He showed me the toy machine gun he'd gotten for Christmas. He didn't remember me. I thought I saw a flicker of a smile from Jane as she watched us together, but I couldn't be certain I hadn't just wished it in my mind. When the time arrived for me to go, I kissed her on the forehead. She remained in her chair as I thanked Nadine for letting me stop by. I rolled back to Denton at a more pensive pace than my earlier drive.

After a boring New Year's Eve with the family, watching television coverage of the ball descending in Times Square and then going to bed, I mapped out my cross-country drive to Fort Lewis. Before I left I decided to call my high school frat brother, Speckles, to get the poop on the whereabouts of Bobby Bennett in Vietnam. Speckles' old lady answered the phone.

"Robbie Bender? *John* knows you from high school? Okay, I'll see if I can find him."

A few minutes later I heard that familiar voice coming at me through the wire.

"Robbie, my boy! What's up? Goddam', it's good to hear from you after all this time. You must be *General* Bender by now!"

We had a good time reminiscing for a while, before realizing we'd reached the limits of our common ground. I had no more interest in his domestic doings and carpentry work than he in my military stories. I think we both understood for the first time that the high school graduation party we'd celebrated at Tommy Calderone's house had become ancient history, with little relevance to our present lives.

"Hey, Speckles. I'm heading to Vietnam, man." I'd picked up on his wife's inflected emphasis of the serious "John" versus "Johnny" or "Speckles." I refused to cast aside that high school nickname. "I wonder if you could give me Bobby Bennett's number, or his unit. So I can look him up when I get over there."

A moment of silence had me wondering if we'd been cut off. Then I heard Bobby's best friend reply, and his voice began to choke up. "Jesus, Robbie. I thought you knew. Bobby's not . . . Bobby's not . . . with us anymore."

This is not happening, I thought to myself. Enough is enough. It's time to wake up from the bad dream. I took a long drag on my Pall Mall before I answered him.

"What do you mean?" I watched the exhaled smoke billow, then hang in the air.

"He was killed in Vietnam. Almost a year ago. Bobby's not with us anymore."

I had to get off the phone. "I'm sorry, Johnny. I'm real sorry. I'm sorry for every goddam' one of us." I gently pressed my finger on the disconnect button.

My focus took longer than usual this humid morning. Looking up from the narrow Army bed, I felt myself emerging ever so slowly through a cloudy nebula, noting a sensation of weightlessness and feeling a dull throbbing at the back of my head.

I observed the ceiling in this room to be slick and smooth, without the texture I'd fancied as that imaginary place growing up back home. Probably the difference between plasterboard and real plaster, I thought. *Well, I wonder what my upside-down town would look like now, after a few puffs of the psychedelic herb. I'd drunk a few beers in my day, but I'd never before known anything like that marijuana cigarette. It's a different kind of hangover, too, that's for sure.*

The mortifying events of the previous evening came crashing through the fog. *Jesus, could all this be some nightmare hallucination? No, I remember everybody raining bullets down on that paralyzed black car. Just like that, it was over. I'd talked at length with the provost marshal and my battalion commander. We'd put a friendly allied officer in the hospital, in critical condition. We'd been fortunate we hadn't killed any innocent bystanders on the city street. Hopefully the ARVN lieutenant would survive. Oh yes, and I'd been under the influence of a mind-altering drug while I commanded my men.*

Then I saw Zina's anxious impassioned face, unable to conceal the anguish and despair we both felt as she gradually dissolved behind the hotel door. And Jane just sat there in her chair, with no expression on her face. *And Bobby Bennett's dead. He'd been killed right here in this miserable stinking country. Now it's my turn.*

How had I managed to get myself so far, so fast, from my friends and my previous life? What ever happened to my dreams and aspirations? I hadn't prepared myself for this chaotic, alien world. What in God's name am I doing here?

CHAPTER 24

It didn't take long to realize the vast differences in the cultures of the United States and Vietnam. After our nerve-racking flight from the sampans of Vung Tao to Tan Son Nhut Air Base at Saigon, our military transport plane having made a steep climb and descent trying to avoid Viet Cong sniper bullets, I led my 528th Military Police Company onto Army busses for the ride to our inner city billets.

First observations enlightened me regards the heavy density of population on both streets and sidewalks, and the squalid living conditions. The streets were jammed with an assortment of curious modes of transportation, from the preponderance of bicycles and noisy motor bikes to the taxi-prone rickshaws, *cyclos* and pedicabs, peculiar three-wheeled three-passenger vehicles with foot pedals. Tiny automobiles, typically French manufactured Citröens and Peugeots, made up the traffic minority.

Pungent scents inundated my nostrils. When we passed by the first of many marketplaces everyone on the bus started coughing and feigning asphyxiation from the putrid stench of rotting fish. Breathing came to be a challenge, the odor was so bad.

Many native heads were covered by pointed, conical straw hats to ward off the blazing sun. Pretty, petite girls dressed themselves in satiny *ao dais*, consisting of a blouse with flowing panels complimenting long baggy pants. My troops' enthusiasm at the sight of these young sidewalk maidens diminished somewhat, however, when one of them squatted at the curb, calmly pulling her pants forward from her buttocks, and defecated into the gutter.

"Aw, jeez," someone moaned, from the front of the bus.

"Welcome to Saigon, the Paris of the Orient!" someone else reacted, to the amusement of everybody.

Settling into our new surroundings, the biggest adjustment had to be coping with, and accepting, the poverty and verminous quagmire that was the lifestyle around us. I knew the slums of New York City, in the south Bronx and Harlem and lower east side Manhattan, and in Newark and Jersey City, but none of those areas compared to this sewer existence.

Legions of the capital's frail, hideously undernourished souls set up residence on the streets, improvising with ingenuity to create some manner of shelter, be it a concoction of cardboard boxes or the more elaborate fabrication of a piecemeal shack. The city was a maze of convoluted streets and alleyways that required alertness on the part of pedestrians. This held especially true at night, when the pathways became cramped with scores of families and individuals settled into their patchwork abodes and vulnerable makeshift beds.

I'd never seen so many orphans, begging for any morsel of sustenance, most of them adorable little waifs deserving someone's love and affection. My MPs reported that during routine security checks they observed hundreds of persons, including many of these forsaken children, resorting to find refuge within the network of sewage pipes that lay beneath the city streets. We sometimes captured Viet Cong infiltrators mixed among civilians in these advantageous hideouts.

Just as vexing were the overt black market activities taking place in broad daylight all through the city, even in the well-trafficked commercial districts. However corrupt governmental deals and political/economic influences may have played a part, sidewalk peddlers flagrantly displayed stolen American goods. Anything you could imagine, from toothpaste to stereo sets to jewelry. Many items intended for the military PXs never reached their destination. Sometimes the "deuce and a half" Army supply trucks that carried them disappeared too, hijacked out of convoy somewhere between Vung Tao and Saigon. The detachable components of these vehicles, tires and engine parts, even the seats, could be purchased on the street as well.

Since civilian enterprise lay beyond the purview of our military police, the only available course of action for our patrols was to report the criminal operations to the provost marshal's office for coordination with the Vietnamese National Police. On occasion there would be conspicuous VNP "raids" at prime commerce locations, such as the popular intersection of Tu Do and Tran Hung Dao streets, making "arrests" and confiscating the stolen goods before the inquisitive multitudes that frequented the area. Nevertheless, these black market vendors must have possessed some sort of license of impunity, hand-stamped for carte blanche privileges. Within a few days those very same faces were back at it with their illegal wares, perhaps a few blocks away, business as usual. Seasoned "in-country" MPs learned not to bother wasting their time filing reports on this conduct; they learned to look away just like everybody else.

Many of those attractive, smiling young ladies in their colorful *ao dais* and parasols made their livings in another illicit industry also flourishing at this time, siphoning from the deep pockets of the American soldier. The oldest profession hummed in high gear, working girls decorating the streets and the abundant nightclubs.

Though many *cos* in the bars spoke only a smattering of English, they all knew how to say, "You number one, GI!" when you bought them a "Saigon tea"—merely a coke, or colored water in a double shot glass, at five to ten dollars a pop, depending on the joint. Or, they'd sneer, "You *dinky dau* number ten!" when you refused. There were no numbers in between. It was a black-and-white proposition, cooperatively accepted or rudely dismissed. In the former instance, if the GI spent enough, and played his cards right, he might get the chance to spend even more, at the end of the evening.

It would appear that even General Worthington, commander of all our American troops in Vietnam, was not immune from the contagious influence of corruption and immorality, either. Early on, I heard the stories that filtered up through the ranks concerning our fearless leader. The general's staff car, with its four-star flag flying boldly on the front fender, had been observed by our MP patrols on numerous occasions driving a young Asian woman, rumored to be Chinese, to the various shops in the fashion district of the city. I guess after all the dependents had been sent home, as the war escalated, even the commanding officer became lonely for private companionship.

We sat across the wobbly table from each other. I marveled once again at the familiar blaze of his gemstone blue eyes. He raised his voice just shy of a shout to be heard above the din in the chintzy Saigon nightclub.

"Man! You and I been in some pretty frantic places in our short time together on this planet, Rob. But this crazy goddam' city sure calls for raising up that old chalice again. Here's to the next outrageous chapter in our continuing search for the holy moly."

"To the chalice!"

Clinking our glasses together, as we'd done so many times and places before, I felt amazed just thinking about how our relationship had developed from the locker room at Teagle Hall. Our mutual experience had become an unbelievable phenomenon we shared, going our separate ways and living our individual dramas, yet forever reuniting and continuing the journey in far-flung places of the world. Now we sat together in a bar on Cong Ly Street, somewhere in the ambiguous pith of the Vietnam War.

The time had come to share stories once again, catching up on the latest in each other's lives. Odd as it sounds, I felt relieved that Lenny was now in war torn Vietnam and had survived his daredevil enterprises back home, from the stock car racing and hang gliding to free falling from airplanes high above the mountains of California. It troubled me how he forever pushed himself to the limit, obsessed with seeking new dangerous situations.

Though I continued to wonder about Zina, I refrained from broaching the subject with Lenny. It was disturbing to think I'd even tried to get her pregnant under the circumstances. I suppose I'd come to realize the enormous implications her *ever-after* quest entailed. The hope that we had not succeeded now dwelled in a guarded cloister within my brain. On a subconscious level I prayed she had had her whatever female problem operation, coming through it all with no complications, medical or otherwise. The entire matter had become too painful to discuss with anybody, even Lenny. I had to find a way to move on, for my own peace of mind.

I did tell him about my unit's specialized training at Fort Lewis, designed for a physical security role in rough country terrain. How we'd been perplexingly reassigned to Saigon at the last minute.

He looked at me with that comical expression on his face I'd come to know with fond appreciation.

"Damn tootin' they sent you to Saigon. For Christ's sake, you're not exactly Daniel Boone, you know. They took one gander at you, and knew they had a true-blue city slicker on their hands. I ain't at all surprised. Just look at this wild-ass town here. This is where you belong, pardner."

Laughing together, I had to agree with him.

We bent elbows long into the evening, successful in fighting off the advances of numerous *cos*. As the hour grew late, Lenny realized he needed to get to bed. He had to take his chopper up country to Pleiku first thing in the morning. I'd taken the liberty of using my company jeep, giving my driver the night off. I drove Lenny back to his quarters. Up in his room I pulled out one of my magical cigarettes and lit up, inhaling deep into my lungs before offering it to him.

"What're we doing here, brother?" I took note of one of the very few times I ever saw Lenny bewildered and off-balance.

I raised my hand for a moment, holding my inhalation so I wouldn't be wasting any of this particularly choice cultivation. He stood there watching me, his mouth agape. When my chest ached for air, I let it go.

"It's a joint, Lenny. Marijuana. A different ride from that booze we been doing all these years. Here, try some. You're a smoker. Just hold it in your lungs so you get a good hit."

It was his turn to hold up his hand. "No thanks, pardner. I got to be alert early tomorrow. This particular mission might not be a cakewalk." He raised his other arm and moved toward me. I awkwardly angled the joint away from him as we hugged in the middle of the room. "I'll see you soon, good buddy."

Taking the stairs back down to my jeep, I had the distinct impression I'd just discovered the first taboo in my best friend's unrestrained, indulgent lifestyle.

She looked fragile, vulnerable, and scared as she sat in the chair in my office, her arms handcuffed behind her back. Her frightened eyes were large brown buttons, reminding me of the Margaret Keane lithograph with the exaggerated gaze of contemplation I'd bought at the Nürnberg PX. She looked at me, scanned the room, then set her sights on the uniformed MPs guarding the door. What impressed me was that, unlike what I would have expected from most women in such circumstances, she had not started weeping. Accompanying the fear she had an almost defiant look about her.

We had a thief in our midst. A short while after settling into our Cholon billets, my men began reporting missing personal items: jewelry, watches, cash from their wallets. I contacted the provost marshal's office for advice. They suggested setting up plants to bait and trap the culprit. They provided me with a powder that could be brushed on objects susceptible to theft, something that would invisibly transfer to anyone touching the merchandise. The powder would unobtrusively cling to the skin, and turn purple when combined with water. Almost impossible to wash away, it had to wear off over a period of time.

After a few days of continued pilferage, to include some doctored bills, no purple hands surfaced from the inspections of our water bucket brigade. It had us baffled. Then my Aussie detachment leader, Sergeant MacElvaney, apprehended one of the laundry girls in the act. He brought her down to the orderly room where we again performed the PMO test.

Before we even stuck her arms in the bucket we had a good idea we had the right person. The skin on her hands was red and raw. It appeared she'd scrubbed them with a brush and heavy detergent, attempting to remove any trace of evidence. She'd done a good job; I'm certain the PMO would've been impressed. But not quite good enough. Close examination revealed minuscule remnants of purple stain in the cracks of skin at the joints of her fingers, and some under her fingernails.

Lanky First Sergeant Tomlinson entered my office. "The Vietnamese National Police are here, sir. There's an officer, two *canh sats* and, believe it or not, an interpreter. Whoops—"

The words had just escaped his mouth when the officer pushed past him and the MPs. Stepping right up to my desk, he saluted me and offered his hand, talking rapidly in his native tongue. I stared at a short, stocky man with a mustache. I had no idea what he was saying.

Responding with due politeness, I shook his hand. Without warning he turned and moved to the girl, now standing in front of her chair. With a closed fist he punched her savagely in the face, putting his full weight behind the clout. She hurtled backwards into the chair, stunned by the force of the blow. Blood spurted from her nose. I'm certain he'd broken it.

In an instant, the two *canh sats* wrenched her back up to her feet and dragged her out of my office. The officer and interpreter followed them, creating red footprints in the trail of blood as they went. The speed and brutality of the event caught us by surprise. They made their way halfway down the hall toward the exit before we recovered our composure and reacted.

Lieutenant Chudzinski, who'd been standing just outside my office door, joined Sergeant Tomlinson and me as we ran after them. They'd begun shoving the young woman into the back of their unmarked official car when I grabbed the "interpreter" by the arm.

"I need to talk to you about all this!" I shouted, my voice shaking with anger. "There are many things that need to be discussed!"

"Here is my card. You may call me . . . at your convenience."

The little twerp did speak English after all. I felt my heart pounding hard in my chest and my lungs seemed inadequate to the task of my escalated breathing. I watched their car disappear out the driveway.

Lieutenant Chudzinski was the first to speak. "What the hell happened in there?"

Sergeant Tomlinson answered for me as I walked back inside, shaking my head.

"Those fucking slopes."

"I'm sorry, captain, but we really can't help you with this one. I understand your frustration with the VNP. But that's the way they are. The girl shouldn't have been cleared for working in your building in the first place, living in a VC active location. And, frankly, I can't justify sending our MPs outside the city, which is the extent of our jurisdictional authority here.

"Besides, if she stole all that shit over a period of time, you better believe it's gone by now. She's not decorating her chicken shack with watches and jewelry. Probably sold it all to a fence right here in town. You'd do better hitting the peddlers out on the sidewalks than going way out to her place."

"How about getting the friggin' 'white mice' out there. The way I see it, it's their job, anyway."

"I'll see what I can do."

That was the extent of cooperation I got from the PMO's operations officer. I failed to reach Tran Quang Đúc, the Vietnamese police interpreter. He never returned my calls. The secondary token response from the provost marshal's office informed me that the Vietnamese cops would not go out to search the maid's hovel, either. They confirmed the village had Viet Cong allegiances, therefore considered "too risky" for such an endeavor.

A week later Lieutenant Chudzinski and I returned from lunch at the O-club to find a celebration at the company bar, the bar we'd built with the lumber intended for our original field mission. Once again Sergeant MacElvaney and his Australian cops had gathered as the hub of the commotion. This time First Sergeant Tomlinson had joined them as well, unusual for such an early hour.

"What's the occasion?" I called out, as we approached. "You guys are having too much fun in the middle of the day. Don't you know we're at war here?"

"We got a lot of our stuff back, captain!" one of my squad leaders cried out. "Sergeant Mac and his band o' down under pirates led a bunch of us out to that chambermaid's shanty. Way out in the rice paddies. And guess what? Most everything, even a lot of our money, was still there. Look, sir. I got my bracelet back!"

Unbelievable. These crazy soldiers of mine took it upon themselves to motor some thirty plus miles, toward Bien Hoa, into a known enemy hamlet where both the Vietnamese National Police and American military police were afraid to go. To boot, they'd accomplished their mission, retrieving much of our stolen property.

"Did you know about this?" I asked my top sergeant.

He smiled. "I know about it now, sir."

I had another question for Captain Vogel at the PMO, after I teasingly rebuked him about our successful reclamation project in Charlie territory.

"Say, friend, I understand this young lady we had beat up and thrown in a smelly Vietnamese prison has a daughter. A little girl. My men tell me she was alone at the place when they got out there. So, what's the deal on that? What was she doing left all by herself? If there's no family to take care of her, doesn't she become a ward of the state, or something, while her mother does time?"

"Don't think so. This is not the 'land of the free and home of the brave,' Bender. The French didn't leave these fuckers no Statue of Liberty. As I understand it, seeing as her mother's guilty of a major crime, in the eyes of the GVN she's forfeited all rights and privileges as a citizen. The government assumes no responsibility for the welfare of her offspring."

"What becomes of the kid, then?"

"If there's no family to pick her up? I guess she joins the ranks of all those other kids scratching for grubs on their own."

"So she gets punished for her parent's crime? An innocent child becomes an orphan on the street because her mother was so desperate she had to steal for them to survive? It doesn't make sense."

"Not a whole lot does over here, does it?"

Touted as the first "free election" in Vietnam, the government announced that former Army general Nguyen Van Thieu and Air Force general Nguyen Cao Ky had been selected to lead the country. I guess the titles were premier and president. To be frank, I'm not certain who was really in charge. In conformance with the nation's political vagaries they appeared to have their own independent agendas.

The Viet Cong threatened to bomb the polling booths. Yet American and South Vietnamese newspapers trumpeted exultant headlines about the "record turnout" and "impressive victory for democracy." Of course the men of the 716th Military Police Battalion were right there, on special alert during this propitious occasion, to insure the peace and safety of the city and the many voters.

Our efforts encountered unexpected calm and serenity. No bombs at the polling booths.

Hardly any voters, either.

CHAPTER 25

My big present for Christmas '66 turned out to be the Bob Hope show with the troops. Bob made us laugh with his wry humor. As expected, Joey Heatherton, strutting the stage in her scanty outfits, had all the boys hooting and hollering for more. It seemed strange to see Bob live, rather than on a grainy black-and-white news clip performing for our GIs in some heroic previous war. I realized that this time we were ourselves the patriotic coverage on the boob tube back home. Only this time we all understood that this fight for freedom had not been accorded the same support and enthusiasm as those depicting earlier American soldiers, and their commitment to world peace.

Another present, which I received with mixed feelings, involved a reassignment. In January I turned over the reins of the 528th to another captain, assuming new duties as adjutant at battalion headquarters.

I got somewhat despondent about having to leave the company I felt I'd been instrumental in creating—the men I'd mobilized for action, taken across the Pacific, and commanded in an embattled foreign land. I was so proud of them and the esprit de corps they carried with them as a unit; I had a solid feeling that they, in turn, respected me and were sorry to see me move on. At the same time I felt that administration, especially writing memos and letters, handling correspondence for the colonel, would prove to be a personal forte. I'd long entertained the notion of one day functioning as a battalion adjutant.

Changing billets, since I no longer served as part of the company, became my third dispensation of the holiday season. I remained in Cholon, but moved to a BOQ "hotel" a number of blocks on the other side of the neighborhood officers' club. It impressed me that these quarters came equipped with mosquito netting around the beds. A welcome luxury to help escape the constant invasion of those pesky fellows, and the flies and other obnoxious insects thriving in this climate.

Here I had a designated roommate, 1st Lieutenant Billy Riggins. He'd just been reassigned himself, from an ARVN advisory post somewhere up in the northern highlands to a staff job respite at MACV Headquarters—U.S. Military Assistance Command, Vietnam. As a gung-ho infantryman doing his second tour in-country, he'd received his commission through OCS, Officer Candidate School, after quick promotions through the enlisted ranks to buck sergeant. Unlike most OCS-commissioned officers, however, he'd joined up with a college degree. His advanced education had continued with Uncle Sam. He wore Airborne, Pathfinder and Jungle Expert patches on his uniform. And he looked the part, a rugged individual with an iron physique, a fine-tuned fighting machine with stabbing, steel-gray eyes.

Billy didn't seem pleased about either his new assignment or the city life. He made no bones about it.

"No offense to the job you guys have to do here. But all this is horseshit as far as I'm concerned. Six months in the boonies, trying to teach these people how to fight a war, ain't gonna' get it done. Just when you're making some progress, even communicating with 'em, they pull you out of there. Bring in another guy from some crap desk job like they got me in now. Or some wet behind the ears kid from CONUS. And everyone's back at ground zero, starting all over again."

He sidled past me to our shared closet. I caught his words as he kneeled down for his duffel bag.

"Goddam' it, I loved what I was doing up there. I was real good at it, too. I'm just not cut out for this pencil pushing routine."

That said, he rummaged around in his bag. He pulled out a leather case, unzipping it as he stepped to our small desk. He removed a weird looking pipe and a plastic bag filled with some kind of dark brownish material. My first reaction guessed it to be pot, another surprise from Santa. But as he removed some from the bag and placed it on the shallow screened bowl of the pipe, I realized it had a much denser composition. Like a tiny stone.

He lit a match. As he held the flame to the substance he breathed in deep, drawing from the pipe. The stone glowed and faded. After a few hits, he held his breath and offered the pipe to me.

"Here. Have some. It'll do us both good." His voice squeezed out constrained, like an old man handing out sage advice. He maintained the smoke inside his lungs even as he spoke.

"What is it?" I asked, feeling a bit naïve as my words snagged in the stagnant air.

Eventually he exhaled, long and slow. "Hash, man. Sweet, sweet Vietnamese hash. Nothing finer in the whole wide world."

At this point I had trouble making the transition from the rock hard soldier venting his frustrations to the subdued, tranquil personage I now beheld before me.

"Hash? You mean, like, hashish?"

"Yeah, that's it. Hashish."

"Well . . . I've smoked pot . . . some. What's the difference? This looks like a little stone."

He sat there on his bed, staring at the floor. I couldn't be sure he'd even heard me. An eternal moment later he looked up and answered, in the same bridled voice.

"It's like pot. But condensed. In a resin form. Compact. More intense. But it's a natural herb. Made from leaves and flowers. You'll like it."

I put the match to the charred brown pebble in the pipe. Watched the golden ember glow as I took a puff. It flickered and died. I thought it'd gone out until I puffed again and saw it re-kindle. Warmth blossomed inside my lungs as my mind soared toward ethereal wanderings. With broadened chest I passed the pipe back to my new friend. He wasn't Lenny. Yet I had the feeling we were going to get along.

As usual, we sat at a far corner of the roof, secluded from the other stargazing officers.

"Yeah, man, this is one horseshit war we've got going here," Billy observed, as he took another hit from the pipe. "What the fuck do they think they're doing out there, anyway?"

He pointed in the direction of the copters flying far west of the city. They cracked open the nocturnal darkness as they fired brilliant topaz tracer rounds down upon the earth. We had joined the BOQ's nightly light show on the roof, high enough to view the action outside our metropolitan existence. It was safer than the streets, cheaper than the clubs, and when you'd already seen the flick at the O-club twice, the choice came easy. It also happened to be a great place to get stoned and relax. Billy and I had been doing the roof a lot lately.

On a couple occasions we'd even seen planes dropping Agent Orange or napalm. The herbicide Agent Orange served as a chemical defoliant to strip leaves from plants and trees. Napalm's function went a giant step further. This jellied gasoline functioned as an incendiary that would light up an entire area with roaring flames that destroyed everything in its path. Either way, the intention was to deny jungle cover and, ultimately, liquidate the VC and the NVA, North Vietnamese Army. Beyond the effectiveness, I wondered about the ethics of this—how many farmers and laborers, mothers and fathers and children had been sacrificed per

Charlie guerrilla or enemy soldier eliminated from his Communist cause.

The American media had been feeding all of us Worthy's "statistics" on our adversary's casualties for some time now. But the word filtering back through friendly combat channels suggested that the reporting system encouraged inflated numbers. "Successful" career commanders had become amazingly adept at conducting accurate body counts, even after shadowless hit-and-run guerrilla attacks in tropical thickets during black, waning crescent and new moon nights. The numbers they submitted were often impressive even when hostile action had been thin to negligible.

"You know we're gonna' lose this shindig, don't you?"

"Excuse me?" I couldn't believe what I heard coming from the mouth of my patriot soldier comrade.

"Just look at what we got here," he continued. "Beyond the impossible military situation the boys back home have put to us, which is a whole nother matter, we've allied ourselves with a country that's rotten to the core. The government has no respect for the people, and the people have no faith in their government."

"What're you talking about?"

"Don't you know who we're trying to save from the Commies, all bundled up inside our warm democratic blanket? South Vietnam is run by the rich. Fat-ass aristocrats who don't give a shit about Mister Everyday Man. The big boys here have simply been born into it. From birth, they're guaranteed leadership positions all across the board. Business and industry, government and, yes, the military, too."

I shifted and leaned back in my folding chair, resting my sandaled feet on top of the roof's parapet. "So how's this different from anywhere else in the world?"

"Well, they've got this so-called mandarin system, where the educated wealthy run everything, unquestioned. Unlike other countries, there is no middle class. So there's this huge gap. You have the pompous, often incompetent, minority running the show.

And all the millions of peasants working the construction sites, the canneries, the rice fields—"

An explosion from somewhere in the bowels of the city interrupted Billy's diatribe. Other rooftop sightseers moved in the direction of the noise to investigate. I removed my feet from the wall and started to get up from my chair. Billy ignored it all, intent on continuing his tirade. As he went on, I decided to stay put.

"So . . . these fat cat sons-o-bitches are experts at exploiting their positions. Corruption and cronyism working hand in hand. Shit, it's just expected they're gonna' take care of their friends and family."

He pulled his chair closer, looking straight at me. "Confucius say the family is everything, above all else. Here, like other Asian cultures, though you may be just some poor do-as-you're-told factory worker, your true allegiance is to your own blood. Not only for your wife and kids, but all your cousins, aunts and uncles, grandparents and great grandparents. Reaching back through time, even, to all the family gone before."

"What's wrong with that?"

Their curiosities apparently unrewarded, the majority of the roof-gazers returned to their original perches. I glanced in their direction until Billy's voice pulled me back.

"The problem is, these people here are divided themselves by religion, race and provincial custom. Roman Catholics don't trust Buddhists or Muslims, and vice versa. And they scorn the Jews and Protestants. So, along with mistrusting their elitist government, they're fragmented among themselves. As a result, there's no patriotic spirit, no true national identity."

An MP siren wailed deep down in the city streets. Billy cast his eyes on mine, like he was fishing for some response.

"No wonder ARVN has such a high desertion rate," I observed.

"You got the picture, captain."

I took a long drag on the pipe and handed it back to Billy. I took my time getting up from my chair and stepped to the edge of the roof. Vietnamese pot packed a wallop. One joint could pleasure me for more than one night. Yet Billy's heavenly hash transcended any realm of euphoria I'd ever dreamed possible. I've always had to fight my natural tendency to keep returning to the proverbial well when I'm enjoying myself. With this drug in particular, I had to be careful not to smoke too much of it, to avoid being lost in space beyond the allotted off-duty hours, when I could attempt to temporarily escape our circumstances.

Timidly looking over the wall to the cesspool streets far below, I caught sight of the emaciated orphans that frequented the front door of our building. They had gathered together, about a dozen of them, on the street corner. As distant as they were, I could still pick out "Harry" from that collection of stunted, puny innocents. The cocky little urchin in the dirty red shirt, whose real name was Lanh.

I heard the propellers and tracer rounds from the choppers outside the city, the occasional heavy shudder of faraway bombing or mortar fire. A familiar backdrop of sound rampaging around the indifferent children. A detonation inside my brain had me wondering where that little girl was, an only child. How she was surviving without her mother. The mother I'd put in prison.

CHAPTER 26

"Gentlemen! Can I have your attention, please!"

The string bean sergeant stood tall by the lectern inside the reception hall. He waited until the last few conversations within the large group tailed off to silence.

"I'm Staff Sergeant Warren Reynolds. And I'm here to greet you-all, and introduce you to your week of . . . HEAVEN! Here in the 'city of angels.' Now, before we go any further, let's clear up those first two points so there's no misunderstanding. You-all are here because there's no war in Bangkok. But there is a 'War in' Reynolds . . . your official host and advisor, standing right in front of you-all. Yeah, I know, ha-ha, pretty corny."

Suddenly he turned and jumped up onto the bare metal desk behind him. I suppose he wanted to make sure the people in the back didn't miss his one-man vaudeville show.

"Thirdly, any heavenly angels around here has certainly got their work cut out for 'em. So I'm here to try to save you red-blooded freedom fighters from dealing with all those dee-sciples of the Devil just a-waiting to make your acquaintance."

Lenny leaned over and muttered in my ear. "Is this guy for real? Maybe we should've gotten into Special Services ourselves. Forget flying through VC bullets to pick up wounded grunts, or protecting some stinking rat nest city."

The two of us had coordinated our week of R&R, meeting at Tan Son Nhut Airport for the flight to Thailand's capital. We abided by Sergeant Reynolds' "Rules," negotiating for his "going rates" to hire two cute little brown "escort ladies" from a "recommended" nightclub, who stayed with us, full service, round-the-clock. They toured us through the city, from the Damnern Saduak floating market and the Buddhist temples, a pick-your-pretty-masseuse-in-the-window massage parlor, to the many bars and lively dance clubs.

The girls took us to a jewelry store the first day. We drank free glasses of beer as we perused the merchandise. Lenny and I walked out with receipts for two black sapphire rings, each to be assembled with a stone possessing a reflective star of exquisite clarity, mounted in matching silver settings. The rings would be ready for us by the end of the week.

"Goddam'," Lenny exclaimed. "Talk about a super deal. Under a hundred bucks for rocks like that, perfect cat's eyes, set in silver. You know, the ancient mystics believed these stones represent destiny. Our very own pardner rings, Rob. Brothers all the way to that final sunset."

The next morning I managed to hook up with a hashish contact Billy alerted me to. Lenny pouted about us "fucking with drugs." As angry as I'd ever seen him, he left the girls and me to smoke it up while he went off touring on his own for the rest of the day.

His aversion to this natural, non-addictive substance, like the marijuana I'd offered him in Saigon, his refusal to even experiment with it, took me by surprise. It was so unlike him to be intolerant, or squeamish about trying anything new. He'd always been the one first stimulated by the thought of diving into a fresh experience. Especially when it came to something others might consider "inappropriate" because it was controversial, forbidden, or, best of all, hazardous.

Yet, seeing as he never scrutinized or disparaged me, relative to my own hesitance toward precarious diversions, like my phobia with heights, I felt reluctant to take him to task on this subject. I must admit, though, it piqued my curiosity and urge for speculation.

All too soon the time came to say farewell to our two smiling R&R girls. We hugged them and kissed them, and tipped them generously before departing. Screw that sergeant and his self-serving "Rules." We flew together back to Tan Son Nhut Airport, where Lenny had to catch a Marine helicopter to his base. There we smoked our cigarettes and dallied over cups of coffee in the airport snack bar while he waited on his connection. At one point in our conversation he touched on the issue wedging its way between us.

"You know, I really think the biggest danger you face here in Saigon is the drugs you're getting into. Far be it from me to condemn others. Lord knows I'm no choir boy. But I just want you to be careful with that crap, okay? You're my brother and my best friend and . . . sometimes I worry about you."

I nodded my head, thinking about the irony of that statement, coming from Lenny. I deferred from making any confrontational comment at that time.

A short while later his copter was ready. We clenched each other with firmer grasps than usual. Just after he started to walk away he did an about-face, holding out his fist in my direction. I picked up on his intention. We clicked our sapphire rings together before he turned and left. No words deemed necessary.

CHAPTER 27

"**D**on't know if you looked at today's IR from the PMO, captain, but I highlighted some pretty scary stuff in there."

The battalion sergeant major was very good at his job, almost always a step ahead of everybody else, including the CO, XO, and myself. I don't know when he went to bed, but it had to be long before me and my night owl proclivities. He always beat me into the office every morning, having coffee brewed and his review of the daily Intelligence Report sitting on everybody's desk.

I was glad he'd also verbally alerted me to this particular report. Intelligence sources, whoever they might be, indicated Charlie planned to step up his terrorist shenanigans within city limits.

One attack approach would take the form of *satchel charges*, bombs concealed inside some type of innocuous container, like a knapsack or shopping bag, then placed within a delivery device, such as a bicycle basket. The bike could be secured to a tree, lamppost or street sign near a military bus stop. A timer would then be set to detonate at a popular commuter pickup time, either early morning or at the end of the day. The spinoff tactic would be to monitor other military traffic flows within the city, determining specific times and locations of high density. Then set up timer bombs or guerrilla ambushes to hit American or other pro-ARVN targets.

"Thanks, sarge. Appreciate the info. Looks like things might be getting a little hairy around here. Think maybe I'll take advantage of those spare jeeps in the motor pool for a while."

So I began to drive myself between battalion headquarters and the BOQ whenever I could get my hands on an available jeep. I thoroughly checked the vehicle, underneath and inside the hood, too, before turning on the ignition outside my hotel. I varied my streets and times so no pattern could be charted. Billy had the habit, like many other American officers, of traveling the same routes at close to the same schedule, day after day. Thus I took it upon myself to drive him whenever I could.

I also came to spend more time on the roof, with Billy or on my own, safely smoking my tea or hash, and watching the embellished fireworks. As far as I was concerned, the *co clubs* weren't worth the potential perils of the street. The O-club had the protection of our MPs. Yet I felt leery of the choices of narrow, meandering passageways that lay between that diversion and my bed. I also cut back on my leisure time there.

"Say, Billy, you really ought to be more careful how you get around in the city," I remarked, stepping out of the bathroom. "Taking the same bus everyday, between MACV and the club. Walking the same streets with other officers, at the same time, between here and there. That's why I try to get the jeep. Drive you when I can. And take different ways to get where I'm going."

Billy grabbed his lighter off the night stand and put the flame to the pipe. His chest expanded with his inhale. He leaned forward, offering me a toke.

I deferred, determined to get my point across. "It hasn't happened yet, but those PMO intelligence reports I see every day keep talking about Charlie's new plans. Satchel charges at bus stops. Clocking our repeat traffic habits for a possible strike."

Still holding his breath, it took a moment before he answered.

"I hear what you're saying. And I appreciate your concern. I do. I guess I'm just skeptical about a lot of that intelligence forecasting. Like the weatherman, they're wrong more than they're right. I'm convinced Charlie's behind a lot of it, just to keep us on edge, looking the wrong way. That sure was the case up country, most of the time."

He passed me the pipe. I took a puff as he continued. "Hey, if the shit starts hitting the fan here in Saigon, you better believe I'll have extra eyes in the back of my head. I'll be showing you some new trails in this goddam' hellhole."

I loved to get him going about the war. In most instances this sparked long, verbal rampages about our government's mismanagement, at home and abroad. This night was no exception.

"You know, it's a fucking shame what our government has done with this effort over here. They've handcuffed us, in favor of political expediencies, to the point there's no way we can win. We can't bomb north of this line. We can't chase the gooks when they run over that line, whether it's so-called North Vietnam, or Laos or Cambodia. You don't see Ho Chi Minh putting all these curbs on General Giap, like we've put on Worthy and the Pentagon."

He stretched out on his bed, on his side, propping his head with bended elbow.

"Christ, our own top commanders, who are right here and know the situation in the field, can't make a decision without checking in first with those egotistical white-collar civilian assholes all the way back in Washington. Goddam' selfish politicians looking out for themselves . . . with no clue about the reality of the situation, much less suitable military tactics. The same frigging politicians who're screwing up our own country back home, at the same time."

"And what are those piss ant politicians doing back home?" I asked, baiting him further before I took another whack at the pipe, following that up with a practiced secondary inhale of the external smoke floating toward me in the air.

"God Almighty. More like what they're not doing," he fumed, getting up into a cross-legged sitting position. "Letting special interest lobbies continue to rape what's left of our heritage. It tears my guts out to see what's happening to our natural resources."

All of a sudden he was on his feet, his muscled torso rippling with his words. "Hey, I know you're a city slicker. So you might not relate to what I'm talking about." His face mutated into Rocky Marciano's that split second before the champ threw his haymaker punch. "Our government sanctioning the wholesale slaughter of our land on behalf of their subsidizing industrial megacorporate conspirators. Who're looking to exploit something else to line their pockets, and satisfy their greedy stockholders."

He stalked the room, pressing the attack. "Indiscriminately cutting down our forests, polluting our waters, putrefying the soil, poisoning the air we breathe. Then having the balls to label it 'Progress.'"

I raised the pipe in a mock toast. "Cheers to Progress!"

"You know what really pisses me off?" he continued, ignoring my bent for levity. "Seems like the lack of concern about our environment, the indifferent attitude our government has toward the fascinating piece of the world we snatched away from the Indians, has filtered down to Mister Everyday Man himself."

He glanced around for the pipe as if he'd misplaced it. I held it out to him. He remained standing as he fired up another blow. After a series of quick intakes, he handed it back. Less than a minute later he picked up from where he left off, pacing the room for lack of a podium.

"No one really cares about what's become of our homeland anymore. Parents don't even set the example for their kids. Like 'follow the leader,' everybody's throwing cigarette butts and candy wrappers out the car window, littering the street right by the garbage pail, burning and trashing woods and meadows—"

"Man! This sure is a potent batch we're smoking tonight, isn't it?" I interrupted, enjoying his ride on the high horse I had saddled. "What say we hit the light show up on the roof."

With that, we returned our stash to its hiding place, taped up under Billy's chest of drawers. We floated out the door together.

Billy Riggins and I did have quite divergent backgrounds. While I was growing up in Denton, drinking and carousing New York City and its urban sprawl, joy riding the outskirt Jersey towns, and taking lessons from suburban wise guys and metropolitan hustlers, he was raised as a farm boy in rural Littlefork, Minnesota. His big adventure would be traveling up the road to the "city" of International Falls. Sometimes over the Canadian border into Fort Frances, Ontario. Billy talked about sowing and reaping, hunting and fishing, fording streams and blazing new trails. He was a true down-home country boy who had basked in the warmth of a snow-crested sunrise, bathed in the spectrum of a springtime rainbow, and bowed to the miracle of a harvest moon.

Up on the roof, I resumed our conversation from where we'd left off. "Just to set the record straight. I may be a city dude, but I do understand and appreciate what you're talking about. When I was a real little kid I lived in the country for awhile. Worked on a farm, while my dad was serving in World War II."

The hash had loosened up my mind and tongue as well.

"So I do know something about cows and horses, running across open fields, dozing in the sun at the old fishing hole. I agree with what you're saying. And even though I've spent most of my life with concrete under my feet, and buildings blocking the view, I did go to college in a small town . . . on a beautiful campus, with lakes and huge trees, and gorges and waterfalls."

It was my turn for some of that good ol' soap box oratory.

"But you know, I never realized how much we abuse all this in America until I got shipped over to Germany. I was amazed how everybody over there looks after their corner of this earth. They don't throw garbage on the ground. They clean up after their dogs. They don't clutter their roads with commercial billboards. Why, they even bury their power lines underground. They take care of their countryside, they're proud of it. Families dressed in their Sunday best go out walking together and share it."

Billy's exaggerated eyes reflected the flashes from the bursting sky. "Now that's what I'm talking about! Even after Adolf, they have respect for who they are. Something these sad people here need so god awful bad."

Before the import of his comments nested in my head, I launched my own words burning to be heard. "Anyway, it opened up my eyes to how we take our own great country for granted. How shabby we treat it. In spite of all the millions of people packed into it, it doesn't have to be like that."

"Amen, captain. I knew there was some reason I liked you."

We fell silent for a while. I thought about what had just been said. At the same time I sensed a strange, intruding comprehension of how close Billy's remarks, and my own, had come to piercing some abstruse core of embargoed feelings buried deep inside me. A seismic tremor from a faraway artillery round shook me back to the rooftop and the flickering night sky that once again hosted the helicopters' fiery ejaculations.

"Nice trip?" Billy smiled at me. "Pretty good shit, isn't it? Say, I noticed you're reading a book about American folk music. Ever hear of Bob Dylan?"

I could've sworn a red-hot tracer round had arced from his mouth and penetrated my brain. A look in the mirror would reveal the singe on my forehead. It seemed quite a bit of time passed before I heard my weak reply.

"You . . . you know who Bob Dylan is?"

Now he grinned all his teeth at me, full-bore.

"Of course I know who Bob Dylan is. He grew up in Hibbing, not all that far from Littlefork. His real name is Robert Allen Zimmerman. Fuck, I drove by his house once, just to see what it looked like."

For a while I just stared at him. I guess you could say I was speechless, for one of the few times in my life. I finally formulated a sentence.

"Let's you and me go get ourselves another piece of that pipe. We've got a lot to talk about."

Early one evening I lay stretched out on my bed, listening to the radio on the night stand. *That* rock tune came on again.

"Hey, Billy! Get out here and listen to this! Here's that song I was telling you about. With the catchy beat and bizarre lyrics. I think the group's called the Airplane. Or something like that."

Billy strolled out of the bathroom with a towel around his waist and lather on his face. He had a routine of shaving at night so he didn't have to bother when he got up to go to work.

"Oh yeah, I know this tune. It's called 'White Rabbit.' Like from *Alice in Wonderland*. And the group's moniker is the Jefferson Airplane, actually. The lead singer's a good-looking chick by the name of Grace Slick. Whoa, there. As Dylan would say, 'You could be a poet. Bet you didn't know it. Hope you don't blow it.'"

Looking at me intently, his eyes widened as he raised his eyebrows. "You know, it's amazing they're playing some of this music on the Armed Forces station. Just shows you how out of touch 'the powers that be' really are."

"What's the problem with it? To tell you the truth, I haven't got a grip on the lyrics yet. What's offensive about it?"

He almost dropped his razor right there on the floor. "You got to be kidding me. You . . . Captain Robbie Bender, resident druggie of the local military constabulary . . . protector of the peace, enforcer of the law. You, the high priest of pot, the herald of the Cholon BOQ hash bash light show. You don't know what they're singing about? I don't believe it."

"Well, shit, it's over now. And you were blabbering all the way through it."

Billy raised his upturned hands, shrugged his shoulders and rolled his eyes. He disappeared back into the bathroom to continue his shave. We'd gotten real tight, enjoying the bantering relationship developing between us. I hoped I would be able to have him meet Lenny. The two of them were birds of a feather in many ways. I could picture all of us as a ridiculous re-creation of the Three Musketeers.

I turned off the radio and waited a while, expecting him to answer my question. When he began humming to himself as he continued his project in the mirror, I tried again, hollering to be heard over the melody and the running water.

"So . . . what the hell's the song about? Don't leave me hanging, for Christ sake."

He turned off the faucet and stuck his refreshed face back out the door.

"It's about drugs, you ninny. What'd you think? You've got a pill that makes you larger, another that shrinks you small. Check out Alice when she's, like, ten feet tall. Then go treat your head, man, treat your head!"

I'd heard those particular lines all right. Of course. What was wrong with me?

"Fuck me. And they're playing it on a government sponsored radio station."

"That's what I've been trying to tell you, bub. The folks at the top have all got their heads up their fat asses. They don't get it. They don't see what's going on . . . over here, or over there.

"As Dylan says, 'the times they are a-changin'.' There's a whole lot of shit going down back home right now. I got one younger brother who's marched on Washington as one of them protest leaders. And he ain't even going to college. My other brother's already stepped across the border to Canada. To beat the draft."

I thought I caught an inkling of dew in his eyes.

"I'll tell you, Robbie, the real revolution is just kicking up. And it isn't here in Vietnam, either. It's right back home, in the good old US of A. And you know what? Those candy-ass politicians who're fucking it all up don't even have a clue how bad it is. Or how bad it's going to get. Not yet, anyway."

God, I thought to myself, we truly are living in an extraordinary day and age. I wonder what the history books will tell us when it's all said and done.

J ust as it happened in Nürnberg, the battalion XO called me in to discuss the Pentagon's response to my latest routine request for release from active duty. I figured the worst news would still be better than where I was. Hallelujah. This meeting projected a much different kind of traumatic effect. Come May I would once again be a civilian. *Mister* Robbie Bender. It sounded strange after all the years in Army green. I wondered what I would look like in a coat and tie. Where I would start my new life—my real career.

After all this time I had no plan. I had no idea what I wanted to do with my self. Other than an abstract vision of maybe becoming a famous author. Or more likely, sitting behind a company desk somewhere. With a private office and a secretary who took shorthand. Lord knows what I'd be dictating.

My Army orders had me processing out of the service in Oakland, California. Right across the bay from San Francisco. *That's it. I'd try that exciting city on for size. I'd always heard fantastic things about it. Hey, the Jefferson Airplane is based there. Maybe that's just the place to chase a white rabbit in my very own wonderland.*

The major burst the bubble of my fanciful daydream.

"I thought you might be interested to know . . . now that you're getting out, they're going to have to take your name off the schedule for major. You did make the new promotion list."

Oh no, here we go again. While we're on the subject of rabbits, Uncle Sam sure knows how to dangle those carrots when it comes to re-up time. My reply seemed to bolt out of my mouth, my mind scurrying to corral it.

"That's certainly nice to know, sir. It feels good you're appreciated for what you've done. For your devotion to duty." I inched toward the edge of my chair. "Well . . . I'm going to miss all you good guys I've served with over the years. That part's going to be tough. Kind of like leaving your family, you know? I wish you all the best."

As I started for the door, the major had the last word. "Hey, don't be talking like you're done with us, already. You've still got another month to enjoy our little tea party here."

I'm not certain if I went slack-jawed or it just felt that way. Was that comment mere coincidence or had the major tipped me off to an uncanny ability to read my mind? Whatever, he spoke the truth. I faced one more unpredictable month in the Paris of the Orient.

MIDAFTERNOON

The boy stopped at the bridge, as was his habit to do. He looked down over the side at the rapids of Canadaway Creek. Pleased that they persevered as spirited as ever, he held up his new friend at the top of the balustrade, to share the view. He wanted to give the little fellow the opportunity to become a part of the inspiration of this elusive kingdom.

Satisfied the incipient impression had been made, he moved on across the span. He walked up the side of the country road to the fresh water spring, a pleasant rest spot shrouded in a cool, natural arbor tucked away in the curl of the hillside. Cradling his prized possession in one arm, he bent over and drank long and deep from the spout extending from the cobblestone wall. The underground water tasted cold and invigorating, imposing the price of a short-lived surge of pain to his head as he gulped it down.

Energized, he stepped to the path leading into the woods. He held his trophy before him, so they might both observe the trail and the marvels along the way. Speaking out loud for the benefit of both of them, he extolled the virtues and integrity of each landmark location as they proceeded upward toward his secret place.

Now he was Shelley Forrester once again, in tune with the essence of nature's presence, alive in his reclusive realm, comfortable in the role he'd assumed, vitalized by the fancy of sharing the magic that thrives outside the sphere of the trivial human focus.

The angle of the sun reminded him it was already midafternoon. Not the best time to find night stalker Wee Willy. Yet he hoped he might be fortunate enough to catch his stealthy cohabitant out on the precipice, perhaps sunning himself before his evening hunt. If not, he would try to coax his acquaintance out of his lair with the enticement of his companion. The young pathfinder felt his anticipation escalating in the beating of his heart as he drew closer to his asylum.

Sooner than expected, he stood at the juncture where his indistinct trail cut toward the outcropping of rock that guarded the retreat. He took a firmer grip on his partner and bounded forward through the trees and snarled brushwood toward his destination. The trough in between the boulders extended its courtesy as it had so many times before. The boy wasted no time in assuming the role of bobsled for his rare treasure, supporting him affectionately in his arms as he slid on his rear down to the welcoming shelf.

The lad's intention entailed presenting his decoration to the evasive little neighbor who shared their lofty perch. The potential for another story had nibbled away in his brain ever since he'd won the school's nature contest. He knew Wee Willy would relate to his unique medal. He'd felt shivers up his spine when he first confronted the choices for the blue ribbon award. A stuffed weasel was a token of honor to behold. The boy had become convinced that, in light of their fated contact on the ledge, the ironic relationship between the two deserved to be shared, appreciated, preserved.

The same ominous feeling he'd encountered before prickled his skin once again. This visit didn't require any in-depth special investigation. While a cursory inspection didn't reveal any recent signs of Wee Willy, other than his active den, numerous clues indicated a more blasphemous presence.

Jagged shards of a broken wine bottle, shattered against the rib of stone, accentuated the warning of the impending edge. The shriveled cellophane sleeve from a box of crackers, still partially filled with crumbled pieces, lay prostrate in the trampled grass.

Four cigarette butts, two adorned with traces of pink lipstick, served notice as to the sexual differentiation of the trespassers.

The most upsetting piece of evidence in the youth's mind was the used condom dangling from the frond of a bordering fern. He wasn't certain how that piece of rubber fit into the relationship between males and females. He'd once found a box of the peculiar things left in the bathroom. Out of curiosity he'd removed one, daring to tear its package open and hold it up to the light. It looked weird then. But not slimy and nasty as it did now, clinging to the fern.

Sensing the onset of the nausea he'd suffered earlier, when he first came upon the plundered nearby meadow, he turned away from the offending filth, clutching his taxidermic fetish to his bosom. He moved quickly past the giant oak toward the bank of shrubs concealing that hallowed ground.

Emerging from the thicket on the other side, his torment intensified when he confronted the refuse of yet another orgy of intemperance and gluttony. Discarded boxes and wrappers identified a hodgepodge of snack foods. Crackers, cheeses, chips and cookies. Even caramel coated popcorn and peanut candy. All scattered across the grassy clearing. Countless smashed bottles of beer, twisted six-pack cartons, and splintered jugs of wine contributed to the havoc. An empty cigarette pack lay crumpled in the dirt. Butts lay everywhere. The dingy oval of ashes from the campfire had not only increased in diameter and pitchy remnants, but had been joined by a new, immature, circle of soot.

The cumulative effect of the abuse was alarming, as the fresh garbage mingled with the ripe to spread the contamination. Badly shaken, the boy withdrew to his favorite oak tree. Sitting down in its shade, he pulled out the tablet and pen from his pants pocket. He jotted down three pages of notes, studied them for a time, then stood and crammed them back into his pants. Experience duly recorded, he walked away, hugging his silent idol and desperately searching for answers.

CHAPTER 28

Boldface newspaper headlines validated the merit of the intelligence report warnings we'd been receiving from the Saigon Provost Marshal's Office.

GI'S DIE WAITING FOR ARMY BUS!

A satchel charge at an American military bus stop took out three of our soldiers and injured a dozen more.

It happened at 0727 on a Wednesday morning, just a week after my active duty release notification, at an intersection somewhere in the middle of the hubbub of the city. The Viet Cong selected their location well, and timed it to perfection. The shrapnel that exploded from the bicycle basket tore through the flesh of three enlisted men. None of them made it through the night at the American field hospital. The others had been lucky, positioned a little further from the blast. The forward bodies shielded them somewhat, taking the major hits.

I stepped up my harping on Billy after the incident, but it had little or no effect. It seemed incredible to me that with his advisory duty in venturous northern terrain, much closer to NVA occupied territories, he would be so apathetic about Charlie's threats and their guerrilla activities in and around Saigon. Yet he continued to regard my caveats as overcautious relative to what he perceived to be the reality of risk. I guess after what he'd been involved with out in the high country, though he never went into details even when we were stoned and by ourselves, he didn't see the capital city as being that vulnerable to serious enemy aggression.

When I reminded him it had only been days since three of our men died at a bus stop, in the manner forewarned by our intelligence, he asked why "my MPs" hadn't done their job and neutralized the target area before the killings occurred. Then he observed, "I'll bet at least that many bite the bullet every day in that Big Apple orchard you got in your own backyard back home."

After that crack I dropped the subject. Figured I'd just forget about it and take care of myself. I'd tried. He was a big boy anyway, with all those special combat training patches on his uniform.

Nine days after the bus stop bombing I found myself late once again getting out of the sack. Billy already had his uniform on as I waited for warm shower water. He called to me from our front door.

"You going to have breakfast at the club this morning, Rob? I'll save a place for you."

"Naw, forget about me. Think I'll just head straight over to the shop. But hey . . . if you want to wait a couple minutes, I'll drive you by the club. I've got the jeep."

"That's okay. Knowing how long you can dipsy-doodle around in that shower, I'll just head on over. Say, why don't we meet there tonight? Grab a bite, maybe do a flick, if there's anything decent. Then hit the roof for some more party time."

That sounded good to me. I hadn't been by the club in a while, staying at work later to clean up some job related things before I said goodbye, eating rations from the MP mess hall at my desk.

"Got yourself a date there, lieutenant. How about we add some happy hour to that IT? I should be able to make it around 1730 hours."

"I'll have a stool waiting for you . . . captain."

As I stepped into the shower I heard him close the door.

In as much as I would be coupling the late start with my evening commitment, I got in and out of that tiny stall in record time. I faced a lot to do at the office, to make sure I had everything in order for my replacement. I didn't want to be "pushing that pencil" overtime, as Billy would put it, during my final days on the job. Besides that, the Vietnamese built their facilities, especially the showers it seemed, on such a reduced scale that it didn't present a place for comfortable dalliances.

Fifteen minutes later I tripped out the entrance of the BOQ, still fiddling with the trouser blouse over my combat boots. I noticed some kind of commotion in the narrow street across the boulevard. A crowd of people, both Vietnamese civilians and American soldiers, were yelling and screaming at each other.

Then it hit me. I knew something terrible had happened. Someone once told me it's possible to will bad things into reality if you dwell on negative thoughts. I said a little prayer under my breath that this had nothing to do with my recent concerns. Disturbances like this were commonplace occurrences in Saigon. Billy had left the BOQ at least a quarter of an hour ago. Yet the evil bile had begun to rise in the pit of my stomach.

I dashed across the boulevard, almost colliding with a *cyclo* that clearly had the right of way. The lunatic crowd milled about in front of me, shouting in both Vietnamese and English. Obeying my instincts, I pushed through from the breech of the muddle, finding a slight seam between jostling bodies and clawing my way to the front.

Once there, my most fearful apprehensions were ripped asunder. I teetered at the edge of a pit of flesh and blood beyond my most appalling nightmare. Aghast in this spectral arena, it all unfolded like I'd been snared in a surreal slow-motion warp. It occurred to me that such a scene could only have emanated from the inferno of an irrational, irresponsible, and reprehensible war.

Amidst the debris of death a human body twitched in spasms on the pavement, drenched in its own scarlet sap. A gurgling of terminal mortal gasps could be heard. My only immediate identification was that it looked to be an American soldier, wearing the common camouflage fatigue uniform and boots. Though he lay on his back, he remained unrecognizable, rendered anonymous in that he no longer had a face.

The most individual distinguishable feature of his existence on earth had been literally blown away. In spite of my revulsion I persisted to hold my ground to try to determine the identity of the victim. A commanding voice advised everyone, in English, to, "Stand back! Stand back, everybody! Make room so the medics can get through here! Stand back!"

It was far too late for the medics. There was nothing they could do. There was nothing anyone could have done the instant this annihilation had been dealt.

Then the insignia caught my eye. Though part of it was swathed in raw tissue and blood, a portion of the silver wings showed on the left side of the uniform, positioned a few inches above the pocket—*Airborne.*

Looking across the body to the other side, I located the name tape. It was also covered with muscle pulp and soaked in the ebbing dark fluid of life. *Hold on. A bit of the first letter appears to be visible.* Pushing to my left for a better angle, I fought past some character intent on abiding his morbid fascination. I got close enough to make it out. *The letter "B." Barely distinguishable, but nonetheless a——. No. There's no closing loop at the bottom, as I'd hoped to see. It has to be an——. But wait. It could be a "P." It's only clear on the left side. The spreading stain makes it hard to tell.*

No. Viewing it objectively, it isn't a "P" either. Clearly, a black print line extends down from the lower right of the loop. It's an "R." No doubt about it. An "R."

My own blood curdled in my veins. *Billy. Billy Riggins. My roommate. My new buddy, my friend. Dying right here in this godforsaken alley, this worthless world of corruption and exploitation, filth and starvation, deadly desperation and everlasting hopelessness.*

A wave of sickness and loathing crashed over me. I could no longer control it. Pitching forward into the crowd, I felt myself being swallowed by the horror, colliding with arms and elbows, bellies and legs. They seemed to yield, leaving me without support, and I fell awkwardly to the curb. I vomited there, again and again. Then the shudders and dry heaves took over. They wracked my body and my spirit until I became immune to the pain. The siren wailed and the medics came and took him away. I remained there, still on my hands and knees, long after they'd gone.

CHAPTER 29

Although my mind didn't want to dwell on Billy's death, I had to know the details of that fateful morning. Captain Vogel at the PMO supplied me with all the reports, both MP and VNP.

The separate sets of investigation verified that Billy had been walking with a cluster of American officers up that street to the O-club, as they routinely did. Witnesses, both Vietnamese and American, reported a young couple on a motorbike pulled to a stop about twenty feet behind them. The passenger, a slight Vietnamese girl, dropped off the back of the cycle and ran toward the group. Closing the distance between them with a few quick steps, she pulled an Army issue .45 from her bag. Holding it out in front of her in both hands, her arms extended and locked at the elbows, she aimed the pistol at the soldiers. She fired a round at the middle of the assemblage, falling to the street with the recoil of the weapon.

One American also dropped to the ground. As the remainder of the party dispersed up the street, the girl marched up to the fallen soldier, now writhing on the callous pavement, bleeding profusely. Standing over him, she lifted the heavy pistol once again, pointing it at the wounded man beneath her. She shot him in the head, stumbling backwards with the repercussion of the gun. The male accomplice pulled alongside the girl with his motorcycle as she replaced the weapon in her bag. She remounted behind the driver. They proceeded past the body and on up the street, making the first left turn onto another side street and disappearing into the city.

I received a follow-up telephone call from Vogel. "Howdy, Bender. Here's the poop on your late bunkmate. The *canh sats* have arrested some kid and his girlfriend. Claim they're VC. Charged them with the Riggins homicide. Apparently they've been trying to get the goods on these two for some time. The scuttlebutt is they fixed the evidence to fit their purposes. Par for the course with these guys."

"Thanks for the update there, Derek. Appreciate the call."

Hanging up the phone, I felt sick with the hollow justice. I would imagine, guilty or innocent, a Vietnamese son and daughter will be spending the rest of their lives in prison for Billy's murder. If not subjected to a firing squad.

In my final two weeks of military service I didn't conduct myself much like the *short timers* I remembered in Germany, and at Fort Gordon and Fort Lewis, out celebrating every night till their obligation had been completed. To the contrary, I practically went into seclusion after Billy's death. My short time seemed like "long time," with the hands on the clock somehow shifted to low gear. I made sure I had a jeep every day to transport myself, in variegated routes, between my two destinations of battalion and BOQ. I dusted off my flak jacket, and made sure I wore it when I drove. If not for the verbal abuse I'd have gotten, I think I would've worn it all the time.

My room at the BOQ became a place of unnerving shadows and whispers. Attempting to cope, I smoked up the rest of our stash. But I'm not sure if the escape helped or hindered. The ghost of Billy remained. I heard him on many occasions, the familiar sounds you get to know and expect from someone you routinely come home to. The breathing of deep sleep and the shifting body in the middle of the night. I turned the light on a couple of times. His bed was empty. The murmur of expressions he loved to use, the humming of favorite songs in the shower or during his nightly shave. I darted into the bathroom once to catch the singer. No one there. On another occasion, as the darkness merged toward early morning light, I opened my eyes to the spot where he had slept. I thought I saw a form under the covers. At the crack of dawn it became clear the bed remained tightly made, in accordance with strict military standard.

I attempted to change rooms, but no others were available.

When the sun gave way to the nightly light show on the roof, I found I could not bring myself to go up there anymore.

The joy of flying *Pan American* back to the States became tempered by yet another in transit special assignment, as Uncle Sam drained the last ounce of patriotic duty out of me. I again got put in charge of security for the military passengers and cargo, this time aboard an airplane.

As we rose up above Vietnam I pulled out my map of that wretched land, looking down from my window to see if I could identify actual geography. Eventually we ascended to an altitude above the clouds. But I made a startling discovery looking at that map. If you held it sideways, with the west on top, the country had the shape of a bamboo pole—slender in the middle, with expanded protuberances of land, like rice baskets, dangling at either end. As I thought about that, I realized the country required the basket on the right, that of Communist Hanoi and North Vietnam, in order for it to have balance.

The airplane touched down to refuel in Tokyo. Then, for some unknown reason, another pit stop at Elmendorf Air Force Base, outside Anchorage, Alaska. We all froze our butts off hustling from the plane to the snack bar in our jungle fatigues. My two assigned security guards had a worse case of the shivers when we returned, having to stay with the cargo out on that cold tarmac.

On 19 May 1967, I became a civilian once again. I signed all the papers and happily accepted a Treasury check for $7,863.41, which represented the extent of my accrued Army savings and other entitlements. The government then picked up the tab to seat me on another commercial flight out of Oakland. I hopped a ride up to Seattle, to reclaim my mothballed Austin-Healey, looking to put the past year behind me, and determined to get on with my life.

CHAPTER 30

. . . with violins and the voices of Buffalo Springfield . . .

The vast atmospheric change from war weary, unscrupulous Saigon to energetic, idealistic San Francisco was mind-blowing.

Not to mention the pervasive hippie culture, with all its ramifications in art, music, clothing and lifestyle that engulfed the entire city. I found myself caught up in the outward manifestations of the new flower power society, with its free spirit, eccentric clothing and long hair.

A creative psychedelic music that had become popular while I played my Army games epitomized the cultic vogue. Along with the tapestried revival of art deco furnishings, textured fabrics and avant-garde poster craftwork found everywhere. The city basked in its vibrancy and mirth, an entrancing antithesis to the place I'd been fortunate enough to leave behind. I triumphed in the simple pleasure of being able to immerse myself in the mass loitering taking place daily in the streets and parks, and the nightly intemperance that inspired the crowded watering holes. It seemed as though I'd risen from the soul consuming flames of Hell to the sublime influence of a heavenly firmament.

I'd just visited suburban Sausalito for the first time. Toured the trendy gilt-edged shops and bars, grabbed a lunch of fish and chips at a little takeout place. The food tasted good. I enjoyed it while I sat on a pier in the marina, gazing across San Francisco Bay at the impressive skyline of the city. The famous Golden Gate Bridge framed my view on the right. With no schedule to keep, I'd decided to motor back to my apartment and change clothes. Then continue the search for my favorite neighborhood tavern.

On the road out of town I happened upon a longhaired youth, hitchhiking. His cascading primrose locks pranced in the warm sea breezes. The hair gave him the appearance of a high fashion model of the opposite sex. He wore a flowery long sleeve shirt, open to his navel, exposing a raft of artsy bead necklaces. A handsome leather belt with a large brass buckle held up faded bell-bottom jeans with paisley knee patches. He was barefoot.

"Where you headed?" I asked, after he caught up to my car at the edge of the road.

"San Francisco, man!" he smiled eagerly. "If you're going anywhere over the bridge, that'll be cool." He hitched his rucksack over his shoulders in anticipation of contracting the ride.

"Hop in," I said, hoping I came across casual and cosmopolitan, a regular guy.

"Bitchin'. Thanks a lot!"

After he'd seated himself, backpack between his knees, I vainly gave him a taste of the power of the Austin-Healey's first and second gears. Short of dropping rubber, of course, which every good Jersey lad knows is a sign of immaturity.

"Wow! Riding shotgun in one primo sports car," he yelled, displaying unrestrained appreciation. "What a beauty. So what'll she do? Have you ever had the chance to just let her out? On the open road, I mean."

"Oh yeah."

I felt just lonely enough to take the bait for the brag. "I got her when I was over in Germany. No speed limits on the autobahns, so you can really check out your car's capabilities. Fact is, she's beyond the speedometer. Well, a friend and I had access to the radar equipment the cops use, you know? So we tested each other's wheels. He actually clocked me at 139 miles an hour. And she could've done more. I wanted to keep accelerating. But then there were a couple trucks up ahead on a hill. I didn't want to chance it."

"Far out. Jeez, that's really fast," he exclaimed. "I wish I had the bread to buy one. Oh yeah, the name's Justin. And thanks again for the lift."

"No sweat," I replied, trying to sound equally cool.

Before we even reached the bridge Justin struck a deal with me. He created things out of leather, like the belts, barrettes and wristbands that had become popular with the new generation. He convinced me the car's interior needed his special leather conditioning treatment. We traded his expertise for a ride to his parents' house, somewhere out in the foggy western shoreline district, south of Golden Gate Park.

Even on this gorgeous day, mist blanketed the neighborhood. While he worked on my upholstery we continued to talk. As our conversation developed, it registered that while he applied elbow grease to my car's leather, we were also buffing the luster of an emerging friendship. He educated me on San Francisco and the hippie lifestyle of its younger population. Many arrived as transient runaways and vagabonds. Perhaps escaping some dramatic past, but epidemically drawn by the communal spirit and adventurous pilgrimage of the calling. He declared he'd just turned 19 himself. Yet we shared many common interests—cars and music and good times. I soon felt like I'd known him longer than our short ride from Sausalito. When he finished his work, as I sat back in my car extolling the supple leather, he made me another offer I couldn't refuse.

"Say, man. I'll bet you haven't even been to the Fillmore yet. How about you join me and my friends next Friday night. There's going to be a super concert there. A real happening. You'll dig the sounds. And the vibes."

Excitement stirred within me. "All right . . . man. I'd love to go."

"Here's my card. Give me a call during the week. We'll make arrangements. I'll get you your ticket, so you won't have a hassle with that."

"Thanks. Well, talk to you later then."

"Peace."

On the way to my place, I checked out his business card. Besides his phone number, it simply stated: *justin leather san francisco.* I didn't catch his crafty play on words until long afterwards.

I'd found a studio apartment that cost more than I'd expected to pay, but a bargain by the going rates. I considered myself lucky to have been synchronized with the previous tenants' final failure to pay their rent on time. The landlord, with what appeared to be his bodyguard and enforcer, met me there as they ushered the young kids from the premises. The only happy face was mine.

Though I'd taken up residence in the desirable North Beach area, my clapboard building stood inconspicuously within the bohemian neighborhood that fringed Grant Avenue, bordering on the carnal sleaze of tacky Broadway. In fact, I had a bird's-eye view of that boulevard's flashing neon lights advertising various strip clubs, dirty magazine stores and X-rated movie houses from the window of my tiny kitchenette. My only concern came with the realization I'd have to find outside parking for the Austin-Healey on the steep curbsides of Vallejo or other surrounding streets. As far as Mom and Dad needed to know, their son resided on Telegraph Hill. In the shadow of historic Coit Tower. Overlooking San Francisco Bay. Impressive.

North Beach turned out to be the ideal location for me, however, to escape the trauma of my recent past and venture forth into a brave new world.

Zesty Italian restaurants abounded. Authentic Asian places as well, in nearby Chinatown. I discovered La Pantera early on. I not only enjoyed the food, served family style with a gusto that matched everyone's ravenous palates, but the opportunity it afforded to meet people, both tourists and locals. The procedure they employed seated people from the bar when they accumulated a full table, ten or twelve diners. On many occasions I would paint the town from there, with whomever I'd gotten most acquainted. In most of these instances, the many bars and coffee houses up and down Grant and other neighboring streets provided the social outlets. They also became my temples of salvation from the demons that had trailed me home from across the sea.

Justin and I hooked up on the phone to arrange the Fillmore date. I arrived at his house right on time. Then sat on the couch in the living room for the next hour or so while his outrageous friends straggled in and out.

Their interactive jive had me wondering if I'd landed on another planet. "Outta sight! Look at the groovy threads hanging off you, fool. Hey, give me some skin on your way in. Justin's still doing his thing, so plenty o' time before we cut out."

"Right on, freak. Better believe I was hauling ass to make it here before you-all split. Got a woody just thinking about the heavy sounds going down tonight."

Though all males, they'd grown long hair, down to their shoulders and beyond, some pulled back into ponytails. A few wrapped crazily patterned bandanas around their heads. Like the older beatniks and artists of North Beach, they wore tattered and faded bell-bottom jeans, repaired at the knee and butt with colorful patches, predominately paisley. They scuffed the floor in sandals, cowboy boots or moccasins.

If they had belts they looked handmade, like Justin's, with large, festooned brass buckles. Most of them fastened their belts at the side, toward the hip, rather than aligned over the fly, a strict standard of military convention I continued to adhere to. A few fellows chose to use colorful kerchiefs threaded through the belt loops, again knotted to the side rather than in front. They wore either buttoned shirts with long, draped sleeves, or eye-catching tie-dyed T-shirts; two of them layered Western-style leather vests on top.

A mingling of costume or semi-precious jewelry, most often turquoise, finalized the fashion ensembles. Necklaces, bracelets, rings and earrings combined beads, leather, silver, and stones in the most garish displays. I glanced at my sedate sapphire ring, longing for my soul brother, Lenny. It made me feel a little better that I at least exhibited some silver myself, perhaps my only point in concert. Looking back on it now, I can understand why those boys shied away from me, with my chino pants and rayon shirt from the Army PX.

Quite a few of them had tattoos, prominently exposed, adding the final touch of rebellion. In essence, they looked like a band of pirates marauding through an insecure urban home.

Once again, I didn't see Justin's parents anywhere. And I couldn't figure out what was going on at first. Kids tramped in and out of the house and his bedroom, constantly utilizing the bathrooms as well, while it seemed he lollygagged getting himself ready. Psychedelic music blasted from his room. The TV attempted to counter in the living room, I guess for my amusement. *What could possibly be taking him so long?*

Then I smelled it. The distinct fragrance of pot or hash reached my nostrils from maybe his room, the bathrooms, or both. Over the noise of the stereo and television, I heard the whispers and muffled voices and suppressed laughter.

Those little pricks. They're doing drugs. And they're not inviting me to join them. How rude. And what the fuck is wrong with you . . . dude. If you want some, go on inside and join them.

Somehow I couldn't do it. I felt glued to the couch.

At this point I took stock of myself. My hair, my clothes, my—age. I understood. If I'd been them, I wouldn't even have had me around, sitting right there in the living room. They must've all been asking Justin who the hell I was, what I was doing there. I had to have made them all real nervous. Later I would understand the paranoia, and wicked thrill, of procuring and doing illegal drugs in our free society.

"I got to tell you, Justin, this place is really something else. In all my travels, I've never seen anything quite like it. Thanks for the invite."

At long last I got one-on-one with him, inside the Fillmore Auditorium. His friends gallivanted all over the place, buying apples, chocolate chip cookies and other munchies, socializing and raising Cain with anybody and everybody. They came and they went, but always seemed to know where to find Justin. The roadies labored at setting the stage for the second band of the evening. My ears perked to the sound of exotic voices backed by the likes of mandolin, sitar and kazoo. Some weird, ethereal, nevertheless catchy medieval folk music flitted with breezy abandon from the speaker system.

"Say, what is that witchcraft they're playing, anyway? I kind of like it."

He looked at me with a knowing smile. The whites of his eyes had turned to red, his pupils dilated.

"Yeah . . . man. That's the Incredible String Band. But you haven't seen or heard nothing yet. Just wait till Blue Cheer cranks up."

He strolled away from me toward a young brunette with shiny hair flowing down to her thighs. She'd squeezed into a long tan calico dress, cinched at the waist with a beaded Indian belt. Turquoise gleamed from the anklet above her left moccasin. A flower replaced the feather I expected to see in her hair. She threw her arms around Justin's neck, pulling herself up to his face, kissing him and whispering in his ear. I resumed my tour of the concert hall on my own.

The Fillmore looked to have been an old movie theater. It had been redesigned by a fellow named Bill Graham, a European immigrant now making quite a reputation for himself putting together rock 'n' roll shows, akin to Alan Freed of the previous decade. Unearthing an acorn from my three credits of architecture at Cornell, I realized the structure must've been built back in the twenties or thirties. It flourished the geometric forms and profuse, elaborate garnitures of that art deco period. The high dome ceiling and tall doorways soared in elegant arches. Ornate chandeliers hovered from aloft.

The main floor seating had been removed. Only the balconies continued to offer traditional viewing rows. This provided space for dancing and the freedom of movement and interaction so essential to the full enjoyment of the music and the hippie lifestyle. Bulky stuffed chairs and couches gave the snack bar, lounge and lobby areas a sense and feel of comfort and relaxation. The products offered at the concession counters, apart from the chocolate chip cookies and various chocolate bars, featured more health oriented foods and juice beverages. I didn't see the popcorn, candies, soda pop or assorted junk foods usually found at entertainment refreshment areas.

The human presence, with its fashion and artful ambition, reinforced and further embellished the mood and tone established by the architecture and décor. Beyond the ornamental aura provided by the hippie garb, the audience engaged itself in an assortment of activities. People throughout the place applied phosphorescent body paint on each other. They bedaubed faces, hands, feet, arms and legs, and any other exposed skin, with flamboyant creations. If not inspirational in their invention or originality, they at least contributed to the spirit of participation. "Artistes" in the auditorium got down on their hands and knees, continuing to chalk illustrations on the floor while dancers exulted in freestyle footwork around the graphic salutations.

Blue Cheer didn't please me when they started noisily warming up over the pastoral Elizabethan strains of the Incredible String Band recording. I never did acclimate to their reckless rock 'n' roll mentality. But in spite of my clear head, I'm certain I had to be the only person there totally sober, the technical production that accompanied and supported the band impressed and amazed me. It lent a whole new dimension to the influential dominion of music.

I don't know if Bill Graham deserves credit for the innovation, but his show elevated the new sounds to visual and sensory heights I'd never imagined. Besides the freakout flashing strobe lights, screens had been set up behind and adjacent to the stage for the presentation of film and closed circuit camera coverage of the performers. The crew also employed some technique of projecting psychedelic images in the manner of bubbling, pulsating colored liquids, cyclopian amoebas constantly changing shape and structure. This drug enhancing light show didn't restrict itself to just the fixed screens. The percolators of impressions and color cast illusions across walls and ceiling for an ambient, cosmic effect.

The film pieces themselves crackled as a photomontage of eclectic scenes and actions, sometimes cross-referencing one another on separate screens. Projectors rolled black-and-white representations of comedy routines by the Marx Brothers, Laurel and Hardy and the Three Stooges. Namby-pamby color clips exposed Doris Day and Rock Hudson cavorting in a frilly pink bedroom. Melodramatic pictures exploited the vicarious stimulation of James Dean bailing out of his hotrod just seconds before it plummets over the cliff.

Much of the visuals focused on political issues of the times, subjects of concern that formed the bedrock of the many protest marches and rallies that were widening the rift between the government and older and younger generations. An old news flash showed Adolf Hitler extending his *Sieg Heil* salute in front of a giant draped swastika, superimposed over his goose-stepping Nazi troopers. This intersected with shots of President Lyndon Johnson pontificating about our courageous war efforts in Southeast Asia while Vietnamese women and children race in terror from their napalmed village. These films had a powerful impact observed in conjunction with the angry beat and psychotic guitars of Blue Cheer.

During the break I tracked Justin down, attempting to pawn his over-eager Indian princess with a couple of stoned friends. I waited for a pause in their interplay before jumping in.

"Think I'm going to head out, Justin. Just wanted to thank you—"

"Robbie! Where've you been, man?"

". . . thanks again for letting me join you and the gang. I had a great time. Really enjoyed the light show. Guess I'll see you around."

"Hey! You can't leave now. You've got to at least stay for a toke of this next group, man. That's what we're all here for."

Unaccustomed to being the sole stone-cold sober one in a social setting, I had had my fill of incessant, high energy psychedelic rock, without variation or change of pace. I had my mind set on a strong Jack and soda at my latest bar discovery, the Coffee Gallery on Grant Avenue, in my new neighborhood.

"Yeah, I'm out of here. It's getting past my bedtime."

"What do you mean, man? It's only 10:30. You can't be serious. Look, just at least stay and see what you think about these cats. Get your money's worth, man."

"Jeez, I don't know . . . ."

If he had offered me some of that smoke they'd been doing, I'm sure I would've been in a different frame of mind. Right now I just needed a good old shot of whiskey.

"Who are they, anyway? Have I ever heard of 'em?"

He looked at me with a quizzical expression. "Hey, I don't know who you ever heard of. They're called Big Brother. Big Brother and the Holding Company, actually. Look. Stay for a couple numbers. See what you think. If you don't dig it, you leave.

Simple as that. I'd just feel bummed if I didn't, like, clue you in you might be missing something cool. Know what I mean?"

"All right. I'll stay for a couple numbers."

After tuning up for what seemed like an interminable amount of time, Big Brother and the Holding Company kicked into some blues tinged rock 'n' roll. They sounded okay, but I'd heard better. After the "required" two selections, I again had the itch to leave.

The moment I turned to find Justin to say goodnight, a loud cheer rose up from the audience. I turned back toward the performers. A girl with wild hair halfway down her back bounded across the stage. She brusquely grabbed hold of the center microphone, adjusting it to her satisfaction. She'd dressed all in black, wearing the widest pleated bell-bottoms I'd ever beheld, and a fringed jacket with the longest sleeve tassels I'd ever seen. Only the scintillant beads dangling from neck to waist, and the red workman's bandana tied around her head, broke the ebony image. She leaned into the microphone, caressing it as she took it into her jeweled hands. Drawing it to her mouth, she parted her pearly lips.

The Coffee Gallery had closed its doors by the time I returned to North Beach. I hoped I might find some Jack back at my apartment. I needed a good belt. What I'd seen and heard at the Fillmore will be etched forever in my mind. For over two hours I'd been entranced by the most tormented, raw blues singing I'd ever witnessed. It didn't matter that I hadn't had a drink or a drug. The voice intoxicated me all by itself, lifting me up to the psychedelic ceiling. My life most certainly had been changed. I'd just been introduced to Janis Joplin.

CHAPTER 31

Getting started in my life's career didn't come as easy as I'd thought. Not that I had ever organized any kind of viable plan, or had any definitive goals in place.

A couple of companies that interviewed me on campus my senior year had left the door open for the possibility of a job after my Army obligation. Unfortunately, they must've been East coast businesses. I couldn't find any office listings in the Bay Area. The classified ads in the *San Francisco Chronicle*, and the possibility of a position there as an intern, no doubt fetching coffee for the journalists, didn't whet my vocational appetite. Not really knowing what to look for, I couldn't identify those so-called blue-chip companies who might be seeking Ivy League graduates with a liberal arts degree and military combat command experience. The few interviews I did succeed in setting up, with companies I'd never heard of, turned out to be thirty-minute dead-end streets with no reciprocal interest.

Frustrated after one abrupt, fallow interview, I seized the moment to try to catch up with Justin. I picked up the phone. After seven rings I was about to hang up when a drowsy voice answered.

"Yeah . . . hello?"

"Justin? Is that you?"

A long silence. Then, "Who is this?"

"This is Robbie. Robbie Bender. Remember? I gave you a ride home from Sausalito?"

Another pause. "Oh, yeah. Robbie. Hey! How's it groovin', man? Hope you didn't split while we were all trippin' out on Big Brother at the Fillmore. Missed you at the end there."

"Right. I couldn't find you, so I just made it back to my pad and crashed." I prided myself on my progress with the latest youth jargon.

"Thanks for putting the screws to me . . . making me stay for that last set. Jesus, that Janis Joplin is the most incredible chick singer ever. What a voice. Say, Justin, you going to be around for a little while? Got something I need to discuss with you. Thought maybe I'd stop by."

"No problem, man. Motor on over. My mother's at work, so we've got the whole place for a few hours. I'll play you a couple albums and clue you in on some other cool groups doing some pretty heavy sounds. Ever hear the Doors?"

I hesitated. I had dialed into KMPX, the "underground" FM rock station in town. The name sounded familiar, though I couldn't be positive. Oh, so much to catch up on.

"I don't know, man. Give me a listen. I'll be there in about an hour, okay?"

The hefty beat of Justin's stereo resonated all the way across the street as I parked at the curb. Sitting there for a moment, I wondered what his mom was like, where his dad might be. How they got along with each other, and their neighbors. A warning flash in my brain reminded me of our time constraints. Checking my watch, I realized I'd lost a half-hour at the bank making sure I'd brought enough cash with me. I got out of the car and loped the distance to his front door.

Minutes later Justin and I sat on his bedroom floor, listening to Jim Morrison and the Doors doing "Light My Fire." Like Joplin, Morrison had a marvelous voice, dissimilar from her raspy manna-from-the-soul in that he possessed a true balladeer's romantic tonality. But his delivery incarnated a soothsayer intonation of evil and danger, lurking in the incense of jaded debauchery.

The Doors sounded tighter and cleaner than Big Brother. They ratcheted my excitement up another few notches. I felt electrified by the prodigious strides evident in the new rock 'n' roll's fresh, creative maturity. I picked up their album a few days later, from the cashier's rack in a neighborhood grocery store.

After we compared notes and both gave the Doors rave reviews, Justin spun another of his platter acquisitions. In deference to my expressed intention to discuss something personal with him, he played a softer, folk-like compilation performed by a robust voice named Richie Havens. I wasn't sure how I should broach the sensitive subject. Sensing our friendship bonding with the music, and not knowing how much time I had before his mother came home, I decided to just go ahead. Get right to the point.

"Justin. I guess we've gotten to know each other real well in a short period of time. It's hard to believe just a couple weeks ago I picked you up hitching over in Sausalito. Anyway, I know you're a person I can trust with a private matter. And, well, you're also a guy who's into a lot of different shit. Not afraid to experiment, if you know what I mean. And you've got a lot of . . . connections.

"So, you see, when I was over in—" Suddenly the rancid taste of poverty and pestilence in a single swallow. My throat started closing up on me. ". . . Vietnam . . . well, there wasn't a whole lot to do. Beyond the obsession with the war. I had this roommate—"

Like the burst from a Colt .45 at close range, the memory of Billy Riggins' last day on earth plunged headfirst into my consciousness. The racket in the alley, shouts in Vietnamese and English. Fighting my way through the broiling crowd. Then the blood. Oh, the blood. Everywhere. The ruptured flesh where a buddy's face should've been. My eyes submerged into the drowning pool of abomination and grief all over again. I could do nothing about it. As I lowered my head I felt Justin's arm around my shoulders. His soothing voice tiptoed in my ear . . . .

My hands continued to shake as I drove back to North Beach. I hadn't expected that to happen. Hadn't even thought about the war when I prepared the solicitation in my mind. I thought I had put that grisly morning behind me. Obviously it still lingered there, languishing deep down in the back edge of my brain. It would probably always be there. For the rest of my life.

Back into the safety of my apartment, I surveyed the studio for possible hiding places. After seeing my landlord and his bruiser in action with the previous tenants, I understood I had to be extremely careful. Even in highflying San Francisco, the law is the law. I'd already been keeping an eye on the exact location of my personal things, to be aware of any surreptitious entry while I was away. When I stood before the distressed walnut armoire, I knew I had the answer.

I just needed to go down to the corner store for a roll of masking tape.

San Francisco represented a true slice of paradise after all I'd gone through in Saigon. I loved having my Austin-Healey back, being able to tool around North Beach and the city, drive out to Sausalito or Tiburon. I found contentment hanging out at the Coffee Gallery and relished the wonder of having discovered Janis and psychedelia at the Fillmore. I felt nourished in the simple joy of just having my own place, with its unique view of nasty, neon Broadway. Privileged to listen to the revolutionary new music on my long lost stereo. It had become a heady, inspirational period of transition. Unlike those sorry souls back in Vietnam, it seemed I'd received the blessing of liberation at last.

So, walking down Van Ness Avenue that sunny day to grab a hamburger at the Hippopotamus, I probably had a happy-go-lucky smile on my face. Until the detonations exploded in my ears.

I hit the sidewalk hard and fast, my arms up over my head to protect me from flying shrapnel, shaking and quivering with sparking nerves. In an instant my body heat skyrocketed with the adrenaline rush, my heart pounded like a bongo drum inside my chest, and I felt slick with sweat. Lifting my eyes from the concrete, I saw the black car reeling and rocking as the bullets perforated its metal shell, the Vietnamese lieutenant lying still in a fetal position beneath the steering wheel. Another blast propelled shredded American soldiers across the pavement, and I recognized the twisted smoldering bicycle there at the bus stop. Vomit surged to my throat as I confronted my faceless friend once again, shuddering in his final death throes in that crimson passageway.

Then I heard the laughter.

A little boy's voice cried out. "Look, mommy, that funny man is pretending he was shot!"

Now some older boys' taunting shouts, "Hey, man. What've you been shooting up?"

"Better to shoot up than be shot at, right?"

"Yeah, get up, you asshole. This ain't Vietnam."

As I picked myself back up off the ground, it suddenly dawned on me. It was the fourth of July.

CHAPTER 32

Peace-symboled Haight-Ashbury received more publicity in the sixties, of course, than any other district of the city. Located by the greenbelt area aptly named the Panhandle, bordering the east side of Golden Gate Park, it attracted young hippies, starry-eyed flower children, musicians and artists, Hell's Angels, drug dealers and hustlers, beggars and deadbeats. All there to celebrate their blessed congregation.

In 1967 it achieved its zenith in terms of both social excitement and economic productivity. Though many penniless loiterers cluttered the streets, masses of solvent young people convened there as well, from all walks of life and far-flung parts of the country. The shops, restaurants and bars overflowed their capacities as cash registers jingled with the joy of business enterprise.

Haight Street, from Masonic to the park, pulsated as the mainline vein of commerce. Almost every block afforded establishments selling food, booze, clothing, amusements and interior decorations. Like the head shops offering any kind of drug paraphernalia imaginable, from Zig Zag cigarette rolling paper to the hookahs referenced in the local Jefferson Airplane's national hit, "White Rabbit," the majority of products and services explicitly targeted this psychedelic counterculture.

Record stores not only enticed customers inside with the latest mind-bending stereo sounds on vinyl disc, but emblazoned windows and walls with an array of hallucinatory pop art posters,

available for purchase from swinging display racks. Clothing outlets specialized in all the hippie garments and freaky fad accou-
trements, featuring not only basic bell-bottom pants and jeans,
but wide-brimmed feathered felt hats, wire framed granny glasses,
fringed buckskin boots and jackets, and old-fashioned full-length
dresses, often velvet or cotton print. Besides clothing, endless selections of "antique" costume jewelry glittered behind glass counters
and curio cabinets. Food outlets and dining places joined in the
bustle, merchandising all kinds of chocolate goodies, fruit tarts,
and other gooey dessert items to gratify insatiable drug enhanced
appetites.

I dropped in on this neighborhood often, usually on the weekends in conjunction with some happening in one of the parks, either Golden Gate or Buena Vista. For the most part, however, I
channeled the development of my new life within the North Beach
area, spending a fair amount of time on Grant Avenue and nearby
Washington Square. While I continued to peruse the newspaper
for job opportunities, when necessary dressing up for an unproductive interview, I became increasingly content with the casual
bohemian way of life that surrounded me. Yearning for acceptance
into their artistic community, I spurned the pressurized, ambitious
urgency and organization of the straight-arrow corporate world.
I let my hair grow long. I bought bell-bottoms and moccasins.
A short denim jacket. And I lived off the balance of my waning
military monies.

If I entertained egoistic moments where I thought, as a result
of my accomplishments, world travels and experiences, that I possessed savvy, wisdom, or status advantages over my peers and the
public at large, North Beach quickly dispelled those notions. Like
the incident early on at my favorite bar, the Coffee Gallery.

"Hey, man, this the first time you worn that there jacket out
of the house? I didn't know Levi made denim that dark. Better be
careful. 'Sides fading it out, you just might get yourself some trail
dirt on it, too, out here in the great wild West."

My antagonist personified the epitome of the immaculate hippie, from his weathered and scrupulously shaped cowboy hat brandishing the arched feather in front, to the cracked, pointed metal-toe lizard skin boots. A long, braided ponytail hung down the middle of his back, from underneath his hat. Two silver earrings dangled from his left earlobe. He sported a thicket of mustache waxed into delicate twines at the ends. His ridiculing sneer revealed itself only in the creases in his cheeks, crow's-feet wrinkles at the eyes, and the widening spread of the upper lip hair that curtained his crude mouth. A leather-sheathed chain with a peace sign medallion adorned the neckline of his tie-dyed shirt. He wore more silver on his wrists and fingers, garnished with turquoise. Ragged, patched and sun-bleached bell-bottoms decorated his body below the waist.

"And, man, you sure got your legs poked into some stiff new jeans there. Next thing you know, you'll be needing some knee patches, hee, hee, hee. Naw, more than likely a butt patch, from squatting your ass on one too many barstools. She-i-i-t!"

On the surface, this wrangler looked to be an icon of the idealistic beautiful people, those who espoused love and the gracious tolerance and treatment of all mankind. Reacting within the reality of the moment, I considered he was nothing more than a mirror of the snobbery and prejudice he condemned in stereotypic right wing, conservative society.

Grabbing my drink, I moved my square ass over to the jukebox. I figured the time was right to revisit the choice music this player offered. The owner, or someone in the know, had it well stocked with Dylan and other artists regarded as forerunners and flag bearers of the new culture. I ignored the stoned gaze of my adversary as I stuck a quarter in the box, punching the buttons for Tim Hardin's "You Upset the Grace of Living." While I'd just gotten into the singer and didn't know the tune, the title seemed apropos.

You might say I still had more to learn from another of Mom's tried and true maxims, not to ever "judge a book by its cover." Like the straight world, the cool hippie community had its own frauds and fakers, egotists and elitists, deceivers and dictators. As much as governments, armies, churches and peoples try to make it a black-and-white proposition, good versus evil, the righteous and the criminal, justice or vengeance, it's never that simple. Like Saigon, nothing was absolute in San Francisco either, as to who truly manifested friend or foe, sage or hypocrite, saint or infidel.

Yes, I coveted the pageantry of the hip bohemian lifestyle. Pressed the inspiration of the creative new music close to my breast. The fundamental ideology of a free society served as motivation for me. Yet, as much as I came to believe in the spirit of the peace movement, especially after my inside knowledge of the corruption, deception and obscenity of the Vietnam War, there also existed a tacit awareness that it too was tainted by the universal schizophrenia of the human factor. It didn't matter if the world wore suits and ties, robes and crowns, bell-bottoms or sandals. The common denominator remained basic human nature, with all its foibles, pettiness and self-delusion. There are good people and bad people, with most of us somewhere in between. That's just the way it is. And always will be.

The ambassador of Peace was back in my face. "You know, man, if I were to guess, I'd bet you were one of those killers over in Vietnam. Shooting up those poor Commie freedom fighters in their rice paddies. Booby-trapping their villages. Burning down their little thatched huts. Am I right?"

"What makes you say that?"

"Oh, you just got that there look about you. Kind of the stiff, pompous way you carry yourself. Like some general shoved his fucking swagger stick right up your fucking ass!"

It surprised me that this self-appointed merchant of love knew anything about swagger sticks. I guessed he had had some kind of contact with the military somewhere along the line. I'd had enough of his shit, though.

"Why don't you sit back down on your barstool over there. Enjoy your drunken stupor. Before you get yourself in trouble."

"Son of a bitch. Listen to this goddam' hard-ass. Why don't you just take a goddam' hike, soldier boy! Hike your fucking ass right the hell out of here! You don't belong in here with us peace-loving folk. Motherfucker killer man!"

The rage in his eyes startled me. Nausea began a slow creep inside my gut. It flashed in my mind that my final wrestling match and my last street fight had both occurred before my sophomore year in college, almost a decade past. I'd won my scholastic competition against Penn State with a third period takedown, but lost the brawl outside the bar with thug Hank Nolan. Hopefully someone would blow the whistle before this one got any further.

Two other hippies joined the confrontation.

"Come on, Lowell. Sit yourself back down before they kick your butt out of here. Leave the cat alone."

The second one looked me in the eye. "Sorry 'bout that, mister. Lowell gets a little carried away sometimes. He lost his brother in Vietnam."

My saviors maneuvered Lowell away from me, a spate of F-words accenting the blue streak of expletives he left in his wake.

A short while later I drained my glass. I left the Coffee Gallery early that night. Never did get to hear Tim Hardin sing me my quarter's worth on the jukebox.

Thankfully, that happened to be my most disturbing encounter in all the many hours I hung out at "The Gallery." At the same time, I understood that popular opinion within its walls, like that of the majority of the city, leaned firmly pacifist, opposed to the war in Vietnam. For the sake of my own peace and self-preservation I maintained a low profile regards my veteran status. Only if cornered and hard pressed would I admit I'd soldiered in such a deplorable military enterprise. The feeling I should somehow be apologetic for my participation, and the fact not one person has ever thanked me for serving my country in combat, still festers, a canker sore in my psyche.

Despite the wonderful times I spent at the Gallery I remained pretty much a loner, never able to get accepted into any of the cliques that frequented the joint. Nonetheless, I found myself satisfied just playing my fringe role at the bar, enjoying the music, the action around me, the color slides the bartender screened over the chess table by the front window. These picture presentations, most of them donated by patrons, contributed a neighborly personality to the ambiance—amateur photos of private parties, festive be-ins at the various city parks, motorcycles and hotrods, scenes of folks just hanging out or goofing around, and other social occasions.

I'd take my drink into the tiny theater in the back, appreciating the many musicians and poets who performed their spacy creations with talent and imagination. Of course, the beat atmosphere made it a trip in itself, especially after priming myself with a reefer, or bowl of Justin's spellbinding hash.

After chickening out on many occasions, I packed up my cheap guitar and some songs I'd written during my meditative moments in Vietnam, stepping down the hill for one of the voluntary hootenanny nights held at the Gallery. I suppose I might've been looking to resurrect those old high school thrills when I'd sung with the Velvetones, a quartet of quixotic youths that had performed doo-wop at local sock hops, proms and bar mitzvahs. I sat in the back row of the theater for almost three hours, observing all the folkies and other amateur hopefuls doing their thing. There I procrastinated into my own pit of apprehension and intimidation before grabbing my guitar case and slinking out the door, my tail tucked between my legs.

CHAPTER 33

I felt her hand as it moved down across my abdomen, gliding lightly over my pubic hair, taking hold of me. I heard her voice and those amazing words once again. The words I knew I would never forget.

"My darling Robert Stephen. I love you. I've always loved you. I just never had the courage to tell you before.

"Let's do it. Let's make love. Let's make a beautiful baby. I know this sounds crazy, Robbie. But don't you see, this is our one chance. For our own special kind of ever-after."

Brrrrrnnnng!

Oh, my God, what is that? The jangling bell pierced through my surreal dreamscape, rudely intruding upon the waves of emotion I'd been riding. "Expecting to Fly" with violins and the voices of Buffalo Springfield, I'd hopped on a miracle back to Zina, to that grand old German hotel room in Nürnberg. We'd lain naked and feasting together, feeding each other in between tasty, slippery kisses. We'd floated in space on a cloud of love somewhere between the Oriental rug and the Baroque ceiling . . . .

Brrrrrnnnng!

I felt myself slipping from the consolation of her sanctuary. Then, all alone, crashing down, down—landing on my back, spread-eagle on the sparse carpet in my stingy studio, a reflection of neon flashing on the wall. *Oh Jesus, what a fall. I could've broke my neck from that height.*

Brrrrrnnnng!

Shit. It's the goddamn telephone. Who the hell could be calling at this hour of the night? I crawled over to the table and picked it up.

". . . Yes?"

"Robbie! You old son of a bitch. How the hell are you. Let's pa-a-a-arty!"

". . . Lenny? Is that you? Goddam' almighty. Like . . . where are you, man?"

"Frisco, pardner. You don't think I'd be asking you out long distance, do you? Get your buns down here! I'm buying, and I got more honeys than I can handle right now. There's a neat little chickie I want to introduce to you. Hair down to her ass. I know you like that long hair."

I could tell by his voice he'd already ventured a long way into the libations. He had his own quirky slur and spoke with the staccato speed of an automatic weapon when he got bombed. My reply misfired repeatedly, in striking contrast.

"Oh . . . okay, man. I . . . I'll be there. Oh, yeah, uh . . . tell me, uh . . . where you are. I can hear the jukebox . . . somewhere near you. But . . . uh . . . there's quite a few of them in town, you know."

"Damn tootin'. Well, I'm somewhere west of Union Square. Hey! Where are we? I don't even know the name of this slum-hole . . . ." His voice faded as he sought assistance from his acquaintances. I hung on, listening to a multitude of faraway voices and the static of a jouncing phone.

After a while he came back on the line, full tilt. "Jeez, no one knows the goddam' name of this place. The frigging inn keeper doesn't know his own name. So I sent your girlie outside. She says we're at the corners of . . . what is it? . . . Ellis and Jones. Christ, I can see another bar across the street, on the other corner. But that's it, pardner. If you don't find us in one, I guess we're in the other. Just get your buttocks down here! And that's an order, captain."

I felt the excitement of finally being back with my best buddy again. It had been much too long. Since our R&R together in

Bangkok. Lenny never got to meet my Army roommate, Billy. Nor did he know anything about my traumatic experience surrounding his murder. I needed to share that, to get my usual prescription of insight and inspiration from my confidant.

At the same time, tension gripped me as to where I had to go this night, to catch up with him. Although I'd descended a long way from my spaced-out euphoria when the telephone shattered my passion trip with Zina, I remained high from the hash I'd smoked. Innumerable cops patrolled that downtown area. I would also need to do some spur of the moment planning just to get there. I had to make certain I had enough money for a parking garage to house my Healey. Curbside spaces didn't really exist. The bar's crossroads placed it southwest of Union Square, in that questionable Tenderloin district, where pimps and their prostitutes, panhandlers and drug peddlers dealt with the fuzz and ruled the street corners. It would be difficult enough to navigate that neighborhood with a clear head, much less recovering from a few tokes of mind-expanding dope.

Halfway there it hit me that I should've taken a cab. Standard procedure after doing the pipe. As worried and paranoid as I got about all this, I made it to Ellis and Jones without incident. Sure enough, two ratty bars faced each other, catty-corner on the intersection. A few letters had burned out on one's neon sign; the other looked devoid of identification, probably too ashamed to bring attention to itself. It did take some doing to find a garage capable of handling my transient status at the midnight hour. Before too long Lenny and I were hugging, grinning and fooling with each other like village idiots once again.

He held me by the shoulders, sizing me up at arm's length.

"Holy crap. Just look at the hair and 'stache on you. My man's gone beatnik on me. How about that."

He turned toward his collection of characters. "Ladies . . . and gent." He nodded in deference to the grizzled, unshaven drunk in scruffy clothes who it seems had also garnered Lenny's fellowship.

"Allow me to introduce all of you to my very best friend on this entire lunatic planet of ours. This here's Robbie Bender. New Jersey wrestling champeen. Highfalutin Ivy League grad."

He went on. "An officer and a gentleman who fought for your freedom in Vietnam. Not that you'll ever go there. But anyway . . . raconteur, rabble-rouser, a full-fledged rapscallion. A pillar among men. Er, uh, a connoisseur of fine wine and wild-ass women!

"Folks, raise your glasses, your mugs, your plastic cups, whatever the hell you got there. To my long lost brother!"

Surveying the audience while Lenny spoke, I realized what a motley group of people they were. Haggard faces, greasy hair, vulgar and seedy clothes. I wondered how he had managed to assemble them all and keep them intact for any length of time. I guess free drinks are one way to unite the world. Outside of my old crony they amounted to a sleazy collection of human beings, fitting in perfectly with the shoddy establishment. It wouldn't have surprised me if a couple of the girls earned their livings as hookers.

The "neat little chickie with the long hair" startled me when she first looked in my direction. She not only displayed a beauty mark mole on her chin, complete with a protruding hair, but a nose that gave her face the impression of making a perpetual right turn. She may have been a nice person, beyond her crass language. But she still qualified as homely, in every scientific sense of that word.

Sipping on my fresh Jack, I soon became concerned with the deteriorating style of Lenny's socializing. After his toast on my behalf, he no longer exhibited his usual pungent sense of humor. If it was a consequence of his awareness of his present company, I also worried about the erosion in his taste and choice of comrades.

Due to the sorry circumstances, his drunken condition and my altered state of mind, we neglected to do our usual update on our lives. Nevertheless, since we had stayed in touch, I knew he'd also returned to civilian life, lived somewhere down in southern California, and flew for *Pan Am* out of LA. I suppose this qualified as the first of the post-soldier reunions we'd promised each other.

I did get to ask him when he had to leave "Frisco," as he referred to it.

"Early in the morning," he gibbered back at me. "Got a 0800, I think it is . . . to . . . let's see . . . Dallas. Then, on out to . . . 'Lanta. After that, maybe if I'm good, they'll let me go home."

I twitched from the shock. "Don't you need to be getting off the sauce then? I mean, what're the regulations about drinking and flying?"

He looked at me vacantly. A few seconds later he said, "Ohhhhhh, I guess it's twelve. Or is it twenty-four . . . hours before a flight? Maybe that's the Marines. Think it's twelve, actually. But nobody takes that shit seriously. Don't you worry none about me, brother. You know I'm always ready to do the job."

Now he leaned into my ear, his nose consorting with my lengthy locks. "And, you know, your hair really is getting mighty long, pardner. Not as long as that little chickie's over there, though. So, you going to take her back to your . . . pad . . . my beatnik brother? I detect she's hot to hook up with your jelly roll."

It seemed the time for truth was at hand. I didn't feel good about a lot of things going down at that moment. I took my turn at Lenny's ear.

"I got to be honest with you, Lenny. The girl's a skank, if you really want to know. I'd be scared to let her in my place. And I wouldn't be surprised they aren't all whores, anyway. Jeez, man, these people are bad news. Can't you see that? They're just taking you for the drinks. And whatever else you're buying."

My face felt like an arsonist had doused it with kerosene and flipped a match to it. "I hate to sound like my mother, but you need to be sobering up if you're flying in a couple hours. I don't know all those people who'll be riding in that plane with you. But I know you. And I sure don't want to be attending my best friend's funeral this early in my life."

Everyone's eyes were on us now. I'd tried to keep it down, but my frayed emotions had turned up the volume.

"I'm sorry, man," I said in a hushed voice. "I got to get out of here. To lay it on the line, I think you should, too."

Lenny continued to look straight at me, as if we were the only people there. He stiffened as I attempted to embrace him. I turned to go.

I heard his voice behind me. "Wait a minute. Let's talk about this." He followed me out the door.

The bartender gazed in our direction through the grimy window. I guess the pile of cash by Lenny's glass didn't quite cover the tab. The carnival crowd we'd just escaped stood right where we'd left them, transfixed as well. They gaped at us like stupefied ghouls freeze-framed in some horror movie.

Now it was Lenny's stage.

"Hey, you got a lot of nerve throwing stones at my house. You want to know what worries me? It's those druggy eyes popping out of my best friend's head, that's what. You don't think I can tell what you were doing before you came down here? You don't think I knew the second you picked up that phone?"

We stood almost nose to nose. I wouldn't have been surprised if my burning skin set him on fire.

"I don't know if you got yourself a full-scale addiction yet. But you're getting deeper into drugs, aren't you? You're going to fuck yourself up with that shit long before I crash any goddam' airplane. And if I ever do, you won't have a clue what the hell you're up to at my frigging funeral, anyway."

Suddenly I realized the bell had rung for round two of the disagreement we'd had in Thailand. When a scorching mad Lenny went touring on his own while the two R&R girls and I tripped on some native hash.

Taking a step back, I parried his emotional, naïve counter-thrust by commenting on that previous altercation.

"Look, man. We're right back to that stupid situation we had in Bangkok, aren't we? When you ditched the girls and me to join the tourists with their Hawaiian shirts and camera necklaces.

Posing with the Buddha statues and all that garbage. Just because we wanted to smoke a little hash.

"You know what? In spite of worrying about you, the three of us still had a fine, 'happy time,' as they put it. Enjoying each other and everything around us. Do you really think those sweet ladies were hopeless drugheads? Would you describe them as addicts? I didn't see any track marks on either one of 'em. Anywhere. Did you? And we should know, for Christ sake."

Besides Lenny's group watching us from inside the bar window, we now had a curious street audience, too. We'd attracted a drift of the dregs of San Francisco society, those dissolute parasites representing the underbelly of one of America's most celebrated cities. They shuffled about, playacting like they were into their own devices, yet clearly attempting to eavesdrop on our conversation. I tried to keep my back to them as I talked, which had Lenny and me moving and turning together in an attempt to maintain a modicum of privacy.

I continued my case. "Who do you think tipped me off on a contact for the goodies over there? I told you about my roomie in Saigon . . . Billy Riggins. A real gung-ho patriot soldier, man. Airborne, Pathfinder, Jungle Expert. All that hotshot special training you can relate to. Grew up from solid American stock, in the heartland of the Midwest.

"A country boy, like yourself. Who loved America for all its natural, honest beauty. Concerned about what's happening to our environment. Looking to protect it from all this so-called industrial progress. He was as clean-cut as anybody you ever met. In great shape. Health food nut."

The street people had started jerking and jiving to the pulsing of our turmoil. They looked like ghostly prizefighters sparring in some nether world arena. I tried to ignore them.

"Believe it or not," I raved, "he was the one who really introduced me to the relaxation and pleasure of smoking pot and hash. Like he said to me, it's a natural herb. Harvested from the soil of civilization, man. God put it on this earth."

Stepping to my left and edging toward Lenny, I blocked off one grungy witness who'd gotten closer than I liked.

"There's a big difference with this and synthetic lab drugs, Lenny. We're not talking about sticking needles in your arm. Shooting up an addictive narcotic that's been manufactured. Like heroin, or something. We're not talking about popping pills or sniffing coke. This isn't any different than drinking booze. Or smoking cigarettes. A pothead is just like an alcoholic. Or somebody whose lungs are black from smoking three packs of Camels a day," I cried, really into it now.

"If you're a compulsive user and abuse it, it'll whack you just like anything else. If you have normal self-control, it can be a—" I searched for the right words, ". . . a loyal companion in your life. Helping you get through all the bullshit."

Momentum is a wondrous thing. I wish I'd been this loquacious in my college speech classes. Might've gotten some decent grades.

"This isn't a substance that makes you aggressive, drunk and obnoxious like whiskey. Or crazy, like tequila. And it sure doesn't give you hangovers the next day. It calms you down, man. Makes you aware of things you'd normally miss, or not appreciate. Turns your whole attitude easy and mellow. You're able to see things better, taste food better. Hear music like you never heard it before. You can have real conversations with people, with more imagination, humor and understanding. And sex? Well, that's just unbelievable."

I paused to catch my breath. Lenny remained uncharacteristically quiet.

"Goddam' it, Billy's not with us anymore, man. But he sure didn't die from smoking hash. He died because our idiot government is screwing around where we have no business to be. He was just another one of the good guys sacrificed in the process."

Lenny returned my stare. I think the hashish had enhanced my eloquence and expanded my breadth of vocabulary. And it felt good to purge some of the poison fermenting inside me.

"You were right. I was high when you called. You want to know why? I'll tell you why. I smoke pot and hash because it makes me feel good. Helps me forget all the terrible crap in my life, and remember those few truly special times I was lucky enough to experience. Like when the four of us were all together in New Orleans."

The words, like water streaming from a mountain spring, continued to flow in a steady spew.

"I got high tonight so I could take a trip all the way back to Nürnberg. To relive the last days I had with Zina. I . . . I'm still in love with her. I always will be. There'll forever be a piece missing inside me without her. But I was with her tonight, man. And we were making love all over again, just like that last night we were together."

My gush of verbosity continued unabated. "You know, it blows my mind that you, of all people, are so uptight, so closed-minded about this. You, the fabulous party man, the instigator of good times, the ultimate adventurer. Drinking, dancing, laughing, entertaining, making sure everybody is having fun. Driving your fast cars, jumping out of airplanes, leaping off rocky cliffs. But when it comes to a measly joint, it's like you OD'd yourself on *Reefer Madness*, or something. Maybe I am one fucked up son of a bitch . . . but I just don't get it."

That was it. The well was dry. There was nothing left to say.

He stood there, leaning against the window with his hands in his pockets, looking down at the sidewalk. Somehow he seemed smaller. And profoundly sad. The people on the other side of the glass had gone back to their own conversations, drinking up the last of Lenny's generosity. The bartender had busied himself again at the far side of the counter. Only the street hustlers hung on, grumbling and wheezing, not even bothering now with any staged theatrics. After a while, Lenny raised his head back up to my patient silence. His focus held me tight.

"I'll tell you why." His crystal eyes were azure smoke. "I lost a brother to drugs. He's still alive. But he might as well be dead."

CHAPTER 34

The Old Spaghetti Factory in the alley off Green Street had always been fun, besides filling up the tummy and going easy on the wallet. Nothing fancy about the food, but the choices of unique sauces made it interesting. They had just enough flavor so the pasta slid down effortlessly with the Anchor Steamed Beer from the tap. I also liked looking up at the conglomeration of conversation piece chairs and other bric-a-brac hanging from the walls and ceiling. Another thing it had going for it—the convenient, short walk from my apartment.

The place always seemed to breathe friendliness, too. The bearded fellow eating alone at the next table had engaged me in chitchat this time. He paid his check, got up to depart, then turned back to me.

"Say, don't know if you're familiar with Fred Neil. He's playing the Opera Room tonight. A rare opportunity. He's not out here that often."

I always had an interest in music, of course.

"Where's the Opera Room?"

He seemed surprised I didn't know. "Oh! It's right through those doors over there. Past the restrooms. It's the front part of the building."

"Hey. Thank you very much. I just might do that."

A little while later I had my own choice seat in the small club that shared toilets with the spaghetti joint. The musical performance turned out to be another evening of goose bump revelation. The man with the God-gifted voice and twelve-string guitar fascinated and inspired me.

Hunched over his instrument, he played with the touch and finesse of a jazz musician. Tones and timbre flowed with a feathery vibrato that wove a mellifluous texture through his sidemen's accompaniment. But what most charmed my eardrum was his rich cowboy voice, resonating with a modulation of startling purity ranging between bass and baritone. It rose up out of his throat as a cry from deep within the heart, at times seeming to reach all the way down to his feet and rumbling forth from the very soles of his shoes.

Unlike the bohemian instrumentalists playing with him, and the vanguard audience that obviously worshipped him, he did not look the artistic part. He wore his hair short and unkempt. His clothes consisted of baggy, custodial type gray work pants, a powder blue polyester shirt that had me wondering if he'd shopped the same Army PX I had. His bare feet were stuck into beat-up old brown loafers.

But the blues-tinged melodies and lyrics that bobbed and swayed through the congenial room on this rainy night carried me to faraway places. I wished that Lenny could be with me. To hear it and feel it. To gain insight into the new world I'd entered. So we might bridge our differences and go forward together, once again, as we had before.

Then I felt my eyes begin to melt and I knew Zina belonged there, too.

She bounced into the office full of the holiday spirit, placing the decorated goody on my desk as she giggled her season's greeting.

"Merry Christmas, Robbie! And here's your special little surprise from Santa. Enjoy."

Then she curtsied in a cutesy manner, presented replica gifts to others there, and skipped back out the door.

Belinda Bliss worked across the hall, a receptionist and secretary for Columbia Records. She was a petite girl blessed with big brown eyes and an extraordinary sheen in her raven hair. I think she worked for the recording company more for the doors it opened to meeting musicians than the salary they paid her every two weeks. It seemed safe to assume she fit the term *groupie*, wearing all the latest eye-catching hippie fineries. A far cry from the military brats and camp followers that networked around Army bases in yesterday's apparel.

Preoccupied in a rush to chart the cash values and dividends of a whole life insurance policy for a client I had an appointment with that very afternoon, I failed to respond in my usual affable manner before she was gone. Under normal circumstances I wouldn't have ignored her, an attractive young woman who shared my interest in the new music, and the artists and bands creating it. I'd spent a lot of time in front of her desk, comparing notes on the latest in that stimulating business.

Finished at last with the numbers I'd been working on, I looked over at what she'd left me. How sweet. A chocolate brownie that looked homemade, sitting on a Christmas napkin with a toothpick Santa stuck through the center. I took a tentative bite and found it to be delicious, devouring the rest of it since my stomach had begun petitioning its dissension. A tongue-lashing from Mom would be in order, as I had lunch scheduled with Trent in another five minutes, to preview my afternoon appointment.

Good old Dad. As he'd done for my sister, Barbara, he got me on track for some kind of civilian career, in his wondrous world of insurance. After depleting a good portion of my Army savings, I was concerned about how long I'd be able to continue to pay my rent before the landlord and his gorilla tossed me out into the street. Dad bailed me out when he called about a possible sales position with United Mutual.

"You call Trent Witherspoon, right away. He's an old friend of mine. I ran into him at a recent convention. I told him about you. He said he was already thinking about hiring another rep at his branch. So you get right on it now. Give him a call. Let me know how you make out, and . . . good luck, son."

Dad sounded tired, older than that last time I'd seen him. It was hard to believe I'd traversed America from coast to coast, trained a company of soldiers for combat, shipped across the Pacific, served in the Vietnam War, and settled into a new life in San Francisco since he and I had been together. His voice had a rasp, he seemed short of breath, and he coughed a lot. I tried to picture what he looked like, hoping he hadn't lost any more weight. I had my doubts about Mom making sure he took his annual physicals.

He had sure come through for me. After hiring me, Trent personally trained and coached me for the state insurance exam. I passed it on my first try! Then he helped me devise a plan to approach the market, taking into consideration I had no real contact base of local family, school chums or long-standing acquaintances. While the employment contract had me salaried for the first year, to allow time for building a commissions base, I still needed to achieve a minimum monthly sales requirement to warrant a paycheck.

Trent recognized a specialty niche that might give me a platform to work from. I became the "official conversion agent" of the term insurance policies every GI had in effect when completing his active duty service. The government, working in conjunction with commercial life insurance companies, allowed every military person returning to civilian life ninety days to convert this group coverage to a personal policy. The program prevailed over standard application requirements, to include a physical examination.

I would spend long hours at city hall, poring through microfilm files of draft notices to determine release dates and addresses of those more fortunate young men expected to come home, with ten thousand dollars' worth of group insurance eligible for a sales conversion. It turned out to be a laborious, time consuming and tedious repetitive procedure. But it worked. I had to sell these small policies in volume in order to meet my goals, but I found many prospects ripe for "processing."

Of course, I had to get my hair cut a whole lot shorter to at least look representative of the role I came to play. With a great deal of reluctance, I trimmed back my mustache and resorted to a tight Afro, a conservative version of the hairstyle the militant Black Panthers popularized at the time.

"Ready for some lunch?" I jerked in my chair as Trent interrupted my thoughts. He stood at my desk. "It's that hour, and we do need to discuss your upcoming presentation."

I glanced at the wall clock. Sure enough, its hands pointed straight up at noon.

"I'm all set, sir. Let's do it."

A senior agent at our office joined Trent and me for a sandwich at a nearby Irish pub and restaurant on Market Street. I got partway into my corned beef on rye when I started to feel lightheaded. The next thing I knew I was tunneling through the protoplasmic tissue of the meat, like I'd entered the Olympic trials competition in an insane microscopic version of the luge. *Oh, my God, what is going on here?* I managed to make it through lunch, though I have no idea what we discussed relative to my upcoming sales call. All of a sudden we were standing inside the office elevator again, Trent pushing the button for the seventeenth floor. When we lifted off the base of the elevator shaft and accelerated upward, I found myself freaking out inside a space capsule heading for the moon, privately questioning why we hadn't strapped ourselves in for such a dangerous mission. Back in the safety of the office, I attempted to get hold of myself, to concentrate on reviewing the details for my pending appointment. It was no use. My mind started tripping all over the place, the room tilting like I remained trapped in that awful spacecraft.

Then I remembered Belinda's brownie. *Of course. She must have put something in that Christmas surprise.* I managed to make my way out of the office, down the undulating epileptic hall, into the reception area of Columbia Records. Belinda wasn't at her desk. The older peroxide blonde with the white patent leather boots was there, sitting at her typewriter.

"Connie! Where's Belinda?"

She ignored me, continuing to type.

"Connie. Listen to me. I need to talk to Belinda. Right now. Where is she?"

Finally she looked up at me, a frightened expression on her face. I took it upon myself to unlatch the reception gate between us. I'd socialized at their desks before. I walked over to her.

"Are you all right?"

She started to cry, her mascara blackening her eyes. I thought it seemed pretty ludicrous, a mature woman behaving like a distraught child.

"No. I'm not all right! I have no idea what I'm doing. Look. I can't even type!"

She had that right. Whatever she'd been trying to put on paper made no sense. I gasped at a jumble of disjointed words, phrases and clauses, fractured with misplaced consonants and vowels, numbers, punctuation marks and other assorted typos. All adding up to nothing.

"Did you have one of Belinda's brownies? Connie. Did you eat one of those Christmas brownies?"

After the sobbing subsided, she honked her nose in her hankie a number of times. After a while, she composed herself long enough to answer.

"I had three of them!" She started bawling all over again.

Belinda had disappeared somewhere. Connie had no idea about anything. I advised her of my suspicions, urging her to get someone to take her home so she could sleep it off. I went back to my office and alerted everyone to the suspect treats from Santa. No one else had eaten one yet, though Belinda had left the gift on every desk. Apprising Trent of my own incapacitating predicament, we agreed he should handle my appointment for me. I winced more than once as he stripped gears on my stick shift sports car driving me home, fretfully imagining him grinding up more of the corned beef I'd had for lunch, leaving a trail of that red meat in the street behind us.

Back in my pad overlooking Broadway, I decided the high to be too good to waste. I hit my stash of hash under the armoire and kept the thrill alive. But I forgot Trent had to return my abused Healey after the sales call he made on my behalf. I suffered some embarrassment when he surprised me with his ring of the doorbell. Inside, he delivered an in-depth report of his successful meeting while my fleeting mind glided around my collection of psychedelic posters on the walls and ceiling. When he asked how I felt, I told him I still suffered strong symptoms of vertigo. I thanked him for helping me out.

"Boy, whatever she put in those brownies must be really powerful," he said, his face showing honest concern. I nodded my concurrence.

To this day I don't know if he picked up on anything going on there, from the collection of hippie poster art, the utopian Tim Buckley compositions playing in the background, or the burning incense masking the aroma of smoked hashish. If he courted suspicions about the duration of my condition, he never let on.

Reprimanded for the incident, Belinda came close to losing her job. She wouldn't discuss anything about it until many weeks later. Connie informed me that she, herself, had also gone home early that day, calling in sick the next morning, too. She told me the postman had eaten two of the brownies, becoming so disoriented that the mail delivery got screwed up through much of the building. Those brownies were a seasonable taste of the happy holidays, a la 1967.

CHAPTER 35

All it took for Belinda and me to move in together was a concert date to hear Blood, Sweat and Tears. Of course, she somehow had free tickets and backstage passes through her business contacts, so we also got to meet Al Kooper and the boys in their private lounge after the final encore. Less than a week later we mingled with the industry's fast lane freeloaders, attending a post-performance party for the great Odetta, belatedly honoring her birthday. Odetta arrived late and left early. She listened with patience to our discordant celebratory song and dutifully blew out the candles on her cake. I would guess she spent fifteen minutes, tops, being polite to all the profuse, self-serving well-wishers before staffers escorted her away with her bodyguard attendant.

One Saturday afternoon early on in our relationship, I got to bide my time while Belinda browsed a ladies' clothes shop, right there on Grant, in my own neighborhood.

She called to me. "Oh, Robbie. Robbie! I'd like you to meet someone."

I sauntered over in the direction of her voice, through an isle of antique-styled hippie dresses. She stood by the racks alongside an outlandishly attired woman with a craggy complexion and frizzy hair. Her acquaintance appeared familiar. Belinda beamed at me, obviously having trouble containing herself.

"Robbie, say hello to someone I know you'll want to meet. Janis, this is my boyfriend, Robbie. Robbie, this is Janis."

The light of recognition shone over me as I tentatively held out my hand. When she took it, and held it, granting me a courteous smile, I could feel myself dissolving right there on the floor.

Later, walking down the street, Belinda asked me, "You do know who that was, don't you?"

I answered absent-mindedly, still in a state of wonder, "Oh, yeah, I saw her at the Fillmore last summer. That was Janis Joplin." Simultaneously my inner voice chided me for my inability to rise to the occasion. *Wouldn't it have been nice if I could've thought of something to say to her more intelligent than "Hey, how you doing?"*

We were moving down the block to another store, but I'm still not sure my feet touched the ground.

Such was life, living with Belinda. Famous people who I'd always been content to read about in magazines, see on the TV screen, distant stage, or looking through a window at a secluded table in a restaurant I couldn't afford, I now got to meet face to face. I exchanged polite handshakes and embryonic conversation with them. Whereas I'd never wanted to intrude, kowtow or brown-nose, ever fearful of rejection, she possessed an intrepid sense of self-reliance, mingling in any social setting with audacity and grit. She also had the stamina to challenge my own propensity for living like there's no tomorrow. The candles burned at both ends lit our windows on Vallejo Street far into every night. The tachometer on my hellbent life mode edged closer toward the red.

Her first significant influence on me affected my wardrobe. "We've got to get you into some boss threads," she said.

Before I knew it, I had all the clothes to deck myself out in my hip persona. Leather pants and bell-bottom slacks to compliment my jeans, tie-dyed T-shirts, flowery and psychedelic patterned dress shirts. I even acquired a silky white-on-white Nehru, along with sandals, headbands and kerchiefs, handmade beads, and a distressed brass medallion of a dove in flight, the bird of peace, hanging from a rawhide necklace.

After work we'd get ourselves duded up in our hippie duds, Belinda wearing either tight-fitting bells, a granny dress or mini-skirt with black pantyhose, boots or heels, and a floppy hat or French beret. We'd smoke a doobie or chunk of hash to get our shit together and prime the appetites. Then we'd go trucking on down to some North Beach or Chinatown restaurant. We'd hoof it, since parking a car in the city while on drugs would be much too stressful. And we'd hang out with all the beautiful people in the milieu of sophisticated intellectuality, looking down our noses at the straight-arrow philistines passing by, finishing up drinking coffee and eating dessert cakes at Enrico's on Broadway. Doubt never entered our minds that this had to be the center of the universe, though the Haight would never agree. We lived for *the now* as though it would last forever.

Although we often got too stoned to fully appreciate or remember, we shared many warm, intimate times together, talking about our deepest secrets and most sacred personal thoughts. She told me about the loves of her life, her successes, failures and frustrations. I enlightened her in kind, especially regarding my relationships and everlasting attachments to Lenny and Zina. We helped each other with advice and compassion.

One rainy night at the apartment, we sat cross-legged next to each other on the rug. Belinda worked her Tarot cards as we listened to the morose musical poems of one of her idols, Canadian bard Leonard Cohen. I brought up the situations surrounding those two most significant persons in my life.

"Every day I try to find a way to deal with losing Zina. I want to know how her operation went. If she's all right. I called Marjorie, her American girlfriend. They've remained tight over the years. Got some senile old lady. No help from the phone company, other than that numbers get reassigned. They told me there's no superseding number for Marjorie."

A nerve started a spastic squirm in my left pinkie. I rubbed my hands together, but it wouldn't stop. I snatched my pack of Pall Malls off the floor and lit up.

"As I've said before, I still wake up in the middle of the night sometimes, wondering if maybe I did get her pregnant, like she wanted. Maybe before her operation she had our own little kid. Jeez, if she did, I'd like to at least know. To see him . . . or her. To be able to hold my child, too.

"God, knowing Zina's still in this world, yet beyond my touch, makes it even harder, I think. You can't ever put it behind you. So the hurt's even worse."

Belinda looked at me with true tenderness, putting her hand to my cheek. Her dark eyes were pools of empathy.

"Man, you're carrying one hell of a torch for this girl. I've got to say, from a woman's perspective, if she did have your baby, she's got to include you. It's a matter of instinct and conscience. If she's the good person you say she is, she'll make it happen."

My mouth opened to respond, but my brain had nothing to offer beyond bewilderment. Then my scrambled mind went blank.

Belinda stepped into my outer space. "I don't profess to be an expert with these cards. But let's see if we can get any insight at all. What are your signs, babe?"

"What are you talking about?"

"Your signs. You know, signs of the zodiac. Like, when you were born."

"Oh. I'm a Taurus. Born 6 May."

She looked at me, as if waiting for some sort of elaboration. When I just stared back, then shrugged my shoulders, she asked, "And Zina?"

"Ah . . . right. Let's see. Her birthday's early June. I don't know her sign."

"That'd be Gemini."

She went through progressions with the cards, shuffling and spreading, gathering, reshuffling and spreading again. At first I watched with interest, intrigued by the bizarre allegorical pictures. The Knight of Swords, The Fool, the Queen of Pentacles, Strength, the Page of Wands. But soon my attention drifted to the winking candles inside my broken, *verboten* fireplace.

"I hesitate to interpret what I'm seeing here," she began. "What the cards are telling me. Like I said, I'm still learning. And it's so important to you. I don't want you to take my reading as, what would you call it? . . . gospel. I probably shouldn't be doing this."

"Just lay it on me. I can handle it. I've never been a believer in fortunetellers, anyway."

"Well. I'm not at all certain about any of what I'm getting," she replied, continuing to stare at the cards.

As she reshuffled and spread again, I observed more drawings: The High Priestess sitting between columns beneath The Sun, The Lovers standing naked before Judgement.

She started to speak, hesitated, then said, "There's a great event involving a . . . bright, golden light. The glory and wonder of a rising sun. The promise of a new morning?"

"Wow. I'm enthralled. What the hell is that supposed to mean?"

Belinda went on working the cards. I don't think she heard me. Now the Wheel of Fortune had aligned with The Hanged Man and the Ace of Cups lay directly above Justice.

"There's more. Incredible. Just the opposite. How confusing. Here, let me show you what I mean. See these three cards?"

"Come on, Belinda. I'm not getting into this. Just give me your take on it and be done with it."

"Okay. I'm now seeing extreme darkness. Darkness like the sun has set. No moon to light the way. Pitch black. You know, I don't think this is such a good idea." She gathered the cards into a stack, leaned back and set them on the floor behind us, under the end table.

Returning to my side, she gave me a smile. "So what did your big frat-mate Lenny advise you on all this?"

"I haven't told him."

"You haven't told him? Why not?"

"I don't know. Maybe I'm afraid of what he'll say."

"You should tell him, babe. He's obviously more qualified than me to help you handle it."

Once again I considered the faded ray of hope that shone behind the damage from our tempest in the Tenderloin. "I guess you're right. But it might be too late. Now I see Lenny slipping away, just like her. I've always worried about him killing himself in one of his harebrained hobbies. The race cars, skydiving, whatever. He might not. He's a crafty old cat who's probably got nine lives. But after our latest hassle about drugs I just might lose him, all the same. I hate to think what the hell that would do to me."

Belinda retrieved the ashtray from the kitchen table so I could snuff out the cigarette stub threatening to burn my fingers.

"Bad karma. This last time you saw him . . . was he still wearing his sapphire ring?"

I looked down at the splendent piece of jewelry on my left hand. *Jesus. I hadn't even noticed.*

"My god, I don't know. I never bothered to look. That's the link in our lives. Our pardner rings, our . . . destiny, for Christ sake! Of course. Thank you, Belinda. Thank you so much."

"Just be sure you're wearing yours next time you see him," she said, as I closed my arms around her.

CHAPTER 36

In terms of our drug use, I came to be the one that kept a lid on this activity. I unconsciously assumed the role as the governor controlling our joint sessions with illegal mind enhancers. I do believe I helped Belinda restrict the variety and quantity of pharmaceuticals she'd gotten into, as I remained more than satisfied anchored within the safe harbor of marijuana and hashish. On the other hand, she steadied the spyglass for my vision of more distant, complex and adventurous voyages.

"Now, what was it that made Santa's brownies so delicious?" I asked. "I'd really like the recipe. The flavor stayed with me for hours."

At last she felt amenable to sharing her culinary skills, her job apparently intact.

"Well, sous-chef Robbie, if you must know, Benny, my supplier, happened to have some particularly excellent pot. Of course, I personally taste-tested it myself to make sure it was up to the project. And, just to be certain, I also laced the treat with just a pinch of acid. I'm so pleased you liked it."

I rocked backward. It took a few seconds to get my mouth working again.

"Acid? You mean, like, LSD? You put LSD in those brownies? I don't believe it!"

She forced a nervous smile, working to maintain her composure and humorous intent.

"Well . . . as I said, it really was just a teensy-weensy of that. Just to spike that dreamy grass. But, since Connie and the postman didn't like my baking too much, I don't think we'll be doing any more holiday favors. Oh, my." She cupped her hands over her cheeks, like Little Orphan Annie would do, affecting a wide-eyed babe in the woods.

The next weekend we entertained a group of her friends at the apartment, for the first time. The party started with a couple heads she worked with at Columbia. I'm not, of course, referring to department heads. Then she ushered in a few pals from her previous employment at rival Capitol Records, and a spaced-out broadcast engineer from KMPX. The last to arrive were some former roomies from her previous pad, believe it or not, a commune arrangement in a bourgeois neighborhood way out in Tiburon, across the bay.

I had Belinda's promo copy of the jazzy new rock group, Spirit, on the stereo as things got going. We greeted everyone with good vibes at a moderate volume as people arrived and settled in. Belinda acted as the perfect hostess, making sure each guest had a glass of wine and nibblings of cheese and crackers to get started.

Before either of us got to offer samplings from our stash, the sweet perfume of Mary Jane intermingled with the incense. A reefer made its rounds person to person from one side of the studio to the other. By the time I turned up the sound for the Grateful Dead, the first roach clip flashed from hand to hand. Then Belinda lit one of her tightly rolled Benny's beauties. It irked me how she consistently produced a joint like that: firmer, more compact than mine, no matter how hard I tried.

Soon the rubbing of elbows removed all strangers, the mood becoming simultaneously casual and buoyant. Belinda went around the room with a brass serving tray—*now where'd she get that?*—presenting little tan capsules to everyone on freaky psychedelic napkins. *Or those, I might ask?* It began to sink in that, though I might be the technical host, paying the rent, this was her party, with her friends. And that was the only reality presiding now.

"Here's your dainty delight, babe," she smiled, bobbing her head from side to side in feigned girlish folly as she held the tray before me.

"What is it?" I asked, taking the next-to-last capsule while trying to conceal my intimidation and apprehension about the sudden course of events.

"It's a real trip, honey." She hopped on her toes in front of me. "Come on, don't be a party pooh-pooh. We'll dig it together. Right here, with all my friends."

"But . . . what is it?"

She cozied up to me and popped her delicacy into her mouth, washing it down with wine and flicking her eyelashes at me, still caught in the trance of her little girl mode. Then she seemed to catch the seriousness of my drift.

"It's just mescaline, babe. It's really good. We'll have a lovely time together with it. I've already tried some. It's pleasant, really exciting. Please, join me and my friends. They're fun people. You'll enjoy them, too."

Like an impulsive youth eager to impress his peers, the pill tobogganed down my throat on a rivulet of cabernet.

Belinda patted me on the cheek. "There . . . that's a good boy."

The group had formed a circle on the floor, in front of the stereo. They looked to be getting comfortable for their psychic excursion together. Someone had placed a bottle of wine in the center. Another joint made its rounds. For a split second I thought one of the couples looked like Lenny and the skinny coed he met up with at that smoky College Town party, where everyone lay around in a daze. Now I understood what had been going on there.

"Do you have Sgt. Pepper?"

The voice yanked me back from my recollection. One of the male guests had just asked for something.

Belinda turned to me, reinforcing both the request and her hostess role. "You do have that, don't you?"

"I'm sorry . . . pepper?"

Then it hit me, square between the eyes. "Oh! Sgt. Pepper! The Beatles album. Of course."

Feeling oh so awkward, I moved toward my record collection, to the prickly chuckles of our guests.

Before long, John Lennon was singing to me, about *a day in the life*. And I'd never ever felt like this before. *He turned me on.* I vaguely acknowledged the rediscovery of my drifting mind . . . .

I am submerged deep in the lurid green waters of the sea—but now I am rising up—rising up with the sound—multicolored bubbles trailing behind—thousands of them!—red and yellow, blue, every color of the rainbow, every shade in between—trailing behind me, bubbling from my outstretched fingers, my hands—from my head, my ears—rippling from my feet, my toes—the entire spectrum of the rainbow—now I am rising faster—and higher!—the music rises with me—the bubbles are merging into each other, transposing into a multitude of laser beams in kaleidoscopic hues—streaming behind me as I surge upward, upward—violas and bassoons crescendo—beams now expanding into shafts of iridescent tones streaking from behind my body—the water is getting lighter—from green to gold to silver—and the music climaxes in an eruption of sound as I crash through the surface of the water!—then fading, ever fading away while I float there—in the placid, shimmering surface—looking out on infinity . . . .

I lay there on the floor, flat on my back. Belinda held my left hand. Someone else held my right. I stared at the ceiling, with its flickery neon sheen.

"Welcome home, Robbie. We love you." I heard Belinda's gentle voice, in a kind of echo.

"Oh, my god. Oh, my god."

Less than a week later I slipped into Trent's unoccupied office for something or other, saw the morning edition sitting on his desk. The headlines on the front page of the *Chronicle* caught my attention.

SAIGON IN PERIL
FULL SCALE TET OFFENSIVE

For my own self-preservation, I guess, I'd pretty much ignored news coverage of the war. It snowed year-round on most of my TV channels, the only antenna being the adjustable rabbit ears sitting on top of the set. No longer needing the classified employment ads when I landed the United Mutual job, I'd cancelled my newspaper subscription. But this story reported devastating news involving my former battalion. I wondered what this "Tet offensive" was all about. Tet represented the traditional annual lunar New Year's holiday the Vietnamese celebrated; during the war it had always been a routinely negotiated period of cease-fire between North and South.

According to the article, Communist Hanoi had decided to renege on the truce this time. They attacked unsuspecting American and ARVN troops with both NVA soldiers and Viet Cong guerrillas, all the way down into the most distant provinces of South Vietnam. The enemy infiltrated and overran defenses at Tan Son Nhut Air Base, the responsibility of my 716th Military Police Battalion. They'd encircled the capital city of Saigon itself.

The report read a bit sketchy, but stated that a truckload of MPs had been ambushed and totally annihilated somewhere in the vicinity of the airport. Four other military policemen and a Marine security guard had been killed defending the U.S. Embassy. Attacking Viet Cong warriors had at last been suppressed by additional MPs dispatched from the Cholon district. The MPs were successful in securing the embassy compound. Fighting continued in and around the city.

Jesus. Who would've thought Saigon would be on the verge of collapse! Why, it's been just a matter of months since Billy scoffed at my concern about Charlie's guerrilla tactics, disparaged the danger of the strategy targeted at those of us within the shadow of MACV Headquarters.

So, who were the hardy MP heroes that thwarted the enemy's attempt to overtake our embassy? If they'd been called in from Cholon, they had to be "C" Company and/or the 528th, the unit I'd trained at Fort Lewis and commanded right there in Saigon!

I felt a surge of pride welling up inside me. Then the blood from Billy's wasted body leached into my brain. I put the paper back down on Trent's mahogany desk and returned to my metal rendition, determined to somehow get beyond that miserable suffering. It didn't really matter anymore if my former command had distinguished itself. I could no longer cope with either the glory or the pain.

The shower had felt good. Relaxing, after a long afternoon scouting out insurance prospects at city hall. I could've kicked myself for dripping water all the way to the ringing phone. It was more than likely someone for Belinda.

"Hey there, Robbie. Justin. How you doing, man?"

It had been a while since I'd had any contact with Justin. What with Benny supplying anything Belinda wanted, I had no need to drive all the way across town to make a score. Beyond that, I also preferred the so-called "sense-a-million" prime seedless grass Belinda received from Benny. It was more expensive, but closer to the high quality level I'd cut my teeth on in Vietnam.

I guessed Justin might be wondering where my business had gone. But we just rapped for a time and he extended his friendship by inviting me to join him and his cohort at a concert coming up that Saturday night. In that Belinda would be going to Reno for the weekend with one of her girlfriends from her Capitol days, I was free and more than receptive.

"Sounds great. You got any more Janis Joplin's to pull out of your sleeve?"

"She's one of a kind, man. But I do think you'll dig this band from Chicago. Called H.P. Lovecraft. You know, a take on that spooky old horror novelist. They're pretty trippy, definitely worth a listen. Plus, I remember you were really grooving on the scene at the Fillmore. You'll like the feel of the Avalon Ballroom, too. It's the same kind of old artsy décor."

The name H.P. Lovecraft didn't ring any bells with me, but I was no longer the avid reader I'd once been. As for music, I trusted Justin's judgment.

"Let's do it. Just tell me where and when."

Since the Avalon Ballroom was right downtown, on Sutter Street, I welcomed Justin's suggestion to meet in a nearby bar so I didn't have to make the long jaunt over to his house. This time I also prepared myself, polishing off a decent size piece of hash and tucking a joint in my jacket pocket before hailing a cab.

He knew what he was talking about, for I felt right at home with the Old World atmosphere of the concert hall. Even tardier than we'd been arriving at the Fillmore for Janis, this program was already into its second act when we scuffled inside. The bluesy colored performer up on stage, with the curiously compelling name of Taj Mahal, impressed me.

By this time I'd become accustomed to the light shows supporting the performers, understanding now that actual companies of people had been hired to provide this visual aspect of the spectacle, to lend to the psychedelic sensation of the music. Justin confirmed that this night's light group happened to be the very same company that had backed the Big Brother gig last year at the Fillmore.

I managed a few rejuvenating tokes of weed in one of the restroom stalls just before H.P. Lovecraft went on. The band proved to be as entrancing as Justin had said. I especially got into two imposing, illusive offerings, the opening "Wayfaring Stranger," and later, a sullen piece entitled "The White Ship," complete with embellishes of baroque harpsichord.

The light show then became my waterloo. Amidst the mind-blowing illuminations, a sudden sequence of blazing news clips cast simultaneously on various screens had me dazzled. I saw Martin Luther King speaking at an equal rights rally, contrasted by Governor George Wallace barring the first Negro student from entering the University of Alabama—followed by the Ku Klux Klan burning a cross in front of a Second Baptist church. Then Russia's Nikita Khrushchev pounded his shoe on the table of the United Nations, his superimposed bloated face sneering in the foreground as he proclaimed, "We will bury you!"

I soon found my modified psyche lurching through an arcade of personal terrors and apparitions I'd long attempted to suppress. I flinched at the presentation of JFK's assassination in Dallas, Jacqueline Kennedy on the trunk of the topless limousine, clinging to the back of the seat where Kennedy slumped, mortally wounded. With bone-shivering clarity, the images transmuted into Jane Lennox and Jerry Blakely, speeding off the road and slamming head-on into an unrelenting tree. Chills climbed my spine when I swore I saw Bruce Tierney sitting right there in his wheelchair, watching it all from the rim of the grassy knoll. Lyndon Johnson returned to the screen, talking peace once again, over a backdrop of American helicopters strafing jungles and villages in Vietnam. I stood over the ditch of collected corpses, bullet-riddled Bobby Bennett and Billy Riggins lying side by side on their backs, their faces raw flesh smiling through the curse of death. James Dean roared back again, too, still the "Rebel Without a Cause," steering his vehicle toward that consequential Hollywood cliff. Only this time he looked just like Lenny, losing control of his race car and sailing off the edge. A blinding flash heralded an oddly platinum blonde Natalie Wood in a stark white room, stretched out on her back and naked on a marble slab, under a molesting light, her eyes closed shut. Mystified, I moved closer, only to be jolted by the realization I'd been staring at Zina. I felt embarrassed by her nudity. The light dissolved to black and she was gone. As Robert Kennedy eulogized his slain brother from the church pulpit while his child nephew, little "John John," saluted his father's casket, I headed for the door. I hoped I would not be sick before I made the sidewalk.

As luck would have it, a number of taxis had lined up at the curb, waiting for the show's conclusion, or an earlier fare from some strung out druggie like me. I think I paid him too much, but welcomed the relief just to get back home where I could crash as well, in my droopy bed. Once again, I'd left without saying good-night to my young friend, Justin.

CHAPTER 37

Belinda and I picked up from where we'd left off, after her lit-tle gambling excursion in Reno. She was happy she'd only lost $104 playing blackjack and the one-armed bandits. That first weekend back together we went to Winterland to hear Cream, with the fantastic Eric Clapton. Belinda and I arrived tripping on mes-caline again.

"Just hold my hand, babe, and we'll be cool together," she said.

Winterland turned out to be an enormous auditorium, as I remember it, with a balcony that encircled floor level. We found the place packed to the rafters with San Francisco's finest flower children, young hippies and old beatniks, most everyone doped up on something or other for the big show. The crowd went wild when Cream took the stage. Though I'd grown accustomed to loud music, the volume of sound generated by just three musicians overwhelmed me, sending me teetering back into the startled group of people behind us. Clapton's supporting cast of Ginger Baker walloping drums and Jack Bruce stroking bass guitar were im-posing in their own right. The bluster of their three instruments combined for a most bracing effect.

Until I got lost. Not too long into the concert Belinda and I got separated in the shifting audience. I soon found myself stoned and staggering, searching for her in the dark corridors of an erratic rock 'n' roll migration instigated by the guitars and percussion. I circled the balcony a number of times, at available vantage points looking down to the small stage separating the three master technicians from the human caldron. I felt myself swept further into my oblivion by their enveloping message of sound and passion. Finally I just wandered in space, floating somewhere within that constellation of mortal beings and amplified vibrations, disappearing and reemerging unto my own self over and over again, each time finding it harder to engage with the reality of my existence and my surroundings. I have no idea how I got home, but ages later I stood alone on the corner of Grant and Vallejo. A cabbie hollered at me, "Thanks for the fucking tip, pothead." I felt relieved to find my key in a pocket. Then I trudged up the endless hill and let myself back inside my somber abode.

Waking to the surprise of finding Belinda lying beside me once again, I stumbled to the sink to wash the mildew from my mind. The short hand on the clock pointed to seven. The sun was beginning to set. It looked like I'd missed a pretty nice day.

A few weeks later Belinda and I spruced up for yet another musical happening.

"I'm not going to tell you anything about this guy, Robbie. I want you to be free to form your own opinion."

I could tell she'd begun working toward her usual hyper frame of mind that accompanied major social activities. Not even pot or hash could quell that ambitious spirit, especially involving those people she described as "larger than life." This time the attraction happened to be a singer who'd changed his moniker to "Dino Valente."

"Real name's Chet Powers. Believe he wanted to change that?" Belinda was up on it all. "You remember we saw that band Quicksilver Messenger Service one night? He was supposed to be their lead singer, but got himself thrown in jail for drugs. I believe he's out on some kind of parole. So I guess you could call this a rare opportunity."

I recalled the Quicksilver performance. They came across loud and exuberant, but needing the focus of a credible lead singer.

This night Dino Valente took the stage all by himself, at the Purple Onion. He was far beyond what I'd anticipated. This became my second experience seeing someone truly adept at a twelve-string guitar. Valente incorporated an electronic reverberation effect that buttressed his vocals with an echoey textured background. His sensuous voice had great range, evoking strong emotional reactions. His lyrics and melodies transported me to transcendent worlds swirling in another dimension. When the house lights announced intermission, I fought the thought of pinching myself back to reality.

During the break Valente sat on a stool at one side of the foyer, making himself available to converse with his audience. Of course Belinda and I stepped right up there, and she introduced me to this person with the curly black hair and considerable musical talent. To my surprise, he was almost incoherent. He smiled, and he talked, but unlike the brilliant romantic, philosophical ballads he'd authored and sung to us earlier, his spoken words barely treaded the shallows. He rambled on in all directions, digressing into disappointing blind alleys. It didn't take long to see he was drowning in drugs, incapable of constructing a substantive thought about anything.

When the break ended, he went back inside to his guitar and concluded one of the most memorable solo concerts I've ever had the privilege to witness. How he could play and sing so well in such a state I will never know. But I felt thankful that, for the first time in a long time, I'd attended lucid enough to enjoy and treasure every nuance of his magnificent performance. I also thought it ironic that, on this night at least, the entertainer was more whacked-out than his audience.

Later, Belinda presented me with the radio station promo copy of *Dino Valente*, a studio recording of the very same songs he performed during that one night appearance. I take good care of it, and play it only on very special occasions. I don't know whatever became of Dino Valente. After that, I never found a trace of him again. I did hear he'd been busted once more on drug charges. For certain he could've been a star. But I guess maybe he just rambled away from it all. Just rambled away and vanished off the edge of the earth.

"So this is your new neighborhood."

The three of us waited for the walking green to cross Columbus Avenue. Dad seemed enthused about having seen where I lived, and visiting San Francisco for the first time. He even acted as though he liked my little apartment, with all the far-out poster artwork, candles and incense holders, despite Mom's negative comments. I got upset noting how bad he looked and how nervous he acted, though, even thinner than the last time we'd been together, constantly clearing his throat, stopping to catch his breath, and hacking that smoker's cough.

"Quite a diverse mix of people . . . living all around you, Rob. So many Italian restaurants right here at your doorstep. Chinatown just a couple blocks away. And all these . . . interesting characters . . . on the streets."

"Looks like you've gone from defending our country to consorting with all the left wing anti-establishment beatniks and draft dodgers, if you ask me," Mom snarled, for the benefit of everyone within earshot.

I took them to the Golden Spike for dinner that first night. Belinda had thoughtfully elected to get together with Nicky, her girlfriend at Capitol Records, so I could spend time alone with my parents. As usual, table space came at a premium in this popular little Italian restaurant, so we put my name on the wait list and grabbed stools at the bar.

"What'll you have?" the extrovert bartender inquired.

Mom ordered her Tom Collins and I my usual Jack and soda. Dad lit up another Lucky Strike as he perused the beers on tap. The bartender waited with colossal patience.

"You got Rheingold?" Dad asked, at the breaking point of my presence of mind. He exhaled the most recent puff from his cigarette before introducing everybody to his nasty cough.

"Rheingold?" the bartender retorted, loud enough for the kitchen staff in the back. "What the hell's Rheingold?" He had a twinkle in his eye as everyone at the bar and nearby tables contributed hearty guffaws.

"Bet he's from New Yawk!" somebody exclaimed from the other end of the bar. Dad balked in the good-natured ribbing.

I stepped in to get him off the hook. "Try a Coors, Dad. It's about the same. I think you'll like it."

Dad drank Coors for the remainder of their stay.

The next day Belinda joined us. We toured the city in their rental car, hitting all the traditional tourist spots where we would dutifully park and take pictures. I stopped at a traffic light where two flower child nymphets and their hippie boyfriends had their thumbs out for a ride, I would guess heading to the Haight. They wore dilated red eyes and shared generous smiles.

"Just look at these . . . young people here, Eleanor," Dad commented, his cough continuing to intrude. "With all the troubles in this world of ours . . . and all the sourpusses everywhere . . . it's nice to see someone who still knows how to grin. I don't know . . . it just looks to me like they've found . . . you know . . . the spiritual answer our generation's still looking for."

Mom uttered her patented skeptical grunt as the light changed. I slid my sandal to the gas pedal and Belinda kicked my leg to acknowledge, share and contain the humor of the naïve observation.

Chic Belinda preferred her Middle East hookah and our selection of metal and ceramic roach clips. But exercising my working class origins, I suppose, I thought my coffee can functioned as a more efficient water pipe. I also loved to tease her by finishing off the butts of joints using folded matchbook covers. When she became vexed enough to express her exasperation to me, most times because I had the gall to do it in the company of others, I loved to drawl my latest trademark response, "The man ain't got no culture."

This particular Friday night I'd arrived home first. So the burning hash glowed over the ice pick holes in the aluminum foil, wrapped over the top of old Chase & Sanborn. We drew the water-cooled smoke through the mouth vent I'd cut along a portion of the top edge. I felt humming-happy and she excited. We looked forward to double-dating that night with her girlfriend Nicky and comparable live-in, Travis. Belinda had finagled four tickets to a sold-out Hell's Angels fundraising concert at the Carousel.

The first performer had to be one of the most outrageous acts I'd ever seen. "Dr. John, The Night Tripper," as he called himself, weaved and flounced with ponderous steps about the flimsy scaffold that purported to be a stage. With sewn-on tassels flying and sleigh bells jingling from his four major appendages, he spoon-fed us some of his funky homegrown "Gris Gris Gumbo Ya Ya" from a mythic cast-iron kettle, and growled rapturously about walking on "gilded splinters."

"Man, this joker's blacker than my Uncle Delbert," Travis observed. "What a gas. I ain't seen too many white cats who can roll it and shake it like that. And get their sound down 'n dirty into the nitty gritty soul swamp. Right on!"

"That's kosher soul you're talking about," Belinda said, snapping her fingers in time. "Don't ever sell us Jews short when it comes to digging the essence of life's joyful misery. You're not the only race with a birthright to hatred and discrimination, man. With the dance of deliverance in your blood. It's these poor WASPs and

Cat-licks here who had to go to Arthur Murray, you know. And wouldn't you know Arthur is a kike himself, of course."

It was all getting a little too heavy for me. I butted in with a trifling question.

"You're telling me this here bayou witch doctor is Jewish? What makes you think that?"

I should've known better. Belinda stormed right back at me, with her groupie "facts."

"Because his real name's Mac Rebennack, that's why. Born and earned his dues in New Orleans, as you might suspect. But with Hebrew roots, if you dig beneath the voodoo topsoil."

I bit my lip. In my Jersey gut "Rebennack" didn't ring kosher. But I knew Belinda would stray out of her way to footnote the relevance of her heritage whenever she could.

"Wow. That must've been some really good shit you was smoking before you got here, Belinda," Nicky piped in. "I want a few hits of that before the night's up. So's I can jabber that fancy talk myself."

It wouldn't be too long before she got her wish. We'd joined everyone else sitting on the floor of this small, no-seats second story club that functioned as the concert site. In that Dr. John served as the opening act for the Grateful Dead, the crowd had grown much too large for the limited space of the facility. In spite of all the cops outside, the room had to be far beyond the legal limit in "seating" capacity; you could hardly move, and the aura had gotten smoky, stagnant, and explosive.

Earlier, standing in line with our tickets on Market Street, I'd never seen so many pigs, Hell's Angels, choppers and other motorcycles in one place at one time ever before. Nor anything resembling the show of force this event generated. City policemen in riot control gear observed us from just off the sidewalk, stationed every fifteen feet or so. A denim or leather jacketed Hell's Angel faced down every cop, with the height advantage of the curb. In most cases, they had their arms folded in a stance of defiance.

I marveled at hundreds of parked Harleys and other bikes across the street. More Hell's Angels provided cycle security and monitored the police activity before them. The confrontation between opposing forces cordoned the long line of fragile flower children and awed hippie concert goers, wrapping around the corner from Market onto Van Ness Avenue, all the way to the entrance doors of the show. And I don't believe I've ever witnessed a more hushed public gathering. Beholding the legions of police, motorcyclists and hipsters at the scene, the stillness in sound and motion felt suffocating. The cool night air crackled with tension and the anticipation of imminent violence.

Though I saw no heat inside, at least not in uniform, the atmosphere of potential anarchy carried over into the club. Hell's Angels dominated the bar behind the audience, and they'd become raucous and obnoxious, their biker boots having scuffed the threshold of inebriation.

Travis returned from a booze run over there, while the roadies reset the stage for the Grateful Dead. He handed us our soppy, half-spilled plastic cups.

"As much as I want to hear Jerry and the Dead, especially up this close, I'm not sure how much longer it's going to be safe around here."

"What's the matter, honey?" Nicky put her arm around him as he rejoined us on the floor.

Travis glanced over his shoulder, then turned back to us. He lowered his voice.

"Well, for one thing, there's a whole lot of drunken testosterone raging around the old bar, in case you hadn't noticed. And the biggest and ugliest hoodlum over there asked me if you was a real blonde. Not in a particularly gracious way, I might add. I kind of got the feeling he might not be what you call a liberal thinker when it comes to interracial relationships."

The Dead had just begun to tune when a brawl kicked up somewhere on the other side of the bar. We watched as a half-dozen

Angels dragged out some sorry tippler with a bloody face. The stupendous goon Travis had encountered pointed his finger in our direction and mouthed the words, "You're next!"

The bikers threw the terrified fellow down the stairs leading to the entrance door.

Now the barroom was abuzz with macho temper. To our dismay Travis's bully took the initiative to conspire with a cluster of leather cronies at the near side of the bar. Noting his body language, mutual eye contact and flapping lips it didn't take long to determine why we'd suddenly become targets of their hostile attention.

"Think it best we blow this dive," Travis advised.

"Right, and like, *nonchalá,*" Nicky submitted.

Jerry Garcia still hadn't made it to the stage, and the rest of the band continued to diddle with their instruments when the four of us dragged our drug-induced paranoid asses in the direction of that very same staircase. Travis flashed the peace sign toward the bar as we tumbled on out of there.

"Oh well, we'll catch 'em some other time," Belinda observed.

We hit the street and headed for Travis's car.

"Hey," Nicky exclaimed, "let's go have a taste of Belinda's *vocabalary* boosters."

Within a half-hour we'd parked it up on Twin Peaks, overlooking the lights of the San Francisco metropolis.

Travis pulled the cork from a previously opened Napa Valley burgundy vaunting a *pleasing complexity, well-balanced, with a distinctive bouquet and robust character,* if you believed the label. Nicky shared the joint she'd lit up during the ride. Belinda parodied a formal presentation of her notorious, ill-mannered mescaline capsules, in a most humorous, bombastic fashion that had us all coughing out clouds of prime harvest and worrying our sides would split open from cackling so hard.

Everything remains a filmy mist from this point on. I do remember Belinda holding on to me, nibbling on my earlobe as I looked out at the city lights. The Bay Bridge arched to Treasure Island, bending and continuing across the bay to the more distant sparkles of Oakland.

Somehow, we are all together in the back seat of the car, and we are laughing— and laughing—and laughing—I must have dozed, or fallen asleep, for I awaken emerging from a quivering black hole that immediately evaporates—there was a grotesque dream lurking deep down in its recesses somewhere—but it has evaporated too—and there is absolutely no sound—we are encased in a vacuum—an acoustic vacuum—now I find myself in the front seat—with Travis—and the girls are together in the back—I speak out to them and I feel the vibration of tone in my throat—yet there is no sound—nor is there movement anywhere—everything has become suspended—floating in a timeless spatial wilderness—and I want to stay awake—I need to stay awake—I want to investigate—but I am being swallowed up by the black void again—I cannot help it—I cannot stop it—I just keep sliding—sliding deeper—deeper inside . . . .

CHAPTER 38

I'd grown accustomed to out of sync Saturdays. After all, they came on the heels of the premier party night of the week. But this Saturday seemed different. I just couldn't put my finger on it.

Belinda seemed normal, singing to herself in the bathroom, where she'd been bathing and primping for the past two hours. Yet beyond the usual vacillating, abstracted detachment I accepted as a routine part of the mental cope following any drug binge, I had this unsettling, foreboding feeling that seemed to permeate everything everywhere. A nagging sense of tenuous, obscure events and shadowy phantoms I could not bring to mind. I recognized my annoyance that we'd missed the Grateful Dead the night before. But the real irritation, whatever it involved, was more profound than that. I just couldn't get a grip on it. Perhaps, like a deep-seated splinter, it would eventually draw to the surface. I decided to try to set the diagnosis aside for now. If an infection was forthcoming, I should know about it soon enough.

Damn it. I don't believe it. I'm already late. Now I'll be even later. The Healey's got a flat tire, all right. The first flat since my used car and re-tread days back in Augusta. Shit, I don't even know where to start the job, it's been so long. I've got to be too far from Justin's house to even think about making it on foot.

I looked around for a phone. Finally found one outside a corner hardware store a few blocks away.

"Hey, that's a bummer, man. I feel for you. Tell you what. We need to haul ass. You know how to get down there, right?"

Justin had his mouth revving, like he was not only anxious to get going, but maybe on speed as well.

"Just get on the old coast highway. You know, Route I. Take it all the way to Half Moon Bay. The club's at the corner of Main and Mill. You can't miss it. It's a real small town. So we'll see you when you get there. Just look for the table full of assholes."

After a few scraped knuckles and minor cuts, I figured out how the jack worked and where to place it to raise the car. I couldn't find a nail or anything. But the tire, just like all the others, had worn dangerously thin and needed to be replaced. With what I had sitting in my checking account, they wouldn't be Michelins anymore. Thank God the spare had air in it, though I'm sure no longer anywhere near the recommended pressure. The lug nuts were as tight-ass as old Colonel Slater, who'd tried to tear up my officers' commission back there at Fort Gordon. I figured they might be rusted to the bolt. Leaning my weight into the wrench, I dug deep into my old repertoire of curse words, for the whole neighborhood to appreciate.

An hour later the Healey had its flabby spare mounted and ready to rotate. But I'd ended up sweaty, disheveled and discouraged. Forget Half Moon Bay and Justin's latest local rock find. I decided to head on home. A doobie, shower and the stereo sounded like a pleasant alternative. Maybe Belinda and I could hook up for a bite to eat somewhere.

The second I opened the door I knew this would be the last episode in this chapter of my life. Before my eyes focused hard on the sordid sight before me, before the total impact of it registered in my brain, I could feel the chill as my hairs rose from their follicles. I tasted the bitter curdling in the back of my throat. As a kid, my mother had often badgered me with the expression, "I smell trouble." Not until this very moment did I understand the most literal interpretation of its meaning.

Nicky flew from the bed in an instant, reaching for her clothes on the nearby chair, her white buttocks illuminated by the glimmering candles. Belinda remained in the bed, sitting straight up and holding the sheet in front of her, as if to shield her breasts from the violation of my intruding eyes.

It was pretty much your standard "guy catches his gal in the sack with someone else" scenario. Other than the controversy the lesbian and bisexual tangent added to the equation. We've all seen the familiar plot line over and over again, in movie theaters and on television screens. We've read about it in books and magazines. Oddly enough, my mind thought this as I stood there at the door, watching Nicky get dressed while Belinda sat stone-faced on the bed. It occurred to me that in all the representations of this classic scene I could ever recall, pivotal high drama took place in the harsh light of truth. It represented the crucial moment when emotions ran the gamut of human sensitivities, when physical impulses reacted instinctively within the uncultivated province of nature's domain.

In these tragic instances normal people yell and scream, threaten and cry, lash out in anger and pain, recoil in shame or fear. This night, for whatever earthly reason or position of the planets in our constellation, no such sensational hysteria took place. Nicky put her coat on. She walked past me to the door. She wouldn't look at me. Before she went out she turned back to Belinda and said simply, "See ya." Then she was gone.

I sat down in the kitchen, loaded my Chase & Sanborn with the last piece of Justin's fine hash, and lit up. Extending a courtesy Belinda didn't deserve, I waited until her Hamilton Camp record finished. Then I put Procol Harum's "Repent Walpurgis" on the turntable and punched up the volume. I returned to the commiseration of my fond friend and smoked the rest of it, looking out on the lights of Broadway. I considered hiking down to the Gallery, then decided I wasn't in the mood to go anywhere just yet.

Long after the album concluded I got up, undressed, and slid into the sofa bed next to Belinda. She faced the wall, lying with her back to me, her breathing calm, restful. But I knew she was still awake. I lay there for a while, staring at the repetition of flickering provocations as the striptease lights played their cheap flirtatious games with the psychedelia of the ceiling posters.

My lips parted of their own accord. "I want you out of here tomorrow."

She didn't answer. She didn't have to. I knew she'd heard me.

The serenity of that night's experience was merely a mask to disguise the shock and panic, the rage and embarrassment. Wounds beyond mending. Manifestations to be expected from such trauma dawned the following day of reckoning. While she packed up her things, I managed to call her a whore and a slut.

"To tell you the truth, Belinda, it's not that you're apparently a lezzie . . . bisexual, or whatever, that really bothers me. What bothers me is the fact you cheated on me. That makes you a slut. Even if last night 'just happened,' like this hasn't been going on for some time, and we both know that's bullshit, you broke the faith between us. Either way, you chose to deceive me. To make a mockery of whatever we had between us. Plain and simple, you betrayed our special connection. And that's why you're nothing but a whore."

She countered, calling me a hypocrite. Her last words, as she went out the door, jarred me to my very foundation.

"So call me whatever you like, Mr. Pretender. But your hypocrisy is your own self-denial. You're the classic pot calling the kettle black. If you catch my drift."

With that, she slammed the door on our relationship forever. Standing behind the sheer curtains at my front window I watched her wait at the curb until Nicky picked her up. They jammed her junk into the trunk and back seat of Travis's car. Good luck to that poor bastard, I thought to myself, as the old sedan rolled away and disappeared down Vallejo Street.

Not even Richie Havens and a joint could help me shake the cloud of conjecture that darkened my apartment and my mind. *What did she mean by that last comment?* That night of drugs up on top of Twin Peaks kept creeping into my thoughts. *Was she making some oblique reference to something that might have happened up there?* I wished I'd had her clarify that last remark before I let her go. It might have helped to provide some answers, if not remedies, to my continuing uneasiness since that cobweb evening.

I pulled out my valise from the back of the closet. The masking taped hiding place beneath the armoire had become history, inadequate to conceal the bongs, scale, Mary Jane pot cleaner, reefer rolling tool and other druggie paraphernalia to which I'd graduated. I wanted to be certain Belinda hadn't run off with more than her majority share of our stash. My mouth must've fallen open as my eyes widened. She'd left her entire supply of pot, pills and hash, and her own pieces of underground drug gear. Even her choice Middle East hookah was there, all shined up for another trip.

My, my, I thought to myself. *Isn't this something? What a marvelous legacy for her to leave me. How considerate. Why, I just might've found a quick way to escape my little black cloud. This very night, no less.*

CHAPTER 39

The Gallery was packed. Not one bar stool available, every row of the little theater filled. Even the coffee and cake café section crowded.

I planted myself by the jukebox and dropped a buck's worth of quarters down the slot. I pushed the buttons for M63, the Tim Hardin song I'd purchased and never got to hear that night I had the clash with the drunken hippie. Also Paul Butterfield, Jimi Hendrix and a couple other personal favorites. Having swallowed one of the mystery pills from Belinda's stash, whatever chemical I'd ingested should be finding its way to my brain in a little while. I hoped it would mesh with my music selections. I sipped my Jack and soda with satisfaction while observing the action around me.

Then it began. Barely perceptible at first. I started to feel a bit like I was back on the high seas, crossing one of those great oceans. I sensed a shade of queasiness, as if I hadn't taken the precaution of Dramamine tablets. Without warning the tidal wave hit, with such force the place began to turn upside down. It seemed as though God had decreed to invert the gravitational sway, reestablishing the draw from above instead of below. The floor became the ceiling, the ceiling the floor. As if a miracle occurred as a side effect of a catastrophic event, none of the bottles and glasses and ashtrays, or people, including myself, crashed down to that plaster ceiling. Amazingly, even the hanging bar lights maintained their positions. Their interwoven chains and electrical cords stood firm beneath the lamps, like they'd solidified to provide leg support. Of course, they needed to pay allegiance to the reverse drag as well. For some reason I recalled that day in second grade, when Miss Aldemir had explained the earth and the force of gravity. It seemed hard to imagine us all sticking out in space from the sides of the world we lived in, yet we didn't fall off. The plausibility hit me that since the power of gravity now pulled the other way, perhaps the surface of the globe encompassed us from the interior. In essence, we adhered to the inner wall of a giant magnetic ball. Before I had time to consider this preposterous proposition, everything wavered right and left, up and down and around, spinning now, reeling out of control. I had to get away, I couldn't handle it. It all began moving much too fast. I got dizzy with the speed. Somehow I made my way, upside down, to the door leading outside. The moment I stepped through, gravity swung back around. I was hurtled across the sidewalk into the fender of a parked car. Sliding on cold metal before spinning off into the street, I lost my equilibrium as I went. I fell onto the hard pavement to the shrieks of a blaring horn and squealing tires.

Floundering in and out of a topsy-turvy fog, I picked up snatches of conversations above me.

"What happened?"

"Is he all right?"

". . . somebody push him?"

"Jesus . . . flew out in front . . . can't believe I didn't hit him . . . didn't feel like I hit anything."

". . . you didn't hit him . . ." "Did you see it?" "I saw it . . . he just fell . . ."

". . . stoned out of his head . . . ."

". . . God, he looks so white . . . ."

"Come on, guys . . . pick him up . . ." "What should we do?" ". . . put him on the sidewalk . . ." "Grab his arms . . ." ". . . before he does get run over."

"My word, Henry . . ." ". . . one of those hippies . . ." "He doesn't look like a drug addict . . ." ". . . overdosed . . . right here in the road . . ." "Would you believe it? . . . you don't see this in Topeka."

"What's wrong with him, Dad?"

". . . some poor junkie . . . trying to get himself killed . . . Take a good look, son, this is what happens when you get into drugs."

"He's not going to die, is he?"

Somehow I managed to find my way back to the apartment. I must've been outside the door for quite a while, though. I remember coming out of a very long tunnel of icy stalactites and stalagmites, lying on the stoop at the base of my door, my key still in the palm of my hand. It took a long time to work the night latch, but I persevered and made it inside. I woke up to a gravely depressing reality the next afternoon.

That night, rather, Monday night, come to think of it, I received a telephone call from back home. The phone had rung twice Sunday evening, my usual chat time with Mom and Dad. But I'd been in such a shaky condition I'd just let it ring. I remained far from my normal self, my mind racing down cul-de-sacs of logical illogic. I also felt nervous and fidgety, consumed by a fear that I tread on the slick edge of a crevice reeking with the stench of certified mental insanity. One wrong step and I could slip right in, emerging on the other side where the people in white coats held syringes and straitjackets in their hands. I hoped I could find my way through talking to Mom and Dad without them knowing just how bad off I was.

"Robbie? What are you doing?" Mom's voice, honed to razor sharp. She always found a nice way to start a conversation.

"Nothing much, Ma. Just kind of sitting around, taking it easy. Going over some of the insurance projects I need to get accomplished this week." She always liked to hear things like that, relating to responsibilities, work ethic, career commitment, and such. I exhaled a breath of relief for having gotten this far without falling apart.

"Well, the reason I ask is that I think you should sit down and listen to what I have to say. This isn't going to be an easy conversation, for either of us."

It never was with Mom, I thought. But I felt glad she'd be going first this time, so I could finish up talking with Dad.

"Are you sitting down?"

"Yes, I'm sitting down, Mom. What's up?"

I heard a sound on the other end of the line I couldn't make out. At first I thought it might be static. Then I heard her voice again, and I realized she was crying. Something I couldn't remember having ever seen her do.

"I'm sorry. I'm just having a little problem dealing with this. It's so . . . overwhelming."

"That's okay, Mom. Go ahead. What is it?"

Another lapse on the other end. Completely quiet this time. I thought we'd been cut off. Then her voice came back on the line, sounding as distraught as I felt.

"I . . . I think you need to get yourself home, Robbie. It's your father."

A volley of soft static pelted my ear again. Then the stabbing words I suppose I knew all along lurked right around the corner.

"He . . . he's got cancer. He's not going to be with us that much longer. He's got cancer, Robbie. Do you hear me?"

"Yes. I hear you, Mom."

I felt like I'd just dropped into the crevice, chair and all.

CHAPTER 40

Sitting at my desk in the office of United Mutual, I remained incapable of doing any worthwhile work. I kept thinking about the telephone call from the night before. It stood alone as the time I didn't get to talk with Dad. Mom said he couldn't bring himself to speak to anyone just yet. I tried to imagine what he must be going through, having just been issued a death sentence. It had to be worse than the firing squad, I guessed, if you split hairs. At least when the bullets hit you, it's all over. Without the lingering pain and growing fear as you get closer to your undetermined fateful day.

Mom said Dad had lung cancer. The doctors gave him a year, at the most. I should've known, the way he chain-smoked and coughed all the time. Mom should've, too. Why the hell hadn't she looked after him better? She was with him all the time. That probably contributed to it. Christ, she made him so nervous. It's no wonder he smoked like a madman. I wondered how long she'd let him go since his last physical. Lucky Strike. How cruel to name killer tobacco Lucky Strike. Lickety-split, I'd thrown my carton of Pall Mall into the garbage after the news, determined I would not smoke again. Except for grass and hash, of course.

In my tangled state of mind I couldn't make a decision as to what I should do. My finances had gotten critically short. It was daunting just to think about driving cross-country again, this time on my own resources, with no job waiting on the other side. I'd have to invest in new tires to make the trip, for one thing. I could drive at night, to avoid traffic and make better time. Sleep in my car during the day, when it would be safer. That would preclude spending money on motel beds. And they have cheap showers at some truck stops, so I could maybe freshen up when I needed to.

Good lord, I thought, what a terrible way to come home. Pushing 30 years old now, "without a pot to piss in," as Mom would say. I'd have to eat humble pie and stay at the house again. The realization swept me back to Jane Lennox, that summer we'd lived together, after my falling out with Mom and Dad. My God, consider the reign of death that's taken its toll all around me since then. JFK assassinated, just before Jerry Blakely killed himself on Thanksgiving night, leaving Jane behind to languish mindlessly in her living demise. And Bobby Bennett and Billy Riggins found bullets in Vietnam. Then Martin Luther King and soon Robert Kennedy after him, only those national leaders bought it right here in good old peace-loving America.

Now Dad. Dying from bullets of another sort. My boss knew Dad, of course; he'd hired me because of Dad. Maybe I could arrange taking a leave of absence, or something. Return to this job, if things didn't work out back home. Trent and I got along okay. Yet I couldn't bring myself to tell him. Not this day, anyway. I had to make some kind of decision before I said anything. Whether Belinda's mystery pill continued to work its sorcery on me, or I'd become shell-shocked by the awful twists in my life, I didn't know what to do just yet.

Wednesday I played the office game for yet another unproductive day. I headed back to my apartment at five o'clock, still living alone on the drifting isle of limbo.

❧   ❧   ❧

I never saw him until I almost bumped into him. He sat there, on my stoop.

"Hey there, pardner. How you doing?"

"God Almighty! Don't scare me like that!"

It happened like a jolt from Heaven, seeing my old friend out of the blue. I froze in place, standing in front of him. Then I felt the wave of relief wash over me.

"Jesus, Lenny, it's so fucking good just to see you."

I'm sure I surprised him when I hugged him right there, grabbing him by the arm and hustling him inside, giving him a tour of my tiny pad, all the while talking incessantly. He didn't comment on my interior decorating. But I don't think he anticipated the candles, posters, and all the other nonconformist bohemian oddities I'd collected from around the city.

"What're these little china bowls and stuff for?" he asked, picking one up from the lacquered chest and looking it over in his hand.

"Those are incense holders," I replied. "You know, you burn incense sticks in 'em. Like your Music Room honey did back at school."

"Oh. For when you're doing your drugs," he said matter-of-factly, most likely withholding the scorn he felt inside.

"Well . . . not just for that. It gives a nice fragrance to the place. Same with a few of the candles. Some of 'em are scented."

I opened the refrigerator door. "Say, Lenny . . . I've got club soda, Pepsi and some jug wine. Jack Daniels under the sink. Or I could introduce you to my local hangout. Kind of like when you first took me down to the Chanticleer. Remember that? Man, what a night that was."

A smile crept across Lenny's face. "Let's do it. Yeah. Let's go sip a few. I'd love to bop around in your rumpus room." His serious side returned. " 'Course, I can't be drinking too late. I got a flight out in the morning."

"That's all right, man. I won't keep you out long. I promise." The fact that he'd tried to abide my earlier criticism from his last visit didn't go unnoticed.

When we got there I couldn't introduce Lenny to anybody at the Gallery. Outside of one of the bartenders, no one acted like they even knew me. Or really cared, for that matter. But the two of us had a fine time, later moving from the bar to one of the small tables when it became available, so we could talk more in depth to each other.

Lenny's life seemed to be going well, on an even keel. He loved the constant travel of being a commercial airline pilot, the thrill of flying those big jets. Of course, he had a new girl in his life. He showed me her photograph.

"Yeah, might actually settle down with this one, Robbie. Could be a keeper. And she can cook! Her name's Denise. She's a real sweetheart."

Maybe she didn't happen to be photogenic, but she sure didn't look anywhere as beautiful as I remembered Marjorie. She didn't have that twinkle in her eye and mischievous smile, either. But it was only a picture.

I told Lenny about my eye-opening revelation regarding Belinda. We recalled the lesbians I'd inadvertently gotten involved with one night at the old Chanticleer. His bent for humor blossomed once again.

"Oh, yeah. You mean AC/DC Trudy. And her chubby dyke girlfriend. The one with the strap-on! And you thought you might have your first threesome. How appropriate the two of 'em hung out at a place known as the 'Red Rooster,' don't you think?"

We both laughed about that bygone night, like we hadn't laughed together in a long time. At that moment I noticed Lenny still wore his sapphire ring. I felt so much better. We enjoyed a few more chuckles and drinks. Then I took him down the street to La Pantera, where we digested the excellent food and dining companionship. After the cannoli and spumoni Lenny looked at his watch and suggested he hit the road. He agreed to let me drive him to his hotel.

On the way downtown I blurted out the troubling thoughts preying on my mind. Just like that, Zina danced off the tip of my tongue. "I know I never mentioned this to you before, Lenny. Guess I should've. Well, when I last saw Zina in Nürnberg she was supposed to have some kind of surgery, for a female problem. She was worried she wouldn't be able to have any kids afterwards, so I guess it was pretty serious."

After all the time, treasure and trash washed down the river since that final rendezvous, I chose this moment to lay it all out for him.

"She wanted us to make a baby together. Right then and there. She talked kind of crazy. Like a kid would be our chance for some sort of . . . *ever-after*. Yeah, that was her exact word. And she was willing to take the risk in spite of a medical condition where she has to have this operation. I guess she felt having my baby would bond us together forever. Even though she's spending the rest of her life, maybe even raising our kid, while she's married to this Lars dude. Damn . . . I sure wish I knew how she's doing."

Suddenly aware of my sweaty palms, I eased my stranglehold on the steering wheel.

"And now I find out my Dad has . . . cancer." It became more difficult to maintain my composure. "He's not going to make it. And I don't know what to do. I finally got a respectable job, thanks to him. I guess I should just can it and go home to be with him. But I'm flat broke, I need new tires on the Healey . . . ."

Lenny let me get it all out, his blue eyes clasping my brittle mental state in a steadfast gaze. When I finished, his voice responded with reassuring calm.

"You get your ass home, Charley. You only get one dad in your life. Both you and me been mighty lucky in that regard. Think about all the good things he did for you over the years. You probably weren't even conscious of a lot of it, and the rest you mostly forgot. He needs you now, man. It's your turn to give some of that back. Spend as much time with him as you can, while he's still around. Show him how much you appreciate all he done for you. How much you love him."

I stopped for a traffic light. Lenny paused to take in the pedestrians passing before us in the crosswalk. When he continued, it seemed he spoke straight to my inner soul.

"As for Zina, she's one fantastic girl, all right. And you had the good fortune to have experienced an incredible love affair with her. I'm sure if she had your kid she'd have contacted you, somehow. But she *is* married. The rest of her life belongs to someone else. You got to put it behind you, brother. You got to let it go."

This was why Lenny stood alone, unparalleled, my faithful "pardner." Why he'd always be my Prince Valiant. He'd always come to my rescue. He'd never let me down. He knew what was best for me. The light changed to green and I put my foot to the accelerator.

Now he offered more pearls. "You may want to come back out here. That's okay. But before you do, check out your roots, your hometown pals. Check out yourself again, back in your old stamping grounds. It ain't going to be the same as it was. Don't expect that. But neither are you. Maybe you'll want to start a whole new life back there, where you know you once belonged. Maybe you'll find your career calling. You said yourself this gig here is just a job. At any rate, if it doesn't fit any more, at least you know you tried it on."

Another red light. Lead car in our lane again, we went through the same routine once more.

"And don't be all stressed about the money," he said, after the passersby had thinned. "Try to work out a rough figure on how much you're going to need to make the move. You know, the tires, the gas, meals and beds. And enough to tide you over while you decide what you want to do from there. Everything, totaled up. Then you let me know if you need some help. You just give me a number, if it comes to that. If I can't do it all, I'll do what I can. And there's no interest when you borrow from my bank, you understand? That's what friends are for. Besides, I fly into New York and Joisey every now and then, so you won't be seeing the last of me. I ain't worried about getting my shekels back."

Signal sanctioned and clear to proceed, we rolled on down the avenue. I was overwhelmed. "Jesus, Lenny, I don't know what to say. I was really worried about us after the last time you were in town. Until tonight, I wasn't sure you were even wearing our ring anymore. Now you're offering me money to help me out."

"That's because we're pardners for life, Robbie. So we'll always be wearing our pardner rings, won't we?"

"Yes we will," I cried. We tapped those black sapphires together one more time.

I pulled the Healey over to the curb in front of his hotel. As he got out of the car he turned back and leaned his head inside.

"By the way. When we get together back East, I expect you'll be letting me take 'my baby' for another spin when we're out together on the Jersey Turnpike."

With that he closed the door, flipped me a salute through the window, and stepped toward the hotel lobby. I gave him a toot as I pulled away into traffic. Once again, after seeing Lenny, I came away with some answers, and a whole new outlook on my life.

Trent was his usual class act when I told him about Dad and announced I would be leaving the following week to be with him.

"I am so sorry about your father, Robbie. Though I didn't have the opportunity to see him that often, I was always impressed by the way he presented himself. He's a good man. Honest. An agent I think is really concerned about the best interests of his clients. There's just not enough of those kind of people around these days, unfortunately. He will be missed.

"And I'm personally sorry to lose you," he continued. "But say . . . let me check out our agency in New York. If you're interested, you may be able to continue with us back there. Would you like me to do that?"

His solicitude surprised and flattered me. "I really appreciate that, Trent. Yes, I'd like that. At the moment I'm not sure what my future is going to be. But I would be interested in that possibility. And I want to thank you for all you've done for me here. You're right up there with my Dad."

"I don't know how true that is, but it certainly is nice to hear."

That took care of that. Heading home a little early, I stopped by Columbia Records' office on my way out. Belinda and Connie sat at their desks.

"Belinda. Do you have a minute?" She looked up at me. I saw the skepticism etch her face. "I've got some things of yours."

She got up and walked over to me. "Let's go out in the hall," she replied, her voice bated, her tone iced.

I told her she'd forgotten her stash when she left the apartment. She didn't hesitate with her response.

"You can keep that shit, for your head. Let's just say that's payment for my share of the rent. But I want my hookah back."

It astonished me she'd let all those good drugs go, just like that. I wasn't about to argue. She hadn't offered to help out with the rent before.

"Okay. You got it. I'll wrap it up in something. Maybe find a box somewhere and bring it to the office. If that's not a problem."

"That's not a problem," she said curtly.

I searched her eyes as we stood there. I had a notion to ask her about the night up on Twin Peaks. But looking at her smoldering face glaring back at me, I was reminded of the time in my boyhood when I'd nettled a nest of wasps. I decided to just let it be.

"Fine, then. I'll drop it off here tomorrow."

I turned toward the bank of elevators and walked away, feeling her eyes following me. When the elevator arrived I glanced over in her direction. She'd returned to her desk, but stared straight at me, through the glass partition. I stepped inside and punched the button for ground level.

CHAPTER 41

Justin acted like he was real sorry to see me go. We smoked some hash and listened to his stereo. I made my last purchase from him. He made good on getting me the more potent, seedless Mary Jane I craved. Who knows how long it would be before I found a contact back in Jersey. Awkwardness ruled when we hugged each other at the door. It struck me that I never once got to meet his working mom, let alone his invisible dad. A moment later I was back in my car and on my way.

That last weekend I hung out in North Beach, testing the pot and hash I'd just bought, and bidding farewell to all my old haunts.

Of course, I spent most of my time in the Coffee Gallery. Saturday night I'd staked my claim to a stool at the bar when a bunch of Hell's Angels tromped into the place. Unbelievably, Janis Joplin was with them. They seated themselves at the big round table right behind me, at the outer rim of the café section. I watched them in the bar mirror. Janis started drinking her famous Southern Comfort, cackling and cursing like one of the boys. I admired her for her fiery spirit, her "I don't give a crap" demeanor. Yet even in the smoky mirror I saw something else, something we both shared. Her eyes gave it away—somewhere inside, the frailness, the vulnerability of the inherent loner.

"How about you, chum? Gonna' buy a chance on Luke's Harley?"

I turned my head to face a heavyset Angel with a full beard.

"Come on, they're only ten bucks a pop."

"You're raffling off one of your brother's bikes?" I didn't quite get it, and ten dollars is ten dollars.

"Yeah. Luke crashed with some semi out on the highway, man. He's up there with the rest of them Angels in the big sky. We're raising the loot to pay for his casket and funeral expenses. How many you want?"

Amazing. Selling chances on the busted parts of a wrecked cycle. Now that is *chutzpah*, as they'd say at the Rainbow Diner.

"So . . . when is the drawing? I'm headed back East."

He couldn't have cared less. "We're putting on a rock show in a couple months. Probably at the Avalon. We'll pull the winning ticket that night. How many you want?"

"I'm a little short on cash right now."

He just looked at me.

"Well . . . give me one."

"One it is," he snorted. "Ten bucks."

I forked over, thinking this amounted to a senseless expenditure, hastening the depletion of my already strained travel budget. But I didn't need a hassle with the Hell's Angels my last night at the Gallery. Not in front of my heroine, Janis. I tried to look at it as paying my final tribute to the place that had been the catalyst behind my unforgettable times in San Francisco.

Considering Lenny's generous offer, I elected to pass on borrowing any money from him. At least for the time being. I purchased four new B.F. Goodrich tires, on sale, for my street-dented Healey. Made sure my Michelin spare had plenty of air. It appeared I had enough in my checking account to last me a few months; I understood I had Lenny's loan as insurance if I'd miscalculated, or something unexpected cropped up. I didn't know if Mom and Dad would be charging me room and board, as they had the short while I lived at home after college. But I allotted a hundred dollars a month for that, realizing Mom would not likely renounce that moral issue, no matter how dire my circumstances.

I departed San Francisco mid-afternoon on Monday, just before the hectic commuter traffic would start clogging up the highways. Good old Route 80 again, this time for the entire trip. I drove straight through that first night, getting myself acclimated to my planned schedule of traveling mostly after sundown and resting during part of each day.

In the middle of that first segment, I glided along all alone somewhere under a full moon in eastern Nevada, wheels humming to the tune of my autobahn accustomed cruise of 90 to 100 miles per hour. Headlights caught my mirror. I kept my eye on my distant neighbor, figuring the vehicle would not be keeping up with me. When it became obvious it was closing the gap, I felt certain I'd garnered the attention of a Nevada State trooper. I decelerated down to a more respectable 75.

Crossing the border into Utah, the lights crept even closer. I now let my foot weigh heavier on the pedal, edging back up to 85, relieved I'd made it to a different state and assuming I had another fleet civilian traveler behind me. The night seemed haunted, the moon ascending into the Milky Way, lighting up the Great Salt Lake Desert, the terrain eerily similar to what I would have expected on that cratered satellite. I imagined we also glowed, conspicuous in the eternal black vault of the heavens, even more dominant in space from that celestial body's perspective.

The headlights in my mirror disappeared when the white Austin-Healey roared by me. The chase was on. Like wild stallions, identical save for our color, we galloped across the last frontier, focused on the swift trail before us, refreshed by the test of pace and power, proud of our common lineage.

I followed close behind as we slowed through the suburbs of Salt Lake City. Finally free to the open road, piston-pumping engines took turns leading each other in the accelerating tear across the moonbeam earth—90, 100, 110, past Green River and Rock Springs, Wyoming; 115, then topped out on the speedometer at 120 by the blurred signs for BITTER CREEK, TABLE ROCK and RED DESERT.

Though we remained strangers, we'd become meteoric alter egos of the journey. I recalled with nostalgia my drive down the mountain of *lacets* en route to Lenny in Nice, when I raced with the girl in the Alpha Romeo, our spirited goodbye waves sharp contradictions to the blasé seashore splash of the Mediterranean.

Now my new acquaintance and I exchanged places once again, sprinting under the stars and over the basin of the Great Divide. Horsepower propelled our machines well beyond the cap of the dashboard gauge. I acknowledged a sense of reawakening as we took the rise and fall and graded turns across the Rocky Mountains. After slowing for the sparse lights of Rawlins, we again tempted the kick of pulse-tingling speed, the needle once more flat against the max until we reached the outskirts of Laramie.

The white stud resumed the lead as we fell back to that easy drift of 90 to 100. After a time, my pale companion made a signal to exit at the cowboy town of Cheyenne. She raised her jewel-spangled hand to the flash of my headlights, a mutual "farewell forever, my highway friend." A few miles further along, I pulled into a roadside rest stop and parked amidst three trailer trucks. The light of a new dawn had just begun to crack the horizon under that alabaster orb of the night.

CHAPTER 42

. . . "Bob Dylan's Dream" carried us back . . .

After the strenuous intoxication of the road race, the Healey ran into problems crossing the continent. It broke down sixty miles east of Des Moines. The owner of the only repair shop in the nearest small town charged me two hundred smackers, and his country boy mechanic advised me to take it easy the rest of my trip. It seemed I needed a new transmission and additional work under the hood. My ailing deep-green jewel and I limped into Denton in the middle of the night. I slept until supper time the next day while the car dripped fluids in the street outside.

A Fort Lee service center whose sign said they specialized in "European Autos" charged me another fifty dollars to confirm I indeed faced major expenses to keep the car on the road. Dad advised me he would be acquiescing to Mom's interest in buying a "brand-new secondhand Buick," a clean, low mileage '66 Riviera off a nearby used car lot. I could have his old Plymouth. I faced the hard facts of life and advertised my cherished possession in the classifieds. The very first week I ran the ad I opened a new bank account with five certified checks from the father of some 19-year-old kid who happily drove the car away, oblivious to the trail of wet spots he left in the street behind him. I stood on the sidewalk and watched him go, sad in the realization that an era of my life was over. The dream had started with a hitchhike ride up State Street hill my first year in college. It ended eleven years later, right back where I'd been before I even knew about such luxuries.

I became even more depressed during dinner that night, when Mom forced Dad to advise me he'd have to renege on just giving me the Plymouth. He agreed with her that I ought to be responsible enough to pay a nominal three hundred dollars. I should've known better than thinking I'd get something for nothing when it came to Mom. I'd started paying room and board at the Bender house, just like before.

"After all," Mom emphasized, "the dealer offered us almost twice that on a trade-in."

Dad looked even weaker as he quietly sipped his cup of soup at the table.

Yet he rose to the occasion, once again, when it came to my ambiguous career. Trent Witherspoon had been unable to get me a job at United Mutual's New York branch. Despite my relative success selling ex-GI's in San Francisco, they had no sales openings in the entire metropolitan area. I wondered if maybe there might be more to it than that. Nevertheless, as he'd done before, and for my sister, Barbara, now an administrative supervisor with another agency and primary breadwinner in her marriage, Dad secured another job for me. This time I landed a sales position with his company. In fact, he managed an early retirement package for himself, in conjunction with his failing health, negotiating an arrangement whereby I would take over his accounts. So it came to be that a new Bender replaced the old at Gaylord-Slocum Insurance Brokerage. I was not entitled to Dad's private office, however.

The morning had been brilliant, a warm sun penetrating the night's coolness, combining for a comfortably fresh and fragrant summer day. By the afternoon, however, all that changed. Heavy clouds rolled in, spreading a flat layer of iron gray between that ball of fire and the black-clad assemblage gathered in the vast garden of tombstones. If not for the temperate humidity you might've thought you'd fast-forwarded seasons to February.

Dad's sister and two brothers, along with my cousins, traveled long distances to be present. Many friends, neighbors, people from the church and his office also paid their solemn tributes. In addition to the pastor's kind words and blessings, Dad's boss, Bradley Slocum, gave a most eloquent eulogy. Barbara, Patti and Donny joined me in making up for the tears Mom refused to shed. She dabbed at her moist eyes with her handkerchief, but did not display the grief I'd heard over the wires when she called me that traumatic Monday night in San Francisco. I guess she considered the public display of such emotion a sign of weakness. It could well be a human trait she never possessed at all. Or had lost to the lash of my grandfather's belt long before I'd ever been born. Barbara's husband looked like he was suffering in his own inflexible mechanical world, hobbled in a coat and tie and ill at ease with the entire circumstance.

"Hello, Robbie Bender."

A warm voice from the distant past sent an unexpected shiver up my spine.

"I'm really sorry about your dad. I know how hard it must be for you. I want to extend my sympathy."

If not for the familiar tone color I don't know that I would've recognized her. At least not from a casual glance. She'd gained weight, taken on a matronly appearance. She wore what looked to be a bargain basement print dress. Then I looked into her eyes and found myself snagged once more on those seductive hazel enticements. No mistaking the enduring allure of Mandy Hardwick. Three children romped unrestrained around her, noticeably light-complected compared to the baby in her arms. She attempted to calm them down and gather them together.

"Kids . . . stop that, Matthew! I want you to say hello to an old friend of mine. This is Mr. Bender."

The girl obeyed and I shook her little hand. The two boys continued to taunt each other, disregarding the momentous occasion.

Mandy gave up her futile attempts to corral them, content to allow them the freedom of more relevant juvenile antics.

"Boys will be boys," she said, giving me that familiar look I'd seen emanate from a slender, more youthful face so many times before, so long ago.

Out of the corner of my eye I became aware of a white, wide-brimmed hat. Mandy's mom stood there, looking as elegant as ever. As soon as I acknowledged her she stepped forward and gave me a sincere hug.

"Oh, you've grown to be such a fine young man, Robbie. I know your father was extremely proud of you. And he was such a good man, himself. The best deacon our church ever had. You just know he's in peace now."

She gave me a big kiss on the cheek. "Well. I'll leave you two kids alone."

Just as suddenly as she'd appeared, she departed. I turned back to Mandy.

"So, I guess you've been busy," I said, regretting the words even as they spewed out of my mouth.

She let it go. I learned she'd separated from her husband, trying to make ends meet tending bar somewhere in Ridgefield. The three fair-skinned kids were his, the source of the new baby left to my imagination. I told her something about my travels and my continuing companionship with Lenny. Then my sister, Patti, took my arm to rejoin Mom at the limousine.

It was another of those eminent awkward moments you remember for the rest of your life. I didn't know what to say as Patti tugged at my elbow. Mandy seized the vanishing stroke of time for her own precious words.

"Please give my best to Lenny when you see him. I'll always remember the wonderful times we had up at your college. They'll continue to be special memories in my life. Goodbye, Robbie Bender. I'm sorry it had to be this way. But I am glad I got to see you. Well . . . good luck, then."

She was gone again, walking away with her children skipping around her. Goodbye, Amanda Hardwick. And good luck to you, too.

Two weeks after Dad's funeral I received an early evening phone call. Yet another voice from the past, this one going back even further than Mandy.

"Hello there, Robbie. I hope it's not an inconvenient time for you. I'll leave you my number if you'd rather call me back."

The rush catapulted off the charts. Although the vocal timbre had changed somewhat with time, a bit fuller, lustier, I had a pretty good idea who it was. I tingled all over, feeling the heat of excitement inciting the flush of perspiration. Then the blade of skepticism sliced into my elation. I did not want to make a fool of myself.

"Please help me here. I know your voice. But it was so long ago. Let me apologize right up front . . . who is this?"

"Oh, Robbie. That really hurts. I would definitely have remembered your voice if you called me."

I understood she was teasing me now, savoring her transient anonymity. Just as quickly, she became serious.

"I'm so sorry about your father. Please accept my condolences. And pass them on to your mom. I went to the funeral. I didn't want to intrude, so I didn't approach you. Forgive me, but I just had to see you again. Your dad must've been a very special human being. I feel bad I never got to meet him myself. The ceremony was a beautiful tribute to one of those people who clearly deserve it."

The well of tears that had been tapped when Mom first told me about Dad in her cross-country phone call proved to be far from empty. I wiped my eyes with my shirt sleeve and struggled to stifle my emotions.

"Thank you. I really appreciate your words. I don't mean to be rude . . . but . . . could you please tell me who you are?"

Silence on the other end. Then, "Oh! Excuse me. I didn't tell you that, did I? This is Shirley. Shirley . . . McFarlin."

My spirits resumed their climb.

Until the little voice grumbled inside my head. *Hold it. Shirley got married. Way back when you were in college. You witnessed her bachelorette party at the Clancy Street Tavern. What's the deal here?*

". . . Uh, Shirley. I heard that you . . . that you were . . . well . . ."

"Water under the bridge, Robbie."

My optimistic anticipation soared once more, full-blown and unrelenting.

Ah, the thrill of nostalgia fulfilled. I was surprised to find Marty's Soda Shoppe still there on Broad Avenue. Shirley and I shared a large vanilla egg cream with two straws. Key items missing—her poodle skirt and my pegged pants.

"Robbie, this is such fun. But look how weird all these kids dress these days. My god, and our parents thought we were outrageous. We were such innocents."

"You're right, Shirley. But lucky for us, it was a whole lot safer back then. Besides holding on to our virginity for as long as we could, we weren't doing drugs, either. Hell, I thought pounding down a few beers in a vacant lot was high adventure. These teenyboppers today are smoking grass and popping pills . . . then jumping in the sack together."

"Robbie-e-e! You don't expect me to believe you were still a virgin in high school."

We'd started the wade into dangerous waters already. "Hey, you weren't about to let me get past second base in the back seat of any car. Don't tell me you had me going home aching for that dirty mag under my mattress, while other guys were hitting homers."

She wasn't going to slip into my snare that easily. "Wait just a minute, Mr. Most Talented in the class. Remember when we were sophomores? I sure wasn't dating the quarterback on the varsity football team when one certain jayvee halfback was going steady with the captain of the varsity cheerleaders. Seems to me I remember after you dumped her, one of your Omega brothers got her pregnant. And what about all the other girls who paraded around with your nasty skull and crossbones ring hanging over their hearts, at one time or another? I never even got a chance to get a green neck like that. And then, so many more you dated. I couldn't begin to keep score."

An inkling of truth emerged from my most subterraneous subconscious. Something I undoubtedly had denied until now.

"If I remember right, sweetheart, it was you who dated a lot of older guys. Like, you even went with Cynthia St. James' brother for quite a while. And he'd already graduated. You were also the best goddam' dancer in the whole frigging school. The fact of the matter is, and I think I just realized it now, I was actually intimidated by you. You weren't a little girl who I could control. You were . . . uh . . . mature. And you were tough. Deep down inside, I was afraid of you. You scared the shit out of me."

"Like you couldn't dance. Do you remember what couple was the center of attention grooving all over the floor at that big party at the firehouse our junior year? You and me, Robbie. And I wanted you to go past second base that night, riding home in the back seat. But you didn't even try."

Her face blushed toward the color of her ravishing auburn hair. I remember just sitting there at that moment, speechless, twirling my straw back and forth between my fingers and drinking in her beauty.

Then, without forethought, I found myself saying, "Do you suppose we'd freak out all these kids here if I just planted a big wet one on you . . . right here in the booth?"

The spherical parlor lights of the soda shop glinted like diamonds off her smiling eyes. "Why don't we just go find a back seat somewhere?"

CHAPTER 43

We decided not to move in together right away. Shirley McFarlin DeCorso was officially divorced. She also had custody of her 7-year-old son, Frankie. We wanted to let him get to know me first, rather than thrusting me into their everyday lives, under the same roof. Shirley's North Bergen apartment didn't have much space, either. So I set out to find something that could accommodate the three of us, closer to the end of her lease agreement, when we felt Frankie might be ready.

I had some income again, back in the old insurance ploy, and money in the bank, thanks to the sale of the Austin. The attic apartment I found in an old Victorian house in Weehawken was perfect. Besides being an interesting layout of fairly spacious rooms, with top floor features of vaulted and cathedral ceilings, and a stained glass window, it presented a number of other benefits. It just happened to be a short ride from Shirley's place. Also the Lincoln Tunnel into Manhattan, and Roscoe's, a busy Hoboken nightclub I'd been to a few times during vacation breaks from college. And I made note of the nice long ride from Mom.

It turned out to be ideal for smoking pot and hash and playing my stereo. The floors beneath me had been rented as office space for an accounting firm that went home punctually every evening at five o'clock. Soon I had Shirley, already addicted to nicotine, adept at rolling her own joints. As well as enjoying my trusty Chase & Sanborn bong for mind-expanding hits of hash. She'd only smoked pot on a couple of rare occasions, and that was it with illegal substances. But she learned to hold the drug long and deep in her lungs, for maximum impact. The box of lids I'd bought from Justin had been a worthwhile investment.

I remember the first time she tried some of it, surprised by her own reactions after just two or three puffs.

"My god, Robbie. This grass is really strong. And smooth as silk. The few times I tried it before, I didn't get anywhere near what I'm already feeling with this. And that stuff was harsh on my throat, too."

"Hey, honey, you're smoking some of the best wacko weed the West Coast has to offer. And to coin another California phrase, don't Bogart that joint. There's two of us here, you know." I leaned forward, extending my right hand toward her with itchy fingers. "I'd like another hit myself before that beauty's done."

The hash impressed her even more, of course. As a matter of fact, Shirley only did that when she knew she had the time for it, when she'd arranged for Frankie to be with his father or her mom, or had other satisfactory overnight accommodations and supervision. Ever the good mother, she insisted that her son not catch the slightest whiff of our outlawed diversion. We made certain that both of us and our separate residences were always "clean" in his presence.

This did not preclude the Weehawken loft from becoming the studio apartment on Vallejo Street, however, complete with the candles, incense and poster artwork. I went yet a step further, adding a collection of hanging stained glass ornaments we picked up in Greenwich Village, to complement the colorful window that graced a side wall of the living room.

We spent a lot of time in the Village where I took strides to further develop my bohemian proclivities. Shirley was no Belinda Bliss, consumed by a blind compulsion to the beatnik mentality and lifestyle. But her wardrobe did expand to include cowgirl boots, clogs and custom-made sandals, granny dresses and bell-bottoms, synthetic antique jewelry and a fringed, suede jacket. She even wore the black beret I insisted on buying her, which accentuated her garnet tresses and augmented her air of sophistication. We got a late start to one particular party, the very last to arrive, because I'd insisted she embellish that fabulous head of hair with a couple of beaded braids.

Greenwich Village remained as cool and avant-garde as it always had been, catering to the new youth culture, capitalizing on the fad aspect of it in the same manner as Haight-Ashbury.

But the area did not exude the same intensity of spirit and totality of hippie ethic that enveloped the entire city of San Francisco. Granted, its influence had extended longitudinally across Manhattan to the Lower East Side. Bill Graham opened his Fillmore East in another old movie theater, and new businesses had cropped up to serve the delirious appetites of the psychedelic generation. Yet it all remained an island within an island, viewed and visited as a neighborhood of society's oddities—those eccentric artists and actors and musicians, students and political activists, gays, derelicts, druggies and dropouts that served as just another tourist attraction inside the Big Apple.

For certain, the Village flourished in the volatile air of the protest movement and popular anti-establishment philosophies. But it never attained the same degree of energy or influence to make megalopolis New York the cultural mecca for America's young that San Francisco had become.

Looking at this now in retrospect, I realize the Haight's 1967 "Summer of Love" that I'd tasted represented the short-lived pinnacle in its crest of glory. My objectivity had also been skewed by the fact I'd resided right there in the cerebrum of that mind-bending, ideology-shifting, once-in-a-lifetime happening.

Following Lenny's advice, I also made attempts to reacquaint myself with hometown places and sidekicks. Through Shirley, of course, I got to see a few of her old girlfriends who'd become just that, like Ginger Jorgenson and some of the other Tri Gams.

But most of my high school pals had either left the area or had gotten themselves restrained by the leash of marriage. Eddie Mazzoli had dissipated into his own wasteland; his sister finally booted him out of her house on Long Island. She had no idea, nor did she "give a damn," where he might've gone. Though I couldn't bring myself to see Jane Lennox again, I did learn that her sister, Nadine, still took care of her and her son. *Hurrah for the "wayward slut," Mom.*

By way of former hangouts, the Clancy Street Tavern had maintained its teenage customer base with its current owner. I can't imagine how much graft the local sheriff must've collected over the years. T&J Lanes had changed, now sparsely filled with legitimate old-timers. Denton entailed a long drive from my Weehawken pad, anyway. Instead, I ended up making a few new bar scene buddies who occasioned Roscoe's ever so often. Then there was Gabe Kavanaugh, another salesman who worked at Gaylord-Slocum.

I'll never forget the way he approached me, driving us to lunch from the office. A few strands of his blond-streaked hair danced on the draft from his partly-open car window. He pulled a joint from his pocket and held it out to me.

"Here, let's see how good the food tastes after one of these."

Instinctively I took it from him, before realizing the implications and trying to cover my action.

"What is this? You roll your own cigarettes? Thanks, but I quit smoking when my Dad got cancer." I attempted to hand it back to him.

He glanced over at me, his walrus mustache stretching with the smirk on his face.

"Aw, come on now. Let's not play games here. You and I both know that ain't tobacco."

He smiled at me straight away. "Look, I can't light it and drive at the same time."

"Hey, I don't know about you, but I'm spending the afternoon in the office. I can't be doing one of these things in the middle of work." I continued to hold it out to him.

"Oh, don't be such a pussy. I'm going to be in the office, too. And Gaylord's a pothead himself. Can't remember how many doobies I've smoked with him."

I stared at him warily. "What makes you think I'm into this shit? Aren't you kind of taking a chance flaunting it around people you don't really know?"

The cynical sneer reappeared. "Robbie, Robbie. First of all, I don't *flaunt* drugs in front of strangers. I'm not that stupid. But I know damn well you've at least smoked pot before."

"And how do you know that?" I asked, my uneasiness growing by the second.

"Oh . . . let's just say you've got that look about you. I can see it in your eyes. You know, like, maybe it takes one to know one?"

"Well . . . I can't go back to the office high. Maybe some other time."

"All right! Sounds good to me!" He beamed with my admission. Then, still the consummate salesman, "Say, why don't we just do a couple quick hits? You know, to enjoy the burgers."

I gave him a hard look. He was smiling again. We laughed together as we pulled into the takeout line at a new fast-food operation called "Burger King."

I met with some success in my old acquaintance search when I stumbled upon a colleague from my college days. A great contact, by any measure. My talented fraternity brother who'd invited me to live out at the Nitecap, Rupert "Mad" Madigan, had gotten married to his old sweetheart, Mimi Lundeen. They owned a brownstone on the Upper West Side of Manhattan, just a few steps from Central Park.

Mad and I had lunch together, near his midtown Manhattan office. We somehow got onto the subject of drugs. My former mixed drinks and milk punch mentor said he and Mimi had an interest in trying grass. But neither of them had ever smoked a cigarette. I related my Christmas brownie adventure involving Belinda. We agreed to get together at their place for dinner sometime. Shirley and I would bring dessert.

Our first double date turned out to be a significant occasion. My Delta Upsilon brother couldn't contain himself when he called to say he'd procured four tickets for us to see none other than Janis Joplin, performing at the infant Fillmore East. I joked that I would have to get with Janis backstage, asking if I'd won the damaged motorcycle parts from the Hell's Angels fund-raiser rip-off back in San Francisco. Mad gave me his address and elaborate directions, inviting us to come early and partake of Mimi's culinary art. He also reminded me about my commitment to provide "the pudding," as he put it, conjuring up fond memories of his creative vocabulary of real and imagined words.

Mad greeted Shirley and me at the door. He flashed his mouthful of prominent teeth and bowed graciously before us, the medieval lord receiving his honored guests at his castle.

"Ah . . . how doest a knave the likes of Sir Robert Rapscallion manage to endear himself to such a winsome and willowy woman, pray tell? You never cease to amaze me, Sir Robert. Your taste in the feminine form has always been impeccable. Though I do recall a few wanton wenches along the way. But you've outdone yourself on this auspicious occasion, my fortunate fine-feathered friend."

He took Shirley's hand and leaned forward, kissing it gently. "Welcome to my humble dwelling, enchanting maiden. Your presence alone raises the stature, yea, perhaps even the real estate value of these paltry premises. Please allow me to show both of you inside. Lady Mimi awaits with hyperventilating anticipation."

After politely relieving us of the gifts we bore, the box of chocolate morsels and two bottles of wine, Mad led us into their immaculate, restored brownstone house. The interior boasted lofty doors and broad moldings of dark oak. We braced when greeted with an ear-piercing scream.

"Eeeeeek! Robbie-e-e-e! My long lost Robbie-e-e! Where have you been, my precious plum cake? Mimi has missed you so-o-o-o."

The pretty blonde party girl raced up to me, throwing her arms around my neck and her legs around my hips. "Mimi has missed you so-o-o."

As she kissed me on the cheek I looked over her shoulder, rotating past a hysterically laughing Mad until I faced flabbergasted Shirley.

"This is Mimi, honey. As you can see, she's a very affectionate person."

With greetings complete and goblets of Mateus Rosé in hand, we proceeded to put our forks to Mimi's scrumptious meal. In the heady ambiance of the feast I elected to risk posing a ticklish question to her.

"So, how's your sorority sister doing? What was her name? Carolynn . . . that's it. Did she ever get married to that Baylor guy she was pinned to?"

Mimi demonstrated her purposely preposterous self with her response. "Yes, Robbie, Carolynn married that guy, whatever his name is. And they've got three little brats now, living in . . . where is it? Oh . . . Tucson, I think. Isn't that in Arizona?"

Mad and I hummed our concurrences, our uneasy eyes now focused on our plates.

She continued in this faux-guileless fashion. "You know, she liked you very very much, Rob. She couldn't get over the wonderful time we all had, visiting you guys at your little lake house at Cornell. After that week with you, she wasn't at all certain she did the right thing marrying him. Anyway, she was a cute little brunette. But she sure didn't have hair as beautiful as your new lady friend here. Why, we're so delighted to meet you, girl!"

I cowered over my food, wondering why I'd been so dimwitted to bring that up, right in front of Shirley.

"Ho-dee-doh." Mad broke the agonizing silence. "Any-who, I can't wait for that delectable dessert delicacy you two rascals are going to treat us to. We better get a move on if we want to make the performance."

Without hesitation Shirley served our special brownies. Everyone gulped them down with high prospects. Mad pummeled me with questions. "How long will it take to feel something?" "What are the first symptoms?" "Is it like getting drunk on booze?" and so on. I advised them to look for a very different, more calming than stimulating high, something much more subtle. Drawing on what I'd learned from Belinda, I told them there would be a delay in reaction time, since we'd ingested the grass rather than inhale it. Also that the euphoria should last longer too, for the same reason. With that, we scuffled out the door for the concert.

I wished I had a better idea of when we would realize the effect of dessert. We diagnosed ourselves to be feeling normal, simply rosy from the wine and companionship. Mad led us to the downtown subway. On the underground platform he kept looking at me, shrugging his shoulders and wondering when the liftoff of his maiden voyage would occur. I just shrugged back at him.

We had to make a couple changes of trains to get to the Lower East Side. On each new platform Mad had more questions. I became concerned that maybe Shirley and I hadn't put enough pot into the brownie butter. Perhaps the baking cooked out some of the potency, or something.

Not until we'd gotten into the middle of our final ride did our expectations yield satisfaction. I sat across from Mad in the crowded subway car, jiggling in our seats as the clattering train hurtled forward inside the echoey black tunnel. I began to feel that symptomatic mad intensification of the senses shuttling through the corridors of my brain. Looking over at my fraternity brother, I saw him smiling at me. It had to have been the broadest grin I'd ever seen on his face. His eyes were flamenco dancers. I read his lips over the thunder of the subway car. "Boogie time!" I smiled back at him, nodding my head in confirmation. When we climbed the steps up to Second Avenue all four of us had caught the giggles, goofing with each other, spaced-out and glorious.

Janis had her gritty voice belting out that sweet pain once again. Her brassy new band seemed at least an improvement from Big Brother. But the free and easy atmosphere that distinguished San Francisco from New York became woefully obvious in the disparities between Fillmores East and West.

Bags, purses, and other belongings got scrutinized for contraband at the entrance. Security efforts monitoring audience activities remained vigilant throughout the program. Here they had assigned seating. Other than for restroom or snack bar trips, we faced restriction to our balcony seats, by ushers and a zealous security force. From our location Janis represented a tiny figure in a spotlight on a faraway stage.

I caught the occasional odor of weed in the air, minimal considering the size of the audience. Security did remove a few violators not stealthy enough in their covert recreation. The four of us managed to float near the ceiling for most of the show, not that far from our seats, since we'd fortuitously chosen to eat the evidence of our particular vice.

On the way home to New Jersey, Shirley cozied up next to me. Her fragrant breath whispered in my ear.

"You know, Robbie, you don't have to hide things from me concerning your past relationships. I wasn't expecting a celibate monk when I fell in love with you."

"And when was that?" I asked, priming the pump. I remembered back in college how both Bobby and Speckles had commented about her confidential feelings for me and urged me to ask her up to Cornell.

"Oh, sometime back in high school, mister hotshot," she answered, squeezing my hand.

I should've paid more attention to those guys, I thought to myself.

Life was good. Shirley made for an ideal partner and companion in every sense, having all the attributes I'd ever wanted in a woman. She possessed such essential qualities as attractiveness, intelligence, sociability and versatility. She conducted herself with conscience and objectivity in the raising of her son, proved capable of dealing with people and everyday problems, able to adapt to diverse situations. Most importantly, she understood what it takes to love. She cared about other people.

She also held a compassion for sharing the music of life, taking a healthy bite out of the gift of just being alive. At the same time she understood and respected the tragic, mortal essence of it. For all these things I loved her.

Shirley made it clear that her commitment to me came bound as an unconditional vow. She now declared with pride that she'd been in love with me since high school. Who could ever want more than this?

Our private lives involved smoking marijuana and hashish, pretty much the same way the straight world drank alcohol. We used it for the good times—to enhance the pleasure of sharing our personal moments together and with friends, to embellish our intimate explorations and discoveries with each other, and to enjoy music, our favorite pastime.

It became inherent to the music. The deeper involvement provided by the drugs seemed indigenous to the appreciation of the art form itself. The two avocations came to be interdependent entities to us, whether listening to the stereo at home, the radio at the Jersey shore, the vagabond minstrel in Washington Square, or attending a Saturday night session at the Bitter End, the Electric Circus, a full-scale event at the Fillmore. Like my relationship with Lenny, Shirley and I lived for the music. We wrapped it around us as the fabric of our lifestyle.

We attended as many concerts and other musical attractions as possible. With Mad and Mimi and other friends we were enthralled by the mysterious Van Morrison in a cramped off-Broadway cabaret. He played his guitar sitting on a stool so close you could've reached out and touched him. And I did. Attempting to catch a word with him during the break, I bumped into him in my altered condition, almost knocking the drink out of his hand.

Gabe Kavanaugh and his wife joined us with Mad and Mimi to climb aboard an illusory trip of dreams with Tim Buckley at Carnegie Hall. We were all flying so high that night I think we even lost Tim somewhere in the stratosphere.

Shirley and I got into the pastoral folk life up the Hudson River in the little artist's community of Woodstock, New York. We became forever enamored with the place after being introduced to the premier album of a group called Led Zeppelin playing in the town's touristy head shop.

One rainy weekend night up there, toking in the car and drinking at the Elephant, we were treated to a local band uplifted with impromptu musical cameos by folkie Joni Mitchell and bluesman Johnny Winter. In the midst of the music and the thundershower a drunken Tim Hardin lurched through the front door. His oversized drover coat and fisherman's boots dripped water everywhere as he mumbled an incoherent riddle to the amused audience before crashing back out into his own personal tempest. I tried in vain to remember the title of that particular piece of his on the juke at the Gallery, the song I never did get to hear. Something about "upsetting the grace of living." I amazed myself when I recalled the selection number. M63. Of course I wasn't about to hear it this night, either. Anyway, Shirley and I couldn't believe we'd seen three major musical talents just doing their thing one stormy night in a little mountain town.

During another weekend up there, Shirley opted to return early to our cabin after we ran into the great blues harp player Paul Butterfield and a bunch of his cronies at some bar on Tinker Street. Conscious of my distorted state of mind, and recognizing a fast-approaching masculine occasion, she adroitly withdrew. I appreciated the opportunity to tag along with Paul and his pals for a memorable night of stoned bar hopping. A night I admit I cannot recall with much clarity.

Yes, life was good.

CHAPTER 44

This room held the distinction of the top floor, in a different wing of the hotel. The view of Manhattan consisted of the spire of either the Empire State or the Chrysler building, I couldn't be sure. Other than that, it was exactly like all the others.

"Hey there, comrade. Here it is. Blast-off time at the old launching pad."

Gabe Kavanaugh held up a small brown vial. A miniature brass spoon dangled by a thin chain attached to the cap. He handed it to me.

"Is this what I think it is?" I asked, already feeling dumb for raising the question.

"You're gol'dang *tootin',*" he replied. "And that there little old piece of paraphernalia is my gift to you. May you use it in many good trips down the fast lane."

With that, he pulled a plastic bag of white powder from his jacket pocket. He laid it on the table. Then he sat down, opened his briefcase and removed a rectangular mirror, setting it next to the bag. He stared at the objects for a few seconds, as if he might be contemplating the positioning of two new trophies on the display case in his den. Now he reached inside his jacket again, this time producing a piece of folded tissue paper. Unwrapping the tissue, he withdrew a gleaming silver razor blade. He placed it on the mirror.

"Time for a couple lines," he announced in grand fashion, though I was the only other person present at the time. "May the bird of paradise fly up your nose. This is going to be a very special meeting of the minds tonight."

Gabe had introduced me to a group of young men who chased skirts every Thursday night at the sports bar of the Sheraton Hotel in Hasbrouck Heights. The weekly boys-night-out had escalated to chipping in on a room in the hotel every month or so. This served the dual purpose of privacy for drugs, women, or both, depending on the luck of the evening downstairs. Most everyone in the clique worked in some capacity somewhere in the insurance business, or had been inducted as friends of someone who was. This would be the first time, to my knowledge, that cocaine became a participant in the ritual.

Soon after that the terrible nightmares began, the prelude to my unimaginable future. They all seemed to include, more or less, the same unnerving visions and images that had tormented me in San Francisco. I would hear Janis and Jimi singing in a psychedelic din of death. I'd see my own distorted eyes, a looming backdrop behind the black Peugeot in that war-torn street, the vehicle convulsing as lead bullets puncture its iron-hard skin. Then exploding bicycle parts, wheels and spokes, sprockets and chains and handlebars, jagged metal fragments ripping into soft camouflaged bodies. I'd recognize Billy and Bobby laid out in a rice paddy ditch, though their faces are reduced to red meat. I'd be there, cringing, when Jerry Blakely loses control of the car and crashes off the road with Jane, appalled to see JFK sitting in the back seat, gushing blood from the holes in his head. I would cry all over again at the sight of my father lying stiff in his casket, shocked when straight-faced Mom takes it upon herself to lower him into the earth. I'd hear my own screams as naked Zina stares up from the table at the penetrating light. Taste the nausea of vertigo at the moment Lenny swan dives off the top of the cliff. Shudder when I realize the corpse of Bruce Tierney is watching it all from his wheelchair, surrounded by scores of wide-eyed war orphans.

Then the strange soft voice started talking to me, slithering inside my brain like a snake in the woodpile. I'll never forget those words.

I'm here. I'm here for you. When you need me, I'll be here. You know that. I'll always be here for you.

Just three months later I found myself kneeling at the altar of my affliction. Shirley said she had a suspicion something like this had invaded my life. As though I were her second son, she cradled me in her arms and promised she would make me healthy once more.

"I waited too long for you, Robbie Bender. I'm not going to lose you again."

Mad had chosen the restaurant for our little reunion lunch. I crossed my fingers he would also be picking up the tab. I wasn't accustomed to dining in such fancy places, much less shelling out what might equate to a new account commission for one plate of food. It seemed Mad ran in pretty rich circles, the maitre d' greeting "Mr. Madigan" with familiar cordiality as he seated us at a prime corner table. I could see St. Patrick's Cathedral beneath us from our view out the window. I knew the historic, ritzy Plaza Hotel was just a few blocks north of us, also facing out on wealthy Fifth Avenue.

"So this is the famous Top of the Sixes," Lenny remarked. "I didn't know I was such a goddam' important person."

We all chuckled at that, settling ourselves in at the table. The maitre d' waited with professional patience, holding our menus. Our waiter and water boy stood obediently in the wings.

Soon Lenny and I were wolfing down the roast pork sandwich special. Mad displayed his silverware expertise dispatching a plate of veal saltinbocca, whatever that is. A most festive occasion it came to be as we tripped lightly down memory lane, reentering our former world of college one-upmanship, recalling various high jinks from those good old days.

As the chardonnay loosened up our tongues, Mad and I joked about our more contemporary doings, headlining the already infamous escapade involving "Bender's badass brownies." Although I could repeat almost every line of Mad's tale, excepting the new embellishing twists he always managed to add, it was still funny stuff the way he told it. We both laughed with great gusto as Lenny drank it all in, along with the wine.

I can't describe how excited I felt, seeing my brother and best friend after so long. This was our first chance to get together since I'd come home. I'd already arranged to take the rest of the day off. So we said our cheerful good-byes to Mad, who was not only nice enough to foot the bill, but performed a little dance for us on the sidewalk before strutting away to his nearby office. We hailed a cab for the Upper East Side. The time had arrived for some early barhopping to catch up on each other's lives and get a head start on happy hour.

We ended up at September's. Before we got really inebriated, Lenny guided me away from the bar to a private table. His face took on an uncharacteristic somberness.

"Tell you what, Rob. I've got a proposition for you. Just hear me out, for a minute. I don't mean to be a downer here, but I'm real concerned about you and Mad. Especially you . . . with the drugs you're doing. I know, we've talked about this before, and I don't want to rehash all that old crap. But I'm convinced, even though you don't see it that way, that you're on a bad track here. You know I never talked much about my middle brother, Joe. He was on the same treadmill himself a few years ago . . . just like you're doing now, with the marijuana and that other dope you smoke. Then, after a while, he was into the major-league drugs."

Lenny looked to be having a tough time now. He attempted to blink away the moisture in his eyes. Two young men who had taken our places at the bar started clowning with the bartender, probably trying to impress the three girls to their left. Lenny ignored the commotion.

"Now he's fucking worthless. His brain is shot. He was a smart kid, and now he's a goddam' idiot. More rehab joints than I can count. Cost my dad a fortune. It didn't do any good. Every time he came home he was right back at it, stealing from all of us . . . lying to us and himself . . . so he could buy more of that shit."

He paused at this point, taking a long swig from his glass. When he resumed, his voice had shrunk. "Now he might as well be a frigging vegetable."

I waited for him to continue. He just sat there, staring at his drink. It all seemed surreal somehow, as though we'd become suspended in space.

Seconds stretched out like those minutes you're on hold on the telephone. I took the initiative to try to resuscitate his train of thought. "God, I'm so sorry. I should've known something like that can really screw with your mind. But, being you, well . . . ."

His silence continued to weigh heavy. The boys at the bar had succeeded in engaging the three nymphs in animated conversation.

Ever so softly I said, "So, what's your proposal, Lenny?"

He taxied in from his flight of abandonment. "Oh . . . yeah. Now I'm serious about this. It may seem ridiculous to you, but it's not to me. You know I'm no holier-than-thou do-gooder out trying to save the world so everyone can be like me. And I understand you think I'm just overreacting because of Joe. That you ain't him. That you're stronger, got self-control, all that good shit going for you. That may be, but I still don't agree. I seen it before, besides my brother.

"Hey, take your pick. You could join the living dead, like he did. Or maybe take it all the way, you know? The way I figure it, if you stay on the road you're on, it's just a matter of time."

I winced with the stab from that dagger. If Lenny only knew what I'd been going through. How hard Shirley and I had been trying to beat it.

"So here's the pitch, stupid as it may sound to you. I'm going to be back in town in just two weeks, arriving late Saturday night. And I actually got a layover this time until Tuesday night. Now, here it is. I'll spend that time with you, for the rest of that weekend . . . smoking that junk with you. You can set up the biggest pot party you want, whatever. I'll do it all with you, puff for puff. With just you, or all your druggie friends, I don't care. All I need is enough time to get back down to good ol' terra firma so I can fly a plane back up Tuesday night."

His gaze pierced the pupils of my eyes. I fought the itch to look away.

"What do I want from you in return? Just the promise you'll try to stop. Really try. Starting the very next day. No drugs, man. Cold turkey, whatever they call it. No joints, no nothing. Just the promise you'll try to do this. Do it for your best buddy, if not for yourself. Yeah . . . do it for me."

He waited for my reaction. When I just sat there, he picked up from where he'd left off.

"There you have it. A one shot deal. We'll do the bit together, just like all the other gigs we've done. True pardners. But that's the end of it. I'll never do it again. And I'll never offer another deal. If you can't stop after that, you know I'll always be there for you. But I won't bug you about it, or try to stop you. You'll be on your own then. You'll have to find a way to make yourself want to do it. You'll have to do it by yourself."

"That's it?"

"That's my proposition. Now go ahead and laugh. Tell me how idiotic it is. Tell me I don't understand."

I looked at him and smiled. I'm sure he'd begun bracing for the rejection he anticipated. It was pretty absurd. Perhaps when he tried it he would come to understand that cannabis is innocuous, if it's not abused. But I had to find some way to beat cocaine. Some way to get the drug dreams and the soft voice out of my head. Some way to stop the nightmares and that murmur in my ear ever since the first time I snorted the powder in that Sheraton hotel room. The soft voice that whispered to me in the still of the night, while Shirley slept quietly beside me. The soft voice that said those words so clear, every time.

I'm here. I'm here for you. When you need me, I'll be here. You know that. I'll always be here for you.

"I'll do it."

I think my declaration shocked me as much as Lenny.

"You mean it? You really mean it? You're not just fucking around with me?"

Suddenly I felt good about it. I could do it. Hell, I knew how to party before pot. I loved music long before I ever smoked a joint. Maybe this was the only way to escape the voice. And I sure didn't want to join the living dead or the . . . dead.

"I mean it, Lenny. But I've got one counterproposal that requires a commitment from you, too."

He furrowed his brow, in earnest. "What's that?" he said, most likely expecting the worst.

"That you agree to meet my lovely Shirley. Let her fix you a Sunday dinner like you've never known. Her food always tastes great. Especially after some good grass."

Lenny held out his closed hand across the table. We tapped our sapphire rings together. Then he raised his glass to me.

"Here's to two lifelong brothers, Robbie. Once again, let's drink that sweet nectar from the sacred chalice. Here's to our continued voyage together . . . all the way to that final sunset."

We partied through happy hour and long into the night. We even did a round of tequila with a group of one-time drinking buddies.

Shirley had gotten almost as exuberant as me. Of course I'd told her all about Lenny. She couldn't wait to meet her male counterpart. She went out and bought all the ingredients to make us chicken sorrentino, my very favorite of all her sensational meals. Lenny never called. Sunday morning Shirley put everything together and baked it anyway. I anticipated he might just appear, like he had in San Francisco, when he surprised me, waiting at my doorstep. But as the afternoon sun began to set, we sat down and started without him. Lenny never showed up.

CHAPTER 45

"I'm sorry, sir. I don't find any listing for that name."

"Thank you so much, operator," I screamed, with all the venom I could muster.

Exasperated beyond reason, I slammed the phone receiver onto its base so hard I was surprised I didn't crack my kitchen wall. Telephone operators, with their irritating nasal, monotone voices and acerbic attitudes rarely provided any help. They never offered any additional assistance or suggested course of action beyond their easy, insincere regrets.

After a week and no word from Lenny, I'd made every effort to contact him. I got no answer at his home phone, not unusual considering all the traveling he did. But it wasn't like him to miss a prearranged get-together, without some kind of follow-up and apology. This attempt to reach his parents in Ithaca also failed. Either they had an unlisted number, or had moved away. I found it hard to believe not one Morrissey resided in that entire community, but the operator didn't take too kindly to the speculation.

I'd again tried to reach Marjorie, not expecting her to be current on Lenny any longer—more out of desperation, I guess, and an excuse to inquire once more about my lost love, Zina. Marjorie no long existed, if you believed Ma Bell.

Nearly two dead-end months later, the only progress in my search being the news that Lenny's phone had now been disconnected, I received notice of an insured, registered piece of mail waiting for me at the post office. The small package had a California return address, and a name I also did not recognize. D. Jennings. I got agitated with the action of the post office pen when I signed the receipt, my signature on the dotted line coming across unusually sloppy and irregular. Then I realized my hand was shaking, I suppose from nervous anticipation.

Back in my car, as much as I wanted to tear it open, I just looked at this enigma resting on the seat. It didn't take a whole lot of intuition to figure it had something to do with Lenny, and I had an overpowering premonition that the contents would be a lot heavier than their weight. I knew I had to open it up at the privacy—and safety—of my kitchen table.

Inside the package I found a letter and a small box. I opened the envelope and pulled out the letter. It had been written with graceful, symmetrical handwriting on exquisite feminine stationery. The scent of lilac clung to the paper.

July 9, 1969

Dear Robbie,

I think Lenny may have told you who I am. He certainly has told me a lot about you. I still hope that someday we may have the chance to meet. I would like that. Lenny's best friend would have to be a very special person.

Lenny and I dated for almost a year. I was hoping to spend the rest of my life with him. I think he felt the same about me.

I know he was looking forward to a visit with you this past spring, when he had some weekend days in New York. I don't know if you are aware of what happened, why he couldn't see you then. Assuming you don't know, I must tell you with a broken heart that Lenny had a horrible accident on Friday of that weekend. He was off duty, flying a helicopter with a friend. They had some sort of mechanical failure and crashed. Our Lenny was a hero to the very end. He made sure the plane missed a schoolyard of children and landed in the street instead. My only comfort is that he didn't suffer, as he was killed instantly.

Lenny's family has moved to Pennsylvania. I attended his funeral there. His parents were thoughtful enough to give me a ring he wore to keep as a remembrance of him. After I got back home and thought about it I believe it may be the ring he shared with you. I think you have one like it. Anyway, I just wouldn't feel right keeping it, knowing it had personal meaning between the two of you. I do have mementos of the wonderful man who changed my life and proved there is such a thing as true love.

I'm sorry Lenny didn't get to see you that weekend. It would have been so much nicer if the two of you could have had that time together before he passed on. I feel blessed that I did spend some hours with him during his final days.

Perhaps we shall have the opportunity to meet sometime. Selfishly, I think it would help me cope with our loss. I will always feel connected to you through Lenny, whether we actually get together or not. Either way, I know we will both find the strength to go on. To celebrate music and laughter and the dance. To enjoy the rest of our lives, happy to have shared some of it with him. He would have wanted that.

God bless,

Denise Jennings

I sat at the kitchen table for a very long time. After a while I reached into the package and removed the box. I set it down on the table, next to the letter. Stared at it for a few minutes. When I felt ready, I opened the top and removed the upper cotton padding. As soon as I saw the black star sapphire ring my eyes flooded. I had trouble seeing anything after that until the tolling of the phone pulled me from the torrent.

"Hey there. Glad I caught you," Shirley said, her voice as sprightly as a river rock skipping across the water. "I've run into a little problem with tonight. Vinny pulled another fast one on me. Says he's got what he calls a major meeting with some future business associates. Really thinks he's going to be a construction boss and trade in his calluses for a fancy car and a shirt and tie."

I floundered on my end, wiping my eyes with the back of my hand. "Shirley, I have to tell you—"

"Yeah, right. A business meeting on a Saturday night. Believe that. Probably has a last minute date with some new chippie he ran into. Mom's also got her monthly bridge game tonight, so looks like I'll be taking Frankie to the movies, or something."

"Listen to me for a minute." My voice sounded like an old-timer seeking attention at the geriatric home.

She ignored my impersonation. "You could join us, if you like. Anyway, Mom said she could help out tomorrow, even take Frankie with her to Mass, so we could spend some time together."

Retrieving my own voice, I surprised myself when I found I could talk without bawling like one of Frankie's playmates. "Think maybe you should do your own thing tonight, honey. I just found out about Lenny."

"I'm sorry. Is everything all right?"

Now the emotions burst upon me, drenching me in the downpour. I took a shaky breath and labored to continue.

"Got his pardner ring in the mail. With a letter from his California girlfriend. He died in a copter crash the day before he was supposed to fly to New York—"

"Oh, no . . . ."

My mind thrashed in the deluge. ". . . to be with *us*! He died in a goddam' helicopter crash! Missed a schoolyard to save the kids. Jesus, do you know how many times he survived picking up bodies and wounded grunts in Vietnam? With frigging bullets and shit flying all around him? And all the other times he was taking chances with his life . . . racing cars, sky diving, hang gliding. And then it's all over. Flying the aircraft he was most familiar with. In a peaceful neighborhood in sunny California. It just doesn't make any fucking sense."

At this point I broke down, letting it all out over the phone. I couldn't keep it inside any longer.

Shirley waited until I'd calmed myself a bit. "I'm coming over. I'll find a sitter somewhere. Just give me a couple hours to find someone and set it up."

"No, I think I'd rather be by myself tonight. I wouldn't be very good company right now."

"That's not the point, Robbie. I don't care about that. I care about you. You need to be with someone tonight. Someone to help you through this. Maybe we should go to the movies ourselves, or something. Try to get your mind on other things to get past the shock. I'll be over in a couple—"

"Please don't do that, Shirley. I'll see you tomorrow. I just want to sort things out on my own. So I can say goodbye to him private-like."

I listened to my wretched soul screaming above the ensuing silence.

Then I heard her compassionate voice again, hesitant, uncertain. "Are you sure? I can fix you dinner. I'll stay out of the way. But I'll be there . . . if you need me. You really shouldn't be alone."

"No. I'll be fine. I need the time to myself." I had to mourn him on my own, in my own way. And get it behind me. "I'll see you tomorrow."

I smacked my lips together, sending her kisses across the wires.

"You're sure?" Worry trickled from her words.

"I'm sure. I'll see you tomorrow. Okay?"

"All right . . . I guess."

I waited for the click of the receiver.

"I love you, Robbie."

"Tomorrow, sweetheart." I eased the phone back down onto its cradle.

CHAPTER 46

First I went into the attic storage space behind the kitchen. I located that photograph Lenny had sent me in Munich. He looked so handsome standing next to his Chevy stock car, trophy held high over his proud, smiling face. I propped the picture up on the kitchen table, against the ceramic vase Shirley had gotten me for my new apartment, next to Lenny's ring and Denise's letter.

Then I perused the old record collection, looking for those musical creations that held special significance for Lenny and me. Gathering together quite a stack, I attempted to place them in some sort of chronological sequence, according to the times we'd shared in our lives. It turned out to be a more complicated project than I'd intended. So I readjusted my plan, just choosing the music by the approximate age of it, from doo-wop and early rock 'n' roll to more contemporary rock, jazz, folk, and blues. As I listened, I kept refilling my glass from the jug of Folinare Soave in the refrigerator. After a time I hit my stash for a joint.

Stretched out on the davenport, I thought about the cocaine voice that had continued to speak to me, in most instances after one of my bad dreams. I prided myself on not having indulged in the powder since seeing Lenny. I'd even refused toots offered me by Gabe, and when I attended the weekly boys-night-out parties at the Sheraton. For certain I missed the intense rush that came with snorting the drug, craving that feeling of indisputable power and insight it provided. But watching Gabe's life disintegrating like a sandcastle at high tide provided additional motivation to ignore the voice, to hang onto my last conversation with Lenny.

Though hard to believe, inside of a year feeding his nose, Gabe had left his wife and kids, moving into an austere apartment on a run-down street in Passaic with some druggie barmaid he'd met somewhere. I'd also seen him in Mr. Gaylord's windowed office, behind closed doors, hippo mouths threatening to swallow each other in their soundproof arena of fury. The word around the water cooler had it that he'd been placed on probation at the agency, on the verge of being fired, though Gabe never mentioned anything to me, nor did I ever ask.

I got up and walked to the bedroom closet, pulled out my party box and took it to the kitchen table. The depleted state of my drug inventory surprised me. A pipeful of Justin's hash remained. Perhaps a quarter ounce of pot. Belinda's charity, in a beat up naugahyde bag, had been reduced to small amounts of grass and hash, two mescaline caps, and one last mystery pill, the twin of that unknown hallucinogen that had almost gotten me killed outside the Coffee Gallery. I laid everything on the table, next to Lenny's ring. I prickled with anticipation, stoked by a life changing event emerging in my mind.

Mom had taught me well when it came to being frugal and not squandering possessions. What was that old expression she said more times than I could ever remember? *Waste not, want not.* Of course. I just couldn't have thrown out a large cache of dope. Couldn't bear the thought of intentionally kissing off that kind of investment. Even if, in fact, you never paid for all of it.

Here I faced an almost empty cupboard. What better time for a magnificent resolution, to clean up one's life, in a tribute to the last wishes of your departed confidant? This would be the final night. Honoring our pact, I would smoke what I wanted of the grass and hash, and with swift ceremony void the remainder from my life forever. Lenny would know. I would be doing it for me. But it would be for both of us.

After emptying the contents of Belinda's bag, I peered inside to make certain I'd gotten everything. I noticed a slight protuberance in the plastic flooring. Yes, I could feel it with my fingers. A little hump, dead center. Checking around the extremities, I realized the base had a seam on only one side.

Pulling upward from the opposite edge, I raised the false bottom. I discovered a shallow space underneath, from which I removed an aspirin tin. Carefully popping open the top, I found it to be filled with a white crystalline powder.

"Poor Belinda. You forgot about your secret supply of coke when you were so gracious to leave me the rest of your stash."

A twitch of my fingers spilled a tad of the powder onto the table. I stared at the sprinkling for a moment. It seemed to have a more ivory tint and granular texture than Gabe's. *Hold on. Could this be . . .? No, Belinda knows better.*

I stepped quickly to the silverware drawer and returned with a butter knife. After scraping the particles together, I tapped at the small pile until it had spread into a long, thin ribbon. I fetched a straw from the kitchen cabinet and sat down to my creation. In an instant I found myself snorting the bottom half of it. I leaned back in my tilted chair, face up, eyes closed, head resting easy over the support of my shoulder blades, my mind a welcome mat to the power of imagination.

Minutes later I sat up and pulled my chair closer to the table. I bent forward and sniffed up the rest of the line. I felt the comfort of the drug as it enveloped me in its reassuring embrace, like a quilt wrapping itself around me at the bidding of some gypsy wizard. It *was* different from Gabe's coke. It engaged me slow and strong, with peace of mind.

A hollow voice startled me. Not soft this time. It sounded very bold inside my head.

I'M HERE. I'M HERE FOR YOU. NOW WHEN YOU NEED ME MOST. I WILL NOT LET YOU DOWN.

The voice frightened and fascinated me at the same time. Abruptly, pangs of guilt had me regretting my betrayal to Lenny. To myself. But then, this was only one line. Like the pot and hash, it would be my last.

Realizing the tracking stylus had just lifted off the completed record on the turntable, I attempted to escape the dubious moment. I immersed myself in the project of setting up another musical selection.

I managed to settle back into my intended program, tried to pay closer attention to the sounds Lenny and I had savored together. At the same time, I caught myself attempting to compare the relative effects of Justin's and Benny's hash with my trusty old Chase & Sanborn water pipe. And I foraged through the meager inventory of edibles in the pantry closet. While the overcast afternoon faded into the dusk of evening, I succeeded in getting pleasantly spaced. I rejoiced in reminiscing the memories of notable events I'd shared with my good brother, reliving them in my mind with high drama.

The darkness of night began its descent. I removed my sapphire ring and placed it next to Lenny's on the kitchen table. The rings and Lenny's picture, alongside Denise's letter, represented a sort of shrine, I guess. I added the flickery luminance of many candles to the fragrance of the burning incense, continuing the odyssey back through time with my empyreal companion.

As though he'd already been ordained spiritual status, I could sense his presence before me.

"So here we are at the sundown, pardner. Here's to the chalice. Once again, let's drink the nectar together."

Good lord. It's Lenny . . . talking to me.

Suddenly, impossibly, Zina appeared alongside him.

"My darling Robert Stephen. I love you. Come with me. Don't you see, this is our chance. For our very own ever-after."

Like nebulous phantasms, the two of them seemed to have emerged from somewhere in the infinite cosmos. I shivered with the surprise, shock and implausibility of it all as I beheld these ghost angels. *Lenny and Zina. O wonder of wonders. Was Zina now free, to go on with me? This must be a dream. What's happening here? How could it be?*

I rushed back to the attic storage space. I found the photo Lenny had taken of Zina and me holding hands in front of the Old Absinthe bar on Bourbon Street. I also dug out that treasured wine bottle Zina had slipped into my satchel in Nürnberg so long ago. Her words inscribed across the label looked as fresh as yesterday.

Dearest Robbie, You have made my life complete. Love eternal, Zina

I hurried to the kitchen table and leaned the photograph against the vase, opposite Lenny's. I set the bottle there with the rings and Denise's letter. Looking toward the living room I saw Lenny and Zina waiting for me.

"Let's do it, Robbie. I'm ready to dance with my first American boy."

Just like that, I was back at the Chanticleer, entranced after meeting my first European girl.

Lenny's words resounded now with even more significance than when I read them under Marine Corps letterhead years before. "You got to feel great about Zina, man. Not too many cats I know can say they ever had a long term scene with anybody so beautiful. In her looks and in her mind. Take the power you've earned from this. Take it now to a new soul pasture."

I became delirious in the tickling exhilaration of it all. I danced like I'd never danced before, with both of them, prancing in ecstasy through all the rooms of the loft, seeming to step through air, somewhere between the floor and the elevated ceilings. As always, Lenny served as participating choreographer, his ingenuity magically coordinating our freedom of expression.

Having been fortunate enough to find Slim Gaillard and Slam Stewart hiding amongst my vintage vinyls, Zina and I celebrated hand in hand, high-stepping with Lenny to the uproarious "Flat Foot Floogie"—"with a floy, floy." I felt the blush once more as the warmth of her palm mingled with mine. With Marjorie nowhere in sight, this time the enthusiastic spectator applause and boisterous "hey, hey, hey's" were directed at the dance maestro and his new partners, Zina and me, proud and pleased to take our bows.

It became an enchanted night of living in the yesteryears, from the elation of Ithaca and New Orleans to the poignant moments of Amsterdam and the French Riviera, Barcelona and Nürnberg, Saigon and San Francisco.

"Looky here, pal. I do believe that guy's hung better than you!" Lenny chuckled. Streaking with shameless abandon on the nude Île du Levant, I flushed the first mescaline capsule down the toilet.

As we glided past the kitchen table, Lenny spotted our sapphire rings. "Goddam'," he cried, "talk about a super deal. Under a hundred bucks for rocks like that, perfect cat's eyes, set in silver. You know, the ancient mystics believed those stones represent destiny. Our very own pardner rings, Rob. Yes sir, brothers all the way to that final sunset."

We swirled and swayed to a calypso beat along the labyrinth of corridors and chambers. With my lungs full of hashish as we frolicked in the temples of Bangkok, I jettisoned the second brown bomber.

Our dancing feet transported us back to the kitchen. "So this is 'Frisco. Now I understand how my man went beatnik on me," Lenny said. We introduced Zina to the cuisine and camaraderie of La Pantera in North Beach. And we gorged ourselves once again, finishing up with both the cannoli and spumoni. After dessert we watched Belinda's mystery pill circle the watery vortex of the commode, ultimately disappearing down the drain forever.

Feeling a tweak of melancholy, it registered that Lenny would not be joining me in attending the upcoming Woodstock Festival, now just a matter of weeks away. I'd purchased two extra tickets to this heralded hippie event, planning on presenting them to him during that anticipated Sunday dinner. Instead, by way of some token alternative, we now stretched out on the thick Icelandic sheep rug I'd purchased in the Village. I took my sacred friends on an excursion into the realm of my own personal musical experiences and appreciations, gems Lenny dubbed "the anthems of your life."

The trip began in passionate fashion as my divine Janis bared her naked soul with her tortured "Piece of My Heart." Then Fred Neil resounded with his deep satiny voice and twelve-string guitar. Ah, the pleasure that Lenny and Zina could get to hear him at last. And "Bob Dylan's Dream" carried us back to the transitory comradeship of those forever bygone fraternal years. I "revisited Highway 61" with my supernatural company, and soon we were stirred by Dylan bewailing his angst-ridden "Desolation Row." Lenny reiterated those words I remember him saying sometime way back when, about the "joy of sad."

As he put it, "You can't say you've really tasted the marrow of life if you don't know the joy of sad." I think I'd just begun to appreciate the full implications of that now.

Listening to Dylan's lyrics, another thought crossed my mind. Despite the fancy stationery and meticulous cursive penmanship of Denise's tragic letter, and the divergent perceptions and realities of life we each might bear, our binding pain connected us to this cryptic dirge waltz.

Zina curled up closer to me as Jefferson Airplane's Marty Balin continued our pilgrimage with his pensive ballad, "Comin' Back to Me." Her voice was haunting in my ear.

"Oh, Robbie, this song is so beautiful."

I looked into her holy face. "And heartbreaking," I replied, hoping she understood.

Her blue eyes held me tight. "It's heartbreaking that Stefan can't be here to share this with us. To at least get a taste of his true roots. Oh, how he'd love you and your music."

My stomach tensed. I sensed I already knew the answer, but felt the desperate need to confirm the enormity of it.

"Who's . . . Stefan?"

Her eyes never wavered. "My lover, my darling. Certainly you know. After all, it is your middle name."

CHAPTER 47

Lying on my back on the bed of imported sheep hair, in between the two most important people in my life, I have no idea how long I stared at the ceiling. Zina's words kept ringing in my ears.

My lover, my darling. Certainly you know. After all, it is your middle name.

I remembered. That last time in Nürnberg. Somehow she knew my middle name.

Making the segue from somewhere just before, the music played on. My other twelve-string guitar-playing troubadour stood center stage before us, singing his intense compositions about love and consolation, chivalry and deliverance. Dino Valente serenaded our souls about the fragile human spirit contending with the interweaving factors of time and place, dreams and changes. As his voice soared with the inviting plea to join him and his "Children of the Sun," I felt us all rising in concert, as if we had wings, hands entwined, the very essence of our beings ascending together, toward the heavens . . . .

I woke up on the hardwood floor, feeling groggy and disoriented. Somehow in my sleep I must've rolled a good four feet from the fur rug. I found myself all alone. I felt the chill in the quiet apartment. Then I noticed that the lace curtains Shirley fixed for me had begun fluttering off the window sills with the breeze of the night air. I closed the windows and shuffled into the kitchen to check the time. Christ, the hands of the clock pointed to almost 2:00 a.m. The events of the evening awakened my logy brain. *Where were they? Where was Lenny? And Zina? They'd been right here with me. Dancing and drinking wine, smoking hash, polishing off the leftover Italian in the fridge. Listening to the stereo. Where did they go?*

"Lenny . . . my god . . . why did you leave me, too?" I scared myself, jumping when I heard my own voice, crying out so pitifully in the empty apartment.

Oh. And what about this—Stefan?

My hands pressed against my temples. "Zina. My love. We have to talk. I've got to know about Stefan. What happened to our ever-after? Where are you now? Jesus, I need you so bad."

I saw the wine bottle, the sapphire rings, the shrine on the kitchen table. It all started coming back to me. The commitment to Lenny. To myself. I'd cast the pills down the toilet. Now I took note of the aspirin tin. The rest of Belinda's coke. I moved to the table and sat down. After looking at the metal container for a moment, I reached forward and drew it to me. Again, some of the powder spilled out. *Shit, there's more here than I thought. At least a dozen generous lines. What a shame to waste it all. This has to be worth a few bucks on the street.*

I'M HERE FOR YOU. LET ME HELP YOU NOW.

The hollow voice was back. Definitely more brazen than the soft utterances I'd first been introduced to. Yet I didn't leap out of my skin like I had just before, hearing myself. *Why not do it? This would be the end of it, after all. My farewell drug binge. It'd be foolish to refrain from your last taste of cocaine. I can deal with the voice. After awhile, it will go away. Some day.*

LET ME HELP YOU.

I went to the bedroom closet and dug out the mirror. The razor blade was still taped to the back of it. I took it to the kitchen and set everything up on the table. The place had gotten as gray and silent as a morgue. I stepped over to the stereo and put my old buddy Richie Havens on the record player, to bring back some color and warmth.

Returning to the table, I carefully tapped some of the dope from the tin onto the mirror. I took the razor and cut it into three lines.

A voice from afar. "Promise me you'll try to stop. Do it for us . . . pardners to the final sunset."

Another. "My sweet lover . . . we can have our very own ever-after."

Wait a minute. What am I doing? I made a pact. I'm done with drugs. LET ME HELP YOU.

The hollow one, up close and personal.

The interminable ticking of the clock on the wall seemed sluggish and thundering. On impulse I did a line and sat there, listening to Richie. As before, I felt the calm reassurance of the substance flowing through me, a river of peace and love and ever-lasting hope.

When the music finished, I snorted the second line. I went back to the turntable, moving with no apparent effort, as though I'd begun loping in slow motion, cruising out somewhere in space. After turning the record over to the other side, I did the third line. I reentered the living room and slid down onto the fur rug, lying there on my back and staring up at an even more distant cathedral ceiling.

Another voice spoke out. It seemed to be my own this time. "Maybe we can't be together on this planet, Zina. And maybe I shouldn't meet Stefan just yet. Easier on him if he stays where he is. For sure he doesn't need another jolt to his young world. But you and I can continue to love each other. And we can reunite some day. In the afterlife. I can meet up with you and Lenny there. All together . . . in paradise . . . for eternity . . . ."

Suddenly they reappeared. Not that far away. Smiling down at me, and waving. Good lord, they looked so pale. Like ashen angels. They beckoned for me to join them. It was time to go. Richie started singing that song—"Follow." *I will follow. Wait for me. Wait for me! Oh, Zina—Lenny—I love you guys. Wait for me, Lenny—Zina—I'm coming—I will follow—Lenny—Zina—wait for me—wait for me—wait for me . . . .*

SUNSET

The waters of Canadaway Creek gurgled in their northbound glide, spellbinding as always, sparkling fresh crystals flashing in the vermilion light of sundown. The boy held his award on top of the bridge's side rail, so they might both behold the vista of the rapids following their course between the silhouetted trees.

He felt sad knowing this would be his last visit to his favorite place. Upset that he could be the reason they had to leave. His father insisted it didn't come down to anybody's fault, rather a matter of realizing an opportunity to start anew. Yet his mother had been adamant that he had served as "the straw that broke the camel's back" when he dropped those marbles down on his dozing grandfather's head from the ceiling register. He dared not reveal he did it in retaliation for the whipping he'd endured out behind the barn, when they'd been alone together the week before. And his grandfather knew how to make that switch sting a whole lot more than his mother ever could.

Now, adding salt to the secret wounds, she would not allow "Wally" to come with them. She said there wouldn't be enough room in the car. The truth was she didn't like stuffed animals. Especially when they weren't the commercial toy store variety. Double especially when the animal happened to be a weasel.

Such were the circumstances as Shelley Forrester paid his respects to the hideaway ledge that had provided him so many nurturing moments within the arms of Mother Nature. As he approached his sanctum, the plaintive cry of the whippoorwill in his ears and the hounds of departure nipping at his heels, he clutched his furry citation to his breast. He hoped that on this historic occasion Wee Willy would be there for the presentation. With the impending nightfall there would be at least a chance the tiny fellow might be out and about. Confronting the old oak tree, he observed tracks that indicated some creature of his size had been utilizing the hole by the exposure of twisted root.

Additional evidence verified continuing human desecration at the secluded shelf, despite the boy's efforts to keep his spiritual harbor in a pure and natural state. He'd resigned himself to bring a garbage bag with him on most occasions. More cigarette butts and a beer bottle lay on the ground by the ridge of stone.

Stepping over the rock slab toward the waterfall, he wondered how much rubbish he would encounter in his new city life. He imagined it would be far worse, beyond what he could ever cram into a paper bag. But then, any retreat he might establish in that world would be much different than this, anyway. Where would he go to escape the pandemonium, the chaos of a metropolitan existence? How would he contend with those dirty, crowded streets? What would he do to find the blessing of contemplation he'd come to know in this private shelter?

Now he realized he stood right at the edge of the precipice. Like never before, the toes of his sneakers had to be less than a foot from the plunge. With uncharacteristic daring he inched even closer to the drop. He could feel where the soil departed under the soles of his shoes. He looked down, past the waterfall, to the slate banks of the river below. Amazingly, he felt no sensation of the vertigo that had plagued him earlier.

Raising his arms in the air, trophy in hand, he shouted out his celebration of conquering the curse, tingling in the rapture of victory. As he lifted his head, he became further aroused by the deepening sanguine hues of the sunset sky. It was a positive sign, an omen of good things to come. *Red sky at night, sailor's delight.* How often had he heard that proverb before?

All at once, right there at the brink, he found himself dancing an Irish jig he'd learned in school. He soon backed away, feeling like he'd just experienced some sort of catharsis, that he'd somehow purged more than one great demon.

The boy moved to Wee Willy's den near the base of the ancient oak. He placed Wally at the entrance to the lair, propping him up so he'd be supported by the root. Kneeling there, he removed the notepad from his back pocket. He opened it. Brief ceremonial words drifted lightly on the evening breeze.

He took out his pen and sat down, writing diligently for the next few minutes. Observations complete, he rose to his feet, sliding the tablet back into his jeans and returning the pen to his shirt pocket. He withdrew a brown bag from his jacket, picked up the cigarette butts and beer bottle and dropped them inside the sack.

Standing there for a moment all too brief, he surveyed his precious haven. This memory would have to endure forever.

He recalled that his teacher had talked about the excitement of traveling to faraway places and meeting different people. This would be his chance. With a brave spirit and sense of adventure, like his lifelong friend and counselor Daniel Boone, he straightened up and stood tall, throwing his shoulders back. Then he strode off into the darkening woods. The sun had set. Shelley Forrester was ready to go to New Jersey and blaze fresh trails.

THE POSTLUDE

Perhaps the glory of Heaven is the spiritual reunion with lost innocence, the dreams and ideals of our fleeting youth. I hear the music now, and rise to embrace those melodies once again.

It would've been nice to have gotten to know my Stefan. But there you have it. Life on Earth. Seems so far away now, so long ago.

Set the pen down. Close the manuscript.

Time to rejoin my ever-after friends in my new soul pasture.

Notes of gratitude:

To Pamela, always the tolerant ear and word of encouragement

To the Scottsdale Writers Group and their collective critique and advice

To Alison, my business manager, literary agent, gal Friday, loving daughter and courageous mother

Rondo Barnes assimilated rural and city life as a youth during the '50s and '60s. He graduated from Cornell University and served as an Army officer in the U.S. and Europe before commanding soldiers in the Vietnam War. Residing in San Francisco at the height of Haight-Ashbury, he experienced that city's notorious 1967 Summer of Love. These credentials of firsthand knowledge are incorporated into the writing of his debut novel, *Living on the Edge*.

CPSIA information can be obtained at www.ICGtesting.com
Printed in the USA
LVOW031138221211

260694LV00006B/26/P